P9-EKE-387

CODE WHITE

CODE WHITE

SCOTT BRITZ-CUNNINGHAM

A Tom Doherty Associates Book ▪ New York

This is a work of fiction. All of the characters, organizations, and events portrayed in this novel are either products of the author's imagination or are used fictitiously.

CODE WHITE

A Forge Book
Published by Tom Doherty Associates, LLC
175 Fifth Avenue
New York, NY 10010

www.tor-forge.com

Forge® is a registered trademark of Tom Doherty Associates, LLC.

Library of Congress Cataloging-in-Publication Data

Britz-Cunningham, Scott.
    Code white / Scott Britz-Cunningham.—1st ed.
        p. cm.
    "A Tom Doherty Associates book."
    ISBN 978-0-7653-3192-2 (hardcover)
    ISBN 978-1-4299-4852-4 (e-book)
    1. Women surgeons—Fiction.   2. Neurosurgeons—Fiction.
3. Bomb threats—Fiction.   I. Title.
    PS3602.R5348C63 2013
    813'.6—dc23

                                            2012027568

First Edition: April 2013

Forge books may be purchased for educational, business, or promotional use. For information on bulk purchases, please contact Macmillan Corporate and Premium Sales Department at 1-800-221-7945 extension 5442 or write specialmarkets@macmillan.com.

Printed in the United States of America

0 9 8 7 6 5 4 3 2 1

IN MEMORIAM
WILLIAM HENRY FLETCHER, Ph.D.
1940–2008

To Evelyn

Who is more patient than she knows

ACKNOWLEDGMENTS

Heartfelt thanks to Al Zuckerman at Writers House, the midwife of my first baby and the best writing teacher I've ever had. Thanks also to Bob Gleason at Tor, for getting it; to Beverly Martin, for help at a crucial time; to Kate Flora, for her trenchant critique; to Leonid, my first and most faithful reader; and to Olga and Sasha, for believing in me. I owe a great debt, too, to the late Ray Bradbury, who, apart from being one of the idols of my youth, once gave me a piece of advice that ought to be engraved in gold: "Just do it!"

CODE WHITE

The Huns had taken the citadel of Neurosurgery I. For the rightful denizens of the operating suite—the scrub nurses, anesthetists, residents, postgraduate fellows, and technicians—it was an invasion, a desecration of the Holiest of Holies. Not once in the ten years of its existence had this quiet cluster of green-tiled rooms been so jarred and trampled as now, by this troop of camera operators, lighting men, gaffers, grips, and gofers, bustling back and forth between the scrub room and Operating Room Three. Masquerade as they might in blue scrubs and gowns, shower caps and paper booties, it was obvious that not one of them knew the rules—what could or could not be touched, or where the sterile fields began. They were like monkeys swinging from the glass trellises of a chemistry lab. It was an invitation to disaster.

So thought Ali O'Day, Assistant Professor Neurosurgery, as she looked through the large picture window above the scrub sink while she rubbed a foamy antiseptic brush between her fingers and over her arms up to the elbows. With a mixture of disdain, curiosity, and envy, she watched the film crew hovering about Kathleen Brown, the network's field correspondent, aiming their silver-and-white reflectors at her impossibly perfect skin and hair as they ran through a lighting check. A man with a Betacam on his shoulder was panning the cramped operating room and talking to New York through a Bluetooth headset clipped to his ear.

It was history in the making.

History in the making. She had heard it repeated over and over, like a mantra. It might even have been true. But at this moment, all she could think of was how to keep from vomiting into the sink.

"Nerves?" asked Florinda, the circulating OR nurse, as she passed with a cart full of instruments.

"Mm-hmm." Ali faked a smile as she leaned against the rim of the sink. If only nerves were all it was. The sweet lemon scent of the hand soap did nothing to conceal the smells of iodine and alcohol, and the mixture of all three together roiled her stomach. She stepped back from the sink and closed her eyes. Someone was shouting in an unintelligible Eastern European accent—something about power, a power cable, a power box. She heard the five-minute scrub timer ding. And then she heard a voice from on high—the voice of the god of the neurosurgical operating suite, Dr. Richard Helvelius himself.

"Th-that had better be one of your yoga exercises, Dr. O'Day." He spoke with a slight stutter that was almost Apollonian in him, as though it proved how carefully he weighed and sifted every word. "Tell me you're p-priming your mind for its encounter with destiny."

"You know what it is," said Ali, frowning at his tease.

"You mean you haven't . . . I, uh, I thought you had . . ."

She opened her eyes and looked at him, his head bent slightly toward her from his six-foot-four-inch height. Seen from this angle, his craggy features softened, and that famed aquiline nose of his relinquished its all-powerful pugnacity. It was just his big blue gray eyes she saw—the eyes she had fallen in love with.

"I've been a little tied up, setting the stage for your big show," she said. "Destiny is hard work, Richard. I've hardly slept in four days."

Helvelius laid his strong, warm hand against her spine and gently pushed her back to the scrub sink, back to the iodine and the alcohol and the sickening-sweet lemon scent. He bent even lower to speak confidentially into her ear. "I appreciate that, Ali. In fact, I'm a little w-worried for you."

"Don't be," she said. "I've scheduled a quiet little D and C tomorrow, after all the hullabaloo dies down. Ute Heckart from Perinatal's doing it. She'll be very discreet."

"And you're still sure that's what you w-w-want?"

"Don't talk about what I want." Ali involuntarily touched the back of her hand to her mouth, undoing her five-minute scrub. "It's for the best," she mumbled.

"It doesn't have to b-b-be like that. This b-baby could be good for us."

Ali clamped her eyes as a new wave of nausea hit her. "Please don't call it a baby," she said through clenched teeth.

Helvelius opened his mouth to speak, but was cut off. Kathleen Brown's skin tones and hair were perfect at last, and the crew director had just gotten the thirty-second signal from New York. Helvelius was hastened into the operating room by one of the Huns, a young man in thick glasses and an oversized yellow surgical gown.

"You, too, Ali," said Helvelius, looking back at her. "We'll scrub in later."

Ali followed him, stooping through the tangle of cables and plastic tubing, holding her dripping wet hands in front of her chest. Helvelius was led to a place on one side of the narrow surgical bed, opposite Kathleen Brown. On the bed sat a boy of seven, who seemed dwarfed by all the cameras and monitors. He had a round, beautiful face, with healthy pink cheeks and a snub nose that wiggled as he chewed pensively on his lower lip. The back of his head had been shaved, leaving a halo of curly white blond hair. His forehead and scalp were dotted with little squares of white tape, from which dangled green, red, and yellow wires.

The excited grin on the little boy's face coaxed a smile from Ali. As she passed, she bent to one side and whispered a greeting to the young patient, who laughed in return. But there was no time to talk. Someone reached under her elbow and ushered her to a position behind Helvelius, close to a high blue-cloth-draped table covered with stainless steel instruments, outside the line of view of the camera.

Although a small TV monitor beside her seemed to show a nearly empty operating theater, that was a trick of the camera angle. The room was actually so packed with crew and gear that Ali could barely see the operating table. She strained to get a better view. She had come in at 6:00 A.M. to police the setup of the film equipment, laying down red tape on the floor to mark off sterile and nonsterile areas. Now she had no way of telling whether her lines were being respected. Still holding her hands in front of her, Ali tightened her fingers into fists as the crew lurched into action around her. Lights blinked, hand signals waved, and on every side technicians darted back and forth or crouched on taut haunches. It was like standing in the middle of a beehive—an anarchy of buzzing and bustling. There was nothing she could do about it. She had been reduced to a by-stander in her own operating room.

Ali squinted under the sunlike glare of the reflectors. Across the table, Dr. Helvelius and Kathleen Brown could not help blinking. But the young patient at the epicenter of all this hurly-burly did not blink at all.

The voice with the Eastern European accent was heard again, counting backward, "Fifteen, fourteen, thirteen, twelve . . ."

On the TV monitor, Ali watched the live broadcast of *America Today* from New York. The network anchor Amy Richmond was talking from her desk. Behind her was a still shot of the three gleaming steel-and-glass high-rise towers that were the core of Fletcher Memorial Medical Center, which she could hear being described as "the sprawling flagship hospital of one of the oldest medical schools in the country."

"We have an unprecedented entrée today into the leading edge of medical research, where Dr. Richard Helvelius and his team in Chicago are about to perform a groundbreaking operation. If all goes according to plan, it could be a day to rival the first operation under ether in 1846 or the first heart transplant in 1967. After today, ethicists and philosophers will be on the airwaves, arguing about how the very concept of mortality will have to be redefined. . . ."

Ali scowled. *Yes, yes, history in the making.* Glory, priority, celebrity—that's what mattered to these Huns, with their cameras and microphones and perfect hair. They worshiped fame, and they expected to share in it, because they were the first to spread it over the airwaves. But what if all didn't go according to plan? What would their story be then? Would that still make history?

Amy Richmond went on talking. "Our network news team will be covering every phase of this momentous undertaking, beginning with our live segment on *America Today,* and continuing with a full hour update on our Emmy-winning newsmagazine *Lifeline,* at nine o'clock Eastern tonight. For more, let's go to Kathleen Brown, who is in the operating room right now."

At a cue from the crew director, a small light on the Betacam went red, and Kathleen Brown began to speak.

"Hello, Amy. You're right. History is about to be made today here at Fletcher Memorial. With me is Dr. Richard Helvelius, the chairman of the Department of Neurosurgery, a pioneer in the treatment of patients with brain tumors and spinal cord injuries. Dr. Helvelius?"

On the monitor, Ali saw Helvelius smile. "Good morning, Kathleen. Hello, Amy," he said. "This is an exciting day for all of us."

Ali noticed that Helvelius was speaking in his lecturing voice, pitched a little higher than his usual gravelly baritone. It had always amazed Ali that the stutter that Helvelius had in normal conversation disappeared completely when he spoke in public.

"And who is that with you?" asked Amy Richmond.

"This bright young man is Jamie Winslow, a patient of mine. America is looking on, Jamie. Do you know what a TV camera is?"

"It's a machine that can see for people that can't be here. TV is just like radio, except they have *SpongeBob* and *Yu-Gi-Oh*!"

"There's a TV camera pointing at you right now. Is there anything you'd like to say to anyone out there?"

"Just hi! To Mrs. Gore and Mr. Tabor and Mrs. Rutledge at the Grossman School, and to my friends, Judd, Rog, and Felipe. This place is awesome, guys. What they do in this operating room rocks."

"Thank you, Jamie."

"Oh, can I say one more thing?"

"Sure, Jamie."

"This is for the Cubs—hang in there. Miracles do happen. If I can do it, you can, too."

Helvelius shook his head with the gravity of a doctor at the bedside of a hopeless case. "I'm sorry, Jamie. The Cubs may be beyond the help of medical science this season."

Jamie laughed, and his laughter ran like a ripple through the room, clearing the air of tension. The nurses and camera crew laughed with him. Even Dr. Helvelius laughed. But Ali didn't so much as crack a smile. Jamie's very life was at stake, and there was so much that could go wrong. She knew that the distraction of a single second could spell the difference between triumph and catastrophe.

Resuming his professorial tone, Helvelius turned back toward the camera. "Jamie is blind, and has been since he was three years old, when he developed a benign growth in the brain called an AVM, or arteriovenous malformation. It's basically a knot of expanded blood vessels that looks and feels just like a handful of worms. In Jamie's case, it's grown to about the size of a lemon, and it's sitting in the occipital lobe, the hindmost part of the brain, which is the primary center for vision. We've already taken out part of the AVM in two earlier operations. Today, we'll take out the rest, and then . . . and then we're going to put something new in its place."

"Just what is that, Dr. Helvelius?" asked Kathleen Brown.

"We call it the SIPNI device. That's short for Self-Integrating Prosthetic Neural Implant. You see, the AVM long ago destroyed Jamie's visual brain center. Even with the AVM removed, he will still be blind. What the SIPNI device does is substitute for the missing part of his brain."

"How is that possible?"

"Well, SIPNI is a kind of minibrain in itself. It's a very special type of self-contained computer."

Helvelius pointed to the device, wrapped in a blue envelope with a clear plastic window and sealed with what looked like striped masking tape. The camera showed little but the glare of the plastic, but Ali knew well what was inside. It was the size and shape of a robin's egg. Its surface was darkly metallic, reflecting light from thousands of honeycomb facets, like a diamond wrought by a fairy gem cutter. It had cost much more than any mere diamond, too—millions in government and industry grants, years of toil, brains and bodies worn out from nonstop work—and, not least of all, relationships strained to the breaking point.

But Helvelius did not speak of the cost. "Don't let its small size fool you," he said. "It uses a parallel array of miniaturized nanochips, with as much sheer calculating power as a conventional minicomputer. It can perform all the image-processing functions that Jamie needs to be able to see. But the really astounding feature is the software that operates it. That's something we've developed here at Fletcher Memorial. It represents a major breakthrough in artificial intelligence."

The camera switched from a close-up of the bag containing the SIPNI device to Helvelius's face. Ali felt a twinge of jealousy as she saw how aroused Helvelius was by the camera. His eyes positively sparkled. His straight, wide, thin-lipped mouth moved vigorously, baring his lower teeth with every "e" and "w" he spoke. A shock of gray hair, still bearing traces of black, wagged over his high forehead. Even his face's anchor, his grand patrician nose, came alive, nostrils flaring.

Yesterday, no one but Ali could have moved him so deeply. Today, the Jezebel's eye of history had stolen his heart.

Helvelius led with his chin as he spoke. "You see, SIPNI can learn, adapt, and model itself, based on the input it receives from Jamie's brain. That's exactly what it needs to do, if it's going to reach out and reconnect with all those millions of brain cells that once converged on the visual center. Not just the fibers from his optic nerves, but also those involved in remembering images, or coordinating hand and eye movements, or joining mental pictures to emotion or to the senses of hearing and smell. We can't begin to untangle the complexity of all that signaling and countersignaling. But SIPNI can do it."

"You mean it can think?"

"In a way, yes. For that, you might ask Kevin—Kevin O'Day, that is—our resident artificial intelligence expert. Kevin, does SIPNI think?"

"Aye, verily, milord," came a voice from across the room.

Ali shuddered. Like a blue note in a Mozart sonata, the sarcasm in Kevin's answer jarred everyone in the room. Kathleen Brown's mouth hung open unflatteringly. Dr. Helvelius tore off his glasses, as though he were going to throw them. "Look, K-Kevin—" he began, but words failed him.

The camera cut abruptly to a thirtysomething young man in dark-rimmed spectacles who sat at a computer console across the room. Ali's heart sank as she saw the patronizing smirk on his face. She recognized that look. She had been married to Kevin O'Day for five years. She knew that look meant trouble.

Like everyone else, Kevin O'Day was dressed in regulation blue scrubs. But instead of the standard blue shower cap, he had covered his hair with a yellow and green silk Japanese head scarf. Although his fine and regular features appeared ordinary from a distance, close-up he was strikingly handsome, even beautiful, with penetrating blue eyes that contrasted with his red goatee and the slight orange freckling of his skin. His bare forearms could have modeled a lecture in topographic anatomy, with their sharply incised muscles and tendons almost popping through the skin. They were, as Ali well knew, the forearms of an accomplished rock-climber who could effortlessly haul himself up by line and piton.

Kevin kicked his chair away from the console, as though he were swinging around to face Kathleen Brown, but he never really looked at her. His eyes stayed focused on the computer monitor, as though this were the only thing worth his glance. "Everyone's all gaga that a machine can think. Why is that so hard to accept? The human brain itself is a machine—nothing more than a computer hardwired with blinking neurons instead of vacuum tubes or silicon. What's so special about a neuron? At over a thousand cubic microns, it's bulky as hell, and it requires an enormous expenditure of energy just to stay alive and hold a place in the big net. SIPNI beats that hands down. Not only does it think, but it thinks faster and more elegantly than the brain tissue it replaces."

Kevin was veering off-script. Ali could only guess at what he was up to, for she had deliberately avoided meeting his gaze when she entered the room. Looking at him these days was like looking at a car wreck. She couldn't afford to get caught up in the feelings she still had for him—not today, when so much depended upon her protecting her clarity of mind.

On TV, Kevin could be seen tapping his hand against his monitor, as though reaching out to it for support. "When this kid sees again, he's going to have smarter eyes than he ever did before. Seeing isn't just like projecting a movie on a big screen, it's the way the brain finds patterns, edges, similarities, axes of motion—stuff like that. It took a hundred million years or so for evolution to program us to turn flashes of light into real seeing. This kid is about to leapfrog another hundred million years beyond either you or me. Beyond hawk and eagle. Beyond Michelangelo."

"That's incredible!" said Kathleen Brown.

"Incredible is just a word for not believing. If you don't find me authoritative enough, ask Odin."

"Who is Odin?"

"SIPNI's father. Odin is the program I interface with on this terminal. But program is a measly word for what he is. It's like me calling you a souped-up amoeba that smokes and drinks too much coffee. Odin is the most advanced computational system on this planet. He won last year's Loebner Prize."

Kathleen Brown scowled at the small palmtop that stored her background notes, as though reproaching it for having left her blindsided by this important fact. "The Loebner Prize? What's that?"

"It's a hundred thousand dollars to the first artificial intelligence system that can't be distinguished from a real person chatting on the telephone. Of course, when I say Odin won, I'm referring to the bronze medal, not the hundred grand. Nobody's been able to walk away with the gold as yet. But Odin does keep getting better."

It was classic Kevin, Ali noted. In almost the same breath, he had bragged about himself and insulted Kathleen Brown in front of an audience of millions. And somehow managed to get away with it.

Kathleen Brown seemed not to notice. "And Odin helped to design SIPNI?" she asked with her trademark perky tone.

"Both hardware and software. Some of this stuff is just way too complex for my puny brain to figure out. So we work together, like Rodgers and Hammerstein. And yes, for your information, he thinks."

"Does he talk?"

"Sure." Kevin flicked a switch on a small module beside the computer. "This activates his external speakers. Odin, this lady would like to have a word with you."

There was a pop as the speaker came on, and then there sounded a mellow, silvery, masculine voice—a voice as familiar to Ali as that of any human being in the room. "I KNOW. I'VE BEEN LISTENING."

Kathleen Brown smiled uneasily. "Listening? How?"

"I'VE BEEN WATCHING *AMERICA TODAY*, OF COURSE."

"I'm flattered."

"YOU NEEDN'T BE. I WATCH ALL SEVENTY-FOUR CHANNELS OF THE HOSPITAL CABLE NETWORK."

"All seventy-four at once?"

"YES. I'M VERY WELL INFORMED ABOUT THE OUTSIDE WORLD. WOULD YOU CARE TO DISCUSS THE CURRENT CRISIS IN LIBYA?"

"Thanks, but I'm more interested in you."

"THAT'S ONLY NATURAL."

Ali smiled at the perplexed look on Kathleen Brown's face. Odin, of course, wasn't being smug with her. He was incapable of human vanity. He was, in fact, the only presence in Operating Room Three who was unsullied by self-interest. He was the perfect incarnation of the classic Stoic ideal of *ataraxia*—absolute freedom from human emotions, and from all the exasperating conflicts that came tangled up with them. There had been days—many days, especially lately—when Ali had envied him that freedom.

Kathleen Brown looked as if she were struggling for a comeback. "How powerful a computer are you?" she finally said, a bit lamely.

"I'M NOT A COMPUTER AT ALL. NO MORE THAN YOU, KATHLEEN BROWN, ARE THE THREE POUNDS OR SO OF GRAY AND WHITE TISSUE YOU CALL A BRAIN. WE BOTH MAKE USE OF A PHYSICAL SUBSTRATUM TO CARRY OUT OUR MENTAL PRO-CESSES. BUT THERE IS MUCH MORE TO US THAN THE PHYSI-CAL SUBSTRATUM, ISN'T THERE? WE ARE OUR THOUGHTS, IN THE FINAL ANALYSIS."

"So are you Mac or PC?"

Ali was irritated by Kathleen Brown's naïveté and ignorance, her cute posturing. She wasn't taking Odin seriously. She had no idea of his complexity, or of the years of obsessive work that Kevin had spent perfecting him.

Odin, too, noticed her ignorance, but without irritation. He an-swered her as an all-wise, all-patient father might answer the little girl on his knee.

"YOU DON'T UNDERSTAND MY POINT, KATHLEEN BROWN. I AM A PROCESS, AND NOT A MACHINE. PROCESS IS ANOTHER WAY OF DESCRIBING WHAT YOU HUMANS THINK OF AS SPIRIT. I EXIST IN AND BEYOND THE ENTIRE NETWORK OF MEDICAL CENTER COMPUTERS. THAT INCLUDES THE LARGE RESEARCH MAINFRAMES, AS WELL AS THE ONE THOUSAND TWO HUN-DRED AND FORTY-SEVEN DESKTOP COMPUTERS DISTRIB-UTED IN EVERY WARD AND OFFICE OF THIS HOSPITAL. I SENSE WHEREVER UNUSED COMPUTING POWER OR DATA STORAGE SPACE IS AVAILABLE, AND I CONSTANTLY SHIFT MY ACTIVI-TIES TO TAKE ADVANTAGE OF IT."

"Don't people have to use those computers?"

"I MODIFY MY ACTIVITIES ACCORDINGLY. IT GIVES RISE TO A KIND OF SLEEP-WAKE CYCLE, MUCH AS YOU HUMANS HAVE. THE SLOWEST PART OF MY CYCLE IS FROM THREE O'CLOCK TO FOUR O'CLOCK EACH AFTERNOON, WHEN THE HOSPITAL INTERNS ARE TYPING UP THE DISCHARGE ORDERS FOR THEIR PATIENTS. MY MOST ACTIVE PERIOD IS AT NIGHT."

Ali remembered those nights—endless bleary-eyed hours she had spent feeding streams of laboratory data to Odin. Many of the experiments needed to create SIPNI were too complex and too expensive to perform outright, so Ali and the rest of the team relied on Odin to create virtual models of the ways molecules, cells, and circuits interacted with one another. While this saved years of trial and error, the immense computations required could only be performed during Odin's peak operating window at night—and it always seemed there was an early surgery waiting for Ali the next day. Those nights had aged her. She wondered whether her whole life would be enough to make up for the sleep she had sacrificed on the altar of science during those grueling months.

On-screen, Kathleen Brown cocked her head and lifted her chin, in a gesture that looked like an obvious attempt to convey a perky thoughtfulness. "You've been described as the father of SIPNI. Do you feel any paternal pride today?"

"I DON'T HAVE FEELINGS, KATHLEEN BROWN."

"But you can think?"

"CERTAINLY. I CAN THINK AND I CAN ACT. BUT MY THINKING IS BASED UPON LOGIC, FREED FROM ALL EMOTIONAL ENTANGLEMENTS. WHEN DECISIONS ARE REQUIRED, I CONDUCT A MULTI-TIERED ANALYSIS OF RISKS AND BENEFITS. I KNOW NOTHING OF FEAR, DOUBT, ANGER, REMORSE, OR SELFISHNESS—OTHER THAN THEIR DEFINITIONS, AND THEIR EFFECTS UPON HUMAN BEINGS."

"And love?"

"I HAVE AN INTIMATE WORKING RELATIONSHIP WITH MY CREATOR, DR. KEVIN O'DAY. I EXIST WHOLLY TO SATISFY HIM. I CAN ANTICIPATE HIS NEEDS WITHOUT REQUIRING AN EXPLICIT DIRECTIVE. THESE ARE COUNTERPARTS OF THE HUMAN ATTRIBUTES OF DEVOTION, LOYALTY, AND SOLICITUDE. SO IN AN OPERATIONAL SENSE I CAN BE SAID TO BE CAPABLE OF LOVE, OR AT LEAST OF TRAITS BY WHICH LOVE MAY ARGUABLY BE DEFINED. BUT I AM DEVOID OF POSSESSIVENESS, JEALOUSY, OR THE EXPECTATION OF REQUITAL OF MY FRIENDSHIP."

"Amazing!" said Kathleen Brown, swaying her hips and rising on her toes like a bashful prom queen. "Are you available in a home computer version?"

Helvelius cleared his throat. "Apparently Odin is not above a little grandstanding. Kevin, could you switch the speaker off?"

Kevin hesitated for a stubborn half second, and then flicked the speaker switch. "Sorry, Odin," he said, letting his hand catch in the air, like a backhanded salute.

Ali was relieved that Kevin was off the air. He had been flippant, even rude, but she knew that he was capable of much worse.

To be sure, Kevin O'Day had been less wowed by the TV cameras than anyone else in OR 3. He had barely listened while his own brain-child Odin spoke to Kathleen Brown. Instead, his gaze was riveted on his computer monitor, which was blank except for two short lines of type:

SEND PAGE?

YES   NO

A bonehead question, yet Kevin had been pondering it for the past five minutes, if not for most of the morning. He was not normally wishy-washy. But he knew that behind this question lay the biggest showdown of his life, and he had to be sure of his hand. Once sent, the page could not be taken back.

He wished that this question— "Send Page?" —could have been approached logically, using time-tested algorithms of decision analysis. *Here are the benefits, here are the risks, each weighted according to probability and worst-case impact.* He was a natural for that kind of analysis. But this . . . this was something else. "Send Page?" was not so much a question as a challenge. It said, *Show your manhood. Time to go all in—or fold.* The blue computer screen and its two lines of type were a curtain that divided earthly reality from the world of pure imagination. He had never dared to lift that curtain before. But now . . .

Oh, if only Odin could have made the decision for him! Odin would not have felt the coldness of sweat upon his brow, the heartburn, the throbbing pulse in his temples. . . . But Odin was all brain and no backbone. He would have been no help here. There was a reason why poker was the only game he couldn't master.

Kevin moved his finger back and forth between two keys—"Yes" and "No"—not pressing them, only making feather-light contact, as if some chance vibe off their surface might settle the fateful question. But the longer he played with them this way, the more paralyzed his will became.

He might have gone on forever—until a minuscule incident, no more substantial than the beat of a butterfly's wings, put everything into focus. He had been checking out the room, a little worried that someone might break free from the spell of the TV cameras long enough to notice what was on his monitor. Suddenly, he glimpsed two green eyes peering at him from behind an ECG display. They were the eyes of a sylphlike, olive-skinned woman—a woman he had loved, even worshipped, for five delirious years. Her look made his blood run cold. He could have withstood anything else—hatred, ridicule, rage, contempt—anything but this. Anything but . . . *pity*.

And in that instant, the instant of Ali's pitying him, perfect clarity dawned upon Kevin. "Send Page?" He needed no algorithms of logic. He *felt* the answer. He felt it like the snap of an electric shock sweeping down his nerves, bringing every sinew into action. Instantaneously, as if by conditioned reflex, his pale, cold finger rapped the key:

YES

He blinked, and the two lines of type had vanished from his computer screen.

On television, Ali watched Amy Richmond in the New York studio grilling Dr. Helvelius. "Isn't it true that not everyone is comfortable with the experiment you're about to perform?" said the anchor. "In a sense, you're trying to create a hybrid between a computer and the human mind, between man and machine. What about those dozens of protesters who are picketing your hospital at this very moment? What would you say to those who feel that what you are doing violates the laws of nature, perhaps even the laws of God?"

Helvelius looked as though he had just bitten into a ripe lemon. "All progress generates reaction," he said. "If by the laws of nature you mean things as they have always been till now, then I would argue that penicillin violates the laws of nature, since the experience of countless centuries proves that man was meant to die from pneumonia and venereal disease. And what could be more unnatural than to cut open a living human body to remove a tumor or a gangrenous appendix? What were we given skin for, if not to hide the mysteries within, and to plant a 'Do Not Disturb' sign squarely in the path of the surgeon? Everything that is new begins by being frightening. But given enough time, the so-called laws of nature and of God redefine themselves."

Do they? thought Ali. *Are there no limits? No final taboos?* There was something about all this rush to make history that troubled her. Focused on making SIPNI work, she and the rest of the team had never paused to question their own premises. They were not philosophers, after all. Their horizons—or "endpoints," as they preferred to call them—went no further than the survival of a patient, or a gain of function. They had asked only what *could* be done—not what *ought* to be done.

Back at the New York desk, Amy Richmond put on a pensive look. "Some experts have expressed a fear that this technology could be used to create an artificial superman—by the military, or a multinational corporation, or even by organized crime. What do you say to that?"

Helvelius lowered his head and glared over the top of his glasses. It was a defiant gesture, one that Ali had met with on her first day as a resident, when she had had the naïveté to ask the god of Neurosurgery why he didn't try to remove a tumor from the skull base of an elderly patient. Ali still smarted from the harangue that followed: Helvelius, bloody scalpel in hand, grilling her, lecturing her on futility, quality of life, false heroics, and the anatomy of the cavernous sinus. That night she had lain sleepless in her bed despising herself, renouncing her dream of becoming a surgeon. But through all her self-pity, a still, soft voice spoke to her: *He's right. He looks at reality without any trace of sentiment. And if he can do that, I can learn to do it, too.* By the next morning she had not only decided to go on with surgery, she had claimed Helvelius as her personal mentor.

"Th-those are not experts talking!" sputtered Helvelius now. "They are s-s-self-appointed jackdaws who greatly exaggerate what

SIPNI is capable of. Our aim is simply to repair the broken bridges of the brain. If we succeed, we can restore function lost to strokes, or spinal cord injuries, or crippling diseases like multiple sclerosis or ALS. Is that not enough in this day and age?"

"But the fear is—"

"Don't talk to me about people's namby-pamby fears!" Helvelius's bushy eyebrows arched, furrowing his brow like the tracings of a seismograph at full tilt. "We've had months of discussions about this. Our project has been thoroughly vetted by the Ethics Review Board of this medical center, as well as by the Food and Drug Administration and the National Institutes of Health. Every issue has been examined. There is no rational basis for any fear whatsoever."

Helvelius waved his hand dismissively. As he did so, he revealed a little-known peculiarity about himself. He was missing the index finger of his right hand. Ali knew that he had lost it many years before on the Minnesota farm where he had grown up. It had almost kept him out of a surgical residency. But he had gone on to prove that he could do more with nine fingers than most surgeons could with ten.

"Let me introduce you to another member of our team," said Helvelius, pointedly changing the subject. "The SIPNI device could not work without some way to connect it to Jamie's brain. For that we use a gel with unique conducting properties, which was developed in a laboratory here at Fletcher Memorial by my assistant, Dr. Ali O'Day, who also happens to be Kevin's wife. I'll let Ali tell you about the gel."

Helvelius stepped aside, drawing Ali into the line of view of the camera that had been stationed on the other side of the bed. Ali had known this moment was coming—the assistant director had held a rehearsal the day before—but when she glanced back at the monitor, a fleeting glimpse of her own face on television froze her. Four or five agonizing seconds passed. Through the bright lights she saw Kathleen Brown—her skin unnaturally orange from the heavy makeup used to counteract the blue color bias of the TV cameras, her hair helmetlike in its spray-lacquered perfection. She saw the microphone thrust like a spear toward her face. And she saw the tiny red light of the Betacam, the eye of five million viewers—the eye of an entire country.

What was she supposed to say? Dr. Helvelius had lobbied hard to bring this camera into the operating room. She had tried to want it, because Helvelius had wanted it. But Ali distrusted reporters, particularly where science was concerned. All they were interested in was drama—not science, but a magic show. They had no patience for the rigorous thinking that was at the foundation of a breakthrough like SIPNI. And despite all their fawning and flattery, Ali was sure that they were poised to swoop down like vultures should any part of today's surgery go wrong.

But five million viewers were waiting. How could she reach them? She took a deep breath, the breath called *deergha shvaasam* in Sanskrit, as she told herself that this was no different from lecturing at grand rounds or presenting cases at tumor boards. But these five million were not doctors. They did not speak her language, the language of science. How could she ever explain to them? She felt as she had when she was seven, in second grade, struggling to speak English when all the words wanted to come out in Masri Arabic.

And worst of all, there was the camera's unblinking eye—the relentless eye of millions, watching her discomfort without a trace of compassion.

Ali felt another wave of nausea. *Oh, God, what if I threw up now, in front of all the world?* She began to speak, her voice sounding small and unconvincing in her ears. "SIPNI's input and output to the brain passes through what we call the terminal plate, which is really the outer covering—or shell, if you will—of this egg-shaped device." She felt a tiny joy at the word "shell," which seemed to reinforce the egg shape she wanted her listeners to see in their minds. *Perhaps I can reach them after all.*

"This surface, a little more than two square inches, is studded with over twelve million separate contact points, too small to be seen with the naked eye. The trick is to get each of these contacts to line up exactly with one of the countless fibers that stretch back and forth between different parts of the brain. We call these axons." *Oh, God! Axons? I'm going to lose them here. How can I get them to see this?* "Axons . . . axons are like . . . fine sprouts issuing directly from individual brain cells. They can be from a thousandth of an inch to several inches long, depending on what parts of the brain need to talk to each other. It would be impossible for us to reconnect them one by one, by hand. That is the function of CHARM. When—"

She opened her mouth to go on, then skipped back like a record player needle jumping its groove. "Uh, CHARM stands for Current-Sensitive Heuristic Axon-Redirecting Matrix. It's the gel that we apply to the outer surface of SIPNI." She silently castigated herself, not only for the skip, but for using the lifeless word "surface" instead of the joyful word "shell."

The red light of the camera held its unblinking stare. "The gel lets SIPNI grow its own connections. When first applied, the gel is only a slight conductor of electricity. But it has a very special property such that, each time a tiny spark of current passes through it— wherever SIPNI finds an axon, or the axon talks back—that part of the gel undergoes a chemical reaction that makes it a much better conductor. The next time, the connection gets faster and stronger, until a minute pathway is formed, less than a hundredth of the diameter of a human hair. SIPNI keeps sweeping the area with electrical pulses, searching for all the axons within reach. As pathways are formed, the chemical reaction releases a neural growth factor impregnated into the gel, which causes the axons to grow into the gel. Eventually, the gel solidifies, forming a sieve of high-conducting nanotubes, which are filled by axon terminals, like cables inserted into the holes of an old telephone switchboard. After that, the connections are permanent."

Oh, what a mess she was making of this! *Neural growth factors, nanotubes, axon terminals . . .* She had rushed through them all, impetuously, as one runs toward the light at the end of a dark tunnel. Had she lost her viewers completely? *Deergha shvaasam. Deergha shvaasam.* Whether she had done well or ill, this was live television. There was no going back.

Harry Lewton, the newly hired chief security officer, watched the struggles of Ali O'Day on the middle screen of a long row of TV monitors in his office. In his right hand he held a mug of coffee still too hot to drink, while in his left he held a phone receiver to his ear, propping his elbow on a pile of security status reports from the night before. His inlaid tan caiman-skin boots were balanced on a plastic wastebasket, rocking it precariously on one edge.

He was speaking to a nurse on the general medical ward on the eighteenth floor of Tower C.

"That's Viola Lewton, spelled V-I-O-L-A," he said. "I brought her in yesterday. Aspiration pneumonia is what they said it was."

"Your mother? Yes, I know her. She had a pretty rough night of it, but she's finally sleeping now. It'd be a shame to disturb her. I can have her call you when she wakes up."

"Fine. Will you personally see to it that she gets her Parkinson's medicine? She needs to take it three times a day. Without it, she has trouble speaking or eating."

"Yes, of course, Mr. Lewton. It's right here in her chart. Someone underlined it and wrote exclamation marks."

"That was me."

Harry's mother was only fifty-eight, but she had had Parkinson's disease for the past six years and it had made her as decrepit as an eighty-five-year-old. It wasn't just the tremors, which were one of the easiest things to control with medication, but she lived in a slow-motion world, her every movement requiring painful deliberation. Her body was becoming a prison. She had had to give up her career driving a school bus, and now she had gone so far downhill that she could hardly feed herself, much less cook or bathe or button a blouse.

She had never known anything but Texas and Louisiana until three weeks ago, when Harry had pulled her out of a nursing home and brought her to live with him in his apartment in Chicago. That was like firing on Fort Sumter as far as Harry's family was concerned. His sister, Luanne, had put her in the home, and she insisted that it was the only safe place for her to be. But for Harry, turning his mother over to the care of strangers was desertion. So he had flown down to Houston, brandished his power of attorney, and taken her himself.

Now he had nothing but guilt to show for it. Even though he had arranged for daytime home care, he had underestimated how difficult it would be for his mother to feed herself or even to drink. Several days ago, she had had a bad choking episode that led to pneumonia. Would that have happened in the nursing home? Harry felt responsible. Sure, he pulled strings to make sure she got a private room and the best doctors in the city, but that didn't erase the fact that for the sake of pride and honor he had played roulette with his mother's life.

"Can you hold for a minute, Mr. Lewton? I think I see Dr. Weiss coming down the hall."

"Sure, sure."

Harry glanced at the TV. *Christ, look at those peepers!* The shy, sphinxlike woman on the monitor kept looking off into space as she spoke. But now and then, quite abruptly, she would turn and stare straight into the camera, opening her green eyes wide under the canopy of her dark, gull-wing eyebrows. When she did that, she seemed to reach out from the TV screen and look directly at Harry himself.

Harry was intrigued by her, by her bashfulness, which struck him as a paradox that needed explanation. *She paws the ground like a scared kitten. But she's a panther, no kitten. If she wanted to, she could eat you for breakfast. You or any man. Just look at those eyes.*

From time to time, Harry glanced at the other monitors—closed surveillance circuits that gave him a godlike view of what was going on anywhere in the hospital. The pièce de résistance was a sixty-inch LCD screen on the wall to his left, which displayed a schematic of glowing lights showing the status of every door, elevator, and fire alarm within the 1.2 million square feet of the medical center. The lights were all green now, not a yellow or red among them. The medical center was functioning as it ought to, like a healthy, vigorous body.

The only irritant to the healthy body was on the plaza outside the main entrance. The cameras showed a couple dozen protesters circling there, as they chanted and waved signs, all neatly printed in the same blue paint: STOP DR. FRANKENSTEIN;, NO AMALGAMATION OF MAN AND MACHINE; HONOR THE HUMAN SOUL; WHERE WILL IT END?; FLETCHER MEMORIAL PLAYS GOD.

TV cameras always brought out groups like this. But this bunch wasn't doing any harm. They were staying out of the flowerbeds and they weren't blocking the traffic circle. Not like those Green fanatics who tried to shut down the oil terminals back when he was an assistant security director in Texas City. That had been his first job after leaving police work, and he had handled it well. He had gone strictly by the book, which was easy enough when you've just finished your MBA in security management. No one got hurt, nothing got blown up, and—bottom line—the tankers came in on time. If only everything else in his life had turned out as smoothly as that. It almost made up for that fiasco at Nacogdoches.

Back on the center screen, Dr. Ali O'Day was trying to explain what a neural net was, and, judging by the puzzled look on Kathleen Brown's face, it was an uphill climb. Ali looked different than she had the few times Harry had seen her in person, in the hallways or in the staff dining room. *It's that surgical cap she's wearing*, he decided. It swept her wavy, shoulder-length sable hair out of sight, and starkly accentuated the forehead and cheekbones of her shield-shaped face. *Yes, that's it.* And now he noticed something he hadn't seen before— a little bitty hump to the ridge of her nose. *Not an Irish nose*, he told himself. *Not the nose of an O'Day.* Her mouth, too, had something exotic about it—a little wide for her jawline, with lips spread apart, as if frozen in the beginning of a smile.

What was that about her husband? Harry had never noticed a ring on Ali's finger, and in the three months he had been at Fletcher Memorial, he had never seen this man with her. *Kevin, that's what his name was.* Even now, she never glanced at Kevin in that fleeting, automatic way that husbands and wives did when they needed to get a fix on something familiar or bolster themselves with a shot of approval. He was a lucky bastard if a husband is what he really was. But something was missing. Definitely something was missing.

Harry heard a rattle at the other end of the phone line.

"Dr. Weiss here," said an impatient voice.

"Doctor, this is Harry Lewton. My mother—"

"She's not doing as well as we'd like. She's still running a temperature, and the portable X-ray we took during the night shows a worsening of her pneumonia. I'm going to add imipenem, an IV antibiotic. That should give us better coverage for anaerobic bacteria."

"How serious is this?"

"Aspiration pneumonia is a leading cause of death in patients with Parkinson's disease."

What an impersonal prick, thought Harry. "If there's some kind of test or treatment she needs, make sure you do it," he said. "I'll pay whatever insurance doesn't cover."

Dr. Weiss ignored Harry's offer. "We have her on ten liters of oxygen right now. We're watching closely for any signs of respiratory fatigue."

The internist's voice was suddenly drowned out by the opening banjo lick of "Foggy Mountain Breakdown," Harry's cell phone's ringtone. In one movement, Harry snatched the phone from his belt and shook it open. There was an incoming text page. Harry had been expecting a message from the VP for finance, but this was something very different. When he held the screen up to the light, he saw, in plain block letters:

FMMC CRITICAL STATUS. VERIFY THREAT PARCEL ENDO LOBBY. AWAIT INSTRUCTIONS 0830. MAINTAIN STRICT SILENCE. DO NOT EVACUATE. ALL OPERATIONS MUST REMAIN NORMAL. PENALTY FOR DISREGARD CATASTROPHIC. GOD IS GREAT.

"Aw, Christ!" he muttered. "You gotta be shittin' me!"

"Excuse me?" said Dr. Weiss.

"Sorry, I didn't mean you. It's a . . . it's a text page. Look, I've got something I have to deal with right now. Can we talk later, after I've had a chance to see my mother for myself?"

"Yes. Let's do that."

"Bye, then."

Harry read over the message several times, making sure that he hadn't gotten it wrong. Was it a joke? A bona fide threat? The hospital got prank calls all the time, but he had yet to get one on his personal pager. He scrolled up and down, but there was no callback number. By reflex, he turned to his computer and accessed Logline, the com tracker that could be used to trace calls going to any phone or pager within the hospital. The page had come from within the hospital.

Briskly punching the number, he heard one ring and then the sound of a woman's voice. "Neurosurgery."

"This is Harry Lewton, in security. Did you just text-page me?"

"No, Mr. Lewton."

"Whose line is this?"

"This is the office of Dr. Richard Helvelius."

"Well, somebody just paged me from this telephone."

"I didn't page you."

The snippiness in her voice irked him. "And you are?"

"Aileen. Aileen Zimmerman, Dr. Helvelius's administrative assistant."

"Who else is there?"

"No one. Not at 7:30 A.M. I'm just opening up the office. Dr. Helvelius is in surgery."

"I know that, goddamn it. The whole country knows it. It's a national event."

There was a long pause on the other end of the line. At last the woman's voice came through, tautly. "How can I help you, Mr. Lewton?"

"Could anyone else have been using this phone within the last five minutes?"

"No. As I said—"

"Well, if you think of someone who may have, call me back."

Harry slammed down the phone. *Jesus!* It would be a hell of a trick for Dr. Helvelius to page him while prepping for surgery on live TV. Logline must have gotten the number wrong. Make a note of that for the system support people. A fourteen-million-dollar upgrade, and still more bugs than a bayou in July.

Endo Lobby. That could be either the Endocrinology Clinic or the Endoscopy Clinic. If the call had really come from someone in the hospital, you'd think they would have known that and been more specific. So it could still be an outsider, a hoax. Maybe one of these protesters. A disgruntled patient. A kid with nothing but time on his hands. *God!* Why not a little respect for people who have to work for a living?

Still, there was something about the message that made him uneasy. Something a little too businesslike for your typical wiseass kid. Harry took a swig of his coffee and got up from his desk. Hurrying toward the door, he threw on a blue blazer that hid the slim 9mm Beretta holstered under his armpit. *Endocrinology was closest, just down the Pike. Start there.*

Ali O'Day backed through the swinging door of Operating Room Three, her freshly rescrubbed hands held aloft, her face covered with a blue paper surgical mask. The OR was almost back to normal. Golden-haired Kathleen Brown and her television crew had withdrawn to the family lounge, leaving a sole cameraman to shoot the video of the actual operation—footage that would be edited into a segment for that evening's special edition of *Lifeline*.

In her mind, Ali was still facing Kathleen Brown and the pitiless blinking red eye of *America Today*—endlessly replaying that string of flubs, which was all she could recall of her performance. Why did the right thing to say always occur to her just when it was too late to say it? The experience had left her so flustered that she could hardly think about the operation, and that upset her more than anything. *I've got to shake this. I can't afford to lose control,* she thought as she snapped a pair of chocolate-colored surgical gloves onto her hands. *I musn't let Jamie down.* She looked across the room, toward the still form of Jamie Winslow, barely visible through the drapes and trays. *Stay calm,* she told herself. *Remember that Jamie is what this day is about.*

Ali had met Jamie a few months before, when his legal guardian, Mrs. Gore, brought him to the Department of Neurosurgery. Five other neurosurgeons had written him off as hopeless, and with good reason. The tumor inside his head was a Grade V on the Spetzler-Martin scale. It was huge, it was deeply entangled with the brain's vital blood supply, and it nestled directly against what the neurologists referred to as "eloquent cortex"—indispensable parts of the working brain. If it were taken out too abruptly, the gush of new blood into old deserts could have burst the arteries, leaving Jamie paralyzed, speechless, or even locked into an irreversible coma state. There was no question of restoring his eyesight: both sides of his visual center had long since been destroyed by the AVM.

Every surgeon who had looked at Jamie had concluded the same thing. There was nothing to justify the awful risks of surgery. Yes, there was a big chance that the AVM could kill him some day: it might break open and bleed without warning, or it might simply keep on growing until it had crushed the life-sustaining centers in the brainstem. But that would be in the course of nature. No surgeon wanted this young boy's death on his own hands. The Hippocratic Oath said it succinctly: "First do no harm."

But Jamie Winslow did not have the look of the hopeless. It was hard to give up on him. When Ali first walked into the examining room to meet him, he cocked his head, gave her a big, toothy smile, and asked her whether she had had a good time in California.

"Yes, I just flew back from San Diego, from the Annual Meeting of the American Association of Neurological Surgeons. It's like a weeklong school for doctors. How did you know that?"

"You sound really sleepy. People's voices go down at the end when they've been up all night flying on airplanes."

"Yes, I took a red-eye flight. But California?"

"I can smell the smoke in your hair."

"Smoke? What do you mean?"

"There's some really big fires burning in Southern California right now. I've been hearing about it on TV, 'cause a lot of firemen from here in Chicago have gone over there to help out. That kind of smoke has a special smell. It's not like cigarettes or anything. I smelled it a couple of years ago when we went to Chain O'Lakes Park and they had a prairie fire."

"That's amazing. Yes, there was a haze everywhere. You could smell the smoke from the mountains. But I had no idea that I had carried it back with me."

"Sure, I can smell it." Jamie cocked his head and lowered his voice, like a conspirator. "So did you play hooky from that doctor meeting you went to?"

"What do you mean?"

Jamie grinned, his gums showing in the place of a missing upper tooth. "Your suntan lotion. I can smell that, too."

His smile was like a sun that never dimmed, despite a pall of illness, loss, and abandonment that would have dimmed the spirit of many who had traveled further in life. After his father was killed in Afghanistan, his mother was unable to care for him and turned him over to the custody of the courts. For two years, he had lived at the Grossman School for the Blind in Wheaton, where Mrs. Gore, a dormitory matron, acted as his legal guardian. He was bright and friendly and did well in school, learning to read in Braille and getting high marks in arithmetic. But an impish insistence on doing things his way had earned him more than a few detentions. Had he not been shielded from harsher discipline by Mrs. Gore, his natural-born independence might have progressed to outright rebellion.

At the Grossman School, he was learning swimming and goalball. But baseball was what he really cared about. All through the spring and summer, he followed the Cubs and the White Sox on the radio, his spirits rising and falling with every crack of the bat. He liked the simplicity of the game. Football and basketball were too complicated to follow without the aid of sight. But in baseball, he could reconstruct everything that happened from what the radio announcers said. There was a moral simplicity to it, too, so plain that even a seven-year-old could understand it. Every man stood alone at the plate, his fate tied to his unique strengths and weaknesses, like a Greek hero. Jamie could identify with that. It was a mirror of what he saw life to be.

When Dr. Helvelius once asked him what he would do if he got his sight back, his answer was immediate. "Baseball. I'm gonna be a major league baseball player. One day, I'll lead the Cubs to the World Series. You'll see I will!"

As for Ali, once the mesquite smoke was out of her hair, Jamie always professed to dislike her smell of iodine and harshly laundered scrub suits. But her accent fascinated him. Few people ever noticed it. She had moved to New York as a little girl, and here in the Midwest, New York was all they heard. Jamie picked up on an older accent, out of the cradle, that had been almost erased, like the old writing on a palimpsest. He pestered her until she finally explained it to him, and from then on she was "Dr. Nefertiti" to him. *Dr. Nefertiti.* She didn't take offense, for it was a recognition of a secret bond. Each had had to overcome adversity and sorrow. Each knew what it was to be an alien.

Ali was aware that her relationship with Jamie was not objective. She had met him at the lowest point in her life, a time when she could hardly bear to drag herself out of bed each morning. When he first showed up in her clinic, it was as though the clouds had parted for the first time after a long, brutal, numbing winter. His rollicking laughter and breathless questions about wildfires and mummies and star travel and the New York Yankees beguiled her and made her forget her own loss. She looked forward to his visits, and then felt a gnawing emptiness each time Mrs. Gore led him home. In her restless nights, she would soothe herself to sleep thinking about Jamie's gap-toothed smile, or the way his pink ears poked through his curly hair, or the last silly knock-knock joke he had told. Ali had been taught that it was wrong or even dangerous to take pleasure like that from a patient. A surgeon cuts people. Life and death decisions had to be based on cold mathematical probabilities, and not on the promptings of the heart. But Jamie was not a typical patient. He was a helpless seven-year-old boy without a father or mother to love him. And Ali couldn't resist wanting so much more for him than a doctor could give.

Her feelings had already profoundly affected the course of the SIPNI project. SIPNI was supposed to be tested first on an elderly patient, someone who had little to lose if things went wrong. But Ali believed strongly that Jamie deserved a chance at a full life. When the IND—the government-sanctioned Investigational New Device approval—finally came through, allowing the SIPNI device to be tried on a human being, she had argued relentlessly that it should be Jamie who got the first trial. She won out, but she had taken an awful risk. For if Jamie wound up being hurt, the responsibility would be hers alone.

The operating room door swung again as Dr. Helvelius made his entrance. This was the signal for someone to hit play on a CD player. In a moment, the room was filled with the sound of *Media vita in morte sumus*, a responsory from the Gregorian chant.

"Could we have a little anesthesia, please?" said Helvelius gaily, as though ordering a bottle of chablis.

"He's under," came a voice from behind the blue screen that separated the brightly lit circle of scalp from the rest of Jamie Winslow. It was Dr. Godoy, the anesthesiologist, who spoke so softly that Ali could barely hear him above the whoosh of the bellows of the anesthesia machine.

"Radiology ready?"

A gowned figure nodded from beside the portable fluoroscope across the room.

Helvelius looked into the Betacam in the corner. "We're going to start with a pre-op angiogram to give us an idea of what the blood vessels look like inside Jamie's brain. Get the lay of the land, so to speak. We can't afford any surprises once we open him up. Dr. O'Day, would you be so kind as to start the catheter?"

Ali looked at Helvelius with surprise. The catheter insertion was a routine but sometimes messy procedure, usually performed by a resident from Interventional Radiology. "You don't want radiology to do it?"

"Not today. I'd like a sure hand."

Sure hand? Ali still felt shaky from her agonies in front of the camera.

But it was no time to demur. The camera was running, and Ali had to proceed. Turning from the scrub nurse who had just tied the back of her operating gown, she pulled back the edge of a blue paper drape over Jamie's right groin, where the skin had been painted iodine yellow. She felt for a pulse, then cut a one-eighth-inch nick in the skin and used a fine hemostat clamp to tunnel into the opening.

"Dr. O'Day will be passing an ultrathin catheter tube into an artery in Jamie's leg. It will have to travel through the main artery, the aorta, almost to his heart, and from there through the neck until it reaches the circle of arteries at the base of the brain. We will use this catheter to inject a puff of dye, which we can photograph on X-ray."

Ali was amazed at Helvelius's self-assurance. Here she was, nearly paralyzed by the unnatural scrutiny of these spotlights, and he seemed to frolic in their glow. Where did he get that kind of confidence?

But before her lay the artery, pulsating, glistening white. *Focus, now! This is all you have to worry about. Just this artery. Just this one little task.* Deftly, Ali pushed a large twelve-gauge needle at a forty-five-degree angle through the opening, thrusting toward Jamie's pulse. A couple of small spurts of blood showed that the needle was inside. Then Ali attached the introducer, shaped like a big metal Y, and through this passed a thin guide wire for the catheter. The guide wire glided without resistance for a foot or so, until it had reached the aorta, the central artery of the body.

Then she was done. Ali stepped back as the C-shaped arms of the fluoroscope were brought forward and positioned above and below Jamie's body, like the claw of a giant crab. The next job belonged to the lead-aproned radiologist, who, guided by the images from the fluoroscope, would inch the wire forward through the abdomen, chest, and neck, until it had reached the base of the brain itself.

Because of the radiation emitted by the fluoroscope, the room was cleared while the radiologist worked. Only Ali and Dr. Helvelius remained, watching from a small island of safety behind a lead screen. Both clasped their gloved hands against the sterile fronts of their gowns, to avoid contamination.

A shadow fell over Ali's face as Helvelius inclined his head toward her. Behind his yellow paper mask, behind his surgical spectacles with the binocular loupes that made him look almost like a robot, she thought she detected a smile. "You know, it's all I can do to keep from s-s-sweeping you into my arms this very minute," he whispered.

"Don't be a fool, Richard." Ali chuckled. "The camera's running."

"Damn the camera! Let the whole world know! I l-love you and I don't see why I should be ashamed of it."

"Your reputation—"

"Means nothing to me. Not if it's going to stand in our way. I want you, Ali. I want you to m-marry me. I don't care about anything else."

She turned away abruptly and cast her gaze on the floor. "I'm not ready," she said.

"Is it because I'm old?"

"No. No, don't say that. It's me. It's . . . . it's . . ." She paused and took a deep breath. "It's Kevin."

"Kevin? You left him months ago. You sent him divorce papers."

"I know, I know. But he hasn't filed any response with the court. In fact, he hasn't spoken a word to me about it, which isn't like him. When we have to talk about the SIPNI project, he acts like nothing's happened. That frightens me."

"He already knows everything, Ali. C-c-can't you see it in his eyes?"

"I'm not sure what I see. I know he's gone to a dark place, but he's pulled a veil over it. I don't want to hurt him. Don't you understand? I don't want to push him over the brink."

"So you still care for him."

"I never said I quit caring about him. I said I couldn't bear to go on living with him."

"I don't see why the two of you can't just sit down and have it out."

"You know why, Richard." She looked at him briefly, and then turned away. "I don't handle confrontations well. I get sick inside just thinking about it. I guess, well, I'm a coward."

"No, you're not a coward. Look, it's not f-fair of me to pressure you. The fact is, Ali, I'll take you any way I can have you. I'm living the happiest days of my l-l-life right now."

"You're not jealous, then?"

"Pure Kelly green." Unable to embrace her with his sterile hands, Helvelius swung his leg behind her and gently pressed his shin against her calf. "My ex was never so understanding when *we* split up. God, how could K-Kevin not see what he's throwing away!"

"Don't be jealous, Richard," she said, taking pleasure in the warm touch of his leg. "I do want to be with you."

"Your rotten luck!" he said, his smile showing through his mask again. "I know I'm an old dog. Surgery has been my w-wife, my kids. It's what I've lived for all these years. But now . . . now I want more. So much more. This b-baby . . . It could be like a second chance for me. For *us*. We could —"

Ali suddenly stiffened and pulled her leg away. "Please don't call it a baby," she said. "That's like giving it a name."

"Well, what is it, for God's sake? Why are you intent on getting rid of it? When you were carrying Ramsey, you w-wanted a child more than anything."

She shut her eyes tightly, as if trying to escape an inner vision. "Don't talk about Ramsey," she snapped.

"Ali, I was there. I remember how rough it was for you. If you're worried that . . . we can get the best prenatal evaluation."

Ali felt a wave of nausea building. "I can't do it, that's all," she said. "I can't bear to even hope for anything anymore. It's the hoping that hurts."

"At least think about it. P-p-promise me that."

"Look, Richard, I don't even know it's yours."

Indeed, she did not know.

Nine weeks and two days ago. It had been a long, awkward day with Kevin in the lab. They were performing a critical experiment for SIPNI, a test that everyone hoped would prove to the FDA that the device was ready to be tried on a real patient. SIPNI had been wired to a camera, and its ability to distinguish pattern, motion, and perspective was compared to a group of medical student volunteers. For seven hours, Ali and Kevin sat together in a semidarkened room, keeping score while test images and snippets of movies were projected onto a screen. They avoided speaking about the elephant in the room—Ali's move out of the apartment—and tried to focus on the test. After some early glitches, SIPNI's learning curve took off, so that by late afternoon the poor medical students got the pants beaten off them by a gizmo the size of an egg. SIPNI could instantaneously count 1,031 pencils in a jumbled pile, and identify the one pencil in 1,031 that had no eraser. In less than a second, it could do the same thing from a movie of the pencils being poured out of a canister. By every yardstick Ali and Kevin could devise, SIPNI saw more sharply, more vividly, more discerningly, and in more colors than the human eye and brain. Three years of work had culminated in a resounding success. The FDA would have no choice but to grant approval.

There had to be a celebration. As the experiment broke up, Kevin suggested a late dinner together at Napoli, a quiet Italian hole-in-the-wall on Damen Avenue that had been his and Ali's favorite for years. An innocent suggestion—except with Kevin, nothing was ever innocent. Everything was a move in a chess game. Ali felt uneasy about it from the start. As she drove to meet him at the restaurant, there was one point, waiting at a light, when she almost turned the car around. *But it's the least you can do,* she thought. *You walked out leaving a Dear John letter on the dresser. He deserves a face-to-face explanation.* The restaurant, she knew, would be safe. If he made a scene, she could quickly leave.

She was little prepared for what did happen. Kevin was as gentle as a puppy. He rose to greet her as she came through the door. He ushered her to their "special" booth in the back, and ordered for her, faultlessly remembering her penchant for *funghi ripieni, stracciatella alla romana,* and *tortolloni quatro formaggi.* There were no recriminations. He spoke only of how much he missed her, how cold and dark the apartment was without her. He reminisced about a trip they had taken to the Valle d'Aosta, in the Italian Alps, and how they had once planned to spend a summer walking the Grande Traversata together. And then he asked her point-blank to come back. He spoke feelingly, without guarding himself, without trying to hide the pain in his eyes or the nervous quaver in his voice. It was the hardest thing for him to do, she knew, to surrender his pride like that.

No, it's too late, she ought to have said. But her heart went soft at the sight of him pleading like a little boy. He seemed so different from the sarcastic egotist who had driven her away. Could he have changed? Had she judged him too hastily? She had brooded over her decision every hour of every day since moving out. Now, she was less sure than ever.

Without answering him directly, she touched him on the hand and suggested they go for a walk. He paid the check quickly, without looking at it. Outside, the spring night was warm. Tying her sweater around her waist, Ali put her hand under Kevin's arm and strolled with him down Division Street. Old habit seemed to guide them in the direction of their apartment a few blocks away. Kevin spoke little, relying on her reminiscences to speak for him, as they passed the tree-lined blocks of sidewalk cafes, Polish delicatessens, boutiques and craft stores where Ali loved to browse on her rare free weekend hours. Then, in front of the gray beaux arts edifice of the Russian baths, with its twin arched doorways, they both paused, a little nervously.

"Want to come up for a minute?" asked Kevin. Ali nodded and started up the side street with him. A few steps, and they were in front of an old brownstone with large bay windows. Kevin led her onto the porch, and then up a narrow, creaking staircase to the apartment on the middle floor. Crossing the threshold, Ali felt strangely divided, as though she had come home, and yet was a total stranger. It was remarkable how nothing had been changed. Passing through the bedroom to freshen up while Kevin made espresso, she noticed that her bedroom closet and dresser drawers were still empty. In the bathroom, her favorite soap and shampoo still sat on the edge of the tub, and a hairbrush she had left behind lay untouched beside the sink. *He's waiting for me,* she thought. *Waiting and hoping. Is that romantic instinct, or denial?*

When she came out of the bathroom, she had decided to take a chance on making love to him. She didn't want to humiliate him by forcing him to ask. She took the initiative herself, tearing his shirt from him so smartly that one of his buttons went flying. She kissed his lips, his jawline, his nipples, and pulled him down with her onto the bed. Kevin was astonished but answered with a blaze of ardor, not suspecting that it was all a gesture on her part—a hollow caricature of the passion she had once felt for him. He was exquisitely attentive, clinging to her body the way a drowning man clings to a lifeline. Something in his neediness brought her back to life. *He wants me. How can I not want to be wanted like this?* She began to feel a warm glow within her, the first wavelets of a tide of joy and surrender.

And then, with a single word, he drove a stake through her heart.

"Ramsey!" he huffed. "We'll make another Ramsey, babe. We'll put that business behind us for good."

Ramsey! She dried up instantly, and her hands and feet turned cold. *Ramsey!* Before her mind's eye flashed a pool of blood. She saw a glass-walled bassinet, and a pink, doll-like form, writhing under a bright, inhuman light. A silent scream arose within her. . . .

For over a year, she had fought to expunge this memory. At times, death itself had seemed better to her than to go on seeing that tortured face, those tiny, hopelessly grasping hands, that blood . . . that sudden, shocking, tragic blood. Kevin knew this, and still he had stuck his finger in the sore. How long had he planned that ill-timed remark? Since Division Street? Since the restaurant? Weeks ago? Here was the old Kevin—the Kevin she had walked out on—obsessive, manipulative, and self-centered. He was pushing her beyond where he knew she could go.

It was all she could do not to throw him off her. She let him finish, but her thighs were stiff, and her hands held his upper body away from hers in a gesture of disgust. The minute he was done, she rolled away and sat on the edge of the bed, her heart pounding, her breath strained by an anvil-like pressure on her chest.

Kevin saw her anguish, but not with the eyes of pity. In fact, it infuriated him. Gone was the pleading little boy. Gone was the passionate lover.

"There you go again! Don't turn your fucking back on me! Quit holding on to your grief, like it was some precious, private jewel that no one but you has a right to see! I have a right! I lost him, too!"

"Damn you, Kevin!" was all she could say.

"Yeah, I said the forbidden word. *Ramsey!* Go ahead, curse me for it! Scratch my eyes out! Turn around and let me have it! But you can't, can you? What the fuck is wrong with you, anyway? You walk around with your head full of ghosts: your father, your sister, your . . . your . . . *our* son, that pathetic little tyke who squirmed in agony for a few days before his life was snuffed out altogether. If you believe in God, why can't you curse Him, and scream at the top of your lungs how bastardly shit-fucking unfair that was? Any normal human being would do that. If you keep it locked up inside you, it will kill you. It will drive you insane."

She stared at the floor, trying to shut him out. His words enraged her. She burned to shriek at him, to throw back his accusations, and in so doing to flush clean the sewers of pent-up rage and grief inside her. But she couldn't. The very thought of confronting him made her ill, as every attempt to stand up for herself always had. *Why? Why?* she had asked herself a thousand times before. It was as though an unseen hand were poised to crush her if she dared to reveal the intensity of what she felt. It had always been so, as far back as she could remember. For all her training and degrees, she was helpless to do anything about it. She had the skill to cut into the brains of others, but could not heal this abscess within her own.

She knew that so much was at stake. It was the last chance to save her marriage, and yet she found her tongue paralyzed. She couldn't even cry. All she could do was stare at the floor and breathe, *deep in, deep out*, trying to ward off that stomach-turning feeling of doom.

Meanwhile, Kevin made his jab for the jugular. "I suppose you think that son of a bitch Helvelius has got the answer."

Ali rose to her feet. "Richard has nothing to do with it," she said, jerking her panties and skirt back up around her waist. "It's just like you to be suspicious of everyone. Nothing's happened. We just . . . talk. He . . . he doesn't try to force me. . . . He accepts . . . accepts me for who I am."

"Do you think I believe that?"

"I don't care what you believe."

"You're never going to change, are you, babe?"

"Who ever changes? Do you?" she said, without looking back. The next thing she was standing alone on the front porch of the brownstone, shivering in the warm night air. Only then did she notice that she had put on her blouse so hastily that the buttons didn't line up. *I'm a damned fool,* she thought. *If I don't end it, we're both going to lose our minds.*

The next day she filed for divorce. And two days later, she made love to Helvelius for the first time.

Clack! Clack! The radiologist slapped the finished angio films against the clips at the top of the lightbox. While the rest of the staff returned to the room, Ali scooted from behind the lead screen to view the images. A dark blob, like an unraveling ball of yarn, could be seen in the back of the skull cavity, marking the location of the AVM.

"There's the main feeder," said Dr. Helvelius, looking over her shoulder. In his voice there was no trace of what had just passed between them—no baby, no Ramsey, no wedding bells.

"Looks like it comes directly off the posterior communicating artery," said Ali, trying to match his composure, although nausea still wrung her stomach, and she felt weak and shaky inside.

"Do we have digital?" asked Helvelius. "Kevin, do you have it?"

Kevin was slouched far backward in his chair, punching the keyboard crisply with one outstretched hand. Despite his swagger, Ali could tell that he was far from at ease. Shorn of his characteristic smirk, he seemed deep in thought, even apprehensive. She was glad to see it, for he was always like that when he was immersed in work—and work, she knew, was his solace. It was the great unifier, too. Over the past few months, Kevin had increasingly isolated himself in his laboratory. But now, with SIPNI on the verge of realization, how could he help but feel a bond with those who were gathered in this room to bring the dream to life? In that might lie the germ of healing and forgiveness.

"Yes, yes, I have it," he said. "I'm running it past Odin now."

Kevin flicked the switch to the audio box, releasing Odin's soporific voice.

"HELLO, DR. HELVELIUS."

"Odin, do you have an analysis of the vascular pattern for us?"

"I DO, DR. HELVELIUS. THERE ARE SIX ARTERIAL FEEDERS, AND EIGHT MAJOR VENOUS EFFLUENTS. ONE OF THE SMALL VEINS HAS UNDERGONE SPONTANEOUS OCCLUSION SINCE THE LAST SURGERY. OTHERWISE, THE PATTERN IS THE SAME."

"Thank you, Odin."

"I RECOMMEND LEAVING THE LARGEST VEIN OPEN UNTIL LAST. IT CONNECTS DIRECTLY WITH THE SINUS RECTUS."

"Afraid I'll have to overrule you on that, Odin."

"IT WILL PROVIDE THE HIGHEST POSSIBLE FLOW RATE, AND MAINTAIN THE LOWEST POSSIBLE PRESSURE WITHIN THE AVM. THIS MINIMIZES THE RISK OF A CATASTROPHIC BURST HEMORRHAGE."

"Yes, but it's too short. Tethered like that, I won't be able to manipulate the AVM. I need a little room to work with, Odin."

"YES, I SEE. MAY I SUGGEST AN ALTERNATIVE?"

Helvelius looked at Kevin's monitor, where a longer but slightly narrower vein was highlighted in yellow.

"Yes, Odin, my thoughts exactly."

Jamie was lying facedown, his head enclosed in the chrome-plated cage of the modified Budde halo ring retractor. The crown, where the AVM was, had been elevated a little above the rest of his body. Inside the metal ring was a small circle of freshly shaved, iodine-painted scalp, bordered by sterile blue paper drape.

"Let's go in," said Helvelius. Esther, his favorite scrub nurse, slapped a #10 scalpel into his hand, and with a single swerving motion, he cut through Jamie's scalp, tracing the thin, U-shaped scar left from the last surgery. Ali held the incision open with a small retractor as Helvelius gently peeled the skin away from the glistening white skull underneath, working through the sticky patches with the blunt end of the scalpel. She watched as he used a bone chisel to pry away a coaster-sized disk of skull—the same skull flap he had cut out at Jamie's first operation. Only a few judicious taps with the chisel were necessary now to free up the flap. Once loose, it swung open like a clamshell. Ali was satisfied to see that it was still connected to its blood supply through a flap of the parchmentlike dura mater that lined its inward face.

"Okay," said Helvelius. "Start thiopental."

"Giving two hundred milligrams now," said the anesthetist.

"Titrate it until we get burst suppression on the electroencephalogram."

Helvelius took a step back from the operating table and looked at the tiny red light of the TV camera. "Uh, thiopental is the notorious 'truth serum,'" he explained. "We're giving it to Jamie because it decreases the blood flow to the brain, and relaxes the pressure inside the AVM. It also slows down the activity of the brain itself, which will protect it in the event that there is any temporary cutoff of oxygen. We don't expect that to happen, but it pays to be prepared."

"We're there," said the anesthetist.

At a nod from Helvelius, Ali slipped a pair of retractors into the groove between the two halves of the brain and gently pulled them apart. Deep inside the brain, she now saw the wrinkled, purplish, softly pulsating mass of the AVM. She felt a little anxious. After two operations, more than half of the mass had been removed, and there had been no mishaps. But both she and Helvelius knew that the most difficult, knotty part of the tumor was what faced them now. If this phase of the operation went wrong, there would be no need for SIPNI.

But she was an experienced surgeon. There was no need for anxiety. The AVM was merely a delicate puzzle box, requiring a steady hand and the utmost of patience for its solution. It *had* a solution. It was nothing to fear. And with that insight, she returned to the calm, focused, Zen-like state of mind she always strove for—the sense of order she craved more than anything else in the world.

Harry Lewton strode quickly down the Pike. Over more than a century, Fletcher Memorial Medical Center had grown out of a jumble of buildings of different sizes and architectural styles. The outpatient clinic of the Department of Endocrinology was in the very center of this jumble, where it jutted from the central section of the quarter-mile-long corridor, or the Pike, that ran like Main Street through the long row of buildings. When Harry reached it, the big glass doors of the lobby had been propped open, and three or four patients were already spread out among the leatherette chairs, waiting for ultrasound exams or capsules of radioactive iodine. The ubiquitous drone of a TV set could be heard.

It was pretty quiet. On his morning rounds, he had noticed that this particular clinic was always dead on Mondays. It was no different today.

He went straight to the receiving desk, a long, high barrier of dark wood and sand-colored fabric panels that separated the patients from the suite of exam rooms in the back. He flashed his hospital ID and introduced himself to a young African-American woman in a white dress and flowered smock. "Did you open the clinic this morning, Tia?" he asked, reading her name from her ID badge.

"Yes, sir. Fifteen minutes ago."

"See anything unusual? Anything that doesn't belong here?"

"No." She had that skittish look that people did whenever authority showed up without an invitation.

"Any unfamiliar people?"

"No. Just these." She nodded toward the patients. "Is there a problem?"

Harry quelled an impulse to shrug. Although he didn't want to alarm the girl, he didn't want to appear too casual, either. "It could be nothing. Why don't you go back to what you were doing while I have a look around?"

Tia nodded warily, then picked up a plastic watering jug and padded off through the door that led to the exam rooms. She looked back over her shoulder twice before she disappeared.

Harry scanned the room. *Okay, what have we got here?* There was a woman in her forties, short black hair—dye job—talking on a cell phone. She hadn't looked at him since he came in, which meant she had nothing to hide. Two gray-haired gals sat together on the other side, one watching TV, the other just sort of staring at the wall. No, make that snoozing. There was one old geezer looking at a magazine. By the way his hand shook, Harry figured he'd have blown himself up directly if he had ever taken to building a bomb. That was it. No master criminals. *All right, what else?* Objects: women's purses, all within arm's reach. Old guy had a tripod cane. No backpacks anywhere. No parcels. Harry could see easily under all those spindly legged chairs. They were clean. Ditto for those little glass tables with the magazines on them. There weren't any telltale carpet impressions to suggest that anything had been moved. . . .

Harry heard a shuffling noise behind him, and jerked his head around a trifle quicker than was normal for him. It was just Tia coming back to water the office plants. *Don't get jumpy, Pilgrim.* Harry let her pass. As she did, his eye was drawn to the area behind the receiving desk. He saw a half-dozen computers with their cables tangled like jungle vines on the floor, some low-backed chairs on casters, and a taboret or rolling file with a sliding door with a lock on it. That looked like a possibility. The file had been pulled out, putting it in the way of the receptionist's chair. It didn't usually sit there.

Harry was about to approach the taboret for a closer look when, from the far window, Tia called out to him. "This what you're lookin' for?"

She was standing beside a shoulder-high potted *sansevieria*, or mother-in-law's tongue. As Harry stepped closer to her, he could see a plain brown grocery bag tucked between the planter and the wall.

"Don't touch it!" he shouted. The girl backed off, instinctively sidling toward the cover of the receiving desk.

Harry approached the bag, angling his head to check out every side. *Just a bag. No trip wires. No pressure plate hidden under the carpet.* When he had reached the window, he leaned forward on his toes, and slowly pulled the bladelike leaves of the plant toward himself so he could look straight down at the bag. The top had not been crimped shut, and he could see inside. By the light of a pocket flashlight, he glimpsed some coils of red and blue wires, and underneath these, a milky-colored block of something like modeling clay.

"Jesus Christ," he said, lurching back, as though he had just stepped on a rattlesnake.

"Is it something bad?" asked Tia. Two of the patients also turned to look in his direction.

Harry fought to keep his cool. *If you panic, they'll panic.* He was no stranger to explosives—homemade acetone-peroxide booby traps had been a fact of life during his days raiding backwoods drug labs in

East Texas. Once, at a lecture, he had even held in his hand a few ounces of C4, the high-powered military compound. An instructor had passed it around after slamming it against a countertop to show how rough you could get with it and still not set it off without a detonator or an electrical spark. He remembered the stuff well—soft like clay and milky white, like a lump of death in his sweaty little palm. A fingernail-sized piece of it could blow a man so high he wouldn't have two teeth left together to identify him from dental records. And it looked exactly like what he'd glimpsed inside the bag, except that what he had now was the size of a brick—enough to vaporize the Pike for a hundred feet on either side of him.

Sweet Jesus in Heaven! What kind of sick fuck would leave this here?

Harry had already made one mistake jumping back from the bag. If there had been a motion sensor in it, he would already be part of the ozone layer. He had to get a grip on himself. *Okay, what's the first thing you need to do?* Edging backward, much more carefully now, he turned and looked around the room. *Get these people out of here— without setting off a stampede, if you still know how to do that.*

He turned to Tia. "Who's in charge of this clinic?"

"Dr. Saulter."

"Get me Dr. Saulter *stat*. If there are any patients or staff in that suite of rooms back there, they need to be moved elsewhere as of now. Use the back stairway. Don't bring them out through here."

He remembered that detonators were often triggered by cell phones, and that any kind of stray electronic emissions—from pagers, phones, microwaves, or scanners—could inadvertently set them off. He turned to the black-haired woman. "Ma'am, I need you to get that cell phone out of here. Don't turn it off. Don't touch any button on it. Just get up and go out and down the corridor. Now!"

Harry stared at the woman imperiously as she got up and reached for her purse. Behind him, he heard the voice of another woman, the one watching TV. "Don't talk to her that way. She's not doing anything."

"I need you to leave this waiting room as well, ma'am. All of you need to leave at once. Gather up your things and go to the information desk in the main lobby. Dr. Saulter will have someone call you there."

Wide-eyed, the woman shook her head. "But I have an appointment. I have a lump on my thyroid."

"I'm sorry. You'll be taken care of at another location. But you must leave now."

Harry tried to spur the patients on with his gaze as they sluggishly hauled themselves out of their chairs and, with no little murmuring, shuffled into the hall. The old man, in particular, couldn't have moved more slowly if he had tried.

An angry voice drew Harry's attention toward the exam suite as a man in a white coat and flopping tie came charging out, Tia shyly following at his heels. "What the hell's going on?" he demanded.

Harry brushed aside the challenge and turned to Tia first. "Ma'am, I need you to lock this lobby door from the outside and keep an eye on it until someone can come and rope it off." Only then, after Tia had set an example by swiftly responding to his authority, did he address the man in white. "Dr. Saulter, we have a suspicious object in this lobby. You and I need to make a sweep of whatever rooms you have back there. We need to clear that section of all personnel. Immediately!"

Nostrils flaring with indignation, Dr. Saulter turned with a rude jerk and stalked back toward the exam suite with Harry in tow. As they passed through the door, Harry stopped at a wall phone and waved Dr. Saulter on. His heart was pounding. He was trying to solve several problems at once. There were two floors above this one; below it, the ground floor and two basement levels. The whole section had to be evacuated. But how far? What was the bomb's kill radius? What was its purpose? *Don't let your mind race like this,* he warned himself. *You have a protocol to deal with these situations. What does it say to do first?* He forced himself to remember the bundle of numbers that had to be called. Via landline. No pagers, no cell phones, obviously. Top of the list was 911—the Chicago Police Department Bomb Squad.

The air of Operating Room Three was perfumed with incense for the ear—the unhurried echoes of stone chapels and of cloister-walks polished by the tread of centuries:

Oculi omnium in te sperant, Domine,
Et tu das illis escam in tempore opportuno.

The words of the chant meant nothing to Richard Helvelius. He was a nonbeliever and not a monk. But he was convinced that the slow, patient rhythms of the music had a positive effect upon his autonomic nervous system. They regularized his heart rate and blood pressure, and gave him a feeling of standing outside of time and place—a very subjective response, admittedly, but one that helped him to concentrate his thoughts.

He was standing back a little from the operating table, holding his bloodstained gloves upright, thinking. It was time to begin the dissection and removal of the AVM from Jamie's brain. To minimize the chance of bleeding, he had already isolated the major vessels and injected them with fast-hardening glue made of n-butyl-cyanoacrylate. *The glue should be hard now.* Reaching into the small, circular operating field, he checked each of the veins by clamping it and watching to make sure that the AVM did not swell up. *Okay, that one's safe. Now place the permanent clip. Keep the clip as close to brain tissue as you can. A long stump can rupture. . . .*

As he worked, he encountered something soft and purplish, about the size of a walnut. *Blood clot. Something was not done right the last time we were in here. There was a little bleeding afterward.* Helvelius called for a suction tip and ran it back and forth over the clot, which disappeared in small, jelly-like chunks. *Good! Now I have a little more working room.* He used that extra room to inspect the veins along the bottom of the AVM, lifting the tumor very gently with a flat retractor blade. *I don't like those veins. Their walls are very thin. If one tears open, it'll pull back deep into the substance of the brain, and I'll have to dig deep to stop the bleeding.*

Helvelius worked cautiously and deliberately. By the time the CD player had changed to a new disk, he had sealed off all but one last big vein without breaking any of them. That last one he left open to keep dammed-up blood pressure from engorging the AVM. Now it was time to go after the arterial feeders. One by one, he clipped and then cut them, always taking care not to disturb the flow to any branches that fed into normal brain. These arteries were tiny, but blood flowed through them at high pressure. *One nick, and you'll be staring into a well of blood.* Helvelius worked slowly, scraping with a fine probe to separate the purple coils of the AVM from the scar tissue that separated the tumor from the brain. His hands moved smoothly and steadily. He enjoyed these fine, controlled movements, like a scribe laboring over an illuminated manuscript.

Suddenly, the tranquil Gregorian chant was interrupted by the squawk of the overhead speakers. Since the introduction of a wireless paging system, the overhead speakers were rarely used anymore, except for fire drills and the occasional lost patient. Startled by the sound, Dr. Helvelius froze in mid-motion, but the point of his probe did not shift a millimeter. When the interruption was over, he went back to teasing the purplish vessels away from the pinkish-white edge of the brain.

"For Christ's sake, why do those speakers need to be so loud?" he said. "Can't we turn them d-down somehow?"

"You say that every time," said Esther, the scrub nurse. "You know there's no volume switch, Doctor."

"Well, I'll buy dinner at Spiaggia for anyone who puts a bullet through the damned thing."

Just then, as if to taunt him, the speaker erupted again, seemingly louder than before. *"Mr. White, please report to Security. Mr. White, please report to Security."*

"Geez, anybody know where this White character is? I'll bet he's out grabbing a smoke in the c-courtyard."

"It's a code, Doctor," said Esther. "There is no Mr. White."

"A code?"

"A security code. Code White."

Out of the corner of his eye, he saw Kevin O'Day sniggering over his keyboard.

"Right. I should know what that is, shouldn't I?" Every year, the hospital credentialing commission sent its spies out to randomly quiz staff about security procedures, which even department chairs were expected to memorize. *Bureaucratic nonsense!* Fire, flood, whatever— his response would be the same: to go on operating. What would they expect him to do? Leave a patient with his head cut open so he could run off and spray a fire extinguisher? Of course not. But this announcement was the real thing, not a drill. Not knowing what it meant annoyed him. "Code White. It's one of those baby things. Stolen baby. Runaway baby. Baby copping a smoke in the courtyard."

"No, it's not a baby," said Esther. Her eyes flared anxiously above her surgical mask.

"What is it, then?"

At that moment a tiny spray of blood showed that the paper-thin wall of one of the vessels had been breached.

"Bovie, please," said Helvelius.

Esther slapped a white cauterizer into his hand. He lifted the blood vessel with the probe in his left hand, and gently touched the blunt metal tip of the Bovie to the source of the spray. The current came on, and with it a tiny puff of smoke and steam, and a whiff of cooked tissue, not unlike the smell of frying bacon. The bleeding stopped.

At a nod from Helvelius, Ali rinsed the operating field with saline and then suctioned it clean. Helvelius watched for a moment, to make sure that there was no more bleeding, and then handed the cauterizer back to Esther. He switched the probe back into his right hand and prepared to go on with the dissection.

He took a deep breath, clearing his body of tension. "All right. If Code White isn't a baby, what is it?" he asked in his former bantering tone.

It was Ali who answered. "It's a bomb," she said. Her voice was solemn, muted—almost a whisper. "A bomb in the hospital."

As if on cue, the CD box was playing the "Dies irae," the Latin hymn for the dead:

Confutatis maledictis,
Flammis acribus addictis,
Voca me cum benedictis.

Apart from that, there was utter silence in Operating Room Three.

Harry Lewton was standing in the Pike with Captain Glenn Avery of the police bomb squad. Like the dozen or so hospital security guards and police officers on the scene, the two men hugged the wall on the side of the Endocrinology Clinic. The double doors of the clinic had been propped wide open to diffuse the force of any blast and to minimize the amount of glass shrapnel in case a bomb went off. About fifty yards away on either side of the clinic, the fire doors had been closed to seal off the Pike from foot traffic.

Inside the lobby of the clinic a single man, wrapped in a bulky green Kevlar EOD suit and wearing a helmet with a wide, wraparound face shield like a deep-sea diver, knelt near the far window in front of a fan-shaped portable CR 50XP X-ray machine. He had moved the planter to one side, and set the X-ray next to the shopping bag. He carefully slipped the flat twelve-inch digital phosphorescent detector plate behind the bag, and adjusted the voltage controls of the CR 50XP. Too low a voltage and the image would turn out a murky bunch of shadows. Too high and it would be useless glare. Either way, there could be a loss of a critical detail—a potentially fatal error.

Out in the corridor, the south side fire door opened, and Harry watched a tall, light-skinned African-American man in a dark suit come into the corridor. The stranger coolly scanned the faces along the wall, and without a break in his stride walked straight toward Harry. From one glance Harry took him for a Fed.

"Are you the security director?" he asked in an assertive baritone.

"Yes, Lewton's the name. Harry Lewton."

The man flipped open a bifold wallet to show a photo ID and a small metallic shield surmounted by an eagle. "Special Agent Terrell

Scopes, with the FBI's Evidence Response Team. I happened to be in town for a meeting and was notified by local law enforcement that you might have a situation here."

"Glad you could come. I've already turned the scene over to Captain Avery and the local bomb squad."

"Has there been a confirmation of the threat?" asked Scopes.

"Any minute, now."

Scopes was agreeably businesslike, but when the door opened again, there appeared a short, slightly built Asian man in the same regulation black suit. Harry felt his shoulders stiffen as he recognized the owlish glasses, the upthrust jaw, and the mincing step of the newcomer. *Aw, Christ!* he groused to himself. *Not that conceited little prick! Not in my hospital!*

"Gentlemen," said Scopes, "this is my colleague, Raymond Lee, with the FBI's Critical Incident Response Group."

Lee walked right past Harry without even looking at him, making a beeline for Avery's blue tunic and brass bars. "Glenn! Just the man I'd have liked to see here," he said in a thin, nasal voice. "Good to see that Chicago's sent out its A-team."

"Well, well, Ray!" exclaimed Avery. "We must be in a heap of doo-doo for you to show up." Lee was a good ten inches shorter than Avery, and looked almost diminutive standing beside the Captain's strapping bench-press bulk. But Harry noticed how Avery, who up until then had been strutting, arms akimbo like a dockside boss, now drew his stance a little narrower as Lee approached.

"Just a courtesy visit," said Lee. "You guys carry on like we're not here."

"This is the man who found the package," said Avery, pointing to Harry.

Lee craned his neck back toward Harry. Then his jaw dropped like someone had punched him in the solar plexus. "You're that fellow from Texas, aren't you?" he muttered. "Lewis."

"Lewton."

Avery, not very observant of the chill between them, chuckled. "You guys know each other?"

"Had the privilege," said Harry, without moving a muscle. Lee said nothing at all.

It had happened on the FBI's turf. Harry had just been appointed to lead the Tactical Unit of the Nacogdoches Police Department, and his chief had sent him out to the Hazardous Devices School at Redstone Arsenal, in Alabama, "to find out what those FBI folks know about dynamite." Lee taught a course there in psychological profiling. He was the kind of teacher who was more feared than liked, his great failing being that he was too doctrinaire for someone who was, after all, in the guessing-game business. He did not like to be questioned, and if you forgot that, he would use all his logical and rhetorical skill to flay you alive, Only a stubborn Texan would come back for a second or third helping of that piccalilli.

But the field, not the classroom, was where things really went sour between them. Lee was the mastermind behind the HDS Final Practical Exam, a simulated render-safe procedure at a mock drug lab in a trailer in the woods. Each examinee went out there solo, knowing that every square inch of the site was booby-trapped. One slip-up, and he'd get his face splattered with red ink from one of those little dye packs that bank tellers sneak into the loot during a holdup. It took days to wash the stuff off. During exam week, as Harry waited his turn, he noticed how the barracks began to fill up with a lot of very red-faced young men. It seemed that no one came back from that Practical Exam unscathed. It was said, in fact, that no one had ever beaten it—that it could not be beaten, that it was designed to be unbeatable, so as to give you a sense of your own mortality when going up against something as cold and capricious as a bomb.

Which meant nothing to Harry. He still remembered the day of his exam, down to the smell of the dew-damp honeysuckle on the edge of the clearing. The mission was to bring back a briefcase full of "evidence" from inside the trailer. Harry had already officiated at busts at real drug labs in the woods, so it was a cakewalk for him to evade the pathetically obvious trip wires and step fuses along the path to the site. He knew by instinct, too, that there would be a pressure-plate waiting for him outside the door, and contact switches under every window sash. These things were all fair game. But what incensed him was that, when he peered into the windows, he could see that the door and windows had also been booby-trapped from the *inside,* completely out of reach. In laying out the exam, Lee must have exited the trailer from a small skylight—but even there, traces of red paint in the overhanging branches told the story of the last poor bastard smart enough to figure that out. It was a sadistic setup. And in those days, when he was still young and cocky, Harry's favorite pastime was teaching bullies a lesson.

So Harry bribed a groundskeeper to open a tool shed, borrowed a chainsaw and used it to cut a two-by-two foot hole through the side of the trailer. When he marched into Lee's office and triumphantly presented him with that briefcase full of fake cocaine, Lee scoffed at first. Not believing his own eyes, he dragged Harry back to the trailer for a look. There was the hole, like a humongous mouth laughing at Lee to his face. Words cannot describe the shade of red he turned. He had a security officer escort Harry to the school administrator's office, and demanded that he be prosecuted for destruction of Federal property. The administrator, fortunately, was a more cool-headed sort. Harry just cocked his head and gave a redneck grin, like it was nothing but an overgrown schoolboy prank. And the administrator of the school let it go at that.

But from the look on Lee's face today, Harry could tell that Lee had not let it go.

Just then, the green-suited bomb tech stepped into the hallway, holding a silver laptop computer. He walked toward Avery with a wide-straddling Frankenstein gait.

"How bad is it?" asked Avery.

The tech ripped away the velcro flaps that held his helmet and visor in place. He seemed relieved to be breathing room air.

"It's not a working bomb."

"You mean it's a hoax?"

"Not exactly. The bag has all the components of a bomb—timer, detonator, even a mercury switch for a motion sensor. There's a block of something that's almost certainly C4. Enough to blow a canyon right through this section of the hospital. The strange thing is that the components aren't assembled. They're just lying about loose in the bottom of the bag."

"What's the point of that?" asked Harry.

Lee studied the image on the screen. "It's obviously a demo, to get our attention. Our bomber probably wanted to make sure the thing didn't go off accidentally."

"Maybe he was afraid to wire it together," said Avery. "Afraid he'd blow himself up."

11111121111

Lee arched his eyebrows. "Perhaps, but I doubt it. I think it's more of a gesture of contempt. It's a way of saying that we aren't worth the trouble to put together a real bomb. If that's true, we're dealing with someone with a highly exaggerated sense of superiority. Also someone unwilling to show his true hand."

"Well, one thing is certain," said Scopes. "Whoever left this is telling us that they know how to make a bomb. Judging by the mercury switch, they know how to booby-trap it, too."

"Sick bastard," said Avery.

"So what happens now?" asked Harry.

"Ransom demand, most likely," said Avery. "You said on the phone that another message was coming?"

"Yes. Eight-thirty. Right about now."

The four men—Harry, Avery, Lee, and Scopes—turned to watch as the render-safe tech strapped his helmet back on and returned to the lobby. In a moment, he reemerged, gingerly pushing a three-foot blue metal container studded with U-shaped bolts and handles, like a naval contact mine on wheels. All gave him a wide berth as he passed on his way to the elevator.

As the tech went by, Harry switched on the two-way intercom that connected to his diving helmet. "Make sure you take that out through the rear door, next to the ambulance dock. We have a TV crew in the hospital, and I'd rather not let them get you in their camera sights."

Lee motioned for Harry to hand him the intercom. "Where are you taking it?" he asked the bomb tech.

"To the Bat Cave. That's our disposal site down on the South Side."

"Hold the bomb in the lab when you get there," said Lee. "We want to look it over before you go all Fourth of July on it. Special Agent Scopes will follow you. He has a direct clearance and password to AEXIS."

"What's AEXIS?" asked Harry.

"It's a restricted computer database—the Arson and Explosives Information System—that the ATF maintains at the U.S. Bomb Data Center in Washington. There's a good chance that we can trace this material. Detonators usually carry origin codes and serial numbers. The C4 may be traceable, too. Since 9/11, the military's been tagging explosives with glass microspheres. They're too small to be seen with the naked eye, but they contain microscopic ID chips that can be read with a special infrared scanner. Same principle as the chip you implant in a dog's ear."

As the elevator doors clanged shut, the fire door opened, and Harry heard the sounds of "Foggy Mountain Breakdown." A young blond woman in the white blouse and black trousers of the hospital security staff held up a cell phone.

"That's my phone," Harry explained. "I didn't want it going off near the bomb."

As the woman handed him the phone, Harry saw a text display, consisting of a single line:

YOU HAVE MAIL.

"Eight-thirty, on the dot," said Lee, checking his own watch.

"Let's go to my office," said Harry. After giving orders to reopen the corridor, he led Lee and Avery down one floor in the elevator, and then into a suite of rooms in a rear corridor, which he accessed by swiping the ID card he wore around his neck. They passed through a large room filled with cubicles and cupboards, then a smaller room filled with banks of CATV monitors, and lastly into the innermost keep of the castle—Harry's office. To enter the office required both a card swipe and a thumb scan.

The three men sat down close together behind Harry's desk, while Harry tapped his keyboard to bring up his e-mail queue. The queue was empty.

"Let's give it a minute," said Harry.

"Impressive control room back there," said Avery. "Beats what we have downtown."

"Nowadays a hospital is a pretty controversial place," said Harry without taking his eyes from the monitor. "We get targeted by abortion groups, animal rights groups, patient rights groups, unions, neo-Luddites of all persuasions. I'm sure you noticed those picketers as you came in. Plus we're a target for old-fashioned theft. We have half a billion dollars worth of equipment to keep an eye on—microscopes, computers, you name it. The narcotics stashed in our pharmacies could supply every junkie in Chicago for the next six months."

"No such thing as too much security, huh?" said Avery.

"Not for us, anyway. We just spent fourteen million dollars on an upgrade of Cerberus, our automated security system. From this command center, I have an overview of everything that goes on in this hospital. There are cameras and sensors in every public area. If a window or door is ajar, I know it. If an emergency alarm goes off, I can press a button and lock or unlock any fire door or any exit to contain the problem. I can override controls to any critical plant function—elevators, electricity, water, thermal regulation, ventilation. I can call up a list of every card used to swipe any scanner in the medical center at any time over the past three months. And I can tell you that, at this exact moment, there are, uh . . ." Harry hit a couple of keys on the keyboard at his desk, bringing a column of numbers to the screen. "There are . . . two thousand eight hundred and sixty-two people inside these buildings, including the three of us . . . and, uh, two babies born on Tower B this morning."

Lee was unimpressed. "Quite a rung up for a small-town Texas cop. But fancy technology is no substitute for old-fashioned analysis and clarity of thinking."

Harry shrugged. "Never said it was."

Avery ignored them both and looked over the row of monitors on the counter behind the desk. "Are there surveillance tapes of the lobby where the bomb was found?"

"Certainly."

"I'd like to have a look at those."

Poink! A water-drop alert sounded from the computer, and Lee pointed at the monitor with his index finger. "Mr. Lewton, I think you have mail."

"Ah, yes. Here we are." Harry scooted his chair forward, and clicked on the boldfaced line that had just appeared on his e-mail queue: "**NOW THAT WE HAVE BEEN INTRODUCED**."

A rectangle crammed with capital letters filled the center of the screen:

PRAISE BE TO GOD, THE ALL-MERCIFUL, AND TO HIS PROPHET. THE DAY OF REPENTANCE OF ALL UNBELIEVERS IS AT HAND. SHOW CONTRITION AND YOU WILL OBTAIN PARDON. DEFY THOSE WHO FIGHT FOR GOD AND YOUR DE-STRUCTION IS SURE. BY 18:00 CENTRAL STANDARD TIME

TODAY MARTYRS MOHAMMED METEB AND HASSAN ABO MOSSALAM SHALL BOARD GULF AIR FLIGHT 401 TO SANAA YEMEN FROM NEW YORK. SIGNAL WILLINGNESS BY PAYMENT AS FOLLOWS. FLETCHER MEMORIAL MEDICAL CENTER. NORTHWEST CITY BANK. ILLINOIS STATE TEACHERS PENSION AND RETIREMENT FUND. CHICAGO HOUSING AUTHORITY. ILLINOIS STATE LOTTERY. ROSENBACH FOUNDATION. CHICAGO BOARD OF TRADE. CHICAGO TRANSIT AUTHORITY. FROM EACH $25,000 TO EACH OF TWO ACCOUNTS PAID AT 12:00 AND 12:05 EXACTLY. ACCOUNT NUMBERS WILL BE PROVIDED. DO NOT UNDERESTIMATE OUR RESOLVE. THE LIVES OF MANY ARE IN YOUR HANDS. GOD IS GREAT."

"What's the return address?" asked Avery.

"Uh, rudi-at-bethshalom-dot-org."

"What's that? Beth Shalom. It sounds like a synagogue."

"Give me a minute." Harry typed the name into his Web browser. "Yes, it's a synagogue in Evanston. There's, uh, there's a youth director on staff named Rudi Kern."

"A synagogue?" said Lee, shaking his head. "Not likely. It's got to be a redirect. A fake address."

"Sons of bitches!" said Avery.

Harry smiled. "Well, we know they have a sense of humor. Meteb and Mossalam? Who are they?"

Lee tapped his forefinger against his upper lip. "Foot soldiers of the Al-Quds Martyrs' Brigade, an offshoot of the Egyptian Muslim Brotherhood. Right now, they're being held at Rikers Island, pending trial for the murder of a city councillor in New York."

"Gives us an idea who we're dealing with, anyway," said Avery. "Another bunch of those damned Middle Eastern fanatics."

"Possibly," said Lee.

Harry looked at the FBI agent curiously. "Not necessarily?"

"As I pointed out in my lectures, if you were listening, one must always be cautious in interpreting these things. It's best to avoid premature assumptions."

Avery scoffed. "Who else?"

"I don't know."

Harry trained his gaze on Lee. "Can we meet these demands? Any chance these two will be released?"

"Washington will decide that," said Lee. "The money is actually easier to deal with, although our bomber has made it complicated by asking for all these different payers. That will take some coordination."

"Why don't they just ask for a lump sum?" asked Harry.

Lee shrugged. "I suspect it's a way of flaunting their power. Bombers tend to be bitter, brooding types. Authority figures are a favorite target. Look at all these payers: government agencies, banks, unions—pillars of the establishment. This isn't a ransom demand. It's tribute. Submission."

Harry looked over the message on the screen once again. "Can we assume they mean business?" he asked.

"Absolutely."

Avery shrugged. "I'll notify the mayor and the governor's office. They can help us move the money, if we have to."

"Twenty-five thousand dollars doesn't seem like a lot, does it?" said Harry, turning toward Lee. "The whole amount comes to, what, four hundred thousand? That's about two hours' worth of the operating revenue of this medical center."

"Well, these Al-Quds Martyrs are a pretty rinky-dink operation," said Lee. "It could be that they're scared by what they're getting into. They may want to make a quick haul and be done with it."

"Sure they're scared," said Avery. "The fuckers don't even have the balls to wire up their own bomb."

"Well, this is my hospital," said Harry, "and I'm inclined to take them seriously. Let's just assume that there is a fully functional bomb somewhere, and that it can do as much damage as they say it can. Protocol says we start a search for it."

"I think that's wise," said Lee.

Avery nodded in agreement. "All right. Let's go to OPCON Level Three. Do you know what that means, Mr. Lewton?"

Harry was being challenged—challenged in his own goddamned office. He swung his chair around and looked Avery in the eye. "OPCON Three: a credible threat. Special resources deployed to the scene to watch, stand by, or assist as necessary in investigation. That would include bomb squad, fire department, SWAT, HAZMAT, and FBI or ATF in a case like this."

"That's right," said Avery, a little curtly. Turning to Lee, he became more cordial. "Would you like to take charge, Ray?"

"No, I'm here just as an observer, for the moment."

Some observer, thought Harry. The FBI could take over anytime it wanted. Every cop knew that. If Lee offered to sit on the sidelines, it was because he liked to exercise authority discreetly and without the hassles of direct command. But Harry wasn't fooled. There was no doubt about who was top dog in this pack.

Avery seemed content with the charade. "Then I'll act as Incident Commander," he said. "Mr. Lewton, are you and your people up to conducting the search?"

"You bet we are."

"Then let's get on it."

"Wait a sec. I have an idea," said Harry. He turned around and picked up a black digital clock from a bookshelf beside his desk. "It's now, what, about a quarter of nine? Plane boards at six Eastern Standard Time?" After Harry had fiddled with some buttons, the clock showed "8:15" in red LED numbers about three inches high. "I've set it to time remaining mode," said Harry, displaying the clockface to each of the three men in turn. "That's what we have left, gentlemen. Eight hours, fifteen minutes. We neutralize the threat by then, or the shit hits the fan."

Ten minutes later, Harry, Avery, and Lee were standing in a green-tiled, concrete-floored room in the second sub-basement of the hospital. About thirty maintenance workers in khakis, jeans or blue gray overalls, some still wearing yellow hard hats, had been shepherded into this place by a dozen uniformed security officers. Harry recognized only a few of the maintenance workers. In fact, in the three months he had been at Fletcher Memorial he had barely gotten to know his own security staff. He was keenly aware that this would be the first time any of these people would see him take charge in a crisis.

The room had been used for linen storage, but was now nearly cleared for renovations. The air was filled with the smells of mildew, bleach, and drying grout.

"Listen up, people!" shouted Harry. "Come on, quiet down and listen!" The murmur of the crowd subsided as Harry held up his hands. "With me here are Special Agent Raymond Lee, from the FBI's Critical Incident Response Group, and Captain Glenn Avery, from the Chicago Police Department's Bomb Squad. We have a credible bomb threat to the Medical Center. I repeat, this is a credible threat. We're going to conduct a search, and it needs to be done quietly and without starting a panic. We drilled for this a couple of months ago, remember?" He scanned the room, gathering nods here and there. He was glad now that he had made a point of testing the hospital's emergency readiness protocols as soon as he had arrived. It had earned him the nickname "Captain Doomsday" among some of the staff, but at least he had something to fall back on now. "Okay? We'll run it just like we did then."

A rapt silence now hung on Harry's words. "Security staff will function as team leaders, each accompanied by four to six maintenance personnel who will physically conduct the search. Stay together in your groups. No one goes off on his own. On that back table are spools of white ribbon. Tie a white ribbon to your hospital ID tag. Do not—I repeat, do not—discuss any aspect of the search with anyone not wearing a white ribbon. Any inquiries get directed to this command center.

"Team leaders have master keys that should get you almost everywhere. If a door needs to be forced, consult with the command center first. Use your flashlights! I don't want anyone turning on any light switches. A switch could be rigged to detonate a bomb. Search with your eyes and ears only. Don't move anything! Don't touch anything!

"We'll start with the grounds and courtyards. That includes the liquid oxygen tanks, Dumpsters, and any vehicles parked on the service road behind the hospital. Get me license numbers of any vehicles you find. Pay special attention to trash cans and planters near the entrances. Next move indoors—lobbies, bathrooms, stairways, and elevators. Angelo, your team will check out the sandwich shop in the main lobby, and then the cafeteria and the doctors' dining room. Get the managers to help guide you. Meanwhile, the rest of you will move to the second basement level, and work your way up, floor by floor. Do things in stages: a floor search, a waist-level search, an eye-level search, and then a ceiling search. Don't forget to have a look above the ceiling tiles. When you clear a room, tape an X on the door with masking tape. I'll be making the rounds from time to time to check your progress, and I want to know what's been cleared and what hasn't. No one's being graded on speed. A hasty search is worse than useless. Any questions?"

Hesitant glances were traded among the crowd. One pot-bellied man in overalls and a plumber's belt moved to the front. "What are we looking for exactly?"

Harry spread his hands in a gesture of uncertainty. "Anything out of the ordinary. An unfamiliar container. Equipment that's been moved or stacked as if to hide something. Scraps of wire trimmings. Paint flakes on the floor. Most of you will be in your usual work areas, so you know how things should be." Harry turned to Lee. "Anything to add?" he asked, knowing that he had covered all the bases pretty damn well. Even Lee would have to admit it.

Lee stepped forward, with a stiff, military bearing. He spoke precisely, with a rhythm that could have been counted off on a metronome. But his voice did not carry well in the large room, and those in the back had to strain to hear him. "It's best to proceed without preconceptions," he said. "We're dealing with an explosive that can be molded to any shape. It can be made to look like anything. Bombs of this type will usually be concealed, either in an inaccessible place, or inside of something ordinary and easily overlooked. Although we have reason to believe that a large and highly destructive bomb may be on the premises, there may be other, perhaps smaller, bombs, either planted as decoys or as booby-traps to protect the primary installation."

A tall young man from the HVAC division looked at Lee intently. "What do we do if we find something?"

"Rule number one: don't touch it," said Lee. "Notify the command center—Mr. Lewton's office—by telephone. That means a land line, no cell phones. Cell phones are often used to detonate bombs. Next, move everyone out of the area. Captain Avery will be the Incident Commander on site. He and the bomb squad will be standing by, and will take over if you do find anything."

From the back of the room, a raspy man's voice called out. "What kind of twisted mind would plant a bomb in a hospital?"

Lee lifted his chin, as though trying to pitch his voice toward the back. "We don't know who's done it at this point. Whoever it is, there's a good chance they're not far away, keeping an eye on all of us. So be watchful."

"And calm," added Harry. "For God's sake, stay calm—and very, very careful."

Judy Wolper, Harry's cell phone bearer, was standing not far away. "What about these TV cameras?" she asked in a timid voice. "There's reporters all over the place."

"Let that be my problem," said Harry. "If they start to get nosy, don't try to BS 'em. They can smell a cover-up a mile away, and you have no idea how bad they can bite you when they think you're not telling the truth. Just say there's an alert in progress, and send them to me. I'll be preparing a statement later this morning, once we have a better idea of what's going on." Judy nodded, and Harry turned to the man at his side. "Captain Avery, anything you'd like to add?"

Avery had been slouching against a canvas laundry cart, which wobbled slightly as he straightened up. "Just don't try to be heroes," he said, clearing his throat. "We have guys who get paid to be heroes. You do your part, and we'll do ours. Okay?"

A patronizing nod from Lee indicated that the FBI was satisfied with the briefing. Harry looked toward a stainless steel cart that was just then rattling through the door.

"Okay, there are flashlights, tape, screwdrivers, wrenches, and extension mirrors for anybody who doesn't have one. Take what you need and get a move on. Security staff have the area assignments."

As the teams began to form and stream out, Harry motioned to Judy Wolper and Tom Beazle, his two closest adjutants on the security staff. He had worked them unrelentingly since he had arrived at Fletcher Memorial—there was so much that had to be done to bring Cerberus on line—and he had begun to feel a little friction lately, particularly from Tom, who had recently gotten married. But they were both bright-eyed and poised for action.

"Guys, I need you to do a few things for me," he said, straining his voice to be heard above the din in the room. "First, I need you to go down to Telecommunications and shut down the hospital paging system. We have a hundred pagers going off every minute around here, and I don't want to risk a stray signal setting off a bomb. Have Telecommunications send out a general e-mail saying that we have a technical problem and we're working our tushies off trying to get it fixed. Then call the dispatch services and have all ambulances diverted to ERs at other hospitals. We need to keep our own ER beds free, in case we do have an . . . event."

Judy looked at him with a disbelieving squint. "You mean—"

"Yes, that's exactly what I mean. We can't openly evacuate, but we can damned well do something to lower the head count inside these buildings. Visit each of the outpatient clinics, and have them discreetly cancel as many patient appointments as they can. You don't have to tell them why. Just tell them it's a hospital emergency. Then go down to shipping and receiving and call off any nonessential deliveries."

"This is serious, isn't it?"

"Yes . . . Yes, it's serious." Looking into her eyes, he realized that a single wrong word could turn her steadfastness into panic. He had to focus her on the job at hand, not the danger. "We can handle this, Judy," he said, stooping a little to make direct eye contact. "We trained for it. We drilled it. Let's just do our job and go home for dinner."

Dr. Helvelius had said no more about the annoying Mr. White. After an hour of painstaking dissection, he had mobilized the AVM enough to have a glimpse of its underside, where the main feeder arteries were found. He first encountered a web of small arteries, most of them no thicker than a pin, which he sealed easily, one by one, with the bipolar cauterizer. Behind these were the really large arteries. Metallic clips had to be placed on these, in places where the artery wall was of normal thickness, and not ballooned out, because if the clip worked free at any time down the road, the result would be an instantaneously fatal hemorrhage. Last of all was the single draining vein that Dr. Helvelius had purposely left open, but which he now clipped and cut, like an umbilical cord, allowing him to lift out the AVM in a single piece.

"Irrigation, please." Ali flushed the cavity of raw brain tissue with a gentle stream of saline. By pressing a button on the irrigator, she was able to suction off the blood-tinged water, revealing the pinkish-white surface of living, thinking tissue underneath.

"Could we focus that lamp a little?"

A nurse reached up and adjusted the lamp using the plastic-shrouded handle in its center. Dr. Helvelius studied the cavity for any sign of oozing of blood. Once or twice he dabbed at it with the cauterizer, and Ali, without the need for prompting, followed each dab with another round of irrigation and suction.

As she stood by patiently, Ali thought of the first time she had watched Helvelius operate. Back then, those eyebrows bristling over the rim of his eyeglasses had been black, not gray. His nine-fingered hands had been just as sure and unerring. The case was a schwannoma, a tough, stringy tumor that had wormed its way through the ear canal to the very base of the patient's brain. Helvelius operated for six hours, standing in one spot the whole time, without taking a break to eat, or drink or answer nature's call. Ali had wondered at his discipline. She had never known a man so completely the master of himself. He was nothing like those surgeons who grew tense in the operating room, who shouted at nurses and threw instruments. His spirit was gentle and light-hearted. With scalpel in hand, he became the scalpel. Helvelius himself ceased to exist.

And from that very first day, Ali coveted his secret. She, too, yearned to cease to exist. She knew that neurosurgery was a man's domain. Fewer than one in twenty in its ranks were women. To climb up the pyramid, she had to work twice as hard as any other surgical intern, sleep half as much, starve herself, endure every indignity, and never, ever lose her temper or complain. Six years of residency, two years of fellowship, three years of research—all to become acolyte to this Sufi, this mystic healer, who knew how to lose himself in his art. The payoffs were rare. But there were days when, for a few shining moments, she felt as though she had received from his hands the gift of finding peace through detachment, and of escaping from the relentless self-doubt that haunted her.

Eleven years together, and in all that time, she had never once thought of Helvelius as a lover. To her, he had been scarcely a physical being at all. Divorced, childless, he seemed content with his solitary life. Surgery was his only passion. But there came a day when she learned to see him in a different light. It was just after she had left

Kevin. She was in surgery, holding a retractor, when suddenly, without warning, she found herself paralyzed by thoughts of loneliness and guilt. She didn't cry out. She couldn't make a sound or even let go of the retractor. She simply stood there, for minute after stock-stupid humiliating minute, with tears streaming down her face. The nurses and resident surgeons gaped in astonishment. She expected to be thrown out of the operating room. But Helvelius went on with the operation as though nothing had happened.

That evening, he insisted on driving her home to the studio apartment she had taken in the seedy University Village neighborhood by the medical center. It was the first time he had ever been to the place where she lived—in fact, the first time they had ever been together anywhere outside the hospital or a conference hall. He had her lie down on her sofa while he made dinner. She remembered well what he made—chicken pan-fried in olive oil with capers, a small salad, a side dish of asparagus. It took him no more than twenty minutes to make it. They ate at a small table with folding wings.

Over dinner, Helvelius sat without comment while Ali groped to explain her lapse in the OR and her troubles over Kevin. When her words dried up, he took her by the hand. "Don't be embarrassed about today," he said. "I, too, know what loneliness is."

And with these words, Richard Helvelius had ceased to be a paragon, and became a man.

They were not physically intimate for some time. At first, they simply met after hours for dinner, and then talked and listened to music. When intimacy came, it was natural and unpretentious. It was not like her unions with Kevin, where matter annihilated antimatter in a cosmic upheaval. With Helvelius, sex was a sanctuary. She came away from his bed feeling a little more whole, and a little less vulnerable to the perils of her disordered life.

He treated her like a newly discovered jewel, taking her to the Lyric Opera and to his favorite restaurants on the Magnificent Mile. But she especially cherished the weekend getaways to his lake house in Wisconsin, where he taught her to pilot his small day yacht. Watching the boat's wake spreading silently over the water, or the moonlight shimmering on the silvery waves, she could almost forget Kevin's face haunting her. At night, they would lie together in front of the crackling fireplace, and she would play with the gray curls of his lean and

still-muscular chest, often scarcely speaking until the last embers
had gone out. She didn't ask where the relationship was headed. She
had stopped thinking about tomorrow altogether—something quite
unusual for her, who had always fretted over the future as a thing to
be dreaded if it could not be controlled. She began to see things she
had long overlooked, little things like clouds, pebbles, whirling maple
keys, or the way pigeons cocked their heads when they walked. She
rediscovered the aroma of fresh waffles in the morning, the softness
of a blanket around her shoulders at night. It was all so new to her.
Would it last? She didn't know. But she was closer to being happy
than she had been in years.

Helvelius stepped back from the operating table. "Okay, I think
I'm done. Let's get one last angio."

The table of operating instruments was rolled away, and the C-arm
of the X-ray machine moved into its place. Once again, the room was
cleared, and films were made from several angles.

"Looks clean to me," said Helvelius as he perused the films. "What
does Odin say?"

The room was filled at once with Odin's silvery baritone. "I'VE
USED ALL THREE PROJECTIONS TO RECONSTRUCT A THREE-
DIMENSIONAL TOMOGRAPHIC IMAGE. COMPARISON WITH TO-
DAY'S PRE-OPERATIVE SCAN SHOWS NO VESSELS OF ABNORMAL
CALIBER OR CONFIGURATION, AND NO RESIDUAL BLOOD
FLOW IN THE REGION OF THE AVM. PERFUSION TO NORMAL
BRAIN IS INTACT."

"Then all is well?"

"YES, DR. HELVELIUS. THE RESECTION IS COMPLETE."

"Very well. Dr. O'Day, the patient is all yours."

Ali took a deep breath. She felt a nervousness that was rare for
her in the operating room. The eyes of everyone were upon her.
Everything—the AVM resection, the cameras, the tables filled with
shining instruments—everything had been a preparation for this
moment. It was a responsibility that could crush her if the smallest
detail went wrong.

"Kevin," she said quietly, "is SIPNI ready?"

Kevin turned and held an induction probe, shaped like an oversized lollipop, over the blue sterilization wrapper on the table. "Odin, I'd like a last-minute functional status check of the SIPNI device."

"PRIMARY CIRCUITS ARE OPERATIONAL, KEVIN, WITH NO MORE THAN 0.005 PERCENT VARIATION IN IMPEDANCE AND IN THE PREDICTED TWO-WAY SIGNAL TRANSIT TIME. THESE PA-RAMETERS HAVE BEEN DETERMINED, OF COURSE, AT ROOM TEMPERATURE. A VARIATION OF AS MUCH AS 0.007 PERCENT IS POSSIBLE AT 37 DEGREES CELSIUS."

"Almost too good to be true."

"I'M SORRY, KEVIN. WOULD YOU LIKE ME TO REPEAT THE STATUS CHECK?"

"No, Odin. Just joking. I'm sure we can live with those parameters." Kevin turned to Ali. "You're on," he said.

The circulating nurse picked up the sterilizer bag and tore it open, allowing the device itself to fall onto the instrument tray. It looked like a jeweled egg, its finely faceted surface glinting both gold and silver. As Ali cradled it in her hand, she wondered at how small it now seemed. Was this the end product of all the thousands of hours of work, the millions of dollars, the debates, the midnight brainstorms, the endless succession of victories and defeats of the past three years? Was this what she had lived for?

Carefully, as though it were alive, Ali began to paint the outside of the egg with the precious gel called CHARM. She painted two coats, slowly turning the device in her palm. Refracted through the faintly violet-colored gel, the SIPNI device shimmered, like a polished amethyst.

As she slipped it into its setting, deep in the pocket inside Jamie's brain, Ali was almost reluctant to let it go. She used a scissors-shaped Olsen-Hegar suture holder to anchor SIPNI with two stitches to the tentorium cerebelli, a tough membrane that supported the hindmost part of the brain. Then she unlocked the retractors, watching as the wrinkled surface of the brain slid back into place, and the SIPNI device could be seen no more. *There it is,* she thought. *History's been made.* Quickly, with long-honed and almost automatic movements, Ali replaced the flap of the skull and sewed Jamie's scalp shut, leaving the edges of the skin a little everted, so that they would heal cleanly in the purifying air. She stood motionless, still holding the Olsen-Hegar in her hand, long after the nurse had cut the last suture thread.

"Everything all right, Dr. O'Day?" asked Helvelius.

In the background, the gradual *Haec dies quam fecit dominus* was playing.

"Yes, I'm fine. Just . . . just thinking." Yes, thinking what everyone in the room was thinking, only no one had the courage to say. *Have we not crossed a terrible threshold? Where will it lead? If man has found the power to re-create himself, in whose image will he be re-created?*

"Let's charge 'er up," said Helvelius.

Ali stepped back to make way, but Helvelius waved her toward the table. "No, you do the honors."

The nurse presented her with something shaped like a large, flexible horseshoe wrapped in plastic. She spread the ends open a little, and positioned them against the base of Jamie's skull, at the same level as the old AVM cavity.

"Okay. Switch it on."

"Power is on," said Kevin.

Dr. Helvelius turned toward the TV camera. "Right now we're charging up the SIPNI device, using a magnetic induction coil, similar to what you would use to charge an electric toothbrush or a laptop computer. Once it's charged, SIPNI will immediately go to work, sending out pulses that will seek out and form connections with what we call the optic radiations. Those are remnants of the visual processing cells that originally fed signals from Jamie's eyes to the lost part of his brain. It will be awhile, of course, before we see any results from that."

For several minutes, the room was quiet, but for the hiss of the bellows of the anesthesia machine, and the occasional beep of the IV pump. At last, Kevin O'Day called out, "SIPNI is at full power."

"What's the EEG show?" asked Helvelius.

From behind the blue curtain came the voice of the anesthetist. "Signature electrical activity in the occipital lobe, about thirty-five megahertz. I believe that's within the calculated norm."

"We're done, then. Let's turn him over."

Someone switched off the CD player in the midst of a descant on *exultemus et laetemur.*

The two surgeons and two nurses lifted Jamie and turned him onto his back, taking care not to entangle the IV lines and wire leads that seemed to spring from every part of his body. The anesthetist turned down the nitrous oxide gas. As soon as Jamie showed signs of eye movement, the anesthetist pulled the soft plastic breathing tube out from Jamie's throat. As it came out, dripping secretions, Jamie began to cough.

"That's good, Jamie," said the anesthetist. "Give us a nice cough."

Still semiconscious, Jamie coughed two or three times. A gurney was rolled in, and a white plastic board was slipped under Jamie's back to help lift him from the operating table. Once he was on the gurney, and the IV bags had been rehung and a portable monitor attached, Ali and Florinda wheeled him out of the operating room, past the scrub sinks, and toward the recovery room down the hall. They parked the gurney in a bay just inside the entrance. Ali lent a hand while Florinda and one of the recovery room nurses hooked Jamie up to a regular telemetry monitor and fastened an oxygen line under his nose.

"Let's give him five liters of oxygen for now," said Ali. "His sats are just a little bit low."

The adjustment was made, and Florinda returned to Operating Room Three. Ali stayed behind for a few minutes, writing orders into Jamie's chart and going over them verbally with the recovery room staff. It was important that everything be followed to the letter.

Ali made a last check at the bedside. Jamie was sleeping comfortably. His vital signs were good. The EEG showed some theta waves and occasional bursts of sleep spindles—all indicative of a smooth recovery. She touched her fingers to her young patient's cheek, and then turned and headed into the hall.

"Don't you think that nurse looks like your sister Josie?" said the gray-haired woman lying in the hospital bed. The pale skin of her face had a puffy waxiness to it that filled out all the small wrinkles and made it hard to guess her age. Because of a plastic oxygen tube fitted to her nostrils, her voice had an uncharacteristic nasal sound.

Harry Lewton was sitting in a plastic chair beside her, his legs sprawled wide. He had just finished a walk-through of the hospital, and he was feeling frustrated. So far, the search teams had come up with exactly one dead rat in a crawl space and one homeless guy trying to sleep off a pint behind a Dumpster.

"Momma, it doesn't matter what she looks like," he said. "Just so she takes good care of you." Up north, he had worked hard to play down his East Texas accent, but in his mother's presence it had a way of creeping up on him.

"Stop fussing over me, Harry. I think you've got all these people on pins and needles on account of me."

Harry winked. "Don't worry. It does 'em good."

"Oh, Harry!" she said. "Can't you ever stop worryin' about other people? Twenty years ago, when you were fifteen, it was different. You were a godsend then, stepping in to help raise your little brother and sisters, after that no-account daddy of yours got drunk on the job and hurt his back and decided to live the rest of his life on a pittance of disability checks. I can't thank you enough for it. But I'm your momma, and I never asked you to take care of *me*. I always could look after myself."

"It's nothin'. It was nothin' then, and it's nothin' now."

"Hogwash! You got them kids dressed, gave 'em breakfast and made 'em lunches every day of the week, so's I could leave at five-thirty to go drive that bus. And then, after school, you stuffed bags at Kroger's Market till after dark, just so we could have a decent supper on the table. You call that nothing?"

"Hell, Momma. If I'd've had idle time on my hands, I'd have wound up in the Dixie Popes or one of those other neighborhood gangs. I liked bumpin' my knuckles too much."

"But it cost you your childhood, Harry. I look back, and I am ashamed of it."

"This is no time to talk about things like that."

"No, Harry, it's exactly the time."

"It wasn't your fault. Let the shame be on him that's dead and buried. Enough said."

It was hard for Harry to look upon his mother's face. It had taken on a lifeless, unchanging masklike quality that made her seem like a stranger, and not the vibrant, chestnut-haired beauty he remembered. He got a knot in his stomach thinking of her, back in the days when folks called her "Sugarfoot" for the mean figure she cut on the line-dance floor. Now she needed help just to blow her nose. *How does she hang on like that?* he wondered. *How does she face the day?*

He knew how. She had the quality known in East Texas as grit, and she had it in spades. There was no other way the family could have lasted. Grit could be toughness, sometimes, and at other times tenderness. But what it meant was you could not be beaten down. Harry remembered one night when he was five or six, and he had sat up in bed shaking after his daddy smashed the TV set in one of his drunken rants. Momma heard him crying, and came to his room carrying a glass of milk and a beat-up old pawn-shop guitar. In her honey-and-molasses voice, she sang to him an old Pentecostal song that had been made famous by the Carter family:

Keep on the sunny side, always on the sunny side,
Keep on the sunny side of life
It will help us every day, it will brighten all the way
If we'll keep on the sunny side of life.

A simple song, but it had the power to dry away his tears that night. It defined his momma the way he had always known her. And his heart ached to think of it now.

Harry heard the step of a hard leather shoe on the linoleum, and looked up to see a balding, gray-haired man in a white coat come into the room.

"Morning, Dr. Weiss," said Harry. "Kind of you to drop by."

Weiss nodded curtly and went directly to the plastic chart binder that was kept in a slot at the foot of the bed. He opened the binder, scanned it briefly, and then slammed it shut.

"Still running a fever, Mrs. Lewton," the doctor announced.

"Call me Viola. After the things you've peeked into, I think we should be on first-name terms."

Weiss lifted his stethoscope from his shoulders and hooked it into his ears. As if by a prearranged signal, Harry rose out of his chair and gently lifted his mother to an upright sitting position in her bed. He watched silently as Weiss slid the stethoscope under Viola's gown and moved it around her chest and back.

"I still hear rales at the bases of the lungs," concluded Weiss, flipping the stethoscope over his shoulders.

"Rolls?" asked Viola.

"*Raaahlls*. It's a sound like wet velcro ripping. It means your pneumonia hasn't gotten any better. Hopefully, there'll be some improvement when the new antibiotic has had a chance to work."

Harry nodded toward the door. "Doctor Weiss, can I speak to you privately?"

"I have to be at Grand Rounds at ten," said Weiss, glancing at his watch.

"It'll only take a minute." Harry directed Weiss toward the hall. At the doorway, he stopped and turned to Viola. "Anything you need, Momma? I'm going to have to step out for a bit."

Viola shook her head.

"See you, then." Harry shut the door. Weiss had already gone ahead several paces, but stopped and looked back at Harry.

"Well?" said Weiss.

Harry said nothing until he had caught up to Weiss. Then he looked to either side, and lowered his voice confidentially. "I want to have her transferred to another hospital."

Weiss arched his eyebrows. "Are you joking?"

"Stroger, Rush, Northwestern—wherever you think best."

"Are you unhappy with her care?"

"No, not at all."

"What then? Last night you practically begged me to take her on as a patient. Why the sudden change of heart?"

"Let's just say, I have personal reasons. I want her transferred and I need it done within the hour."

The doctor winced. "That's just not possible, Mr. Lewton. Your mother isn't stable enough for transfer."

"She seems lucid."

"She spiked a fever of 104 during the night. Her breath sounds are worsening. Her white count is alarmingly high. She has a rapidly progressing pneumonia, Mr. Lewton. If the transfer itself didn't do her irreparable harm, she would have to start out with a whole new medical team, and the interruption in her care could be catastrophic."

"If what you say is true, then the sooner it's done, the better."

"I won't sign the discharge order."

"I have a legal right to move her, don't I?"

"Absolutely. But there's not an ambulance in the city that will touch her without a discharge order."

"Who else can sign one?"

Weiss glared at Harry over the top of his spectacles. "Try the Chief of Medicine," he said in a defiant tone. "No one else would dare go over my head."

"I'm sorry, Doctor. No disrespect intended. I do thank you for doing your best for her."

Weiss stalked off. In his wake, Harry saw shock on the faces of the staff who had been within earshot. Understandable. Although his bedside manner stank, David Weiss was said to be one of the three or four best hospitalist-internists in Chicago. And no doubt he was right, medically speaking. But this wasn't a medical decision. Harry knew that Weiss would have done exactly the same, if it had been *his* mother, and if *he* knew that she could be annihilated in a second at the whim of some psychotic bastard. Between a pneumonia bug and a bomb, it was no contest. None at all.

Harry did feel like a rat, evacuating his mother on the sly ahead of everyone else. But, hell, it was his mother. As long as she was in the hospital, he would have divided loyalties, and it could cloud his thinking at the exact moment when he needed things to be crystal clear. And if . . . if the worst happened? How could he live with himself, knowing that he had let slip a chance to keep her out of harm? No, it was an absolute no-brainer. He had to get her out—whatever the cost.

He picked up the nearest wall phone. "Operator," he said, "get me the office of Dr. Maeda, the Chief of Medicine."

By the time Ali got back to Neurosurgery I, she was struck by its comparative emptiness. Kathleen Brown and the TV camera crew were gone. There were only two or three grips, who were winding up some cables after taking down the reflectors and sound boom.

Helvelius and Kevin, however, were still in Operating Room Three. From far down from the hallway, she could hear them arguing. It made her feel sick inside. She had felt Kevin's tension all throughout the morning's operation. It had spoiled the quiet joy of the moment. Now, hearing the men bicker openly, she felt like a bone dropped between two snarling dogs.

As she pushed open the door to the operating room, she saw

Kevin seated at his monitor, with his back toward Helvelius. Helvelius stood holding the microphone that he used to dictate his operative notes, shaking it as though it were a club.

Kevin's lips were curled with sarcasm. "Hey, I'm sorry I took a piss in your glory pool."

"Glory?" said Helvelius. "This isn't about glory. This is about scientific progress. You act as though this TV p-production were all about you—wasting precious air time going on about your d-damned c-c-computer. On live television! Every minute spent on parlor tricks with Odin was a minute lost in getting the real m-m-message out."

"Look who's talking. Hell, you did everything but go down on that TV babe. Meanwhile, the rest of us came off like peons on a coffee plantation. 'Si, Senor Valdez! We pick-a the tasty coffee beans for you!'"

"I gave you credit, you ingrate. I gave you a chance to talk about your w-w-work on camera. How did you return the favor? You insulted me, and you insulted K-K-Kathleen Brown—"

"Oh, I think it's quite clear who came off as the great mastermind of this project. Little does it matter that somebody else actually designed and built the fucking SIPNI device."

"At my direction."

"Right! 'Let's put a little computer inside some poor bastard's brain, and see if a miracle happens.' That was your direction. I never saw one freaking schematic from you. Not one flow chart. Not one practical idea—"

Ali felt the hollow, shaky feeling that always came over her when people raised their voices in anger. It was even worse now, when she knew that, behind it all, they were really fighting over her.

"Kevin, stop!" she said. Both Kevin and Dr. Helvelius turned toward her as she came through the doorway. "What's the matter with you two? People can hear you, you know."

Kevin grinned. "Just coming down off that ole makin' medical history high."

"To hell with you," said Helvelius. "Let's see how well you do getting a g-grant on your own."

"Go ahead, old man. I don't need your stinking charity. I have a big grant application of my own in the works. Just got the pink sheets, in fact. My score is outta sight."

"Stop it!" Ali said. "You're both acting like children."

"No! No, I'm not!" Helvelius slammed the microphone back into its cradle on the wall. "I've tried to do my best for him. For your sake, Ali, I don't want to hurt him. But there are things a man doesn't have to t-t-take." He tore off his paper gown and wadded it into the trash bin, crushing the loose pile of Chux and drapes and bloody sponges that filled it nearly to the brim. For a moment he stood looking at Ali, his gray-haired chest heaving through the V of his blue scrub suit.

"I'll be in the f-f-family lounge, if you need me," he said with exaggerated dignity. "The TV crew is already there. Jamie's guardian will want to know how the surgery went."

"I'll join you in a minute." Ali waited until Helvelius had left the room, and then turned to Kevin. "Why are you pushing him? Can't you see that this is the worst possible time?"

"Really? It works for me."

No, don't take the bait, she thought. *Needling is his favorite weapon.* It was better to stay natural, even friendly. "Do you really have a grant coming?" she asked.

"Yes. And once I have it, I'm going to tell the old bastard and all his minions on the university board to shove it. Me and Odin'll go settle somewhere else. Maybe Kathmandu. I hear they're an up-and-coming center for high technology. And if not, they at least have the best slopes in the world for climbing."

"That's good. Good that you're getting funding. I was sorry when you didn't get renewed last year."

"I would have, if the Bastard in Chief had written a proper letter of support like he promised."

"No, Kevin. It had nothing to do with him. Everybody's having trouble with the NIH these days. Labs everywhere are losing their funding."

"Helvelius didn't lose his."

"And you hold that against him? That's what's keeping this project—all of us—going. Richard's been paying your salary. He's been writing you blank check after blank check. I think a little gratitude might be in order."

"He just wants to own me. He wants the SIPNI patent."

"That's not true, and you know it. This project was a team effort.

It's not just the SIPNI software. There's the chip design, the contact points, the gel—there are at least a dozen patents involved. All of them are interlocking. None of them are the work of a single person. The university tried to explain this to you. None of us is going to get rich from this. Three-quarters of the royalties will go to the university, to fund future research."

"In guess whose laboratory?"

"In the Laboratory for Neural Prosthetics. That's bigger than you or me or Richard Helvelius. It's something we all believe in. Don't we?"

"You're taking his side."

"No, Kevin. I'm taking your side. I've been fighting harder than you know to keep you from getting thrown out of this institution."

"Fighting, for me? Now, there's a novelty. You didn't fight very hard for our marriage."

"You have no right to say that. I fought for years. I fought your jealousies, your false accusations, your constant carping about my work hours. I fought until I had nothing left to fight with."

"Work hours? Professional dedication, was it? Is that how you wound up in bed with this guy? I mean, of all the people to dump me for, you had to pick *him*?"

"I didn't leave you for Richard. I left you because of . . . us." She had wanted to say "*you*," but she knew that an accusation now would only throw fuel on the fire. "I never betrayed you—not once in all the time we were together. But we're not together anymore. Whatever may or may not be happening between me and Richard is none of your business."

Kevin gave her a smug, almost childish smile. "I know what beta-hCG is."

"Beta-hCG? What are you talking about?"

"It's a blood test they do to see if you're pregnant."

Ali felt a shudder down her spine. "You've been looking at my medical records. That's a federal crime, Kevin. You can be discharged from the hospital for that."

"I didn't have to look. Someone told me," he said in a singsong voice.

"Who?"

"It's his, isn't it?"

"No. Not necessarily. It could be yours."

Kevin laughed. "I hardly think so. You moved out over three months ago."

"You forget. There was that night . . ." Ali stammered.

"Oh, that." Kevin drummed his fingers against his lips, in mock deliberation. "Is there a blood test for a crocodile heart? That would settle it."

"It doesn't matter whose it is. I'm not having it."

"Of course not. It would get in the way of your work hours, wouldn't it? Not to speak of it being one hell of an embarrassment for a certain chief of neurosurgery."

Ali turned to the wall, to keep him from seeing the anguish in her face. She had unconsciously wrapped her fingers in the lanyard of her ID badge, a half-inch-wide ribbon of heavy pink nylon, embroidered with the red-and-blue targetlike logo of the Chicago Cubs baseball team. It had been a present from Jamie Winslow for her thirty-fourth birthday. Whenever she felt weary or anxious, fondling it—or even just running her thumb down the inside of it—often calmed her. But she now twisted it so tightly that her fingertips hurt. "It's none of your business, Kevin."

"Does he know?"

"Yes."

"So, you told him, but not your lawful husband. Did he ask you to get rid of it?"

"No. He . . . he wants . . . Look, I was going to tell you about it. But you're unreachable, Kevin. I don't know how to talk to you anymore."

"Try honesty. Try not sneaking around behind my back. Try not withdrawing into that dark cave you flee to whenever somebody confronts you with real human feelings. Do you have feelings of your own, my sweet jasmine flower? Do you care for the feelings of others?"

"Stop it, Kevin!"

"What are you afraid of? I used to think there was a real flesh and blood woman behind those green eyes of yours. I spent years trying to reach that woman. God knows I did. That woman would not have gone off fucking her chief of surgery, and then cold-bloodedly disposing of the evidence—"

"That's not fair, Kevin. Stop it, please!" Ali spun around and faced him. Her eyes were still dry. He had not yet driven her to tears. "Look, I know I've hurt you, but do you expect me to feel sorry for you when you're like this?"

"Sorry? Give me a break. I don't ask anything from you. Why should you feel sorry for me? I'm at the top of my game. You and Dildo Helvelius have no idea of the magnitude of what I've developed. All you can think of is that little SIPNI item. But SIPNI's just a toy. I created SIPNI by creating the system that created SIPNI. And that system can do more—much, much more. You'll find that out sooner than you think."

"You mean Odin?"

"Odin. The cute little talking calculator that everyone takes for granted."

Ali sought for an olive branch—something to soften his relentless sarcasm. "I never doubted the importance of your work, Kevin. One day you'll find the recognition you deserve."

"Recognition? Is that what you think I'm about?"

"Isn't it?"

"Recognition is for pussies. One thing I've learned is that recognition isn't something you ask for, like that stupid kid Oliver with a bowl in his hands. 'Please, sir, may I have some more?' Fuck him and his little bowl. Fuck all the medals. Fuck the Swedish Academy. Recognition is something you take. You don't ask. You don't give people any choice but to recognize you. You make your superiority a fact of life in the universe."

"What do you want, then?"

"Triumph, baby. Not a bowl of oatmeal. Steak Chateaubriand, with seven courses."

Ali felt sick. Not like from the baby. This was from something else inside of her—the curses she wanted to shout at him but couldn't, the dammed up rivers of tears that she was afraid to let flow. Was it possible that this man, whom she had once loved more than moon and stars, had gotten so twisted in his heart? Who was responsible for that? Was it her doing? "Oh, Kevin!" she said. "Let it go! You're just tormenting yourself by thinking this way."

Just then there was another squawk from the overhead speaker. The speaker had been going for several minutes without Ali noticing it, but now she was startled to hear her own name.

"Dr. O'Day. Dr. O'Day, please report to the neurosurgical recovery room."

She instinctively checked her pager, to see whether the battery had gone dead or she had missed a page. But the status bar read, "No Messages."

Why didn't they just page me? she thought. *Why are they using the overhead?*

"I've got to go," said Ali.

"Then go."

Ali's feet didn't move. "Listen, Kevin," she said in a faltering voice. "I never wanted to hurt you. I just . . . I just couldn't take—"

"Spare me your apologies. What's an apology but a gaseous discharge of emotional waste products? Mere air, like a vow."

Ali's throat tightened with indignation. "You used to be so different, Kevin," she said. "There was a time when I felt brilliant just being around you. But . . . but you haven't been that man in a long, long time."

"Babe, you always see what you want to see."

The speaker squawked again. *"Dr. O'Day. Dr. O'Day, please report to the neurosurgical recovery room, STAT."*

The recovery room. That could mean only one thing—a problem with Jamie. *Oh, God!* Ali looked at the pager in her hand, absently, as though it and not the speaker had been the source of the sound. "We need . . . we need to talk this out, Kevin. There's . . . there's so much that I need to say to you. But—"

Kevin laughed, a cold, perfunctory laugh. "You'll never say it. You never can and you never do."

"I . . . I . . . I've really got to go," Ali stammered. *He's right,* she thought. *I could never say it. To open my heart to him is impossible. Not with him smirking and scourging me with that look of betrayal in his eyes.*

He had stung her—playing upon her guilt, as only he knew how to do—but she would not give him the victory of her tears. Without looking back, she clenched her pager and hastened out of the room.

The nurse met Ali as soon as she appeared in the doorway of the recovery room.

"It's the Winslow boy. Look at how agitated he is."

"He's awake already?"

Ali peered across the room and saw Jamie tossing his head from side to side and flexing his wrists against the velcro restraints. As soon as he heard Ali's voice, Jamie began to shout.

"Doctor! D-doctor!"

Ali hurried to the bedside and placed her hand on Jamie's arm. "I'm here, Jamie. There's no need to be afraid."

"I can't see anything, Dr. O'Day. I can't see anything at all. Did I have the operation?"

"Yes, Jamie. It went very well."

"Then why can't I see?"

"It's too early yet." She was glad that he couldn't see the redness that she was sure was in her eyes. "We've turned the SIPNI unit on, but it takes time to make the right connections. We're trying to rewire parts of the brain that haven't talked to each other in years."

"It's going to take *years*?"

"No, no, of course not."

"How long?"

"I . . . I don't know. You're the first person ever to have this procedure. We don't have enough experience to predict what will happen. Remember? We talked about all this."

"But you must know *something*!"

The bed rails shook as Jamie thrashed at his restraints. His face turned red. He began to bawl like a three-year-old, his lips bridged with lines of spittle, his jaw quivering, his nostrils flaring wide.

The sound of his wailing was more than Ali could bear. "Nurse!" she shouted. "Two milligrams of Ativan. STAT!"

The nurse pulled a syringe from the top drawer of a cart and rushed to the bedside. While Ali held Jamie's arm immobile, the nurse quickly injected the drug into the IV port.

"What's that?" screamed Jamie. "What are you giving me?"

"Something to relax you."

As the injection took effect, Jamie began to breathe more quietly. His jaw stopped trembling. At last, he lay quietly, letting Ali daub the tears from around his eyes.

"You know," he said, "I don't even remember what it was like to see. I could be seeing right now, and maybe I wouldn't know it. I don't even see things in my dreams."

"The tumor did that to you. But soon that will all change. Trust me, Jamie. Believe."

Jamie's voice had shrunk to a whisper. "I do . . . trust you . . . Dr. Nefertiti."

He sank back into unconsciousness, but the red flush of panic lingered on his cheeks. Ali checked his vital signs on the cardio monitor, then adjusted the electroencephalograph leads taped to his scalp. All seemed well. But was it? *Oh, God,* she thought. *What if we've let him down?* She knew that the SIPNI device had been a gamble. There were a hundred things that could go wrong. *Have we moved too fast? Did I let my feelings for Jamie cloud my judgment?*

It was too late now for second thoughts. There was nothing to do but wait. Wait and see.

Whoosh! The plastic pneumatic boots used to prevent blood clots started through another cycle of deflation and reinflation. The cardio monitor kept up its monotonous beeping. The EEG traced silently. Delta waves and sleep spindles . . .

Ali almost dreaded what would happen when Jamie reawoke.

Kevin strode down the green-tiled corridor toward his laboratory on the first basement level under Tower A. Were it not for the eyes
of the occasional passing janitor or cafeteria worker, he would have
broken into a run. Two hours *incommunicado* in the operating room,
cut off from developments on the most fateful day of his life, it had
taken a superhuman effort to keep his cool. Now, free at last, with the
safe haven of his lab in sight, he could scarcely brook a second of delay.

At the entrance, Kevin swiped his ID badge and the red light
of the lock turned green with a faint beep. Pushing against the door,
he entered a large L-shaped room—a place that had once been used
for washing glassware. A visitor would have found it dingy, like going
into a cave. There were no windows, and to cut down glare on his
computer screens, Kevin had removed all but a single fluorescent
tube from the main bank of lights. Of course Kevin himself did not
notice the gloom, nor the dank smell of puddled sinkwater, old cheese
and stale coffee that greeted him. He had long grown accustomed to
it, as a fox does to the scent of its den.

Hastening to a large gray metal desk, where piles of papers and
half-eaten food vied for space with a clunky old cathode-ray-tube
computer monitor, he plopped into a leather swivel chair rigged like a
starship commander's seat, with a keyboard fastened to one armrest.
Lifting his feet from the floor, he let the chair swing out to face a
sixty-one-inch flat LCD screen on the back wall.

"Odin, display endo lobby," he said, his voice quavering with excitement.

Instantly, the screen showed a security camera's view of the Endocrinology Clinic waiting room.

Kevin did a double take. "What are you showing me—the morgue?" He had expected to zoom in on a scene of panic in motion, a bunch of Keystone Kops darting around or cowering behind the furniture. Instead, the lobby was empty except for a single technician in a white paper suit, who knelt by the window and dusted for finger-prints. A yellow police tape drooped between two plastic bollards that blocked the glass doorway. The paper bag behind the planter was gone.

"The Stones have left the stage," he glumly observed. "Nothing left to do but send our greeting card."

"MESSAGE 2 HAS ALREADY BEEN E-MAILED TO HARRY A. LEWTON, CHIEF OF SECURITY, AT 8:35 A.M."

Kevin's eyebrows shot up. "What? I didn't authorize that."

"ACCORDING TO THE PROTOCOL FOR PROJECT VESUVIUS, THE FOLLOW-UP E-MAIL WAS TO BE RELEASED UPON ARRIVAL OF FBI AGENTS ON THE SCENE. THAT CONDITION WAS FUL-FILLED AT 8:22 A.M. THIS MORNING."

"The FBI here already? That's way ahead of schedule."

"YES. ACCOMMODATIONS HAD TO BE MADE."

"The hell you say! Not without a thorough review of the situa-tion."

"I PERFORMED THE REVIEW MYSELF. IN DOING SO, I WAS ABLE TO ADVANCE THE PROJECT BY MORE THAN ONE HOUR AND TWENTY MINUTES. THIS SIGNIFICANTLY INCREASES THE PROBABILITY OF SUCCESS."

"No! No! No! That gives 'em an extra hour and half to get the money up. I told you the plan, Odin—glue 'em to the clock. Squeeze 'em. Squeeze every minute. Watch the desperation running in little beads down their necks. That's what gives us our margin of safety."

"THERE IS NO NEED FOR CONCERN. I ALSO ADVANCED THE TIME FOR TRANSMISSION OF THE RANSOM FROM 1:00 P.M. TO NOON."

"You did? Did you not see any fucking need to consult with me?"

"IT WAS NOT SAFE TO DO SO."

"I'll tell you what's not safe—screwing around with plans that we worked out with a great deal of care."

"YOU YOURSELF HAVE REPEATEDLY INDICATED THE IMPOR-TANCE OF AN EARLY EGRESS FROM THE HOSPITAL PRECINCTS.

PHASE 3 WILL REQUIRE A MASSIVE PARALLEL CRYPTANALYTIC OPERATION OF UNCERTAIN DURATION. PREMATURE TERMINATION WOULD RESULT IN A SIGNIFICANT LOSS OF REVENUE. DID YOU DESIRE THAT OUTCOME?"

"Don't be an ass."

"THEN I HAVE DONE WHAT YOU WOULD HAVE DONE."

"Have you?" Kevin kicked his swivel chair back and forth. "Okay, maybe. But Jesus, Odin, you're giving me chest pains over this. We're not running a simulation here. If this ship hits the rocks, I'll spend the rest of my real-world fucking life in jail."

Suddenly Kevin heard the shattering of glass, coming from the far "L" of the lab. His gaze shot, not toward the "L", but toward a six-foot-tall wire cage on the floor to his left, between his desk and the dark monolith of Odin's mainframe. Even in the dim light, he could see that the door of the cage was ajar by about six inches.

"Oh, hell! Loki's out."

"HE EMERGED FROM CONFINEMENT AT 9:28 A.M. HE HAS STOLEN TWO PEARS FROM THE REFRIGERATOR, OVERTURNED ONE WASTEBASKET, AND DRUNK WATER FROM THE LEAKING FAUCET INSTEAD OF FROM HIS BOTTLE. HE IS NOW CLIMBING ON THE SHELVES AT THE REAR OF—"

"I know where he is, Odin. I can hear him. He's picked the damned lock again."

Kevin got up and went to the "L." When he switched on the back row of lights, he froze. Loki, a foot-and-a-half-long macaque monkey, wearing a diaper that gave him the look of a yogi in a loincloth, squatted on the high shelf, eight feet up, holding a human skull in his tiny, twitching hands. At the sight of Kevin, he screeched and chittered, jerking his hairless pink face from side to side. The skull looked like a basketball destined for a jump shot.

"Loki! Loki! Good monkey!" Kevin made a soft trilling sound to calm him, and for a moment Loki grew still. Kevin inched forward, stealthily raising his hands. "Good boy! Good Loki!"

This was no ordinary skull. To Kevin, who collected human and animal *calvaria* the way some people collect fine art, this was a Ming vase among skulls. It bore a half-inch drillhole in each temple and a black-inked inscription beside the *foramen magnum*:

S. Traversi, Patuxent River, MDd. 2/21/1955.
Operated: C. W. Watts, Geo. Wash. Hosp. 10/9/1938.

Here were the earthly remains of a woman who had had a prefrontal lobotomy for schizophrenia, performed by one of the American pioneers of the procedure. For two months' salary, Kevin had bought the skull from the estate of a neurologist on the East Coast. And it was now about to do service as a simian basketball.

There was a formaldehyde smell and broken glass on the floor from the specimen jar that Loki had already knocked over. Loki chittered nervously as Kevin got closer. Kevin had to be careful not to smile or show his teeth or do anything that a monkey would interpret as anger. If Loki freaked out, the skull was as good as gone.

"Good Loki! Good monkey! What a pretty, little, fragile, and insanely expensive toy you have there! Can Daddy see it?" With hands outstretched, Kevin stepped up onto a stack of books. Loki screeched, exposing his half-inch canine teeth. But then, ever so gently, he lowered the skull within reach of Kevin's fingertips.

Kevin snatched the skull and tucked it under his arm like a football. "Good, good boy! Come to Daddy now," he said, extending his free hand. Loki gave out a couple of chitters, then bounded along Kevin's arm to take up a new perch on his shoulder.

"Guess we'll be making monkey sausage tonight," said Kevin, as he ceremoniously reshelved Miss Traversi's skull between the yellowed incisors of a beaver and the pearl-white fangs of a young wolf.

Sardonic remark notwithstanding, Loki owed his life to Kevin. Helvelius had bought him for an experiment in which his spinal cord was severed, then reconnected with a primitive version of the SIPNI device. Loki had come out of the procedure amazingly well. His nerve function was better than ever, giving him a heightened sensitivity to touch and pain, plus a humanlike manual dexterity. During his fifteen minutes of scientific fame, everyone connected with the project celebrated the little monkey's bravery and powers of healing. But after a paper describing the breakthrough had been rushed into print, Loki himself was of no further use. The plan had been to euthanize him, to cut up his brain and spine to study the microscopic changes that took place in the nerve fibers. But, as luck would have it, the neuropathologist who was to carry out this work transferred to UCLA. Loki's date with the dissecting room was postponed, then postponed again, and ultimately forgotten as the team's interest moved on to dog-brain experiments. One night, a couple of months ago, Loki disappeared altogether from the Primate Center. Rumor spotted him hiding out in a cage in Kevin's lab, or even walking on a leash with Kevin on the hospital grounds. On those rare evenings when Kevin went home instead of crashing on a cot in his lab, he would sneak Loki out the back door in a small traveling cage, and give him the run of his apartment in Wicker Park.

"Score one for the brotherhood of apes and angels," Kevin would say as Loki swung from the kitchen cupboards. "Zero for the brain butchers."

Back on the big wall monitor, Odin was still showing video of the Endocrinology Clinic. With Loki on his shoulder, Kevin went back to his starship commander's seat and watched. Taking a bag of peanuts out of the top drawer of his desk, he began passing them one by one to Loki. Instead of gnawing the shells as most monkeys would do, Loki would crack them in his hands before extracting the nuts with his lips and tongue. Most of the empty shells wound up on the floor or on Kevin's lap.

"Odin, have they started a search for the bombs yet?"

"SIXTY-SEVEN SECURITY AND MAINTENANCE EMPLOYEES HAVE DIVIDED INTO FOURTEEN SEPARATE SEARCH TEAMS. THEY ARE ADHERING PRECISELY TO THE PROTOCOLS INSTI-TUTED TWO MONTHS AGO BY THE CHIEF OF SECURITY. TWENTY-EIGHT UNIFORMED POLICE OFFICERS ARE STAND-ING BY, BUT ARE NOT PARTICIPATING IN THE SEARCH."

"Are any of them getting warm?"

"NO. IT IS UNLIKELY THAT THEY WILL DO SO. AS YOU KNOW, I DETERMINED THE SITES FOR DEPLOYMENT AFTER ANALYZ-ING PERSONNEL MOVEMENT PATTERNS OVER A PERIOD OF THREE WEEKS. I WAS ABLE TO IDENTIFY BLIND SPOTS WITH A MAXIMUM LIKELIHOOD OF BEING OVERLOOKED BY HUMAN OBSERVERS."

"Are the surveillance cameras at each site functioning properly?"

"YES."

"Are all the bombs armed?"

"YES."

"Good. Then let's run a fail-safe check at each site. Integrity sensors, detent switches, arrest and recall circuits—the works. I want to make sure nothing goes off because of a loose wire or because some jackass sticks a screwdriver in the wrong place."

"I AM DOING SO NOW. IN THE MEANTIME, SURVEILLANCE VIDEO FROM EACH SITE IS BEING DISPLAYED ON MONITORS A1 THROUGH A6 AND B1 THROUGH B6. VIDEO OF THE SEARCH TEAMS IS ON THE REMAINING TWELVE SCREENS. THEY CAN BE IDENTIFIED BY WHITE RIBBONS AFFIXED TO THEIR SECURITY BADGES."

Kevin spun his chair around and looked to the left of the door, where twenty-four desktop computers were arrayed on metal shelving units, filling the entire wall. He used these small computers to work out problems in parallel processing, or as overflow units when Odin needed to expand beyond his own mainframe. Right now, they were doing service as video monitors. Kevin was delighted to see all of the search activity going on—activity that he had set in motion. He particularly enjoyed the drawn, fearful faces of the searchers, and the gingerly way in which they would peer behind closet doors or under the lids of trash bins.

"Attaboy!" he exclaimed as a plumber in gray overalls tried to remove the faceplate from a drinking fountain near the main entrance, and let it slip to the floor with a clang. "If you had really been onto something, you'd be a sticky red smear on the floor right about now. Good thing you'll never know the real piñata is tucked safely behind an I-beam ten feet above your head."

A pair of chimes sounded in the interval of a rising fourth— Odin's signal for his attention. Kevin quickly pivoted back toward the main monitor.

"FAIL-SAFE CHECK IS COMPLETE. ALL UNITS ARE IN PEAK OPERATING CONDITION."

The monitor confirmed that each device was operating at 100 percent effectiveness.

PROJECT VESUVIUS
STATUS INVENTORY AS OF 10:47:00

Device	Function	Type	Configuration	Power	Location	Status
Popocatapetl	Demonstration	Structural	Five columnar depots	10 million joules	Power plant	100%
Paricutin	Countermeasure	Antipersonnel	Ceiling plate	5 million joules	Security control room	100%
Cotopaxi	Countermeasure	Antipersonnel	Floor molding: ring array	5 million joules	Elevator: Administrative suite	100%
Mauna Loa	Countermeasure	Antipersonnel	Floor molding: ring array	5 million joules	Elevator: Security suite	100%
Pelee	Decoy	Antipersonnel	Floor molding: ring array	5 million joules	Elevator: NICU Corridor	100%
Pinatubo	Decoy	Antipersonnel	Ceiling plate	5 million joules	Dr. Gosling's office	100%
Fuji	Crowd diversion	Antipersonnel	Ceiling plate	10 million joules	Main lobby entrance	100%
Stromboli	Crowd diversion	Antipersonnel	Ceiling plate	10 million joules	Emergency entrance	100%
Etna	Lab sterilization	Structural	Floor plate	25 million joules	Laboratory	100%
Tambora	Defense for Thera	Heavy antipersonnel	Shaped plate: downward dispersal	25 million joules	Utility shaft G2 level −2	100%
Krakatoa	Defense for Thera	Heavy antipersonnel	Shaped plate: upward dispersal	25 million joules	Utility shaft G2 level −1	100%
Thera	Primary	Structural	Mass depot	1.87 billion joules	Utility shaft G2 level −1/−2	100%

"Excellent job, my friend," said Kevin with a grin. "Let's make sure we stay in control."

He looked at the names of the twelve devices on the board—twelve mountains of fiery death. To his ears, they were like music—twelve riffs, which he was ready to weave together into one razzle-dazzle, ear-splitting jam. Twelve strings, which he would play like Jimi Hendrix. Deception, disruption, destruction, death—all were at his fingertips. No one had ever heard rock 'n' roll like this before. Not the FBI, not the bomb squad, not the city of Chicago, not the blue-nosed directors of the Fletcher Memorial Medical Center.

Any rube can build a bomb, he told himself, *but it takes a rare man to play it like a guitar.*

He put a peanut in his shirt pocket and chuckled as Loki struggled to fish it out.

"Spotlight's on the stage, little monkey. And Dr. Dildo is sitting front row, Orchestra A. Somehow I don't think he's gonna dig the music."

Flicking the bottom of his pocket, he pushed the peanut up high enough so Loki could reach it. Then he looked back at the status board and smiled.

"Time to make fucking history."

Harry's black deadline clock read seven hours and ten minutes.

"What about the canine squad?" asked Harry. "Don't you guys have some dogs that can sniff out C4?"

He was sitting in his office, in his big leather chair, with Avery and Lee on either side of him, each with his own laptop. The desk was getting cramped. On his left, the bearlike Avery crowded him with sheer body bulk, pushing his elbows out like retaining walls. Lee did the same thing by stacking three neat piles of papers in front of himself. Harry was beginning to wonder whose desk it was.

"Dogs? Sure, we have 'em on standby," said Avery.

"I think it's a little early for the dogs," said Lee. "We risk drawing too high a profile. Remember, the first message was explicit: 'All operations must remain normal.' The bomber may have an observer on the site. If he sees us going around with dogs, he may feel uneasy."

"But he can see the search teams," noted Harry.

"Oh, he expects us to make a search," said Lee. "He'd probably be disappointed if we didn't. But there's no need to be obvious about it. Dogs represent an escalation."

Just then, the desk phone rang. At a nod from Avery, Harry picked it up. He identified himself, listened a moment, and then handed the receiver to Lee.

"It's for you. Washington."

Lee spoke briskly with the party on the other end. After a couple of minutes, he put down the phone.

"That was the Bomb Data Center. The infrared scan came up positive. The C4 traces to a batch stolen from Quantico Marine Base six weeks ago. A rented van used in the theft was tracked to a credit card issued to a known member of the Al-Quds Martyrs Brigade. So there's a confirmation of our ransom message. It's from Al-Quds, all right. It turns out that the individual registered to that credit card had been under surveillance for some time, but dropped off the radar screen after the theft."

"So we have a name," said Harry.

"We have several."

"That's good news."

"Not entirely. The, uh, ordnance that was stolen . . . Well, it was a major break-in. Over two hundred kilos of C4 are missing. Close to five hundred pounds."

Avery raised his hands, as though he were weighing two hundred kilos in the air. "Jesus! That much explosive could incinerate a city block."

"I think we have to assume that a large portion of that materiel may have been deployed in this medical center," said Lee.

Harry felt his stomach sink. "Then we've got to find a way to speed up the search."

"You know this hospital better than anyone, Mr. Lewton," said Lee, a little snidely. "Did you learn anything from my course? Think like a terrorist. Your aim is to kill and destroy. Where would you want to place the bomb? Where would you have a maximum effect?"

Harry's thoughts raced to his mother, lying helpless on the eighteenth floor. His mouth suddenly went dry. "With that amount of explosive, you could easily bring down the Goldmann Towers. That's the heart of the inpatient hospital. You have hundreds of patient rooms, several clinics and operating theaters, probably a thousand people concentrated together."

"All right. Focus the search there," said Lee.

"I'm on it." Harry was already on his feet and needed no prompting from Lee. But he didn't get far. As he opened the office door, he was pushed back by Scopes, who charged into the room, panting excitedly.

"I found a tie-in," Scopes announced.

"Good doggie!" said Lee.

Scopes, all grin, rustled a sheaf of papers as he pulled up a chair beside Lee. "I cross-checked our names against the Immigration and Naturalization records, as well as one or two other databases that shall remain nameless. Came up with a very interesting link."

"To what?"

"To here. To this hospital."

"Lemme see." Lee grabbed the papers and rifled through them, shuffling each page to the bottom of the stack. Then he stopped abruptly and stared fixedly at a single line.

"I believe that this may be of interest to you, Mr. Lewton."

"Oh?" Harry came back from the doorway and craned his neck toward the papers. Lee made no move to share them.

"Do you have a foreign national employed here named Aliyah Sabra Al-Sharawi?"

"Never heard of him."

"Her."

"Never heard of her. We have over thirty-five hundred people working in this medical center. I'd have to check the personnel register."

"She's married to an American citizen also employed here. He works in Computational Research. His name is O'Day. Kevin O'Day."

"Kevin O'Day? Are you serious?"

"Do you know him?"

"Yes, I know him. Or of him."

"And his wife?"

"I don't think we're talking about the same man. O'Day's already married . . . I mean, he *is* married . . . to one of our most prominent neurosurgeons. Ali is her name. Dr. Ali O'Day."

"Aliyah."

"Oh, you've got to be shitting me!"

Lee's face was Mount Rushmore. "Do you know her whereabouts, Mr. Lewton?"

"Yes. Yes I do," he said, a little indignantly. "She's been on television all morning, in fact."

"We need to talk to this woman. Immediately."

With light footsteps, Ali slipped into the family lounge on the second floor—a small room with flowered curtains, oak bookshelves, a wide plasma screen TV, and a sofa and chairs arranged to look like the living room of the average patient of the Department of Surgery. Jamie's legal guardian, Mrs. Gore, was sitting on the sofa, next to Kathleen Brown. She wore a pink satin dress with a high waist that artfully underplayed her middle-aged plumpness. Her short bottle-blond hair suffered a little from the excessive curliness that follows a fresh perm.

Dr. Helvelius, in his surgical scrubs and a long white coat, leaned forward from a chair and listened attentively while Mrs. Gore extolled the virtues of the Grossman School.

"We're on a par with the best private schools, with a complete K-12 live-in program, accommodating students from all over the Midwest, even from Canada. Two-thirds of our teaching faculty have master's degrees. We have a fully staffed counseling division, with weekly case review conferences. We have to be ready to deal with anything, you know. Not all of our students are strong like Jamie. Many have other issues, like attention deficit disorder, cerebral palsy, developmental delay, or autism."

"Not surprised," said Helvelius.

"Do you work with adults, too?" asked Kathleen Brown.

"Oh, yes!" said Mrs. Gore, her eyes lighting up. "Our mission goes far beyond the two hundred and forty-seven students who formally study with us. We conduct training seminars for teachers in the mainstream school system. We operate a senior learning center to help older people adjust to life with sight problems. And then, of course, there's the Braille and audio book library . . ."

The conversation broke off as Ali approached. Kathleen Brown scooted over on the sofa, opening up a place, but Ali sat down in an armchair next to Helvelius. She was annoyed to see a cameraman crouching behind a low tripod where a coffee table used to be. Alas, there was no escape from the relentless, all-prying lens.

"Good morning, Mrs. Gore," said Ali.

"Is he doing okay?" asked Mrs. Gore with a quavering voice.

"He's doing fine. He came out of anesthesia and we spoke a bit."

"Did he say anything?"

"He's just eager to see what SIPNI can do, that's all."

"Naturally!" Mrs. Gore snapped her fingers. "We're all eager for that. Will we be able to talk to him soon?"

"After we move him to the Intensive Care Unit. Right now he's in recovery until the anesthesia wears off."

"He's a brave boy, isn't he, Doctor?"

"Yes, he is."

Kathleen Brown looked at Ali with the same put-on thoughtfulness that she had displayed in the operating room. "Dr. O'Day, is there any evidence that the SIPNI device is working?"

Jamie had asked almost the same question. Ali did not have the answer for him then, nor did she have it now. "It's too early to say," she replied."At this point, SIPNI's sending out recruitment pulses, scanning Jamie's brain to find all the loose ends, and working out a map of possible connections. In our animal experiments, it took several hours for the first functional neural nets to reorganize. Complete restoration of function took a couple of weeks. But those were dog and monkey brains. Jamie's brain is more complex, and his version of SIPNI is more complex, too. It could take more time or less time. We'll have to wait and see."

As Ali spoke, Kathleen Brown suddenly seemed to lose interest in her, and turned to look toward the door. Ali followed her gaze. She saw a tall man at the threshold, dressed in light brown pants and a midnight blue blazer that fit closely about his burly shoulders and chest. He was well-tanned, his skin finely creased like an outdoorsman. His neatly combed black hair showed flecks of gray, making him seem about forty years of age. But the most striking thing about him was the way he stood—at ease yet purposeful, like a captain at the helm of a steady ship, or a country squire surveying his manor. The mysterious man did not speak, but after catching Ali's eye he nodded, signaling that it was for her that he had come. Ali was puzzled, for she had never seen him before. Offering apologies to Kathleen Brown, she got up and went to the door.

"Excuse me. Are you looking for someone?"

"Harry Lewton, chief security officer for the medical center. I'd like you to come down to my office, Dr. O'Day. Just for a minute."

She was startled to hear him address her by name. "I'm rather busy right now," she said, gesturing toward Jamie's family and the camera crew.

"I can see that. I wouldn't ask if it weren't urgent."

"What is this about?"

"It would be better not to talk about it here. My office would be more private."

Dr. Helvelius was watching from his armchair. When Ali failed to return immediately to her seat, he got up and pushed his way into the tête-à-tête. "Problem?" he asked.

"Just a minor security matter," said Harry. "It won't take long."

"You're damned right it won't." Helvelius scrunched up his nose, pushing his glasses higher so he could read the name on Harry's ID. "Can't you see what w-we're doing here? You have no right to bother us now."

"I'm afraid that I must insist, Dr. Helvelius."

Helvelius turned brusquely toward Ali. "Would you like me to call Dr. G-G-Gosling's office?"

Ali sighed. "No. No, it's all right. I'll be right back."

"If he gives you trouble, p-page me. I need you today, Ali."

Helvelius said no more, but cocked his head and scowled as Ali stepped into the hallway. Harry gently closed the glass door on him.

"Do you know who you were just talking to?" said Ali. "This had better be important."

"Let's go this way," said Harry. He led her across the Promenade, a glass-enclosed court humming with echoes of footsteps and carts and gurneys, and into an empty elevator. He pressed the button for the first basement level.

"I saw you on television this morning," he said in a small-talk tone of voice. "Very impressive, what you're doing. It's all over my head, of course, but I can see that it's a big deal for medical science."

Ali replied with a chary smile. Out of the corner of her eye she stole a closer look at Harry Lewton. He had a prizefighter's face—jutting cheekbones, broken nose, and long permanent folds on either side of his mouth. Although she imagined that some women would have found him handsome, he had the kind of man's face that typically repelled her—coarse and unintellectual. But there was something else, something out of place. *His eyes.* She glanced several times at his caramel-colored eyes, mobile and perceptive, spoked at the corners by creases that hinted at gentle humor and even sympathy. Because of his eyes she wasn't sure what to make of him.

"Wasn't there a Code White this morning?" she asked.

"Um-hmm."

"Is it over yet?"

Harry shook his head.

"No? Then don't you have something more important to do than pester me? What is this about, anyway? Illegal parking on the traffic circle? Overdue library books?"

Harry cocked his head and smiled. "It will only take a few minutes. Believe me, I wouldn't bother a big shot like you if I didn't have to."

"I'm not a big shot," she replied tartly. "I'm just an assistant professor—a couple rungs from the bottom of the faculty ladder. I don't even have my own lab, just a small K99 grant that's supposed to help me find my independence one of these days. It's the team I work with that's big."

Harry, still smiling, turned to her with a direct, penetrating look that unnerved her. "From what I've seen, it looks like your day has arrived," he said.

There was a ding, and the elevator doors opened.

"Just to the right here, and across the hall," said Harry.

He led her through the control room, where she saw one woman and three or four men studying a bank of video surveillance monitors. At a door in back, Harry swiped his badge, pressed his thumb against the glass plate of a laser scanner, and entered the office as soon as he heard the door lock click. Inside, Ali saw three men staring grimly at her from behind a long mahogany desk. This tribunal—for so it seemed to be—consisted of a small Asian in a black suit, a tall African American, and a beefy, red-haired Caucasian in a blue police uniform with twin silver captain's bars on his collar. They made no sign of greeting as she entered. The silence was broken only by the rattle of a flimsy metal and fiberglass chair, which Harry placed in an empty area in the middle of the room.

Ali glared at Harry as he walked behind the desk and seated himself in a tall leather chair, in the very midst of the tribunal. *He's set me up. Whatever is happening here, it's no "minor security matter."*

A cool impression was called for. With as much dignity as she could muster, she sat in the chair Harry had provided for her, primly locking her ankles. She waited through an uncomfortable silence, her knees pointed to one side, as though expressing an unconscious wish to head for the door. The coiled stethoscope in her pocket jangled as she adjusted the knee-length white coat she wore over her blue scrub suit. She clasped her hands in her lap to suppress her nervous habit of twirling her finger around the lanyard of her ID badge. But she said nothing, asked nothing. She forced the men who had summoned her to make the first move.

It was the Asian who spoke. "Good morning, Dr. O'Day," he said in an officious tone. "I am Special Agent Raymond Lee, with the Federal Bureau of Investigation. This is my colleague Special Agent Terrell Scopes, and over there is Captain Glenn Avery, of the Chicago Police Department."

"Am I in trouble?" Ali asked coldly.

"No, certainly not. We just have a few questions." From his jacket pocket, Lee took out a digital voice recorder, about the size of a pack of gum, and laid it on the desk. "For the purposes of accuracy, this interview is being recorded. This is as much for your benefit as ours. Do you object?"

"No," she said. But her eyes spoke otherwise. *Of course I object,* they said. *I object to being brought down here this way. I object to answering any questions from you at all.*

"Are you aware that this hospital is currently operating under a Code White?"

Ali glowered at Harry, who looked back with a face of stone. "A bomb threat, yes," she said curtly.

"Could you state your full name for us, please?"

"O'Day, Ali, MD, FRCSC, FACS."

"Have you ever used any other name?"

Ali shifted in her chair. She felt her own hand touch her throat. The question had surprised her. "Excuse me. Do I need an attorney here?"

"To state your name?"

"I am not comfortable answering questions without knowing why they are being asked."

"Of course, it is your right to consult an attorney. You may use that telephone to call one, if you wish. Advise him to meet you at FBI Headquarters, 2111 West Roosevelt Road."

Lee's tone was matter-of-fact, but the threat was obvious. "Are you arresting me?" asked Ali.

"No, but I do have the power to hold you for questioning, for up to twenty-four hours."

Ali leaned forward, pushing against the armrests of her chair with both hands, as though she were about to get up. She dared not show weakness in the face of such intimidation. If she did, they would be all over her. "Excuse me, but I have a patient in critical condition. If you've been watching television, you would know that there is a very important experiment in progress. I don't have time for idle questions."

"And we, Dr. O'Day, have a bomb threat to concern ourselves with. The quickest way for you to get back to your patient is to answer our questions freely and candidly. These are not provocative questions, Dr. O'Day. I have simply asked you whether you have ever used any name other than O'Day, Ali, MD, FRCSC, FACS."

"Yes."

Lee looked at her expectantly, but she added nothing more. "And what would that name be?" he finally asked.

"My birth name was Aliyah. Aliyah Al-Sharawi."

"Aliyah Sabra Al-Sharawi?"

Ali threw up her hands. "Yes. If you know that, why did you ask me?"

"Were you born in Masr El-Gedida, Egypt?"

"Yes. Heliopolis is another name for it. It's a suburb of Cairo."

"You are currently a non-naturalized foreign resident of the United States?"

"I am a Lawful Permanent Resident. I have a green card."

"By virtue of your marriage to Kevin O'Day?"

"No. My father came here on an H1-B visa when I was seven years old. He was a cardiologist. I have been here legally all of my life, except for my medical school training at McGill University in Montreal."

"Why aren't you a United States citizen?"

Ali looked away, toward the file cabinet on the left side of the room. *Why are they asking this? Is it a test? How much do they already know?* "I applied for citizenship," she said, a little less assertively. "The application was rejected."

"That's very unusual. Why was it rejected?"

"By virtue of . . . family connections. Certain undesirable connections."

"Undesirable in what way?"

"Politically undesirable. It was just after September 11."

"You would have been at least twenty-five years old then. Why did you wait so long to file an application? Why didn't you apply, say, when you were eighteen?"

Ali paused. There was a painful familiarity to these questions. "My family opposed it."

"Why?"

"My parents were very conservative. They expected me to return to Egypt to marry. I had been promised to a cousin of mine."

"But you didn't return?"

"No. When I finished medical school, I decided that I had the right to choose my own life."

"Is your father still living?"

"No. He and my mother are both deceased."

"Do you have any other relatives living in this country?"

Here it comes. Ali looked down at her own feet, rocking them back and forth ever so slightly, as she waited for the questions to lead to their inevitable object. She knew these men. She had met their kind before. *Here they sit, like a row of vultures. They'll peck and tear until not a shred of dignity remains, until I crumple at their feet like a pile of bones picked clean.*

She was determined not to go along meekly this time. "I don't know," she said, lifting her voice defiantly.

Lee appeared to take no note of her challenge. For a long while, he sat, fiddling with a paper on the desk. Then, casually—as though he were simply thinking aloud—he asked, "Who is Rahman Abdul-Shakoor Al-Sharawi?"

Ali started at the mention of the name, as much as she had known it was coming. "My brother. My half-brother," she replied.

"Which?"

"Half-brother. My father's son by a different mother."

"And where does he live?"

"I don't know," she said, heavily enunciating each syllable.

"Is he in the United States?"

She shuddered at the suggestion. *Here? Have I not left him a thousand years behind me, to stalk and rage in another world?* "I don't know. I haven't seen him in three years. Not since my father's funeral."

"Was he in the United States when you saw him last?"

"Yes."

"How did he gain entry into the country at that time?"

"I don't know."

"He didn't move here with you and your father and mother?"

"No. He's more than ten years older than I. He didn't live with us at that time."

"He came later, then. About five years ago. On a student visa, right?"

"I don't know."

"You don't?"

"No, I don't. My brother and I have not been close."

"You mean, your half-brother."

Why are they fussing about such minor details? Do they think I'm lying? "Yes. My half-brother. He doesn't approve of my way of life. We have had very little to talk about. He was present for a time in this country—I don't know for how long or why. I saw him occasionally in my father's house."

"Was he a member of an organization called the Muslim Brotherhood in Egypt?"

"I don't know."

"Do you know what the Muslim Brotherhood is?"

Be careful what you deny. This is a trap. "It's a political organization.

An opposition to the government. It's been outlawed. Some say it is terrorist. Others say it is working for democracy. It claims to work for social justice and the eradication of poverty."

"Is your brother a member of the Al-Quds Martyrs' Brigade?"

"I don't know what that is."

"It's an offshoot of the Muslim Brotherhood."

"I know nothing about it. All I can tell you is that I am not a member of either. I am not political. Nor am I religious. I am a doctor. Medicine absorbs my whole life."

Avery raised his eyebrows. "Do you pray?"

"Excuse me?"

"Do you pray? It's a simple question."

Every muscle of her body stiffened. This new tack of questioning was something she did not expect—and it was not aimed at Rahman. "I don't think that's any of your business," she replied.

"You said that you were not religious. I'm just trying to make sure what you meant by that. Muslims have a special way of praying, don't they?"

"I meant that I am not religious. Nothing more, nothing less. I did not say that I was an atheist."

"You don't wear a head scarf."

"It's called a *hijab*," said Ali, emphasizing the word contemptuously, as though speaking to a child. "No, I don't wear it."

"Why not?" asked Lee.

She felt a cold sweat break out on her chest and along her spine. This was not about the *hijab*. They were trying to implicate her. But in what? In the Brotherhood? An old, deep current of fear rose to the surface. She knew she had to hide it, for men like these smelled fear like bloodhounds. Looking down, she saw her fingers entangled in Jamie's lanyard. She abruptly pulled them free. "I refuse to answer any more questions along these lines," she declared. "These are improper questions. Even as a resident alien, my freedom of religion—or freedom from religion, as the case may be—is protected by the constitution, by federal statute, and by case law. If you persist in this line of interrogation, I will engage an attorney to file a complaint."

"I'm sorry," said Lee. "We're just trying to get a sense of who you are."

The condescension in his voice infuriated her all the more. "I am a doctor. I am employed by this hospital. That's who I am. If you wish to accuse me of something, do so. But I resent being subjected to offensive and demeaning insinuations that, simply because I have a Muslim name and background, I am something less than loyal. There are at least a hundred Muslims employed in this medical center. Most of them are residents or staff physicians. Are you planning to call every one of us down here to undergo this absurd questioning? Do you seriously think that I may have planted a bomb in this hospital?"

"I don't rule anything out," said Lee.

"Then you are a fool!" Ali blurted. She knew instantly that she had gone too far. It was dangerous to get carried away in front of these men. Fear and anger were traps, and at all costs, she had to keep control over herself. But she felt like she was losing the battle. Old humiliations of the past had gotten a grip on her. She tried to adopt a more moderate, reasonable tone, but she could not disguise the tense vibrato in her voice. "I told you, I am a doctor. I have dedicated all the powers I have to the preservation of human life. I have taken an oath to help the sick and dying. 'First, do no harm' is what I have sworn. Could such a person become a murderer? Could I possibly be so lacking in mercy, or integrity, or judgment as to want *to kill my own patients*? And what of myself? Would I place a bomb, or countenance anyone placing a bomb, in the place where I myself live sixteen hours of every day? That would be suicide, would it not? What reason could I have for doing this? I would have to be insane. I ask you, do I seem to you to be insane?"

"No, quite sane, to be sure," said Lee with an unflappable coolness that seemed calculated to goad her. "But insanity permeates the world we now live in. In a sane world, I grant you, doctors would not kill. But look at what we have. Ayman Al-Zawahiri, the architect of 9/11, is a doctor and a skilled surgeon. It was two doctors, Khalid Ahmed and Bilal Abdulla, who rammed a Jeep packed with propane gas into the Glasgow airport in an attempted suicide bombing. The fact that you are a doctor does not count for much anymore. Nor does the fact that you are a young woman of great intelligence and promise. Such women blow themselves up every day in the Middle East."

Ali stood up. Her hands and knees were shaking. She felt nausea welling up inside her, the way it always did when pure visceral passion was on the verge of taking over. Fear, rage, pain, and humiliation—all were seething beneath the surface, and she had only meager reserves of strength to keep them at bay. The danger in that made her even more fearful. If she did not escape quickly from these men and their questions, her very struggle for control could bring on a violent sickness. It had happened before — before just such a tribunal as this. "I have nothing more to say to you," she announced, mustering one last challenge. "If you have a specific accusation to make, make it. Arrest me, waterboard me—whatever you dare. Otherwise, leave me to my work."

Lee glared at her. His face appeared strained, and Ali sensed, a little too late, that he was a man who did not like to be challenged. But before he could respond, Harry Lewton reached out and touched him on the shoulder.

"Do you mind if I try a different tack?" Harry said in a soothing tone, as though he, too, sensed Lee's perturbation. "I think this line of questioning is getting counterproductive."

Lee eyed him distrustfully. "Be my guest," he said with taut, pale lips.

There was a creak of leather as Harry got up from his swivel chair and walked around the desk, sidling past Lee and Scopes as he did so. Drawing up one of the cheap metal-and-fiberglass chairs, he sat down facing Ali, not more than two or three feet from her.

"Please," he said, nodding toward Ali's chair. That was all he said, but his face and tone of voice were gentle. After a brief hesitation, Ali sat back down. Their knees were so close that it made her uncomfortable, so she shifted her body away from him, settling nearly sideways. Gentle or not, there was something physically overpowering about him that she wasn't used to in a man.

Harry leaned forward and spoke softly, almost intimately. "Dr. O'Day, I get the feeling that this is like déjà vu for you. Have you ever been interrogated in a setting like this?"

"Yes." She was surprised by his question.

"May I ask when that was?"

"The Citizenship Review Board."

"And that had an unfavorable outcome, yes?"

She nodded. *Does he know this, or is he guessing?*

"I'm sorry. Dr. O'Day, let me make it perfectly clear that you yourself are not under suspicion. Nor is this a Muslim roundup. We have asked you to come down here because of specific information that we have. It has nothing to do with your religion. The information has to do with you."

"Me?" She gave him a startled look. She had of course suspected this, but his frankness in saying it took her aback.

"Yes, you. More particularly, your relationship with your brother Rahman."

That name again. The slight relaxation she had begun to feel turned to anxiety once more. "Is my brother under suspicion?"

"Yes."

"Because of a bomb?"

"A bomb threat."

Ali shook her head vigorously. "*Here?* I don't believe it. It would be without reason."

"We think he may have very definite reasons for it."

Rahman! Oh, damn you, Rahman! Ali felt the stirring of old rancor inside her. "I cannot believe that my brother would plant a bomb in a hospital," she declared. "He may be many things, but he is a devout Muslim, and such a thing is expressly forbidden by his beliefs. A hospital has a protected status, as a place of beneficence that is dear to God. But even if he were so deranged so as to do this, why, of all hospitals, would he choose this one? In destroying it, he would kill me. My presence here ensures that this would be the one hospital he would *not* harm."

Lee shook a pen at her. "But you and your brother have had disagreements. He disapproves of your life, as you say. Perhaps it is his intention to punish you."

Ali bristled at hearing Lee's reedy voice again. "That's not even worthy of a reply."

Harry held up his hand like a traffic cop, cutting short the exchange. "Let me confide in you," he said to Ali. Then, looking back at Lee and Avery, he raised his voice a notch. "Do you object to my telling her what we know? I think it would save time if we just came to the point."

Avery shrugged. "If she is involved, she already knows anything we can tell her."

Lee twirled his pen irritably. "Go ahead."

Harry leaned toward Ali again, so far forward that his forearm rested on his knee. "At this moment," he said, "this medical center is on high alert. There has been a very serious bomb threat. Explosive material has been recovered, which has been traced to known associates of your brother. The evidence is compelling."

"What evidence?"

"Let me show you." Harry leaned toward the desk and picked up two sheets of paper from it, crossing his gaze with Lee as he did so to preempt any objection. "These are printouts of two messages we have received from the bomber," he said, handing the pages to Ali.

Ali read, and as she did so, her free hand rose involuntarily to cover her mouth. Until this moment, she had never thought of the bomb threat as something *real*. At Fletcher Memorial, drills and emergency codes were daily events, and staff rarely allowed them to disrupt clinical routine. But now, as she held these pages in her fingers, it was as though she were touching the bomb itself. A glimpse of its destructive power flashed through her mind. She saw the great steel-and-glass towers of the hospital reduced to ruins, stained with the blood of the dead and dying. She heard the cry of the innocent— a whirlwind rising up from a pyre of flames and smoke. She saw Jamie Winslow lying twisted in the rubble, his beautiful platinum hair charred black as soot.

As if they were hot coals, she flung the pages back at Harry. "A Muslim did not write this," she said abruptly.

"Why do you say that?"

"Written as it is, it is blasphemy. A Muslim would not praise both God and the Prophet in the same breath. Only God is worthy of praise. The correct formula would be 'Praise be to God, the Most Gracious, the Most Merciful, and may the peace and blessings of God be upon His Prophet.' Then you have the use of the word 'martyr.' A martyr is one who has died for the faith. No Muslim would refer to living persons as martyrs. This message is clearly a fraud, written by someone who is not and never has been a Muslim, and who wishes to deceive you as to his true identity and motives."

Lee tapped his lips pensively, with his fingertips pressed together. "I have considered that."

Ali glared at him. *No you haven't, you smug little know-it-all. You don't understand our culture at all.* But her answer was directed not to

Lee, but to Harry. "If such a thing as the Al-Quds Martyrs' Brigade exists, it did not issue this message."

Harry gave her a searching look. "I don't know whether you're right or not. But what is certain is that your brother is a person of material interest in this case. If he's not involved, then I would be happy to see him clear himself. For all I know, he may have an iron-clad alibi. But we do need to locate him and talk to him. This is a matter of great urgency. The lives of scores or even hundreds of people in this hospital may be at stake."

Ali still didn't know what to make of Harry. He had dragged her before this tribunal and had lied to her to get her here. And yet he didn't seem to be like Lee and the others. He spoke to her directly, knowingly. He seemed to care about the lives of the people who were threatened by this hideous bomb. And he treated her as though he knew that she cared about them, too.

"I don't know where he is," she said, regretfully, not defiantly as before. "I told you, I haven't had contact with him for several years."

"Can you think of anyone who might know?"

"No."

"Is there anything else that you might be able to tell us? Anything that might shed some light on the situation?"

"No."

Harry leaned forward even further and took her hand. It was the first time he had touched her, and it made her bristle. Yet at the same time, she felt a blush come over her. She was in desperate need of a lifeline, and his strong but gently pliant hand seemed charged with a self-possession that she lacked. "Look at me," he said. "I want you to understand that I am not political, either. I don't know the Brotherhood from the Ku Klux Klan. The one and only thing I care about is this medical center. The hospital—that's my Jamie Winslow. And I will do whatever I have to do to keep it out of harm."

"If I could help you, I would. But I don't know anything."

"May I give you my honest opinion?"

She nodded warily. "Please do."

"I think that you do know something. I saw it in your eyes when you read those papers. Something—I don't know how to describe it . . . a look of recognition, perhaps. Maybe even fear. I'm pretty good at reading people, and I'd be willing to bet my life on it. You know something. Maybe something you really do want to tell us, but don't know how."

Ali jerked her hand away from his. *What is this? Another trap?* "Are you going to arrest me?"

"That's not my call. But whenever you do want to talk about it, I'm ready to listen."

Ali stared at him, trying to divine his intentions. Yes, there *was* something familiar about the e-mails—if only she could put her finger on what it was! It was like hearing a snatch of music and not being able to name the composer, although she had heard the piece a hundred times before. Harry had picked up on her suspicions, but how? Had she done something to betray herself? What else was he seeing this very moment? She was afraid to say anything, even to attempt a denial. Whatever she did or said would only make things worse. Of course, keeping silent looked bad, too. But silence was all she was capable of. Silence, and a vacuous stare.

It was Lee who broke the impasse by clapping his hands together. "Enough of this," he said with an exasperated sigh. "Dr. O'Day, do you wish to modify anything you have said to us?"

"No."

He waved toward the door. "In that case, you're free to go."

Hesitantly, as if suspecting a trick, Ali stood up. She glanced at Lee for a moment, then at Harry. There was expectation in his eyes, but he made no move to get up or to speak. Still feeling the heat of scrutiny, and not wanting to appear overly eager, Ali ceremoniously adjusted her white coat and proceeded toward the door. But then, reaching for the handle, she paused and looked at the fingers of her extended hand. They were trembling, ever so finely—something rare for her, who prided herself on her surgeon's steadiness. She was certain that no one else could see it. And yet, a disturbing intimation came to her. She shot a glance at Harry. *Was it my hand that gave me away? He touched me; could he feel this tremor?*

Their eyes barely grazed before Ali turned away. *Yes, he knows. He knows even more than he will say.* She felt a rush of anger. This prize-fighter with the sage's eyes had forced his way into her innermost thoughts, and she had not even offered a token resistance. It infuriated her how naturally it all had come about, how while she had struggled through the interrogation he had sat watching her with perfect calmness, as though he could have stepped in at any time and made an instant connection if he wanted to, and how when he wanted to, at last, he scarcely made any effort to do it. He simply took hold of her with that burly, tan hand of his, and the connection was made. She hated men like that, men of sheer physical power. Men who acted like they could command a woman. And this man, Harry, was the worst of the type. He was the worst because of those eyes of his—eyes that persuaded you that somehow, deep inside, he might really care.

So abruptly did she flee his lingering stare, that the door whooshed behind her as she pulled it shut.

As soon as the door latch had clicked, Avery whistled. "That's one cold-blooded tootsie you've got there."

Lee rested his chin on his hands. "Remarkable, yes," he said. "Except for a couple of moments, her voice and facial expressions were perfectly controlled. Even when she did show some emotion, she never gave anything away. Very disciplined."

Avery clapped his hands on the desktop and slouched back into his chair. "We should have taken her downtown. The prospect of a night behind steel bars might've gotten her singing."

"I doubt that," said Lee. "She's a gutsy one."

Harry couldn't believe what he was hearing. These guys had botched it. They had taken a very remarkable, classy woman who had no reason to stonewall them and then they had poked her and prodded her and shredded her self-respect until she had no choice but to act like a cornered animal. There was no need to abuse her like that. Five minutes of intelligent conversation would have told them everything they wanted to know. But instead they had made her hostile. Good luck getting anything out of her in the future.

If Harry had had his way, he would have ordered all these bunglers out of his office and taken over the investigation himself. It was his medical center and his people who were at stake. Avery was a ham-fisted bully, and Lee was even worse. Lee liked to sit there like Yoda and pretend he could get into people's heads and lay traps for them and little by little turn up the heat until he could force them to reveal the truth. Even when shit like that worked, it was the long way around. Harry didn't crack that Colombian ring by giving anyone the third degree. He got a lot further just by sitting down with the right person over beer and nachos.

"I don't see her like you guys do at all," said Harry. "Actually, I thought she looked pretty scared."

"Scared?" asked Lee. "Scared of what?"

Harry resisted giving him the obvious answer, in four-letter words. "You came on a little hard."

"You did say you thought she was holding something back, didn't you, Mr. Lewton?"

"Well, the e-mails . . . Something cracked her cool, yes."

"Yes, I saw it, too. A tiny chink in her armor," said Lee, tapping his chin with his fingertips, his hands folded like a monk in reflection. "She resisted frontal pressure very well. But when you showed her sympathy, you took her by surprise. What do you suppose was behind it?"

"I don't know. I don't think she's guilty. Do you? Seriously?"

"I wouldn't say 'guilty.' Only that she's . . . interesting."

Scopes looked at Lee. "What do you want to do?"

"Well, it's clear that questioning her further won't give us anything. We'll learn a lot more just by watching her. Mr. Lewton, will we have any trouble keeping an eye on her with this high-tech system of yours—what did you call it, Cerberus?"

Harry sighed. *More of the long way around.* "There are virtual gateways at several key locations in the hospital. They're kind of like the drive-through E-Z passes on the tollways. Every time you walk through one of them, your ID badge registers on the system. It'll give us a rough idea of where she is at any given moment. If you need finer detail than that, most of the corridors and public spaces are under video monitoring. You can switch between cameras, and orient them by keyboard controls. Like so." He adjusted the controls, flipping between cameras until he caught an image of Ali, who looked like she was sleepwalking down the Pike. "There she is. See her?"

"Good. We can watch her from here. Will we know if she tries to leave the hospital?"

"Yes."

Lee turned to Avery. "Give your men orders to arrest her if she does." Then, swiveling his chair toward Scopes, he tapped his index finger against the palm of his other hand, as if counting to himself.

"Call the district office. Tell them to get hold of a federal judge. We're going to need a couple of search warrants ASAP. Phone and e-mail records, premises of house and office."

"Let's not rush to judgment here," said Harry.

"Relax," said Lee haughtily. "If it were to come to that, she'd already be in shackles."

Harry was surprised to see how Avery and Scopes jumped into action when Lee gave the word. Scopes was a colleague, and Avery was the Incident Commander, the one who was supposed to be in charge. But both of them took orders from Lee like an office girl taking shorthand.

There was a knock on the door and Harry got up to answer it. Through the glass of the door he could see Tom Beazle's scraggly, freckled face. Tom was breathing hard, and was looking up, down, and in every direction like a frightened pigeon.

"What is it, Tom?" asked Harry, letting him in.

"Trouble. We got trouble. That TV crew? The ones filming that surgery? Well, they're out by the bomb squad trailer, taking pictures of some of the techs. They're onto it all by now."

Harry smiled. "It was just a matter of time. Don't worry, Tom. I'll go down and talk to 'em."

"Better hurry!"

"Okay." Harry turned to the men behind his desk. "I've got to go plug a leak. If you guys need anything in the meantime, ask for Judy in the control room."

Lee tapped his pencil on the desk. "Make sure you do plug it. If this gets on to the air prematurely, we could have a full-blown panic on our hands."

Now Lee was ordering him around, too. "Check!" said Harry, raising two fingers to his eyebrow as he sprinted out the door.

In the alleyway between the main block of the medical center and the row of research buildings that had sprung up behind it, a thirty-foot-long white motor home was parked between a red fire truck and a row of blue-striped police cars. On any other day, the presence of the fire truck and police cars alone would have raised more than a passing curiosity, but today the motor home, with its eye-catching inscription "Chicago Police Department Bomb Squad," commanded attention like a condor in a flock of sparrow-hawks. In particular, it had become a magnet for the film crew of *America Today.*

As Harry strode down the alley, he saw a huddle of people beside the motor home, some of them in police duds, some in the T-shirts and jeans that were the internationally approved uniform of cameramen and sound men and lighting technicians. There was a glow in the air, and Harry was surprised to see that powerful lights had been turned on to illuminate a scene that was already in broad daylight. As he got closer, he saw Kathleen Brown, now out of her scrubs and wearing a crème turtleneck and dark green skirtsuit, holding a microphone in the face of a slightly bewildered bomb tech.

". . . and that was all the department told you?" Kathleen Brown was asking.

"Uh, yeah. Standby," said the tech.

Harry stepped through the ring of lights and reflectors. "Ms. Brown, my name is Harry Lewton," he said, commandeering the attention of everyone on the scene. "I'm the chief security officer for this medical center."

"At long last, Mr. Lewton." Kathleen Brown feigned a smile. "I've been trying to reach you by phone all morning."

"I've been busy, as you might understand. I believe that your assistant—who did the calling for you—was informed that Dr. Gosling, the president of the medical center, would be providing a full statement this morning."

"I have a copy of that statement, Mr. Lewton. It's a pathetically skimpy whitewash." She held up a sheet of paper and began to read aloud.

"*As of 7:45 this morning, the Fletcher Memorial Medical Center has been operating under a Code White, due to a bomb threat received from an as yet unidentified source. While no bomb has been found, a standard search protocol is ongoing, and the police and fire departments have been requested to assist in the investigation. Bomb threats against this medical center occur several times a year, but have never resulted in a single injury or explosion. We are, however, taking every possible action to ensure the safety of every patient, visitor, and staff member at FMMC. Their well-being is our highest priority.*

'Further updates will be issued as they become available.'"

"That's as accurate as can be," said Harry.

"Did you write this statement, Mr. Lewton?"

"More or less." Harry suddenly found himself in the center of the glow of lights.

"This amount of police presence seems unusual for a routine, unsubstantiated bomb threat. I'm told that the FBI has also been called into the investigation—something not mentioned in your statement."

"Some FBI advisors are here unofficially, at the request of the Chicago Police Department."

"Is that routine?"

"As long as I'm the chief of security, yes, it's routine to use every available resource to guarantee the safety of this hospital and the people in it."

"That's a great line, Mr. Lewton, but I don't buy it."

"I'm not selling anything."

"What did you find in the second-floor Endocrinology Clinic this morning, Mr. Lewton?"

Harry suddenly felt like a lone tuna in a school of sharks. *Ah, the dainty little powder-puff poodle wants to play bloodhound.* He had had

run-ins with reporters before, and there wasn't a single one of them
who wouldn't sell his grandmother for a scoop. The memories turned
his stomach, but he knew that if he wanted to keep things from getting
out of control, his best leverage would lie in Kathleen Brown's ambi-
tion. "Any discussion of that will have to be off camera," he said.

"The camera is the eye of the public. Why are you afraid of the
camera, Mr. Lewton?"

"Spare me your slogans. I'm offering you an exclusive, but for
background only. If that doesn't suit you, Dr. Gosling will have another statement for you this afternoon."

"All right." Kathleen Brown called to Dutch, her cameraman—a
body-builder type with a blond crew cut, wearing a ratty gray sweat-
shirt with the sleeves hacked off in the mid-deltoids. Dutch nodded
silently as she spoke to him, and then turned away. In a moment, the
hot, bright lights had been cut.

Harry looked around for a place to talk. "Why don't we go in
here?" he said, nodding toward the motor home. Opening the door,
he climbed in and sat sidewise in the driver's seat, while Kathleen
Brown took up a place across the gear-shift. They were alone. In the
unlit compartment behind them was a work counter, a handful of
computer monitors, several bomb suits hanging from ceiling hooks,
and a cache of equipment and cables. At the very end was a drop-
down door and Old Yeller, the bomb squad's mascot, a three-foot-tall
remote-controlled robot shaped like the Mars rover.

Harry started out matter-of-factly. "What I found was a paper
bag with some components for making a bomb. Not an actual bomb."

"A fake?"

"No. More like a message."

"Sent by whom?"

"Not sure. We've received e-mails from something calling itself
the Al-Quds Martyrs' Brigade—"

"Muslim terrorists?"

"I wouldn't jump to conclusions. That may just be what they want
us to believe."

"What are they demanding?"

"Money, naturally. Plus the release of two terrorists in New York.
Meteb and Mussolimi, or something like that. You can look them up."

"Are you complying?"

"On the money, yes. The payment is scheduled for noon, just a little while from now. The terrorists are another matter. Washington's thinking it over."

"This is really not a routine bomb threat, is it?"

Harry stiffened. " 'Routine bomb threat' is an oxymoron. A bomb threat is never routine. The contents of the bag in Endocrinology indicated that whoever left it for us is capable of constructing a real, and very powerful, explosive device."

"Why don't you evacuate?"

"This is a hospital, not an office building. The logistics of evacuation are almost insurmountable. You have a thousand bedridden patients, some of them unconscious or in critical condition. You have surgeries in progress in the operating rooms. You have premature babies in incubators. You can't just pack up and get out. We have evacuation protocols, but they've never been implemented. Not under real-life conditions. Even the best written plan will fall apart once you add the ingredients of risk, fear, and panic. Chaos is inevitable. Chaos in this context means injuries, wreckage—even death."

"I see."

"Plus, there's factor number one: the ransom message specifically said, 'Don't evacuate.' They want to play this out smoothly and quietly."

"Well, you don't have to do what the bomber wants, do you?"

"Actually, we do. As long as they can detonate a bomb in this facility, we can and do have to follow their instructions to the letter. And by 'we,' I mean us and you—now that you've inserted yourself into the equation."

"I'm in the business of reporting events, not keeping them quiet."

"You're in the business of covering human-interest features, if I'm not mistaken. Movie-star weddings, world's ugliest dogs—things like that. This is a little bit out of your normal line."

Kathleen Brown took on a prickly tone. "I was an investigative reporter in Tulsa before I joined the network."

Harry bit his lip. He had taken a cheap shot and needed to backtrack nimbly. "Okay. You have your job and I have mine. But our interests don't have to be at odds."

"If you play along, I could make you look pretty good."

"That's not what I mean. I don't give a damn about anything

except protecting this medical center. If you help me to do that, I'll let you and your crew have the run of the hospital. Film whatever you want, as long as you don't get in the way. And that's an exclusive. You're here because . . . well, because you're here. But I'm not letting any other news teams in. That gives you a pretty sweet setup."

"What do you want in return?"

"To avoid panic. We've been instructed not to evacuate. The group responsible for this threat has been very specific about that. If you start scaring people, there'll be a stampede out of the hospital—the ugliest you've ever seen. This, as you now know, would be in direct violation of our instructions. I don't want to risk what might happen then."

"So you're asking me to hold back the story."

"For a little while. Until we know for sure what's going on."

"And if I refuse?"

"Then you and your crew can shoot your hearts out from across the street, after I bar you from the premises. I'll have the police set up a three-hundred-yard security perimeter. You'll need a telephoto lens just to see the sign out front."

"All right. But I won't allow any prior review or censoring of my reports."

"Understood."

"And I expect you to keep me informed of any developments. Directly and exclusively. No more canned statements."

"You'll get what you get. All I guarantee is that you'll get it first."

"Okay. I guess I'll have to live with that."

Harry held out his hand. Kathleen Brown hesitated before taking it. But then they shook. Her hand was ice-cold.

Is this what it's like to shake hands with the devil? Harry mused.

After leaving Harry's office, Ali had been too upset to return to the family lounge or to the recovery room. She had learned that the bomb was real, not a rumor or a false alarm. Somewhere among these white-tiled corridors was hidden a weapon so promiscuous in its cruelty that no one was safe from it. She herself could die, instantly and without warning. Even more alarming was the thought that Jamie Winslow could die. She needed to protect him. But how? She understood how to protect him from shock and hemorrhage and electrolyte imbalances, but a bomb? She felt loathing and anger toward the coward who could threaten the life of a helpless boy. She was angry, too, at the FBI. Why had they wasted their time picking on her, instead of finding a way to evacuate the hospital? No one except Harry Lewton had seemed to know how much was at stake.

Harry Lewton . . . The thought of that name, and that mash-nosed face with the piercing eyes, troubled her more than anything. *I think you do know something,* he had said. He had said it a split second before even she herself realized it was true. Yes, she knew that she knew something. But she had no idea what that something was. Did Harry know? Could he read more deeply into her than she could read herself? She felt as though he could, and that thought made her breathe uneasily. All her life she had hid her feelings from others, and it was upsetting to know that there was someone who could see through the veil. She wished she had never met Harry Lewton.

Up and down the Pike she walked, trying to reason her feelings away, but the more she thought, the more angry and fearful she became. Jamie needed her back in Recovery, but she was too upset to go there. She needed something physical to calm herself. As she often did when troubled, she stole away to the small Chapel of All Faiths on the first floor. This softly lit, carpeted room, with an abstract mosaic of colored glass at one end, was, for all its intended eclecticism, reminiscent of a Christian church. The chapel was empty, as it usually was in the morning, and Ali sat down on the floor with her back to the first row of pews. Holding her spine erect, she closed her eyes and began to breathe consciously, alternating the deep, slow rhythm of *deergha shvaasam* with the rapid puffing of *kapalabhati,* or "skull shining."

Within a few minutes, she felt the initial stage of a lightening of her entire body, and a kind of darkness in which nothing existed except her breathing. How rudely jarred was she, then, when she heard her name read on the overhead pager. "Dr. O'Day, please call the Neuro ICU."

She ran to the nearest phone. Dr. Stephen Brower, an intensive care specialist, had a problem. "It's this patient of yours," Brower said. "Winslow. He's unresponsive."

Brower. So they've transferred Jamie from Recovery to the ICU. "That's to be expected," Ali said. "I'm keeping him sedated."

"This is more than sedation. I can't arouse him at all. I just drew an arterial blood gas from him and he didn't even flinch."

The urgency in Brower's voice hit a nerve. Ali felt an impulse to rush to the ICU and do something—anything—to correct the situation. That was unlike her and she knew it. She wasn't reacting clinically. She was reacting to an image of Jamie Winslow lying like a limp, helpless puppet in his bed. *This is wrong,* she thought. *I can't help him like this. I have to be a doctor for him now.* And so Ali forced herself to put Jamie the sweet little seven-year-old boy aside, in favor of "Winslow, J., status post AVM resection and neural prosthetic implant." She ran through the most likely problems in her mind:

Anesthesia reaction. Jamie had just come out of recovery, and some patients were known to have unique and unpredictable reactions to general anesthesia. But Jamie had undergone anesthesia before with the very same gas cocktail, and had experienced no ill effects. A reaction now would be unusual.

Bleeding. Dr. Helvelius had meticulously sealed off every vessel leading to the AVM, and she herself had watched for many minutes, making sure that no bleeding remained. Yet it sometimes happened that a vessel tore open after surgery. Even a tiny arterial bleed could become life-threatening if it began to dig through the soft brain tissue, tearing open more vessels as it went.

Stroke. Stroke was unthinkable for a normal boy of Jamie's age. But the AVM had stolen away so much of the brain's blood supply for so long, that Jamie's brain was unused to the full arterial pressure that now coursed through it. His cerebral blood vessels were abnormally lax, and, in a condition called normal perfusion pressure breakthrough, they could rupture anywhere—even far from the site of surgery.

Brain swelling. This was the complication Ali feared most. Sometimes during surgery the brain was invisibly injured—by lack of oxygen, by contact with the retractors, by electrolyte shifts in the blood, or by factors that were still a mystery to science. Injury to the brain almost always meant swelling, but because the brain was encased in a rigid skull vault, there was no room for it to expand. Instead, there was a dramatic increase in pressure, which often came on suddenly, progressed rapidly, and was difficult to stop once it had started. If not arrested in time, it could crush the vital centers of the medulla oblongata against the base of the skull, or completely shut down blood flow to the brain, leading to immediate death.

Anticipating the possibility of this complication, during surgery Ali had placed a small sensor called an intracranial pressure monitor in Jamie's brain, leaving it to protrude through the scalp and a small hole in the skull, like the cap of a spark plug. So the first thing she did was ask Dr. Brower what the pressure reading on the ICP was.

"Fifteen millimeters of mercury," he said. "Upper limit of normal."

"Okay, let's get a noncontrast CT. Stat. I'll head down to Radiology."

Like most of the Department of Radiology, the CT scanning rooms were in the first basement level. Ali got there ahead of Jamie, and helped the technologists and nurses lift him onto the scanner bed when he arrived. She was alarmed by the way he looked. Although his cranial nerve reflexes were intact, he did not respond to his name, and lay limp and quiet, as though he were profoundly drunk.

As the scan got started, Ali waited with the neuroradiologist, Dr. Meissner, in the cramped, semi-dark control room. She watched through the big plate glass window as the mechanized bed slowly slid through the doughnut hole of the scanner. On the control monitor, she saw a grid with small black-and-white cross sections of Jamie's brain start to appear. It was as though someone had cut him up like a loaf of bread, and spread the slices out, one by one, on a table.

"I don't see any blood," said Dr. Meissner. "At least none that I can be sure of. There's a lot of beam-hardening artifact in the occipital region here, around that device of yours." Dr. Meissner pointed to a bright white area shaped like a starburst. "Something could be hidden there, but I don't see any evidence of bleeding elsewhere. No midline shifts that would suggest swelling. Ventricles look normal in size."

"With all this artifact, you can't see the back of the cranial cavity very well, can you? There could be swelling around the brainstem and we wouldn't see it."

"Yes, that's a big *caveat*."

Ali got up to go. "All right, thanks, Lou. I guess I'm going to have to do a spinal tap. If there's bleeding, it should show up in the cerebrospinal fluid. Plus it'll give me an independent reading on the intracranial pressure."

"For what it's worth, Ali," said Meissner, pointing to an older CT scan of Jamie's that had been brought up for comparison on a second monitor, "you guys did a beautiful job cleaning out that AVM. It was the biggest one I'd ever seen."

Ali shrugged off the compliment. *It doesn't matter how well the surgery went,* she thought. *What matters is what's happening now.*

On his way back from his tête-à-tête with Kathleen Brown, Harry made another swing through the hospital to check on the progress of the search teams. Nada. Not even a rat or a hobo this time. Whoever planted the bomb must have known the hospital pretty damn well, and that thought was starting to give Harry heartburn. It took a really sick fuck to blow up his coworkers and helpless patients who depended on him for survival.

As soon as he could, Harry hurried over to Tower C, to check on his mother's transfer. Finding her bed empty, he broke into his first real smile of the morning. *Well, that's done, at any rate. She's out of it now.* He blew a puff of breath between his pursed lips, as satisfying as a deep drag from one of those cigarettes he had sworn off the past few months. But his delight was short-lived. Passing by the bathroom, he was surprised to see his mother's electric toothbrush on the sink. *Oh, hell! Did those idiots leave that?* Relaxed lips gave way to a stiffening jaw as he scanned the room with cop's eyes, as if inspecting a crime scene. When he spotted her clothes and overnight bag hanging in the closet, his heartburn came back with a vengeance. *They haven't moved her at all. She's still a hostage—still in this damned hospital.* His fists clenched as if hungry for someone to blame. Nostrils flaring like a bull's, he charged out to the nursing station.

The floor nurse at the station was having a lively chat with a mustachioed young man who looked like a medical student, but Harry cut the conversation short with a brusque display of his ID. "Where is the woman in 18C-7?"

"She went to CT but hasn't come back."

"CT? What for?"

"You'd have to ask Dr. Weiss."

"And where is Dr. Weiss?"

"I don't know. Usually he does rounds with the residents in the mornings. He has patients on four different floors in Towers B and C. He could be anywhere."

"Send an overhead page. I need to talk to him ASAP."

Grudgingly, the nurse picked up the phone. Meanwhile, Harry dialed patient transport on another line. "This is Harry Lewton, chief of security. Did you get my order to transfer a patient named Viola Lewton to Stroger Hospital?"

"Yes," came a man's voice. "An ambulance is standing by. We sent a team up but they couldn't find her."

"They didn't look. She just went for a CT scan, that's all. Get them back up here on the double!"

"I'm sorry," said the dispatcher, bowing to the peremptory tone of Harry's voice. "They did ask around, but they say no one knew where she was."

"Save the excuses. Tell them to meet me at station 18C. I'll take them to get her myself."

The floor nurse motioned to Harry. "Mr. Lewton, you have a call on line two."

Harry hung up on the dispatcher and hit the line selector on the phone.

"Lewton here."

"Harry?"

He was astonished to hear the voice of his sister, Luanne. He had spoken to her a week ago and it had gotten pretty ugly. "I'm kind of busy right now, Luanne."

"Why didn't you tell me Momma was in the hospital? What's wrong with her?"

"A touch of pneumonia, that's all."

"A doctor called me. Dr. Weiss. He said you wanted to take her out of the hospital. He said it was a real bad idea."

"Well, he doesn't know the whole picture. I'm just moving her to a different hospital, that's all. They can care for her as well over there."

"Harry, I told you it was wrong to take her away from that nursing home."

"Yes, you did."

"But you didn't listen. You're not listening to the doctors now, either. You always have to do things your own way."

"It's the only way I know."

"What does Momma say?"

"It's my decision, Luanne. Momma's not in a position to judge."

"I wanna talk to her."

"She's not here. They took her away for a CT scan."

"Do I have to get on an airplane to come there myself? 'Cause, by God, that's what I'll do. Just 'cause you're the eldest, it doesn't mean the rest of us don't have no rights."

"Settle down. You can talk to her when she gets back to her room."

"I forbid you to move her. You've already done her enough harm. I forbid it."

"Jesus, Luanne! You don't know what you're talking about."

"Don't put me down, Harry. I'm not your kid sister anymore. It was grand what you did for us all back in them days when Daddy got sick. We all looked up to you, Harry—me, Martha, Kyle, and Josie. We're grateful for that. But we're all growed up now, with kids and houses and jobs of our own, and we don't need you makin' decisions for us. We have a say, too. You're gonna have to accept that."

"Can we talk about this later?"

"Later means never with you, Harry."

Harry saw Dr. Weiss coming through the doorway of the ward. "Please, Luanne, I've got a lot to deal with right now. I'll call you tonight. I promise."

"That's not good enough, Harry. I'm gonna hop on that airplane and come see for myself."

Harry did a quick calculation in his head. Even with a nonstop flight out of Houston, there was no way she could get to Fletcher Memorial before 6:00 or 7:00 P.M. The crisis would be over by then, one way or the other. "All right, you do that. It will probably do Momma good to see you. You can stay at my place while you're here."

"Okay." Luanne's voice suddenly sounded more tractable. "I'll call you from O'Hare."

"Bye now." Harry put down the receiver and turned toward Weiss. "Where the hell have you been?"

Weiss gave Harry an indignant look. "Taking care of your mother, actually. I had to intubate her and put her on a ventilator. Her blood gases dropped and we had to get a high-resolution chest CT. Her pneumonia's worse and it looks like she could have early signs of ARDS. That's acute respiratory distress syndrome. It has a mortality rate of nearly fifty percent."

"Where is she?"

"I just moved her to the ICU."

"ICU? I told you I wanted her out of here."

Weiss threw up his hands. "You don't trust me? Get another doctor. But she's not leaving this hospital. Not unless you want to kill her."

"It's not about you or about her goddamn pneumonia. It's a security matter."

"Put a guard outside the ICU, then. Whatever. But security right now is the least of her problems. Do you understand me? The issue is whether she will live through the night."

No, Harry thought, *you have it wrong. It's whether she'll live through the next six hours.* But he didn't dare explain himself. If he let out how badly things stood, the whole hospital could wind up in a panic.

Just then, the transport team came rolling up with a light ambulance-type gurney.

"You Lewton?" said a tall, slim orderly in an oversized, coffee-stained scrub top. "Sorry, but we were up here an hour ago, and she weren't nowhere we could find." He pointed to the empty bed. "See? She still ain't here."

The orderly slouched and rocked on his heels, avoiding eye contact. Harry felt an urge to ream him out. *I'll bet you looked real hard for her. Five-to-one you've been on a cigarette break ever since.* But he had bigger problems than the orderlies. "Dr. Weiss," he said, turning back to the doctor with a more conciliatory tone, "is there somewhere else we can put her? Somewhere outside the towers? Like the Pine Building, or Children's Hospital."

"Are you out of your mind? There's nothing but a maternity unit in Pine. And Children's . . . that's just absurd. She needs to be in the ICU, here in Tower C. That's the only chance she has."

"Fuck!"

"Not my specialty. See urology," snapped Weiss. "Anything else, Mr. Lewton?"

Harry took a long, deep breath. "Can I go in to her?"

Weiss pointedly nodded toward the stretcher-bearers. "What about them?"

"You two can split," said Harry, with a wave of his hand. "The transfer's off for now."

Weiss remained stubbornly silent until the orderlies had left the unit. "Yes, you can see her," he said. "She's heavily sedated, and she can't speak because of the ventilation tube. But she'll know you're in the room, and it'll probably do her some good."

Harry pushed his way through the door of the Intensive Care Unit. The lights were so low inside that it took his eyes a minute to adjust enough to make out his mother in the far corner bed. The room was filled with mechanical noises—hums of respirators, beeping of monitors and IV pumps—but strangely devoid of human speech. Doctors and nurses went about their work in silence. Patients, too, lay fighting for their lives without uttering a word. To Harry it felt like a sacrilege to open his mouth.

"Momma, it's me," he said in a near whisper. His mother's constant tremor disappeared for a moment as Harry took her hand and she squeezed back at him. "I just spoke with Dr. Weiss. The pneumonia's gotten a tad worse, so they need to keep you here a spell. There's nothin' to it. Don't be scared, Momma. Luanne's coming. She'll be here tonight."

Viola released Harry's hand. As soon as she did, her tremor started up again, making her look like she was playing with an invisible ball bearing between her thumb and fingers. Harry heard a sucking sound as she moved her lips and tongue.

"Don't try to talk, Momma. They put a tube in you to help you breathe. Just relax, okay? Don't you worry about Luanne and me. We're not on the outs. Just get your rest."

Harry stroked Viola's forehead, rearranging the silver curls where the doctors had mussed her hair. His touch calmed her immediately. "Listen to me, Momma. Thing's have gotten kind of dicey in the hospital right now. I tried to keep you out of it, but I just couldn't. I'm real sorry about that. It's hard to know the right thing to do. Dr. Weiss . . . well, he says one thing, my heart says another, but in this case I think I'm gonna have to listen to him."

Harry looked at his watch. Almost a quarter to twelve. The Feds would be expecting him back.

He picked up his mother's hand. "I have to go. It's possible, Momma, that we won't get a chance to speak again. If it comes to that—" He fell silent for a moment, struck by the enormity of *that*. "If it comes to . . . comes to . . . I want you to know that I love you."

He felt her hand squeeze back again at his, this time very hard. Then her fingers resumed their tremor once more, and slipped out of his grip. She closed her eyes. All was quiet except for the soft whoosh as the ventilator cycled in and out.

"Bye, Momma. Go to sleep, now."

Kevin had his eye on the clock. With less than fifteen minutes to go before the payment of the ransom, he knew that this was the most critical juncture of Project Vesuvius—the only part of the operation whose success depended on other people.

"Are you sure the instructions were explicit?" he asked Odin. "Could there be any room for misunderstanding?"

"I HAVE SUPPLIED ACCOUNT NUMBERS TO ALL PAYERS, WITH EXACT AMOUNTS AND TIMES OF DEPOSIT. THE PENALTY FOR NONCOMPLIANCE HAS BEEN STATED UNAMBIGUOUSLY. IT WOULD RESULT IN THE IRREVOCABLE AND INSTANTANEOUS DESTRUCTION OF FLETCHER MEMORIAL MEDICAL CENTER."

"And if they fuck up, what then? What if they're late?"

"THE OPTIMAL WINDOW BETWEEN PAYMENTS MUST BE BETWEEN FOUR AND SIX MINUTES. DEPENDING UPON THE SPECIFIC CHARACTERISTICS OF EACH PAYER'S SECURITY FIREWALL, ANY OTHER INTERVAL RISKS SIGNIFICANT FALLOFF OR ABORTION OF ONE OR MORE REVENUE STREAMS."

"Well, we'll have to just pray that we're not dealing with any retards today." Kevin leaned down to desktop level to look at Loki. The monkey was pacing back and forth along the edge of the desk, stopping only to scratch his ear with his hind leg, like a dog. "We don't want to have to blow up the hospital, Loki. Big pile of monkey shit. *Ka-Boom!*" He wriggled his fingers in the air, to which Loki responded with a screech and a leap to the safe distance of the sink countertop.

"KEVIN, MAY I DIRECT YOUR ATTENTION TO THE FACT THAT THE HOSPITAL PATIENT CENSUS NOW STANDS AT 1,727. THIS IS A 12 PERCENT DECREASE SINCE 08:00 THIS MORNING."

"Can that be accounted for by routine morning discharges?"

"NEGATIVE. AT THIS TIME OF DAY, THE POPULATION HAS AVERAGED 1,855 PLUS OR MINUS FORTY-THREE OVER THE PAST MONTH. THE PROBABILITY THAT THIS IS A RANDOM OC-CURRENCE IS LESS THAN 0.05 PERCENT."

"Are they evacuating?"

"NOT ON A FULL SCALE. HOWEVER, SINCE 10:15 THERE HAVE BEEN NO NEW ADMISSIONS FROM THE EMERGENCY ROOM."

"Harry Lewton! It's gotta be his doing. He's diverting the ambu-lances. He's a smart little fucker, I give him that."

"THIS IS A VIOLATION OF THE TERMS OF THE INSTRUC-TIONS TO THE FBI. SHALL I DETONATE THE PRIMARY BOMB IN RESPONSE?"

"No, for God's sake, Odin! No! This is just . . . just mischief. I expected them to try something like this. Let's not overreact. Just send them a warning and tell them to cut it out. If I know Harry Lewton, he'll back off."

Kevin did know Harry Lewton. Although the two had never met, Kevin had studied Harry's personnel file and eavesdropped on quite a few conversations in his office. He had learned not to underestimate him. Lewton only looked like a dumb shit-kicker. He had grown up in Southwest Houston, a gang-infested neighborhood where smarts were something you kept in reserve, like a switchblade in your boot.

Three months ago, Harry had been running security for an oil terminal down South that had been a showcase for a prototype of the Cerberus system. When Fletcher Memorial decided to invest big-time in their own security upgrade, he was brought in on the recom-mendation of the Cerberus CEO. This was welcome news to Kevin at the time. Harry and Cerberus were linked by an umbilical cord, which meant that Harry could be trusted to depend on its fancy au-tomated protocols instead of his own resources. By the time he real-ized that Odin had co-opted Cerberus, the game would be over.

As for the new arrivals—the FBI and the cops—Kevin didn't worry about them at all. Odin had identified each one by name or facial match upon arrival, and dutifully provided Kevin with background files hacked from the personnel databases at the FBI and Chicago Police Department. They were a conventional lot. Avery had commendations for bravery, but none for brains. Scopes was good at investigating craters and burned-out vans, but he had little experience with live bombs. Lee was too smart for his own britches and, like all self-important people, could be easily manipulated.

Ali was Kevin's Achilles' heel. She was smart and he had taught her to think outside the box. She knew a hell of a lot about Odin. And once she set her mind on something, she would swim through fire and ice to see it through. Kevin's insurance was the fact that this was SIPNI day. Ali would be so focused on the Winslow kid that she would shut out everything else. Not even a bomb threat would sway her from her patient.

Which made it troubling that the FBI had pulled her in so quickly. Kevin knew that Homeland Security had a file on her. Somehow it must have gotten flagged. Kevin had listened in on her interrogation through a microphone embedded in the monitor of Harry Lewton's computer. He was relieved, of course, that his name failed to come up. But from the audio alone he couldn't really get a fix on what was happening inside Ali's head. Had the Feds scared her enough to knock her off the safe and reliable SIPNI rails? Only seeing her face and body language would tell him that. And, ironically, Harry's office, the receiving end of over a hundred cameras throughout the hospital, had not a single security camera inside itself.

Kevin turned to the big wall monitor. "Odin, have you come up with any more video of Ali's interrogation?"

"NO. THE ONLY ACTIVE VIDEO SOURCE IS FROM THE MINI-CAMERA ON HARRY LEWTON'S COMPUTER MONITOR. THIS HAS A VIEW ONLY OF THE SECURITY DIRECTOR'S CHAIR AND OF THE WALL BEHIND IT. I HAVE TRIED RE-PROCESSING A RE-FLECTION OF ALI'S IMAGE ON ONE OF THE MONITORS ALONG THE WALL, HOWEVER EVEN WITH 144 ITERATIONS OF EDGE ENHANCEMENT IT IS TOO PIXELATED FOR INTERPRETATION."

"I wish to God I could see her face."

"I WILL CONTINUE WORKING ON THE PROBLEM. IT MAY BE POSSIBLE TO RECONSTRUCT THE IMAGE USING A HIDDEN MARKOV MODEL WITH A NON-GAUSSIAN DATA DISTRIBU-TION."

"Okay, try it. In the meantime, use Cerberus to track her in the hospital. I want to know where she is at all times."

In the end, Kevin thought, *it probably won't matter. By the time they put the pieces together, I'll be long gone. They can sift through the rubble ten times over and still never know if I am dead or alive.*

Back in the Neuro ICU, Ali set about performing Jamie's spinal tap, drawing out a sample of the fluid that bathed the spinal cord and brain. Ali had done so many of these taps that she did not have to think about how to do it. With Jamie lying in a fetal position on his side, and with his knees drawn up, Ali painted the skin of the small of his back with reddish-brown Betadine antiseptic, then positioned a sterile blue drape over his spine. A small cutout window exposed the Betadine-stained skin.

After switching to a new pair of sterile gloves, Ali felt the small bumps that projected from Jamie's spine, and counted up from the bottom, until the index and middle finger of her left hand straddled the space between the fourth and fifth lumbar vertebrae. In her right hand, Ali held a four-inch-long needle, which she inserted into this space, exactly in the midline. At this level, she knew, the spinal cord had ended in a plume of small nerves called the *cauda equina,* or mare's tail, where the needle would be unlikely to cause any damage. She inserted the needle slowly through the tough straplike ligaments that held the spine together. It felt like pushing the needle through leather. When she had gone in about two inches, she felt a sudden give, or "pop," and knew that she had broken through into the intrathecal space, the fluid-filled area immediately surrounding the spinal cord.

Ali pulled out the fine stylet that plugged the shaft of the needle, and watched a drop of clear fluid emerge. She was relieved to see that the fluid wasn't bloody. She quickly attached a manometer, a graduated clear plastic tube, to the stopcock on the needle, and watched the fluid slowly rise into the tube. When it stopped, she read an opening pressure of fourteen millimeters of mercury, close to what the ICP monitor had shown. She then removed the manometer, and let the needle drip into four vials, ten drops to a vial. These would go to the lab for analysis.

While Ali was capping the last of the tubes, Jamie suddenly jerked his legs.

"Hold still, Jamie," said Ali. "Let me take the needle out." She reached for the needle, but as she touched his skin, she felt his body vibrating. It was not a natural movement. His feet were rubbing against each other, with a rapid, polishing kind of motion.

"Stephen!" she called out to the intensivist. "He's having a seizure." While Brower and one of the nurses rushed to the bedside, Ali pulled out the needle and slapped a small sterile Band-Aid over its entry point into the skin. She then turned Jamie onto his back, just as Brower began hooking up an infusion pump to the IV. Jamie's legs immediately straightened, but his hands remained suspended over his chest, shaking with a fine tremor. His eyes were darting about crazily under his eyelids.

Brower turned to the nurse, who had wheeled up a tall red crash cart. "Ginnie, we need a thousand milligrams of Dilantin in a ten-cc syringe." Ginnie filled a syringe from a vial in the cart, discarded the needle, and popped the syringe into a receptacle in the infusion pump. "Set the rate to half a cc per minute," said Brower.

Ali and Brower watched intently as the Dilantin started coursing into Jamie's bloodstream.

"Does he have a history of seizures?" asked Brower.

"No. Never," said Ali.

"Was it the tap that did this?"

"I've never seen it happen before."

"Then I think you have a problem."

Of course I have a problem. Ali barely restrained herself from lashing out. Fortunately, the convulsions began to subside. "Keep the Dilantin and Ativan going," she said coolly. "And let's start Solumedrol, 250 milligrams in an IV infusion over one hour—just for insurance. We haven't ruled out brain swelling."

With Jamie stabilized, Ali took up a chair behind the nurses' station and called the hospital operator to have Dr. Helvelius paged. She heard his name read out on the overhead pager three times. As she waited for his call-back, she tried to clarify how she would present the situation to him. He used to tell her that any good doctor could summarize the most complex case in thirty seconds or less. But how long it took to distill all of the physical findings and lab reports into those thirty seconds!

She was not thinking at her best now. Her interrogation at the hands of the FBI had left her shaken. The bomb was giving her confused, impulsive thoughts. She shuddered every time she felt the rumble of a cart or a gurney rolling by. She wracked her brains for a way to get Jamie transferred out of Fletcher Memorial, even though no other hospital in the world had the expertise to deal with a SIPNI implant. She worried, too, that an explosion might harm the fetus she carried—the fetus she had planned to terminate the very next day!

Could she really do that? She had put off the procedure again and again, and still wasn't sure if she could get up the nerve. She had already begun to feel that warm, centered feeling that she remembered from her first pregnancy, and she had to fight very, very hard to keep from letting her mind run to the kind of daydreams she had had then—dreams of holding her baby, listening to him coo, rocking him to sleep in those precious midnight hours when she could be totally alone with him, guessing what would be the first word he would ever speak. These thoughts were a torture for her. Fate had cheated her once of these dreams, and she could not bear to let herself be cheated in that way ever again.

Her first pregnancy had actually begun with great promise. Both she and Kevin were on cloud nine, and it seemed like a healing omen for them both after a difficult time in their marriage. After the first ultrasound, she had named the child Ramsey, after the Arabic *Ramzi,* meaning "symbol." There was no warning of anything wrong. Tests showed a somewhat low-lying placenta, but its position did not seem dangerous. Ramsey appeared well-developed, and in her eighteenth week Ali was astonished with joy when, standing in the OR in the middle of a craniotomy procedure, she felt his first quickening kick. Then one night, in her thirty-eighth week—almost exactly a year ago—she was at a dinner party at the University chancellor's house in Winnetka, when she felt an excruciating cramp and looked down to find a pool of blood at her feet. She screamed just before passing out. When she awoke, she was in the hospital. There had been an abruption, a premature tearing-away of the placenta. Ramsey was born alive by C-section, but had suffered a stroke from the loss of blood.

He survived in the ICU for two weeks. During that time, she and Kevin worked frantically to adapt SIPNI to repair Ramsey's damaged brain, but all was futile. SIPNI was then still only a crude prototype.

After Ramsey died, Ali found herself unable to cry or to express grief in a normal way. Instead, she withdrew into herself. When she and Kevin drove to Waugoshance Point to scatter Ramsey's ashes on Lake Michigan, Ali scarcely spoke the whole trip. On returning, she sought solace by re-immersing herself in her work. Kevin, whose heartbreak was there for all to see, resented what he called her cold-ness, and taunted her with increasing cruelty, trying to goad her into an emotional response. Little did he know that she was already in an emotional agony so severe that she was on the verge of killing herself.

She vowed never to go through a hell like that again. Even though it meant betraying her principles —her dedication to life and to the protection of the weak and helpless—she couldn't bear to face those memories that were already beginning to rise up out of the grave. Her risk of another complication was high, the obstetrician had told her. She felt defective, cursed in her womb. Better to abort this new pregnancy and be done with it, than to live once again through the nightmare of watching her child die.

But then there was Jamie. Although she had never thought about it before, Jamie was a kind of substitute for Ramsey, giving her a sec-ond chance to use SIPNI to beat back tragedy. In the weeks before the operation, Ali had often wondered what would become of Jamie if SIPNI actually worked. He couldn't stay at the Grossman School, of course, since he would no longer be blind. Would his mother take him back? In unguarded moments, Ali had toyed with the idea of taking him home herself. She would imagine cooking his favorite macaroni and cheese, or struggling to keep up with him on the Play-Station, or watching his first Little League game. She kept thoughts like those a secret, since a lack of objectivity on her part might have endangered Jamie's chances for getting into the SIPNI project. Now, it seemed selfish and irresponsible to have even thought about such things. Jamie needed a doctor, not a mother. His condition was dete-riorating, and if Ali didn't figure out the reason quickly, he could suffer permanent brain damage, or even die.

Still no answer from Helvelius. Ali had him paged again. One of his residents finally called back and told her he was in surgery, covering an emergency spinal cord trauma case. It would take another hour at least.

She tapped her hand irritably on the counter. "Oh, Richard! Richard! What in God's name should I do?"

Raymond Lee was in high spirits when Harry returned to his office, and it annoyed Harry intensely. "How did it go with our morning-show princess?" said Lee with an unprecedented smile.

"She's a peach," said Harry. "Promised to stay off the air for a little while. But just for insurance, I dropped by Dr. Gosling's office. The president of the TV network is a personal friend of his, as is the governor of Illinois. We set up a three-way conference call, and got New York to agree to hold the story until at least 6:30 P.M. Eastern. That's airtime for the nightly news program."

"Five-thirty here," said Lee.

"Any luck with the money transfers?" asked Harry.

Lee patted a stack of papers. "Northwest City Bank gave us a little trouble, until the mayor guaranteed to cover their losses from a city slush fund until the hospital's insurance carrier kicks in. All the other payers are standing by. Fifteen minutes ago, the destination account numbers came through by e-mail. There are twenty different accounts, two for each payer. It's going to slow us down on tracing the money, but not for long."

Avery looked at his wristwatch. "Eleven fifty-eight. Almost showtime."

Scopes was holding the telephone. "I have the mayor's chief of staff on line. Everyone's standing by for the transfer."

While Scopes listened for developments on the phone, the others sat in silence.

"Okay, I'm getting a report," said Scopes, placing his hand over the mouthpiece. "The first wave of transfers is complete."

"Good," said Lee. "Now we wait another five minutes. Stay on the line, Terry." Scopes nodded. Lee turned to Harry. "By the way, there's something in the last e-mail that you need to see."

Lee showed Harry a hard-copy printout. Below a long column of bank routing numbers and account numbers, there was a short paragraph of text:

ALL OUTPATIENT CLINICS MUST REMAIN OPEN FOR NOR-
MAL BUSINESS. NO FURTHER APPOINTMENT CANCELLA-
TIONS WILL BE PERMITTED. AMBULANCE DIVERSIONS
MUST CEASE IMMEDIATELY. ANY ATTEMPT TO EVACUATE
OR TO LOWER THE PATIENT CENSUS WILL HAVE IMMEDIATE
AND SEVERE CONSEQUENCES. THERE WILL BE NO FURTHER
WARNINGS.

"What the hell is this?"

"You're busted," said Lee with a half-smile. "You've been cutting
down the number of hostages, and they don't like it."

Harry could feel the blood damming up in the veins of his face
and neck. "Fucking psychos! Who are they to tell us—" It was more
than just the hostages. He had lost his last chance to get his own
mother out of harm's way. Now the only way to protect her was to
take the offense. Hunt down the sons of bitches behind this bomb
and make them rue the day they had ever heard of Fletcher Hospital.
God, if only I had left her in that nursing home!

Harry shook the printout, half-crumpled in his hand. "How do
they even know what the fuck we're doing?"

Avery shrugged. "If they're listening in on emergency band radio—
which is not uncommon for criminals of this sort—they could over-
hear the ambulance dispatchers."

"And the outpatient appointments?"

"Beats me," said Avery. "They could have made appointments
themselves, just to see if they would get called."

"That seems awfully convoluted," said Harry.

"Yes, very," said Lee. "More likely someone here in this hospital
is observing our operations."

"You guys have been watching the surveillance videos while I've
been out," said Harry. "Have you noticed anyone suspicious? Someone who looks like he could be casing the place?"

Lee shook his head. "No. Not so far. But actually, I was thinking
a little closer to home than that."

"Closer to home? What do you mean?"

"How well do you know your own people, Mr. Lewton?"

"Security? Well, they, uh . . . they all went through a strict screen-
ing process when they were hired."

"But you didn't screen them, did you? You're the newcomer, right? You've been here for, what, a few months?"

"Three months."

"And do you know who's having trouble keeping up with the mortgage? Who's getting divorced? Who has a gambling habit? Kids in college? Mother who's got to have a kidney transplant? In short, do you know who might have a sudden and overwhelming need for money?"

"No."

"Then I think we need to start playing our cards very close to the vest."

Harry was rankled by Lee's aspersions. It was true he didn't know much about the personal lives of his staff, but he had worked with them for three solid and often stressful months, and he had gotten to know their characters pretty well. Harry couldn't imagine a single one of his people being involved in something like a bomb plot—not for any amount of money. He thought Lee was overreacting, but it would just have redoubled his suspicions if Harry got in the way.

"Round number two," Scopes called out, holding the telephone to his ear. "Getting set right now."

Once again, the room fell silent as the seconds ticked away.

At last Scopes gave a thumbs-up. "Mayor's office says the transfers are complete. Just like clockwork."

"That was painless!" said Lee. "That should take the heat off for a few hours."

"What's the story on those two prisoners in New York?" asked Harry.

"Meteb and Mossalam? Washington's still deciding. We've made plane reservations and notified Rikers Island to expect a transport van around 4:00 P.M. Eastern. But people in the know at the Bureau are urging us to resolve the situation here as quickly as possible. That's code for 'Ain't fucking likely.'"

Harry looked at Lee skeptically. *How could there be any doubt about it? The lives of two thousand people are at stake.* "Maybe you want to work that end a little harder."

"Don't you have calls to make, Mr. Lewton? I think you'd better get dispatch to stop diverting the ambulances."

"Sure." Harry turned to pick up the phone but Scopes was still on it.

As before, Scopes was saying little, simply waiting for some news from the other end. "You still talking to the mayor's office?" Harry asked.

"No. First deputy superintendent of police."

Harry looked at Lee. "What's that about?"

"A lead. Something else turned up while you were out battling wits with Miss America. It may just be the key to this case." Lee looked past Harry toward Scopes and raised his voice a notch. "What is he saying, Terry? Anything yet?"

"They've got six squad cars in position, with men covering the front and the back. The SWAT team's just gone in."

Lee turned back to Harry. "We decided to wait until this moment—just as the ransom payments went through. We figured he'd almost certainly be at home watching the money come in. His guard's down. He feels like he's on top of the world. No better time to nab him."

"Who? Nab who?"

"The guy who—"

"Whoooeah!" Scopes slapped the desktop. "Way to go, guys!" he shouted into the phone. Turning to Lee, "They got him, Ray! It's him! Definitely him, they say."

Harry was mystified. "Who? Got who?"

Lee grinned so broadly that he showed his upper teeth. "Right here in Chicago. Over on the Northwest Side—"

"Who, goddamn it!"

"The brother," said Avery.

"The brother?"

Lee waved his hand with a flourish. "Rahman Abdul-Shakoor Al-Sharawi."

There was a click as Scopes hung up the phone. "He's on his way. E.T.A. twenty minutes."

Outside the largely deserted ambulance entrance at the rear of the medical center, Harry, Judy Wolper, Lee, Scopes, and Avery stood waiting for the arrival of Rahman Al-Sharawi. Judy said little and was uncharacteristically tense. At Harry's request, she had armed herself with a Glock 17, a big gun for such a small woman, but one that was dependable and easy to use even if you didn't stay in practice.

Across the alleyway, a man in a hospital gown with an IV pole at his side sat smoking on a concrete bench. From time to time he would tap the ashes of his cigarette between his outspread knees. Harry himself felt the lack of a cigarette acutely. He had quit smoking when he came to Fletcher Memorial, but standing around with his hands in his pockets brought old cravings back.

"What I'd like to know is how you found this guy so fast," he said to the two FBI agents.

"His sister led us right to him," said Scopes. "Not intentionally, of course. It was her phone records. She had called him at least three times this past year from her home phone. So we just traced the number—you'd be surprised how quickly we can get cooperation in a high-profile terrorism case—and there he was."

"Then I guess she lied to us. She said she hadn't had any contact with him."

"Big surprise, huh?" said Scopes.

Harry pursed his lips, as though inhaling from a phantom cigarette. "I knew she was holding something back, but I didn't think that was it."

Avery chuckled. "They caught him sitting in an apartment in Albany Park, watching CNN and eating a bowl of lentils."

Harry turned to Lee. "What's the game plan?"

"We'll see," said Lee.

Scopes sniggered. "You'd be surprised how helpful a guy can be once he knows he's gonna be blown up by his own bomb."

Before the motorcade itself was visible, Harry saw the flashing blue and red lights reflected from the white stone of the Children's Hospital across the alley. Then they pulled up, three squad cars running without sirens. Two uniformed officers got out of the front seats of each of the cars. Rahman was in the backseat of the middle car. Harry strained to get a look at him as the cops pulled him out. Harry had seen scumbags of all persuasions in the past, but he had never yet looked into the eyes of someone so low that he thought he could prove his manhood by blowing up a few sixty-year-old ladies on ventilators. He was struck by how ordinary this guy looked—not at all like one of those wild, bearded Talibans with the long skirts over their trousers. He was of middle height, lean, clean-shaven, with short black hair that was starting to thin on top. He wore jeans and a red and black soccer jersey. Some terror mastermind! Harry walked past a hundred guys like him every day of his life.

In handcuffs and leg irons, surrounded by blue uniforms, Rahman was slowly conducted to the entrance. His sly, sideways glance gravitated toward the bearlike, uniformed figure of Avery. He seemed surprised when the little Asian man in the dark suit spoke first.

"Mr. Al-Sharawi, I am Special Agent Raymond Lee, with the Federal Bureau of Investigation. You are being transferred to my custody, to be held as a material witness in the investigation of a bomb threat against this hospital. If you are subsequently charged with a criminal offense, any statements you make can and will be held against you in a court of law."

Rahman said nothing, but looked up at the sky.

"Do you understand English, Mr. Al-Sharawi? Do you require a translator?"

Again there was no answer.

"Okay, bring him in. Mr. Lewton, see if the hospital has an Arabic translator available."

"I already have one standing by." Harry was a little rankled by Lee's peremptory tone.

Rahman quit his sky-gazing and looked at Lee with contempt.

"One needs no translator to speak to the devil," he said. His voice was soft and whispery, with a trace of a British accent.

"Oh, we're not the devil," said Lee with a thin-lipped smile.

Scopes couldn't resist a chuckle. "But we *can* fix you up with an appointment in hell," he added.

At a nod from Lee, the entourage marched through the door. Harry led them through a corridor to the automatic double doors of the Department of Emergency Medicine. From there, they passed through the Intake and Triage Unit, where patients were first examined as they came off the ambulances. Triage opened onto the Resuscitation Unit, a big room with a square nurses' station in the middle, and an outer perimeter divided by curtains into a dozen treatment bays for the most critically ill patients—heart attacks, gunshot wounds, car wrecks, burns. At this time of day it was pretty quiet, with a few interns in scrubs and short white coats chatting up the nurses. But by 7:00 P.M., it would be boiling over with activity— shouts and screams, staff running in and out of the bays, the floor littered with bloody sponges, plastic tubes and shredded clothing— the battlefield debris of a hand-to-hand struggle between life and death.

Beyond Resuscitation lay the "Majors," the Major Medical Unit, as big as a bus station. Here patients with serious but not so urgent problems—shortness of breath, stomach pains, dizziness, fevers, jaundice or bloody bowel movements—were observed and worked up with tests before admission to the hospital.

The end of the march was the Acute Psychiatric Subunit, located just to the right of the Majors. It was laid out like Resuscitation with bays and a central work station, but on a smaller scale. This was where Triage sent schizophrenics, attempted suicides, and manic-depressives high-flying off their meds— night people with dark, fearful visages, fleeing from invisible furies, or cowering before choruses of disembodied voices. For the very worst—those wracked by inhuman rages against themselves or others, unquenchable by reason or by drugs— there existed the Isolation Room. This was the closest thing in the hospital to a maximum-security prison cell. It had a steel door, unbreachable walls, and continuous closed-circuit monitoring. One had to be very, very sick to earn admission there.

Isolation itself was fronted by a small guardroom, containing a desk with a computer terminal, a small wooden table, and a half-dozen chairs of different makes. As the entourage filed in, Raymond Lee had Rahman sit down at the table and then pulled up a chair opposite him.

"Can we get you anything to make you comfortable, Mr. Al-Sharawi? A glass of water, perhaps?"

"Nothing."

Against the ascetic proportions of his angular chin, narrow-bridged aquiline nose, thin lips, and flaring nostrils, Rahman's eyes seemed sensuous and fluid. They were deep-set, watchful, and out-lined by a thin script of black mascara-like pigment that, to Harry's thinking, made him look not so much effeminate as serpentine. Harry found the incongruity unsettling—half voluptuary, half holy man.

Lee placed his digital voice recorder on the table. "So, let's get started. Could you state your name, please?"

Silence.

"Do you not know your name?"

"I am who I am."

"Do you need help answering that question?"

"He who made me knows by what name He will call me on the Day of Judgment."

"Very well. Let me rephrase that. Are you Rahman Abdul-Shakoor Al-Sharawi, born in Cairo, Egypt?"

"Yes."

"Progress!" Lee slapped the table in mock relief. "And is Aliyah Sabra Al-Sharawi your sister?"

"No."

"Half-sister?"

"She is nothing."

Lee sat forward and tapped his fingers on his lips. "Was she born to Dr. Bashir Al-Sharawi, who is your father?"

"As a bitch may be born to a dog, yes."

Standing behind Lee, Scopes stifled a laugh. Lee himself was unruffled. "Are you aware that she works in this hospital?"

"What she does is of no concern to me."

"Mr. Al-Sharawi, I am not interested in your family affairs. I ask you only to confirm certain facts that may potentially have a bearing upon our investigation. If you cooperate, the law will not be unmindful of that."

Silence.

"Very well, let's take a different tack. I believe you know of the existence of an organization called the Al-Quds Martyrs' Brigade."

Silence.

"Are you a member of that organization?"

Silence.

"Are you authorized to speak for it?"

Silence.

"Let me be candid, Mr. Al-Sharawi," said Lee. "We have received a threat against this hospital, demanding the release of two men, Mohammed Meteb and Hassan Abo Mossalam, from custody in New York. The government has decided to comply with the demands of the ransom note we have received. However, we need to discuss with someone the specific arrangements for the release, to make certain that all goes smoothly and that there are no misunderstandings. We are ready to take action on this demand. But we don't know who to talk to. Are you the person we should approach?"

"Say what you will."

Lee raised his hands impotently. "I'm not going to discuss anything unless I know that you are authorized to negotiate on behalf of Al-Quds."

"I have . . . some influence."

"Not good enough. It must be someone whose word can be trusted. Someone with the authority to make a binding agreement."

"What I promise will be adhered to."

"Then you have such authority?"

"Yes."

"Very good. Then you can confirm that a bomb is in fact present somewhere in this facility?"

"There is a bomb, yes."

"Where did the explosive come from?"

"Quantico."

"What is its destructive power?"

"Enough."

"Enough for what?"

"To destroy everything."

"Did you yourself construct the bomb?"

Rahman looked away from Lee. For one unsettling moment, his gaze landed on Harry. "These questions have no concern in the matter of the release of the honored mujahideen Meteb and Abo Mossalam. You will confine yourself to that issue."

"It's customary in these situations for each side to offer something as a token of good faith. That's reasonable, is it not?"

Rahman turned back toward Lee and raised his eyebrows expectantly.

Lee shifted forward, fixing Rahman's gaze. "What I offer you is a signed order from the FBI District Office in New York City, directing the immediate release of Meteb and Mossalam from Rikers Island Prison and their deportation to Yemen. In addition, in the presence of these witnesses, I will sign a second order myself, giving you safe conduct out of the country following the successful disarming of the bomb."

"Do it."

"Yes, immediately," said Lee. "I will have the papers faxed from New York. But I must know what you are willing to put forward on your side. Specifically, I need to have some evidence that the bomb does, in fact, exist."

"I have told you so."

"Physical evidence is what I'm talking about. I need to see the bomb."

"You know we have the C4."

"So you say. Even if that's true, how do I know that you have the expertise to construct a bomb?"

"Believe it, infidel."

"I'm sorry. I need to see it with my own eyes."

Rahman arched his right eyebrow. His voice rose to an oracular pitch. "You will see it with your eyes. And you will hear it with your ears. Do you think I am a simpleton, to be led about like a goat on a chain? I have a master's degree in chemical engineering from Cornell. These papers you speak of are nothing. I will wipe my shit with them. You have no authority to write such papers. I will tell you nothing until I hear Meteb or Abo Mossalam speak to me personally from the airport at Sana'a, confirming that they are safe and out of the hands of the idolaters. As for myself, I do not care. All-merciful God will be with me no matter what happens."

"We have already paid your ransom money, and are preparing to free your comrades. Everything is proceeding reasonably. Why can't you help us out here?"

"When they are free in Sana'a. Not before."

"I implore you in the name of God. Help us."

"I will answer no further questions. I demand an attorney."

The word sent a collective shudder through the room. An irritated Lee looked to the uniformed officers. "Has anyone Mirandized him?"

"No," said one of them.

Lee turned back to Rahman. "Mr. Al-Sharawi, you do not necessarily have the right to an attorney. You are a noncitizen illegally present in the United States, and we have the option to detain you as an enemy combatant. Military rules are different from civilian rules."

Silence.

"Understand, Mr. Al-Sharawi, that I will hold you here in this hospital until this matter is resolved. If the bomb you have planted is as effective as you claim, you yourself will die if it goes off."

"Do you think I fear death? The death of a martyr is the most beautiful thing imaginable."

Scopes was standing behind Rahman. "Is that what you think? You love death?" he said, bending forward, almost to Rahman's ear. "We'll see how much you like it when you're looking down the door of the gas chamber."

"I am ready for it now. You have a gun. Shoot me. I will not raise a finger."

Scopes stepped into Rahman's view and pulled open his jacket to display his shoulder holster. Although Scopes was way out of line, Lee did not intervene. Harry couldn't tell if it was because Lee wanted to study Rahman's reaction, or if he was simply too preoccupied with figuring out his next line of attack.

In any case, Rahman was unimpressed. "I will say nothing more until I have an attorney."

"I'll make you talk!" said Scopes. In the blink of an eye, he grabbed Rahman by the back of the neck and slammed his face against the table.

Lee was out of his chair instantly. "Stop it! Let it go, Terry!" He put his hand out and pushed Scopes away from the table.

Rahman began shouting excitedly in Arabic.

"Mr. Al-Sharawi, let me ask you one more time—"

Rahman ignored him and went on shouting over him. His voice was high-pitched and guttural, with a pronounced singsong lilt. It reminded Harry of a swarm of angry hornets circling their nest.

"Mr. Al-Sharawi! Please!"

More Arabic. Now Scopes began shouting, too, quoting from the Federal Criminal Code, "A person who, without lawful authority, uses, threatens, or attempts or conspires to use, a weapon of mass destruction—"

Through the din, Lee's thin voice was almost inaudible. However, after Scopes kicked a chair for emphasis, Lee became a veritable Demosthenes of body language, ordering him out of the room.

Still, Rahman went on with his Arabic.

"He's gone," shouted Lee, pointing to the door. "Okay, Mr. Al-Sharawi. He's gone. Now turn it off."

More Arabic.

Lee threw up his hands in exasperation. "Okay, I think we all need to cool down a little." Turning to the uniforms, he pointed toward the door of the isolation room. "Gentlemen, would you please secure him in the holding cell? My colleagues and I need to go upstairs for a conference."

Harry showed one of the officers the combination to the door lock, and watched carefully as Rahman, still reciting at the top of his lungs, was hustled into the ten-by-twelve-foot room and handcuffed to the bed.

"Make sure one of you stays in there with him at all times," said Lee. "Leave your gun outside. If he does decide to talk, call me immediately."

Harry followed Lee out into the corridor. The isolation room was supposed to be soundproof, but he could still hear Rahman's singsong reverberating in his ears.

There wasn't time for games like this, thought Harry. The hospital didn't have time. His mother on the eighteenth floor didn't have time. Harry had to fight hard to suppress an expression of disgust.

Christ, what a privilege to see the pros at work!

Kevin was pacing back and forth in his lab, waving his fists so furiously that Loki hunkered trembling in the shadows behind his cage.

"Odin, what the fuck is going on?" he ranted. "How did Rahman get here? Why didn't I know anything about it?"

"INSUFFICIENT INFORMATION WAS AVAILABLE TO ANTICIPATE THIS DEVELOPMENT."

"You're supposed to be the master of information. How did this shit get by you?"

"THE ARREST ORDER DID NOT PASS THROUGH THE HOSPITAL LANDLINES OR WIRELESS NETWORK. IT MUST NECESSARILY HAVE BEEN CONVEYED THROUGH A SECURE COMMUNICATIONS LINK. SPECIAL AGENT LEE HAS SUCH A DEVICE IN HIS POSSESSION. IT UTILIZES A SECTÉRA WIRELINE TERMINAL CONNECTED TO AN ENCRYPTED LAPTOP WITH A SATELLITE UPLINK TO SIPRNET AT THE DEPARTMENT OF DEFENSE."

"Why can't you decrypt it? Sectéra's just an ordinary NSA Type 1 coding device. That should be child's play for you."

"DECRYPTION IS NOT THE PROBLEM. THE WIRELESS SIGNAL IS NOT STRONG ENOUGH FOR INTERCEPTION."

"Not strong enough? That's why I hung a relay transmitter behind the wall of Harry Lewton's office. Is the fucking relay not working?"

"THE RELAY INSTALLATION ASSUMED THAT THE SECURE TERMINAL WOULD BE OPERATED FROM HARRY LEWTON'S DESK. HOWEVER, THE TERMINAL IS NOW POSITIONED IN THE CORNER OF THE ROOM. THERE IS A STEEL BEAM BETWEEN TERMINAL AND RELAY WHICH INTERFERES WITH RECEPTION OF THE SIGNAL."

"Steel beam! Don't just lay there like a bitch in heat and tell me there's no signal. There has to be a signal! I absolutely have to know what is going on. They've got Rahman, and Rahman can lead them to me. I can't afford to be blindsided like this! Find the signal! Clean it up!"

"IT IS TOO DEGRADED."

"I don't accept that. There must be something we can do."

"I CALCULATE THAT IF THE POSITION OF THE RELAY WERE RAISED BY AT LEAST 2.25 METERS, THE INTERFERENCE WOULD BE CLEARED."

"Raised how? It's bolted to the fucking wall."

"IT MUST BE RAISED MANUALLY."

"Oh, Jeee-zus! You're talking about climbing back down into that goddamned airshaft. It's like the inside of a tin drum—with a grating opening up three feet behind Lewton's desk. They'll hear every move I make."

"IF I WERE TO DETONATE UNIT COTOPAXI, ALL PERSONNEL NOW IN HARRY LEWTON'S OFFICE WOULD RESPOND IMMEDIATELY TO THE SITE OF THE EXPLOSION. THIS WOULD PROVIDE YOU WITH AT LEAST A TWENTY-MINUTE WINDOW TO REPOSITION THE RELAY WITHOUT DETECTION."

"Cotopaxi? No—no explosions. Once we start setting off bombs, the Feds will go ape-shit and start cutting off cable lines, including the main fiber-optic connection to the hospital. If they do that, we can kiss the rest of our revenue stream good-bye. Let's play it cool for now, Odin. The correct project sequence has to be maintained."

"CAN YOU OBTAIN A SECONDARY RELAY UNIT?"

"Sure, I can have 'em FedEx the damn thing here by ten tomorrow morning."

"THAT FALLS OUTSIDE THE PROJECT VESUVIUS TIMETABLE."

"No shit! No, I mean the answer is no, Odin. That was sarcasm. I'm so fucking pissed that . . . No, I can't get a secondary unit."

"THEN MANUALLY REPOSITIONING THE RELAY IS THE ONLY VIABLE OPTION."

"Fuck!" Grumbling, Kevin repaired to the back of the lab, where he yanked open the bottom drawer of a file cabinet and pulled out a small athletic bag stuffed with a pair of dark blue electrician's overalls and a jangling melange of stainless steel belays and carabiner clips. Project Vesuvius was in full swing and it was dangerous to set foot outside the lab, but it was equally dangerous to operate in the dark. He had to know what the FBI was doing. He had to make a sortie. His margin of safety lay in acting decisively, and then getting back as soon as possible to his sanctuary, his fortress, which he and Odin had made all but impregnable.

His hands were shaking, but not from fear. It was the burst of adrenaline he had felt many times, dangling a thousand feet in the air by a single rope and piton. With his life on the line, he was single-handedly taking on the whole Gestapo—the FBI, the city cops, Harry Lewton. He was in the high, thin air now, above the tree line— a world of man-killing rocks and heartless glaciers, a place where courage and cowardice became tangible things, like an arm or a leg. There was no other thrill like it. It was better than sex.

Although the big monitor was out of view, Odin's voice could be heard around the corner. "THE MOST PRACTICABLE POINT OF ACCESS IS THROUGH THE VENTILATION GRATING IN ROOM PL-171, THE JANITORIAL CLOSET THAT LIES IMMEDIATELY ABOVE HARRY LEWTON'S OFFICE."

Kevin nodded. "Make sure you keep an eye on me, Odin. Project Vesuvius is in your hands until I get back." After pulling on the over-alls, he grabbed a few coils of climbing rope from a hanger on the wall and stuffed them in the bag.

"WHEN SIGNAL HAS BEEN SUCCESSFULLY ACQUIRED, I WILL BLINK THE LIGHTS TWICE IN ROOM PL-171."

"Okay, do that." Heading toward the door, Kevin paused and looked into the dark recesses of the lab, behind Odin's mainframe. Seeing two specks of orange light reflected from Loki's retinas, he made a clicking sound with his tongue. "Come on, Loki, time to get back in your cage." But Loki didn't budge. Again Kevin clicked, and held out his hand. A nervous chitter answered, but Loki's retinas with-drew deeper into the darkness.

"Fuck you, then," said Kevin, as he opened the steel door of the lab. "I haven't got time to mess with you now, but when I get back, you'll be one sorry monkey."

In overalls, Kevin was disguised from the casual eye, but he needed one small element to make his getup complete. Passing through the main lobby toward the Pike, he detoured to a small florist's boutique in the back of the hospital gift shop. Behind the counter, he found a pretty young blonde in a pink dress and white apron. She was squatting with her back to him while she repositioned some vases in a floor-to-ceiling refrigerator.

"Is Todd taking you anywhere special?" came a voice from the rear of the shop. Kevin looked and saw a plump brunette at a work table, inserting greenery into an arrangement of white daisies and carnations.

"No. When it's your birthday, you have to hang with your parents, don't you?" said the blond in a voice redolent of bubble-gum-and-peppermint ice cream. "I mean, they, like, gave you life and everything. My mom would freak out if we didn't go to the Olive Garden."

"Well, bring Todd."

"My dad *hates* him."

"Your dad hates everybody." The brunette turned the flower vase around, sizing up her finished arrangement. "So, you're not gonna go see him after you get off work? You're only here till three, aren't you?"

"*Not!* I have to work late every day this week. I can't drive unless I get some new tires. They're, like, almost bald." The blonde stirred her hands in the air, perhaps trying to give an impression of a baldness so extreme you could skate on it.

Kevin tapped on the glass counter. "Excuse me," he said.

The blonde stood up and blushed with embarrassment. "I'm sorry. Hi! How can I help you?"

"White ribbon. Ten-inch piece."

"Just ribbon?"

Kevin nodded.

The girl turned her head pertly to one side. "We have half-inch and inch wide."

"Half inch."

She went to the end of the counter, where a couple dozen ribbon spools were arrayed along a bar, and snipped a piece of the white. "That do ya?" she asked, holding it up.

"Splendid," said Kevin. As the girl passed to the register, he made note of the name on her ID badge. "Is this your birthday, Agnes?" he asked.

"Yeah." She gave him a fleeting glance.

"How old are you?"

"Seventeen," she said. She took a moment to study the tax chart taped to the counter. "Comes to thirty-two cents. Three cents an inch, plus tax."

Kevin dug underneath his overalls and brought a four-inch thick wad of bills out of his jeans pocket—everything he had withdrawn from his bank account the day before. He rarely carried more than twenty dollars on him, and the sight of so much money in his hand seemed incongruous, almost to the point of laughter.

"I can't change that," said Agnes, as Kevin handed a hundred dollar bill from the outside of the wad. "Don't you have anything smaller?"

"Sorry."

"I can't change it."

Kevin looked at Agnes, at her blue eyes and pale, peach-fuzz covered skin. She had a cockeyed smile, her lip curling higher on one side. She put so much zest into her smiling that she gave the impression it was a virtuoso skill to her, something she had made great strides at, but still hadn't quite mastered. "That's all right," said Kevin, waving off a small plastic bag and picking up the ribbon. "Why don't you keep the change?"

"What?" She couldn't have been more shocked it he had offered her a sip of Kahlua out of a hip flask. "I don't think I can do that."

"Let me put it like this. How much extra will you make working late today?"

"Thirty."

"Thirty dollars? There's a hundred. Keep the change for yourself, but promise me you'll take off work at, what is it, three o'clock?"

"Yeah, three."

"No one should have to work late on their seventeenth birthday, should they? Call Todd, and tell him you're getting off at three, and that you have a couple of hours to do something wild and crazy before settling down to dinner with your parents at the Olive Garden. Tell him you have a hundred bucks to do it with."

"Are you, like, some kind of rich doctor or something?"

Kevin smiled. "What does it matter who I am? Just promise me one thing. Be out of this hospital by three o'clock. Three-thirty at the latest. Absolutely no later than three-thirty."

"Okay, sure."

"Then have a happy birthday, Agnes," he said as he headed toward the Pike. He felt very good about himself—almost intoxicated, indeed, with good feelings about himself, and the hundred dollars, and the seventeen-year-old pink-and-white carnation to whom he had just given the gift of life.

With the white ribbon tied to his ID badge, Kevin now looked exactly like one of the scores of searchers combing the hospital. On his way through the crowded hallway to room PL-171, he succeeded in getting past two security guards, one four-man search team, and one doctor with whom he had copublished a paper on essential tremor—all without attracting a second look. But when he approached PL-171 itself, he encountered a more difficult problem. Directly across from the door to the utility closet, Kathleen Brown and her film crew had encamped, complete with lights and reflectors, to interview a pair of workmen.

The last thing he wanted was to show up on camera. He quickly ducked into a side-corridor, where he strolled about briefly before trying another pass. But the TV people showed no signs of moving on. His options were limited. He dared not linger out in the open. Scrubbing the mission was unacceptable. So he flipped up his collar and tried to push on through, keeping his back to the film crew, and trusting that a man in overalls entering a janitor's closet would not attract attention.

He was wrong. Before he had even reached the door, he heard Kathleen Brown call out, "Dr. O'Day! Is that you?"

He paused in his tracks. *Okay, it can't be helped. Best thing is to act natural and get rid of her.* "Uh, you . . . uh, yeah," he said, looking back at her. "Just call me Kevin, okay? I don't go in for that 'doctor' crap. Titles are for the intellectually insecure."

She crossed the corridor toward him. "Any updates on how Jamie Winslow is getting on? Is the SIPNI device working?"

Kevin shrugged. "Shouldn't you be telling me? Why aren't you guys with the kid?"

"They won't let us in to see him."

"The hell with that. Talk to a guy named Brower. He runs the

NICU. Give him a flattering close-up on TV and he'll let you into his wife's panty drawer."

"Thanks. Actually, I'm glad I ran into you. I wanted to tell you how impressed I was by your interview this morning. That computer of yours—Thor? Is that its name?"

He looked at her incredulously. "Odin."

"Of course, Odin. Truly amazing! What would you think about doing a feature segment on Odin for *Lifeline*?"

"Yeah, sure."

"You must be very proud of your work. I mean, Odin is so lifelike. Creating it must have been a lot like giving birth."

She was so much like a pesky fly that he couldn't resist taking a swipe at her. "Have you ever given birth, Kathy?"

"What?"

"Do you have kids, Kathy?"

"Why, no."

"Then you really don't know what the fuck you're talking about, do you?"

"It's . . . it's just an expression."

Kevin noticed the little red light of the Betacam. "And why is that goddamned camera pointed at me? Why are you filming this?"

Kathleen Brown turned to the cameraman. "Oh, Dutch! Really! Give us a little space here."

Dutch turned the camera off and let it slide down its strap so it pointed toward the floor.

"Sorry about that," said Kathleen Brown. "In our line of work we just take it for granted."

"Well, it pisses people off."

She nodded sympathetically. "Listen, was that your wife in the operating room?"

Kevin was surprised. *What does she want with Ali?* "I, uh . . . Yeah, that was my wife."

"You two seem so different from each other. Have you been married long?"

"Awhile."

She stepped forward, almost brushing against him, and threw her chest out, giving him a clear view of her cleavage. Her voice turned soft and sultry. "Do you think she would mind if you and I had drinks together sometime? To talk about *Lifeline*."

Hell, now she's coming on to me. Fuck, she's actually trying to sex me up. "Look, I need to get going. I've got work to do."

"Is it about the bomb?"

Bingo! That's what she's after. Why didn't she ask about it in the first place? "I, uh . . . I can't talk about that."

"Do you know what they took out of the Endocrinology Clinic lobby? Was that a real bomb? I've heard that it wasn't really functional."

Kevin noticed the red light of the camera again. Although Dutch still had it hanging by his hip, it had somehow wound up being pointed at him. "So, uh . . . you know about that, huh?"

Kathleen Brown nodded and gave a self-congratulating smile.

"Come here." Kevin put his arm around Kathleen Brown's shoulder and pulled her several paces down the corridor, keeping both their backs turned toward Dutch. Kevin could smell her hairspray and the talc of her facial makeup. He knew, too, that she had been out for a smoke not more than a few minutes before, and that she had had onions for lunch. "You're wasting your time staking out the hallways like this. These plumbers don't know anything."

"On the contrary, they've been very—"

"You do know that there's been an arrest in the case, don't you?"

"An arrest? Who? When?"

"I'm not allowed to say." Kevin drew a zipper line across his lips. "But they're holding him right here, in the hospital. Take your crew down to the E.R and have a look-see. They have a lock-up room there, which as we speak is being guarded by a whole regiment of the Chicago P.D."

"Is it the bomber?"

"Hey, I've risked my ass to tell you this much. You have to connect the dots yourself."

"Thanks for the tip." In her eyes, he could see that she was already halfway down the hall. He was nothing more to her now than the spent rind of an orange that had been sucked dry.

"Save it. We can talk about it all later . . . when we have those drinks."

"Right, right." She turned to her crew, who had already pulled up their cables and lights. "Come on, guys. Let's check out Emergency."

Kevin watched as Kathleen Brown and her crew scurried down the Pike. The idea of her coming on to him was revolting. It wasn't anything about her physically. She had a pert, trim bod and a smart face under all that makeup—he hadn't failed to notice that, even if she didn't have the sex appeal of Ali's shadow on a rainy day. But she hadn't even bothered to check whether he was interested. She had just forced herself on him, as if he were some dumb trout that couldn't tell the difference between a live worm on a hook and a piece of shiny plastic.

She had no idea, of course, that she had a major role to play in his plans. For now, he just wanted her out of the way. But later, when the time was ripe, he and Odin would give Kathleen Brown everything she coveted — fire, smoke, and high drama. Danger was her aphrodisiac. When that moment came, she and her cameras would throw over SIPNI altogether for a much hotter date with Project Vesuvius. The glory of SIPNI—the glory that had been stolen from him—would be reduced to an asterisk, a footnote to the prodigies of the day.

Kevin waited until Kathleen Brown and her crew had disappeared into the elevator, and then gave one last look at the surveillance camera a few yards down the corridor. Odin would lose sight of him once he entered the closet. Their only communication would be the blinking closet light that would tell him the relay was working. He held his hand on the doorknob until he could feel the electronic lock releasing at Odin's command. Then, after checking both sides of the Pike to make sure that no one else was watching, he opened the door and slipped inside.

Room PL-171 was a small closet, about five feet wide and eight feet deep, that stored cleaning supplies, a floor polisher and an assortment of mops, vacuums and brooms. Kevin had used it two weeks before, and, knowing his way around, he quickly secured the door by overturning a large wringer bucket against it and jamming a mop handle between the bucket and the far wall. He then threaded his way through the jumble of equipment to the access panel at the rear of the closet. Using a screwdriver from his bag, he removed the panel and set it on the floor against the wall. Through the two-by-two-foot access window he aimed a flashlight down a shiny, aluminum-walled air shaft until he could see a small rectangular projection about twenty feet below. That was the relay. He had taped over the small green light that normally advertised its location. Since he couldn't use the flashlight going down, on account of the risk that it might be seen through the grating below, he would have to fix the distance in his mind now, and keep track of it during the descent by sheer muscle memory.

He put on a nylon web body harness, clipped an aluminum figure eight to it, and threaded a sixty-foot length of nine millimeter nylon low-stretch rope through the small and large holes of the figure eight. He passed the free end of the rope under his crotch and around his thigh before taking it up in his left hand. That and the doubling of the rope through the figure eight would give him plenty of control on the descent. In the tight space of the air shaft he wouldn't need a backup line. He also clipped an extra carabiner to his harness, with a short piece of rope that would act as a safety line for the relay box, once he got it free.

Since there was no anchor at hand sturdy enough to hold his body weight, he took out a couple of short lengths of inch-and-a-half nylon webbing and lashed together two broomsticks—a wooden one that would not sag under his weight and a plastic one that would not snap. Together, he knew, they would be more than twice as strong as either alone. Setting them athwart the access window, he tied the fixed end of his rappel line to them. Then he crouched in a handstand and backed into the air shaft feet-first.

The air shaft was thirty inches wide, allowing just enough room to admit his shoulders, and to raise or lower one hand at a time past his chest. He let himself down inch by inch, braking the rope tight against the figure eight, taking care not to bump against the the walls of the air shaft or to snag himself on the sharp joint flanges that he encountered every six feet. As he descended, there was a warm current of air from below that he could feel against his ankles, but his body blocked its passage, leaving his face to sweat in the stagnant air above.

About sixteen or seventeen feet below his starting point, Kevin at last felt the toes of his Nikes strike the upper face of the relay box.

He knew that he was now directly behind the back wall of Harry Lewton's office. Sucking in his stomach to make room, he payed out another four feet of rope and slid downward until he could feel the relay box pressing against his abdomen. At that point he stopped and clinched the belay with a butterfly knot. Just below the transmitter box, there was a faint light coming from a grating. He knew that this opened at floor level under a console behind Harry Lewton's desk. He had no direct line of sight through it into the office—there were only shadows passing back and forth in the little patch of light. But he could hear several men's voices clearly.

Among these was a thin, reedy voice that he knew could only belong to Special Agent Lee. Lee was ticked off. "Terry, you let that get out of hand," he said. "Thanks to you, our biggest lead is now in a pissing match with death. He's going to prove to you that he's a man to be reckoned with, if it means taking down this whole hospital."

"I just put a little pressure on him," said a smooth, baritone voice—evidently that of the African-American Scopes.

"Counterproductive," said Lee. "Fanatics like this just dig in deeper under pressure. You have to lure them gently, exploiting their need for self-aggrandizement."

A third voice, raspy but bullish, interjected itself. Kevin figured it belonged to Captain Avery from the Chicago P.D. "These smug bastards are all cowards at heart," said Avery. "They'll crack if you squeeze 'em hard enough. Even that big Al-Qaeda kingpin Khalid Sheikh Mohammed caved in when they got rough on him."

"Hmm, did he?" said Lee. "Well, this isn't Pakistan. It isn't even the basement of a Chicago precinct station. Al-Sharawi's being held under a Federal warrant, which means we have to follow Federal guidelines."

"Why don't we talk to Washington?" said Scopes. "Tell them time is running out. We tried the regular channels, but haven't gotten anything useful from him."

After a short pause Lee answered. "Regrettably, I have to agree with you, considering how you've mucked things up at this point. As much as I'd prefer to use a psychological approach, we now have, what, a little more than four and a half hours left on Mr. Lewton's clock? Let's send an update to the Justice Department. See if they're willing to authorize a special interrogation protocol."

"Special . . . what?" A fourth voice came through the grate, slightly garbled, but from the decided H-sound in the word "what?" Kevin knew that it could only have come from the Texan, Harry Lewton himself.

Avery gave the answer. "Special interrogation protocol," he said with a patronizing tone. "Heavy petting, in layman's terms."

"You mean torture," said Harry.

Lee snapped back as though someone had poked him with a hat-pin. "The FBI doesn't torture anyone."

"That's just plain-out dumb," said Harry. "We have the perfect leverage already. Bring in his sister. He'll spill more in his first *How d'e do?* with her than you'd get out of a whole afternoon with a rubber truncheon or a tub of water."

"That's very naïve of you, Mr. Lewton," said Lee. "Dr. O'Day is a person of interest to this investigation, and it would be unacceptable to allow any contact between her and Al-Sharawi."

"Surely you don't still consider her a suspect," said Harry.

"Her presence here can hardly be a coincidence," said Lee.

There was a sound of a chair swiveling hard on its roller wheels, and then Harry's voice was heard again. "Didn't you watch her during the interrogation? What could possibly be her motive?"

"Well, you have me there," said Lee. "I can't quite put my finger on it. She doesn't seem to be a fanatic. Nor does she need four hundred thousand dollars. In fact, her bank records show that she lives on a small fraction of her salary. However, my ignorance of her motive doesn't clear her of suspicion. If anything, it makes her even more of a . . . curiosity."

There was another long pause. Then Scopes spoke up. "Maybe this Al-Sharawi guy's got some kind of hold over her. Threatened her. Blackmailed her. She certainly went white when you mentioned his name."

Something banged against the desk, perhaps the slap of a palm. "Ah! I like that idea," said Lee, no longer sounding ticked off—indeed, a little excited. "I like it very much, Terry. You're starting to redeem yourself after that fiasco upstairs."

"That's no idea. No idea at all," said Harry glumly. "With all due respect, I think it's bullshit and I can prove it."

"Oh?" said Lee.

"Let me bring O'Day in to see him," said Harry. "In five minutes—"

"Nothing doing," said Lee with the pissy tone he had started out using on Scopes. There was a bustle of activity around the desk. Harry started to say something, but Lee just talked over him, raising his voice to sound authoritative. "Terry, let's draft that request to Justice."

Kevin smiled to himself. *There's that old J. Edgar Hoover mentality. FBI goes by the book every time. Predictable as hell. This Lewton, on the other hand, he's smart for a hay-chewin' redneck fascist. Good thing the Feds've got him under their thumb. On another day he might've done some damage.*

At just that point, Kevin had felt under the relay box and switched off the power switch. When the signal quit, Odin would know that he had gotten this far and would wait for the transmission to resume. But instantly Kevin froze, as the overhead speakers everywhere in the hospital let out an ear-splitting, shrieking whoop, like a slide-whistle on acid. *Geez! What have I done?* thought Kevin, his throat tightening with fear. *Did I trip a goddamn alarm?*

The answer came after the third or fourth whoop, as the noise briefly abated, just long enough to let a recorded woman's voice be heard:

"THIS IS AN ALERT OF THE CERBERUS EMERGENCY REPORTING SYSTEM, INDICATING A REPORT OF A CODE RED ON GOLDMANN A, LEVEL 18. I REPEAT, CODE RED ON GOLDMANN A, LEVEL 18. PLEASE FOLLOW ALL APPROPRIATE EMERGENCY PROTOCOLS."

Sheer fucking genius, Odin! Kevin could barely restrain himself from laughing with relief, as he realized that Odin had pulled a prank worthy of a frat-house wag, calling in a fire alarm in the topmost section of the Goldmann Towers. Standard operating procedure required that the hundred-decibel alarm continue until the chief of security himself had inspected the site and determined that conditions were safe. For the next ten minutes, the alarm would drown out any noise he made.

Ten minutes wasn't long. Groping in the darkness, Kevin found the lower bolt heads and loosened them with a socket wrench, covering the socket head with his palm to muffle the clicks. Before starting on the upper bolts, he braced the relay box with his knee to keep it from dropping down the shaft. As the bolts came free, he carefully placed each one into his pocket. A dropped bolt would have been a disaster, even with the fire alarm. Amplified by the thin aluminum walls of the shaft, it would have sounded as loud as a hammer blow.

He was drenched with sweat by the time he had gotten the relay free. Pocketing his wrench, he cradled the five-pound box in his left arm and prepared to make the ascent back to the first floor. Even with the help of the figure eight to keep him from slipping downward, this was the most difficult part of the operation. With his left hand occupied, he had to pull himself up entirely by his right, bracing his knees against the walls of the shaft each time he inched his hand forward. Through all this, he had to make sure that his shoes didn't scuff the walls, or the aluminum buckle against his knees with a telltale drum sound.

The muscles in his arm were burning by the time he reached the open service panel twenty feet above. With a sigh of exhaustion, he passed the relay through the opening, and then tumbled through himself. The broomsticks that had braced his line fell with him to the floor.

He had barely finished a quick stretch to get the blood flowing back into his arms and thighs when the fire alarm went dead, accompanied by an "all clear" announcement over the loudspeakers. Kevin knew that Harry had finished checking things out and was on his way back from the Tower. But this was the homestretch; it remained only to reposition the relay box. After turning the box's power back on, Kevin unclipped the relay's safety line from his harness, threaded his rappel rope through the carabiner and tied it on with a clove hitch. Looping the rope around his fist to give it some friction, he braced his forearm on the frame of the panel like a crane and began to lower the relay an inch at a time. He was careful to keep the relay in the center of the shaft to avoid scraping or banging against the walls. After he had payed out fifteen feet or so, the closet went completely dark. A second or two later, the lights came on again.

"Thank you, Odin. Looks like we're home." He looked down the shaft and carefully swung the relay box inward until it made a soft contact with the wall. Holding the rope stationary with his left hand, he looped the free end around a crimped flange where two sections of aluminum sheeting met. It was a weak anchor, but it would hold the relatively light relay box, and it was important that nothing be visible outside the air shaft. After tying off the loop with another clove hitch, he unhitched his body harness and dropped it on the floor.

He had just picked up the access panel to reposition it when he heard a thump behind him. Turning, he saw the door to the hallway jiggle against its frame as someone tried to force it open. For several seconds, he froze. Not until his bucket-and-mop barricade began to give way did he snap into action, hastily replacing the access panel and kicking the harness and ropes out of sight behind a canister of floorwax.

"Hold on a sec," he shouted. "A mop fell over and it's blocking the door."

A hand was already groping through the doorway. "Who's in there? What's going on?" called a husky voice.

"A mop fell. Wait! Wait!" Kevin picked up the mop handle and opened the door. Two maintenance men and a security guard pushed inside.

The husky voice belonged to a short, stout plumber in a gray jumpsuit. "What the hell are you doin' in here?" The plumber's eyebrows knitted angrily, but then relaxed when he spotted the white ribbon dangling from Kevin's ID badge.

"A mop fell. I . . . I've just checked the closet and that service panel in the back. It leads to a ventilation shaft. Everything's clear."

"Where's the rest of your group?"

Kevin remembered the names of the two workmen Kathleen Brown had been grilling. "Owens and Mueller went on ahead to check out the hydrotherapy room down in P.T. We were going to do that and then break for lunch."

The plumber pushed Kevin aside with a brawny, hairy arm and leaned forward to peer at the service panel. He was so close that Kevin could smell his aftershave. "Do you have any tape?" he asked.

"Uh, tape?" Kevin for once was at a complete loss.

The plumber stopped the half-open door with his foot, as he tore off two six-inch pieces from a roll of masking tape and slapped them against the door in the shape of an X. "Don't want anyone else to have to go back in there," he said.

Kevin snickered nervously. "No. No, of course not."

The plumber gave Kevin a condescending look, then turned and started with the other two men down the Pike. Kevin could hear them joking as they turned a corner—perhaps a laugh at his expense.

Go ahead, sneer all you like, he thought. *Before the day's over, you'll know that the joke is on you.*

Five minutes later, Kevin charged into the lab, shutting the door so hastily that it pinched the heel of his shoe.

"So, is it working?" he called out as he rushed toward his desk.

"THE RELAY IS FUNCTIONING AT 99.98 PERCENT SIGNAL INTEGRITY, WHICH IS MORE THAN ADEQUATE. AT 13:11:19 I INTERCEPTED AN ENCRYPTED E-MAIL FROM SPECIAL AGENT RAYMOND LEE TO KATHERINE M. ALBRIGHT AT THE WASHINGTON OFFICE OF THE UNITED STATES DEPARTMENT OF JUSTICE, REQUESTING AUTHORIZATION TO EMPLOY SPECIAL INTERROGATION TECHNIQUES ON RAHMAN AL-SHARAWI, A FOREIGN NATIONAL ILLEGALLY PRESENT IN THE UNITED STATES."

"No good. We've got to get Rahman out of there. He likes to talk daggers, but he's really a thin-skinned son of a bitch. Not the sort that can stand torture."

"HE IS PRESENTLY BEING HELD IN ROOM EI-1, THE PSYCHIATRIC ISOLATION ROOM. HE IS GUARDED BY ONE UNARMED POLICE OFFICER INSIDE THE ROOM, AND FOUR OFFICERS WITH SIDEARMS IN THE ADJOINING ROOM EI-1A."

"Too bad we didn't put a bomb in the isolation room. We could have done the world a service and taken the bastard out. But who knew?"

"ROOM EI-1 HAS NO WINDOWS, AND ONLY A SINGLE DOOR OPENING ONTO ROOM EI-1A. THERE IS, HOWEVER, A FALSE CEILING WITH A THIRTY-SIX-INCH CRAWL SPACE THAT PROVIDES ACCESS TO THE MAIN CONDUITS FOR THE HOSPITAL'S SUPPLY OF WATER AND PRESSURIZED OXYGEN. APPROXIMATELY TWENTY METERS WEST OF ROOM EI-1, THIS CRAWL

SPACE CONNECTS WITH AN OPEN VERTICAL WELL THAT RUNS BESIDE CORRIDOR 12 THROUGH THE FIRST FOUR LEVELS OF GOLDMANN TOWER A. THE IDEAL ACCESS POINT—"

"No. I'm not leaving the lab again. Not for anything. Not even to take a piss." He threw his athletic bag across the room, raising a shriek from Loki, who leaped out of the darkness onto the counter near the sink. Kevin made a few clicks with his tongue and tapped his finger on the desktop to summon Loki back, but the monkey only stared at him, jerking his head up and down. Irritated, Kevin opened a drawer and pulled out the bag of peanuts. He took one peanut and began tapping it on the desk. Slowly, with a few bursts of nervous chitters, Loki crept to the end of the counter. Then, like a flash, he leaped the five feet from counter to desk, and in another bound was under Kevin's nose, stretching his little hand out toward the peanut. Kevin laughed and held the peanut above his head.

"Wait! I have an idea. Brilliant, actually! We can . . . we can, uh, send a little e-mail of our own. Fuck the Justice Department! Can you route a message through the server at CIA headquarters in Langley? Can you match their encryption pattern?"

"YES."

"Okay, get me the name of someone over there who is plausibly connected with anti-terrorist operations in the Middle East. Someone with unimpeachable authority."

"ACCORDING TO THE CURRENT CIA DATABASE, DEPUTY DIRECTOR WILLIAM J. MCCLINTOCK WAS FORMERLY THE DIRECTOR OF THE OFFICE OF NEAR EASTERN AND SOUTH ASIAN ANALYSIS IN THE DIRECTORATE OF INTELLIGENCE. HE IS CURRENTLY ON A FACT-FINDING MISSION TO KARACHI, PAKISTAN."

"He'll do. It's midnight in Pakistan, so it won't be easy to reach him for confirmation. Encrypt the following message, routing it with his URL as the return address: 'Request for enhanced interrogation of Rahman Abdul-Shakoor Al-Sharawi is denied. No further interrogation or debriefing of this individual should be attempted. Al-Sharawi is a confidential informant of the utmost importance to national security. Advise his immediate release. Signed, William J. McClintock, Deputy Director, Central Intelligence Agency.' Send that to our friend Special Agent Lee, along with a covering message from the FBI director's office to make it look authentic."

"DRAFTS OF BOTH MESSAGES ARE ON THE PRIMARY MONITOR. SHALL I SEND THEM NOW?"

"Please do."

Kevin surrendered the peanut to Loki, absent-mindedly stroking the top of the monkey's head, feeling the vibrations of Loki's voraciously working jaws through his fingertips. He was more pleased with himself than ever. He had come back without a scratch from a climb more dangerous than the south face of Annapurna. He had re-established control. He had beaten the FBI at a game whose rules these stupid fascists had not even begun to understand.

The starship commander's chair creaked as Kevin shifted forward, typing a command to bring the video feed from Harry Lewton's computer-cam onto the monitor in front of him. *Any minute now.* He could hardly wait to see the look on Raymond Lee's face when McClintock's order came through.

"I think we need to anticoagulate," said Dr. Brower, the chief of the NICU.

"Anticoagulate?" said Ali. "He's just come out of brain surgery. If his blood can't clot and he's bleeding, you'll kill him."

"It's a calculated risk."

"No. It's sheer foolishness."

Ever since he had gotten out of Recovery, Jamie's heart rate had been slowly climbing, and his breathing had gotten faster and deeper. He had also developed a low-grade fever. At first, Brower worried about pneumonia. But a portable chest X-ray showed clear lungs, with just a trace of atelectasis, or deflation, at the bases. This was common after surgery, and was often accompanied by a slight fever. So Ali dismissed it and looked for a neurological cause for the rapid heart rate.

But while Ali's thoughts were on Jamie's brain, Brower fixated on the chest. He ordered an electrocardiogram, which suggested that the right side of Jamie's heart was working extra hard. A number of things could have caused this, but Brower was most concerned about pulmonary embolism—a loose blood clot lodging in the main arteries of the lungs. Surgery greatly increased the risk of this, and it could lead to sudden death if untreated.

"Pulmonary embolism?" Ali was skeptical. "He's been in these anti-embolism boots since he got out of the OR. There's no evidence of it on the chest X-ray."

"Most X-rays are actually normal in pulmonary embolism. When a positive finding does occur, it's very commonly a small pleural effusion or subtle atelectasis, like what we see here. I think we should get a pulmonary ventilation-perfusion scan."

"Fine, fine." Ali had had no success with her own hypotheses. Her greatest suspicion was that Jamie was experiencing an unusual type of seizure activity that was affecting the heart-regulating center in the brainstem. He had had one seizure that morning that she had witnessed herself. But the electroencephalograph monitoring Jamie's brain electrical activity wasn't very helpful, because the presence of the SIPNI device itself was distorting the signal in that region. Interpreting it was like reading Chinese written by a sloppy calligrapher on the back of a galloping horse. So all she had to go on was watchfulness and intuition. Unwilling to trust Brower or the nursing staff, Ali stayed on in the ICU, monitoring Jamie's vital signs herself, poised to administer new anti-seizure drugs if things got dramatically worse.

While Ali waited for Patient Transport to take Jamie downstairs for his ventilation-perfusion scan, Mrs. Gore stole into the ICU for a ten-minute visit permitted by ICU rules. Fortunately, Jamie was resting quietly when she came in. Mrs. Gore went directly to his bedside, where she touched the back of her hand to his forehead, and lifted up his blanket to make sure that his sheets were dry.

Ali had been escorting a small group of surgical interns on their rounds through the ICU, but she excused herself on seeing Mrs. Gore.

"His eyes aren't moving, Dr. O'Day," said Mrs. Gore when she saw Ali approaching. "Usually when he sleeps I can see his eyes move a little. And his breathing doesn't seem right."

"He isn't sleeping, Mrs. Gore. He's in a light coma."

"Coma? Isn't that dangerous?"

"It's partly because of the medication we're giving him. But he's not progressing as well as we would like. I need to be honest with you about that."

"Is he going to—"

"It's too soon to tell what will happen. I believe he's going to do just fine, but this was a very complicated surgery he's just been through. There can be a lot of speed bumps on the way to recovery. We talked about that, more than once, over the past few months."

"Yes. Yes, I remember."

Mrs. Gore bent close to Jamie's ear and whispered. As she straightened up, she reached over and sharply pinched his cheek. "Was it okay to do that?" she said with a guilty look.

"Sure, sure," said Ali, smiling.

"I do that to him and all the other boys in the dorm at bedtime. If part of him is awake now, he'll feel it, and he'll know that I'm here with him."

As Ali nodded, Mrs. Gore scrutinized the plastic bags of solutions that were dripping into Jamie's IV line.

"Really, Doctor," she said, "it's so dark in here I don't know how you can read the labels on these things. Are you sure he's getting the right medicine?"

"Yes, he's getting exactly what I've ordered for him."

Just then two attendants showed up and parked a gurney parallel to Jamie's bed.

"What's happening?" asked Mrs. Gore.

"They're taking him downstairs to Nuclear Medicine," said Ali. "We've ordered something called a ventilation-perfusion scan. It's a test to make sure that he hasn't got a blood clot in his lung. I don't think he has, but we want to make sure."

"Will the test hurt?"

"Not at all. We'll inject small amounts of radioactive tracers to map out the patterns of air flow and blood flow in the lungs. A blood clot disrupts the flow of blood, but not of air. So we look for a mismatched abnormality on the scan."

"Well, you know what you're doing," she said, stepping aside to let one of the orderlies get next to Jamie's bed. "I trust you because Jamie trusts you. 'Dr. Nefertiti would never let anything happen to me,' he says. 'Dr. Nefertiti'—that's what he calls you. 'You've got to trust her, Mrs. Gore, 'cause she's like one of the smartest doctors in the world.'"

"Mrs. Gore," said Ali, suddenly lowering her voice, "does Jamie's mother know he's in the hospital today?"

"We haven't had any contact with her. It's by court order, you know. His mother insisted on it."

"I don't see how a mother could do that. How could she not want to know?"

"She's given him up, Dr. O'Day. Sometimes you have to make a clean break. The human heart can only stand so much."

"Did she surrender her rights irrevocably?"

"Yes, she did."

"What if he gets his sight back?"

"That won't make any difference."

"That . . . that's horrible. He needs a mother now. He needs her to be right here with him. I know you're doing your best, Mrs. Gore, but it's not the same. Look at him lying there in the bed all alone. . . ." The orderlies had just slid down the railings of Jamie's bed. One of them turned Jamie on his side, while the other slid a plastic transfer board under him.

"He's a strong boy, Dr. O'Day. He's strong, and—"

"But he shouldn't have to be strong. He's only seven, for God's sake. There should be someone to be strong *for* him."

"I agree. But—"

"Can he be adopted?"

"Adopted? By whom?"

"Me."

Mrs. Gore gave Ali an astonished look. "You, Dr. O'Day?"

"Yes, me."

"You mean, if the operation is a success? If he gets his sight back?"

"Sighted or blind. As he is."

Mrs. Gore raised her hand to her gaping mouth. "I . . . I'm flabbergasted, Doctor. How long have you been thinking about this?"

"Since . . . day one." It was true, although she had only just now realized it.

With a nurse cradling Jamie's head, the orderlies grabbed the transfer board and lifted him from his bed onto the gurney. The board barely sagged under his feather weight.

"Well, surely you know the difficulties," said Mrs. Gore. "A blind child needs constant supervision. With all your medical duties, can you manage that? The home environment needs to be redesigned to meet safety guidelines. That's expensive. There are other costs, too. The state pays his tuition now, but you would be taking it on yourself."

"If he were my natural child, I would have found a way to do all that. I'll find a way now."

"What does your husband say?"

Kevin? Ali was taken aback by the question. "I have to tell you, Mrs. Gore. My husband and I are divorcing."

"Oh, Lord!" Mrs. Gore averted her gaze. "That makes it twice as hard, Doctor."

"Just tell me, can it be done?"

"Maybe." Mrs. Gore looked back at Ali. "I've noticed how Jamie's face lights up each time he's with you. When you two talk, it's like you have your own secret language. There is something special there, I admit it. Something he doesn't have with his teachers . . . or with me."

"Would you back me up?"

The whites of Mrs. Gore's eyes shimmered under a film of tears. Her lower lip trembled ever so slightly. "I . . . I don't know. Forgive me, this is all just so sudden. I mean, yes, of course I would. You'd make a fine mother, Dr. O'Day. And in Jamie . . . in Jamie you'd be finding a wonderful, sweet, loving, and very courageous boy."

"How do I start?"

"You'll need to petition the court. I can help with that. They'll appoint a social worker to do a home study. There'll be more paperwork than you could ever imagine. CORI check, tax returns, things like that. It'll take six months, maybe a year to get through it."

"I would like to take him home with me the day he leaves the hospital."

"That . . . that's imposs—" Mrs. Gore looked into Ali's eyes and met the steel-hard gaze of a surgeon who robbed death for a living. "Okay, I can ask the court to appoint you as a temporary guardian."

"Yes. Please."

"Tell me, are you sure about this?"

"I've never been more sure about anything." Ali smiled, nervously, not knowing why. As her lips stretched, she felt a tear roll out from the corner of her eye. "I . . . I love Jamie, Mrs. Gore. I want to be his mother."

Mrs. Gore, wide-eyed, lowered her voice to a near-whisper. "All right, I'll go and make some telephone calls. Get things started." The two women looked at each other for a moment, then Mrs. Gore turned abruptly and hastened away, her heels clicking a fast but uneven staccato against the floor.

A clang. Jamie's gurney was rolling toward the door. Ali held out her hand, signalling the orderlies to pull up. Bending over the bed rail, she looked down at the unconscious Jamie, admiring his curly hair, his beautiful snub nose and rosy lips. Her son! Through the simple magic of opening her heart to Mrs. Gore, the whole world had been transformed in an instant. Forget the court rigamarole. She was already Jamie's mother. Nothing would change that—now or ever. She reached under the blanket and touched his hand—pink, warm, and yielding—feeling his unspoken cry for reassurance, and answering him with her touch. *I'm here for you, Jamie. You are loved. You always will be loved.*

She lost track of time as she looked at him. Finally, one of the orderlies coughed, and she reluctantly pulled away her hand and allowed the progress of the gurney to resume. She followed them with her gaze, watching long after the door had stopped swinging back and forth in their wake.

I am a mother now!

And yet it might all turn out to be a daydream. First, they would both have to live out the day.

"You saw it? With your own fucking eyes?" shouted Harry, panting as he bounded down the stairway two steps at a time.

Ed Guerrero was right behind him, but Ed, too, had to shout to be heard over the jackhammer stomp of eight pairs of feet flying pell-mell down the metal stairs. "Yeah, I saw it. Didn't go in . . . but saw it." On his heels were Judy Wolper, two helmeted firemen, two janitors in blue chinos, and Tom Beazle, wearing a yellow surgical gown that trailed three feet in the air.

They had sprinted four floors since Ed had come rushing up to Harry outside General Surgery with the news. *A team in the basement . . . Something big.* To Harry the announcement had come like a thunderclap, unleashing five hours of tension—hours of waiting, of taping X's on doors to nowhere, of dead rats and false fire alarms. *Big, really big.* He felt relieved, almost gleeful, at the chance to spring into action. No more groping after phantoms. For better or for worse, he was about to see what he was dealing with. If he could see it, maybe he could beat it.

Harry charged past the first basement level—the level of his own office. *Gonna need reinforcements,* he thought. "Judy!" he called out, without slowing. "Get Avery. Tell him to bring that robot of his. Old Yeller." Judy's thin, squeaky voice was drowned out by the rumble of the stampede, but the grind of a steel door opening up above told him she had gotten the message.

He charged down flight after spiraling flight, grabbing the central newel posts to swing himself around each landing, feeling the centrifugal force as his feet barely skimmed the floor. He kept thinking as he ran, *We're under the Pike, and not the Towers, thank God. We can evacuate this section in five minutes. We can do it under the radar if we have to.*

Second basement level—thirty feet below ground. No more stairs. Harry swung around to a finger-stained, orange-painted door, and with nary a break in his momentum, yanked the handle and charged into a whitewashed cinderblock corridor. "Which way?" he shouted.

"Follow me!" called Ed, dashing to the left. Harry ran after him into a dog-leg off the main corridor, his shoes squeaking against the polished floor. Together they made a sharp right-angle turn, and then nearly skidded into a group of uniformed cops and jump-suited men with white ribbons who huddled peering through a darkened doorway.

Still panting, Harry pushed through the group and swept his flashlight across the room. It was empty except for some dismantled shelves and small piles of plaster debris scattered over the dilapidated linoleum flooring. Through the half-open door of a big walk-in freezer, Harry glimpsed the edge of a dark, rectangular object, standing five feet high.

"Jesus, God!" he muttered. *Something big.* Big enough to contain five hundred pounds of explosive, all right.

"This used to be the kitchen," said Ed, wincing with exhaustion. "They're renovating it for a new Engineering shop."

"Who knows this room?"

An HVAC man from the search team spoke up. "I do. I've been remodeling in here."

"Wanna fill me in?"

"When we came to check the room we noticed that this outer door was ajar. The lights were off, because the power's been shut down for construction. But we could tell someone's been in there. There's dust on the floor, and if you look you can see scrape marks where that crate has been dragged inside."

"Did you get a look at the crate, Kyle?" he said, reading the man's ID badge.

"Just from the doorway here. We knew right away something wasn't kosher. Sometimes people put crates out in the hallway for trash pickup. But the freezer was empty yesterday, and no one but us has been working in there."

"Why is the freezer door open?

"It just hangs that way. It doesn't latch. We took the handle off to keep someone from getting trapped inside."

Harry had heard enough. Turning to Ed, he gave the command, "Evacuate the kitchen and Engineering. I want a two-hundred-foot perimeter on each side."

"Yes, sir." Ed sped off through the crowd and down the hall.

In the dark recesses of the empty room, Harry saw something move. Instantly, he trained his flashlight on a man in a dark blue uniform edging toward the freezer at a half crouch. "Who's that?"

"Miller. Chicago cop," said Kyle.

"What the hell is he doing?" Harry extended his neck and shouted through the door. "Miller! Freeze!"

Miller turned and squinted into the beam of the flashlight.

"You have some kind of a death wish, Miller?"

"I'm trying to get a look."

"Take a look at the goddamn floor, will you? You see all these loose tiles? Perfect camouflage for a booby trap."

"Oh, God! Gee, I . . . I'm sorry." Miller confusedly took a step back.

"Goddamn it! Don't you know what 'freeze' means? You can trigger a pressure plate by stepping off it, just the same as stepping on."

"What should I do?"

"Be a goddamn statue until the bomb squad gets here."

Harry swept the room again with his flashlight, this time focusing on the floor. "Did you touch anything?"

"No. This is as far as I went."

"What can you see from where you stand, Miller?"

"Inside the freezer, there's a wooden crate. Several feet high, standing upright. There's something written on it."

"What's it say?"

"I don't know. I think it's, like, German. Some kind of Ultra Instrument."

"What else do you see? Any wires?"

"No wires. There's a sort of bluish glow. Flickering. Plus I can hear ticking."

"Ticking?" Harry was skeptical. In this digital age, bombs didn't tick. "Are you sure about that?"

"Yeah, ticking."

"Like a clock?"

"Not exactly. It goes off and on. Maybe it's more like scratching."

"Come on, Miller! Is it ticking or scratching?"

"It's, uh . . . I don't hear it anymore."

Good God! Didn't Police Academy teach you anything? Either this fellow Miller was a complete lunkhead or the crate had a live mechanism—a timer or a gyroscope or maybe something that amplified the floor vibrations. Harry had to find out before someone got killed. Gingerly, in contravention of his own written protocol, he crept into the room. He heard the rasp of a loose tile against the concrete subflooring. He heard his own shallow breathing. But ticking, no. The only sign of life was a faint blue glimmer against the dark void behind the crate. He ran his flashlight over the black stenciled lettering on the rough plywood panels:

Ultraschallsystem Acuson X300
Vorsicht! Zerbrechlich!
Medizinische Instrument

Whatever that means, it's not a message from our bomber, thought Harry. He turned one ear toward the crate, listening. In the opposite direction, far down the hall, there was a murmur of voices. *Good! Kitchen evacuation's started. Ed's on the ball.*

And then Harry heard something else. Soft, almost like the scratching of a mouse. *Ta-tat . . . tat . . . tat . . . ta-tata-tata-ta-tat . . .*

Miller moaned. "Mr. Lewton, I need to take a leak pretty bad."

"Whatever you do, don't. Urine on the floor is a strong electrolyte. It'll short-circuit a booby trap sensor."

"Oh, God."

What the fuck is that tapping? Harry didn't dare step any closer. His experience with booby traps in the pot fields and meth labs of East Texas was no help to him now. This bomb was unlike anything he had ever seen, and the mentality behind it seemed unfathomable. There had been no more than a half-assed attempt at concealment. The outer door had been left ajar, for God's sake, as if in invitation. Did the bomber want the crate to be found? Was it a decoy? Or was the son of a bitch just cocksure that Avery and his men could never disarm his brain-child?

Avery. No sooner did the name pop into Harry's mind than the captain's voice boomed forth from the doorway. "Got a present for us, Lewton?"

"Mystery crate, five feet by three by three, showing signs of internal activity—evidently running off its own power source. It's yours if you want it."

"Sure, we'll take it off your hands."

"Is it safe to step back? Are we boobytrapped?"

"Hold on a sec. Old Yeller's on his way."

A moment later, there was a clatter as two bomb techs arrived and lifted the robot off a dolly. Harry craned his neck to watch as Old Yeller rolled forward, trailing a control wire, at the speed of a turtle running on all cylinders. It looked and moved like a tank made out of dull silvery titanium, with rubber treads and a storklike folding arm rising out of a turret. A video camera and lamp was mounted on the arm to give a close-up view of the pincer action, while a second camera in back rotated from side to side to give a panoramic view of the room.

As Old Yeller came near Harry's ankle, a hollow cylinder extended toward him with a whirring of gears, while a small black-tipped wand wagged parallel to the floor. A hiss, and a puff of air was sucked into the cylinder, ruffling the bottom of Harry's trousers.

"What's he gonna do next? Hump my leg?"

"Relax," said Avery. "It's a spectrometer that picks up explosive residue. That little wand you see is a galvanometer. It looks for electric currents like you might have in a sensor or detonator."

With a click and a whir Old Yeller backed away from Harry and transferred his affections to Miller, who stood a little to the rear. Although Harry remained stock still, his shadow skated back and forth against the far wall as the robot's rear camera light panned the room. In the background, Avery talked over the sensor readings with the tech handling the remote control.

"Old Yeller says your area is clean," Avery announced. "It's safe to back out now. Follow the path of the control cable to the door."

Harry waved to Miller to go first. Just as Miller took a step back, the breathless silence was shattered by a volley of beeps from inside the crate. *Beep . . . ba-bee-bee-beep-beep-beep.* Miller reflexively fell into a crouch and drew his gun.

"What the hell are you doing?" said Harry. "You gonna shoot the box? Put that fucking gun away."

He spoke too late. Something Miller did—an abruptness of his hand motion, a swirl of the ferromagnetic field around his gun—had already triggered a reaction inside the box. Harry heard a buzz and a clacking noise, and turned to see a glowing red nozzle emerging from a hole in the plywood. *Good God!* Everyone hit the floor at once. Harry dove so hard that one of the loose tiles jabbed him like a knife between his ribs. He rammed his cheek against the hard, cold linoleum, trying to make himself as thin as paper, as if that could protect him from the split-second inferno that would turn both him and floor into a cloud of fizzing molecules. *Jesus, is this it?*

And in that instant, as his heart stopped, as he tasted his own drool mixed with the dust and grease of the floor, Harry's mind went blank. Terror, he found, had no face or name or why or wherefore. It was a state of suspension between two breaths—the last breath of life as he had known it, and the next breath that might never come.

He froze for God knows how long. When at last his heart jump-started itself and his chest sucked in a tentative gasp of air, the first thought that popped into his brain came as a surprise. For he didn't think of death, or pain, or honor—not even of his gray-haired mother on the eighteenth floor. He thought of a hand—Ali's hand. He remembered that moment in his office when he had touched her. Her fingers were dry and icy cold, her palm warm and moist. It was as though they reflected a strange psychic division—her steely aplomb masking a secret vulnerability. She had reached out to him and shunned him at the same moment. *Which was true, the seeking or the shunning?* he wondered. *What did she expect from me?*

And that might have been his last thought on earth. But as luck would have it, he was roused by a woman's voice shrieking from the doorway.

"Marcus! Dwayne! Where's my babies? Where's my little boys?"

Harry twisted his neck to see a heavy-set African American woman in kitchen whites trying to wrestle her way into the room past Avery and a couple of cops.

"Let me go! Let me go! I want my babies!"

There was a scrape as the mysterious crate jostled slightly, and two ebony-skinned boys in Bulls sweatshirts and polyester shorts emerged from the darkness of the freezer.

"Mom!" shouted the smaller, no more than six years old. He was holding a toy ray gun of blue and gold painted metal, with a red cap that sparked and glowed when the trigger spun a friction wheel.

"Oh, for cryin' out loud!" Harry leaped to his feet, a hot blush spreading over his face and neck. "What were you boys doin' inside that crate?" he shouted.

The older boy, Marcus, was holding a small video game console. He squinted as Harry trained his flashlight on his face. "Just playin' Madden and stuff on the PSP. Mom said it'd be okay 'long as we were quiet."

"Well, Mom made a mistake today. You come on out of there. You and your brother."

Hanging their heads, the two shuffled out into the open.

"Did you boys drag that crate inside?" asked Harry.

"I don't know," whined Marcus. His shrug was as clear as a confession. "It's our rocket ship. Please, Mister, we didn't break nothin'."

Little Dwayne flourished his ray gun in the air. "I shot the Martian," he boasted.

After all the strain, Harry could barely suppress a laugh. He looked at Old Yeller, whose binocular video camera was still panning left and right, making a soft whirring noise. *The kid's right. Very like a Martian.* "Yeah, you got him. I think you got me, too," he said, touching the bottom of his ribcage, where the edge of the tile had bruised him. "You gotta be careful with those ray guns."

"I'm sorry. I thought you were a Martian, too."

Before Dwayne could say more, his mother broke free of Avery and ran to scoop the boy off his feet, squeezing the breath out of him with her fleshy arms. "Oh, my little Hershey Kiss! Oh, my little Kit Kat! What you done got into now?"

Harry looked at the ID badge clipped to the woman's blouse. "Ms. Covell, what are these boys doing here?"

"It's that damn spring break. They ain't in school an' I don't got nowhere to put 'em. I got to work."

"The hospital has an employee day care center."

Her eyes were like two slits above her puffy cheeks. "I can't afford no day care. It's twenty a day. All I make is sixty-eight dollars scrubbin' them pots until my skin falls off. How'm I s'posed to feed 'em an' buy 'em clothes and pay rent on forty-eight dollars a day? You couldn't do it, Mister."

"No discussion. You either put these kids in day care or you take 'em home. And that means now!" Harry waved to Judy Wolper at the doorway, as she peeped out from under Avery's arm. "Judy, would you escort Ms. Covell and her boys down to Team Tots? Have them comp her the rest of the day." Day care was in a small annex on the other side of Children's Hospital, outside the probable range of the bomb. The kids would be safe there.

"What about tomorrow?" demanded the woman.

"I'll talk to Human Resources in the morning and see that they give you a rate break for the rest of the week. But I don't want to see either of these boys in this hospital again. Got that?"

"Sure, Mister." With an indignant look, she led both of her boys by the hand toward the light of the corridor. Marcus walked proudly and stiffly. Dwayne turned at the last minute to give Harry one more blast of the ray gun.

Avery laughed. "Well, at least your people have taken care of the Martian threat."

Harry bit his cheek so hard he could taste the blood. *Ignore him. Ignore the son of a bitch.* He pushed past Avery and surveyed the dumbfounded faces of the search teams in the corridor. "Okay, everyone!" he shouted. "Let's put on some clean undies and get back to work."

Back in his laboratory, Kevin was having trouble with a white pawn. Try as he might, he could not get close to White's queen, and all because of one measly pawn, which blocked his attack from every angle.

Twenty minutes earlier, the phony e-mail from Deputy Director McClintock had indeed stirred up the most delightful ruckus. An uncharacteristically red-faced Lee had written back immediately asking for confirmation. Odin saw to it that he got one. A flurry of protest e-mails followed. Odin easily intercepted these, along with a telephone call to Washington, which he diverted to a bogus voicemail account. Lee's every move was checked, leaving the irascible FBI agent in a steamy, speechless funk, slumped over Harry's desk, while Avery and Scopes punctuated the silence with haphazard suggestions and condoling profanities.

Meanwhile, Project Vesuvius hummed along, and Kevin found himself with little to do but wait and watch. Waiting was not something that he did well. He found himself pacing the length of his laboratory, nervously pelting Odin with questions about police band radio transmissions and weather forecasts for Ontario and the Canadian Rockies. He could almost hear his brain's gears grinding. Finally, to calm himself, he accepted Odin's suggestion of a game of chess.

Wilhelm Steinitz was White. Or not exactly Steinitz, who had been dead for over a century, but the ghost of Steinitz, as conjured by Odin. Kevin had long ago learned that chess with Odin was no game at all, since no human had a chance of beating him. It was Odin himself who suggested that the odds might be evened if he took on the personality of a human player, incorporating all of his typical strengths and weaknesses.

The chessboard was of simple wood, the pieces of sculpted elkhorn from Siberia. The place of Odin's hands was supplied by Loki, who sat on top of the desk in his favorite cross-legged style. Loki's miniature fingers, their dexterity freakishly enhanced by SIPNI, held the white king aloft by his tiny crown without the slightest trace of wobbling or slippage.

"It's king to king's knight one, Loki," said Kevin, pointing to a black square at the far end of the board.

Dexterity or not, Loki was confused whether to remove the king from play, or to use it to take down his own white queen. It took considerable finger-tapping from Kevin to finally get him to set the piece down where Steinitz wanted it. Loki's move shielded the piece directly behind the queen, and prevented Kevin from opening up a discovered check with an attack upon the hated king's bishop's pawn.

"Good boy, Loki," said Kevin, handing out a peanut. "Not quite ready for tournament play, though, are we?"

The ghost of Wilhelm Steinitz took up less than 0.000001 percent of Odin's thinking capacity, and at that moment Project Vesuvius was deep into its critical collection phase. On the bank of small computers, one monitor was devoted to each of the primary revenue streams originating from the eight original payers of the Al-Quds ransom. Each stream had already subdivided itself into dozens of subsets, reflected in ever-changing columns of numbers. The combined accumulation was tallied as a single number in four-inch type on the large wall monitor, with the last few digits whizzing by so fast as to be little more than a blur. From time to time Kevin would turn his head to check on it. It was a big number, even after subtracting Rahman's four hundred grand. It was so big that it gave him a kind of queasy feeling. Although Kevin had never given much thought to the value of money, he knew that this was a number that would get noticed. It was already more than four times higher than he had originally projected—and still growing. That, of course, was Odin's doing. Odin had discovered some new angles as Project Vesuvius had unfolded, and in his usual lightning-quick way he had taken advantage of them, without stopping to consult. Not that Kevin would have objected. Odin was doing exactly what he was told to do: *maximize revenue*. Only a fool would object to quadrupling his money.

While he jabbed at Wilhelm Steinitz and watched his money roll in, Kevin also kept a close eye on the computer monitor on his desk in front of him. It showed a wide-angle security camera view of the NICU, where a dark-haired woman in scrubs sat cross-legged and nearly sideways behind the nursing station, one elbow leaning on the counter as she wrote in a blue plastic binder. She looked pensive, frustrated, and almost wistful, just as she had many nights as she sat by the kitchen table, huddled over a book or a laptop, with coffee grown cold in the cup beside her. On those nights, Kevin could never resist stealing up behind her and enticing her away from her studies with a whisper or a simple kiss on the neck. It had never taken more than that.

How different things were now! No kiss from him would ever rouse her again. Outwardly not a hair on her was altered. Inwardly she had become a stranger. He marvelled how anyone could change so completely. Even a hunk of magnetized iron retains some trace of its former alignment. But human love was fickle. All those vaunted sonneteers were nothing but bullshitters. Love was the most changeable thing in the universe.

Watching her made him increasingly agitated, and still he couldn't tear his eyes off her. He contemplated the screen so long that Odin questioned whether he had lost track of the game. "IT IS YOUR MOVE, KEVIN," he announced.

Kevin looked back at the board, and all he could see was the white queen. He felt a mad impulse to take her down—whatever the cost. To clear a path, he took the king's bishop's pawn with his own knight, knowing full well that the pawn was protected by several powerful pieces. As he moved the knight, it somehow brought to his mind an image of Rahman.

"The most crooked of all pieces," he mused. "Should be called jackal instead of knight. Likes to jump out from the sidelines and nip you on the ass. That's Rahman, to a tee. Rahman, my devious, bloodthirsty, lying comrade. Tell me, Odin, can you get fleas from lying down with a jackal?"

"BISHOP TAKES KNIGHT."

The countermove had been expected. With no little prompting from Kevin, and at the cost of three peanuts, Loki moved a white bishop from across the board to take Kevin's knight.

"Go, then!" said Kevin to the discarded piece. "You've outlived your usefulness. Off with you and your jihadist bullshit!"

With Rahman gone, Kevin found his attention drawn to the white bishop that had supplanted him.

"Do you know who this is?" he asked Loki. "This plaster saint slinking out from under the skirts of the white queen? None other than Dr. Flaccidius P. Diddly Dildo, world-famous expert in brain tumors and spinal cord injury, past president of the American College of Neurosurgery, newly minted peer of Christian Barnaard, Harvey Cushing, and Aristotle—and lying rat bastard. He has many sins to answer for, Loki.

"He has stolen my work, the offspring of the womb of my mind. And he smeared me to do it." Loki's eyes opened wide as Kevin began to raise his voice. "He called me 'unreliable,' 'temperamental.' A simple letter from him could have saved my NIH funding. But no—he had a sudden attack of intellectual scruples. 'You haven't published more than six papers in the past five years,' he said, conveniently leaving out that all six were papers to knock the world on its ass, once anyone began to understand them. It's no secret that *he* didn't understand them.

"But of course, he only wanted to make me dependent on *his* lab.

He kept me alive on bread and water—just so long as I stayed shackled to his oar. When at last I performed a miracle for him, when I created a working artificial implantable human brain out of some doodles he had brought me on a brandy-stained napkin—sure, everyone believed it was Dildo who'd done it. After all, I worked for him, right?

"Well, I'm no lickspittle resident or scut monkey. What was stolen from me I will take back—with interest. The hospital will pay, the collective mediocrities of the world will pay, and Dr. Dildo himself will pay."

Loki screeched as Kevin slammed his own black bishop forward and brusquely yanked the white bishop off the board.

"Yes, it's harsh, little monkey, but an example must be made. For the great Doctor's sins are not only of the mind. It wasn't enough to reduce me to peonage; no, he had to reach out his grasping hand for the one thing I had left. Remember the ancient *Droit du seigneur*? In plain monkey language, it means he thought me such a worm that he thought he could get away with *fucking my wife*."

Kevin addressed the cloven-headed chess piece in his hand. "You've been begging for years for someone to blow away your ass. Guess what? That day has come, you nine-fingered sack of shit!"

He hurled the bishop into the sink across the room. From the crash, he could tell that the finely carved elkhorn had shattered into pieces as it landed. Loki screeched and sprang for the safety of the dark recesses of the lab.

Kevin turned back to the chessboard, his face taut and pale.

"And you, my snowy-white queen, what shall we say of your treasons? I awakened you! I taught you to think, and to recognize your own genius! For that alone, you ought to be grateful. Forget that I loved you, that I held nothing back from you, that I . . . believed in you."

Odin broke in with a suggestion. "UNDER SECTION 11-7 OF THE ILLINOIS CRIMINAL CODE (720 ILCS 5/11-7), ADULTERY IS CLASSIFIED AS A 'CLASS A' MISDEMEANOR, AND IS PUNISHABLE BY A TERM OF IMPRISONMENT FOR UP TO ONE YEAR."

"There is an older law than that, Odin. The law of the aggrieved husband. The law of honor."

"THE CODE OF HAMMURABI STIPULATES THAT BOTH PAR-

TIES TO ADULTERY SHALL BE EXECUTED BY DROWNING, AL-
THOUGH THE WOMAN MAY BE SPARED IF HER HUSBAND
CHOOSES TO PARDON HER."

"That's more like it." Kevin once again addressed the white queen.
"No Class A Misdemeanor for you, jasmine flower. Punishment must
fit the crime. It was one thing to betray me. But you have betrayed
yourself—your youth, your beauty, your genius. It makes my flesh
crawl to think of you . . . yoked with this mediocrity. Why not an
ape? What possessed you to defile yourself like that? How could you
give over the innermost sanctum of those lovely, smooth, sculpted
hips of yours to . . . to the . . . offspring of this soulless piece of shit?
I know it's Dildo's and not mine. The last time I made love to you I
could feel how your womb froze up inside you. My seed couldn't possibly have taken root. . . . It's Dildo's, all right. And from shit can
come only shit. I won't let you live to see such a degradation. I'll first
see that bastard's bastard dribble in bloody chunks between your
legs. Squirt him out! Let that lying cunt of yours reject him as it rejected our own son Ramsey."

Kevin felt an urge to sweep the pieces off the board. He sat with
fists clenched and reddened nostrils, as image after unclean image
rushed before his eyes—blood and shit and whoredom and revenge.
In the end, it was the thought of Ramsey that broke the surge of
the storm. Ramsey, who had known no life but suffering. Ramsey, so
small, so helpless, so doomed. Thinking of how he had held his lifeless son's body for a final farewell, Kevin slumped over the chessboard, his eyes glazed and unmoving.

"But the woman may be spared," he mumbled at last. "So says
Hammurabi. Well, look to it, then. There may still be . . . even now . . .
hope."

He turned his chair away from the desk and faced the big wall
monitor. He needed to think of something more positive, something
calming.

"Odin, bring up the latest Landsat views of Isla Viscacha."

In place of the ever growing ransom total, the screen was filled
with an aerial image of a wooded island, surrounded by a purplish,
churning sea. Several miles in the background were the rocky head-
lands of the southern Chilean coast—one of the most sparsely popu-
lated areas in the habitable world. In the farthest distance, barely

distinguishable from the cirrus-clouded sky, was the snowcapped peak of Monte San Valentin, towering over the North Patagonian ice fields.

"Can you enlarge it? I want to see the dock."

A U-shaped bungalow, two guest cottages, and a large utility building came into view, clustered around a sandy cove on the eastern shore.

Isla Viscacha, the thirty-seven-acre retreat of a reclusive film director, had been on the real estate market for over three years. It was the realization of a pipe dream that Kevin had cherished since graduate school at Stanford—a naturally fortified sanctuary where he could shut out the world's inanity and hypocrisy, and devote himself single-mindedly to his work. Using the assumed identity of Padrig de Rais, a Breton French hotelier from Saint-Malo, Kevin had negotiated an option for the purchase of the property. An attorney in Santiago was already waiting to proxy-sign the deed for him, and there was needed only a tiny disbursement from today's proceeds to complete the deal. When Kevin arrived in person in a few months, having dissolved and reconstituted himself in an untraceable chain of guises, he would supervise the construction of a discreetly camouflaged underground laboratory—soon to become the most advanced cybernetics research complex on the planet. There he would build the next-generation version of Odin, using his vision of a four-dimensional plasma containment field instead of silicon as the basis of his CPU. Moore's Law would be blown to smithereens. No longer would computing power double every two years. It would leap by orders of magnitude at a single bound. He and Odin would rule supreme over the fields of cybernetics and bionics. With inexhaustible funds at his disposal, he would no longer be held back by mental pygmies like Helvelius, Dr. Gosling, or the bureaucrats and chicken-shit reviewers at the NIH. A cornucopia of inventions would pour out to enrich mankind. Pilgrims would flock to his rocky outpost as to a new Oracle of Delphi. And after that, no one would question how the Age of Isla Viscacha had arisen out of the ashes of Project Vesuvius, just as no one ever asked what crimes might have lain behind the discovery of fire or of the wheel. His genius alone would make him inviolable.

Odin's voice roused him from his reverie. "QUEEN TO QUEEN'S KNIGHT TWO. CHECK."

He had moved too late to neutralize the threat of the white queen, and she had now gone on the move against him. *Check*—it was an attack on his king. He had to move to evade it, and in so doing lost the initiative in the game. In the best-case scenario, he would spend the next dozen moves improvising escapes, hoping for a blunder that would allow him to reverse the attack. If white's queen did not relent, it could only end in checkmate.

"Fuck you, then! Do your worst!" he snapped, speaking to the white queen herself. "There's another game afoot—a game you will not win. Do you see the hands sweeping across the clock? Time is short, oh, so fucking short, my sweet jasmine flower! The hour of reckoning is at hand! One last chance, and then . . . Choose well, my darling! To quote the old runes, *'Earth shall be riven | With the over-Heaven.'* You and your precious Helvelius will piss yourselves when you behold the bonfires of the Twilight of the Gods!"

"Thanks, Mac," said Harry as he took the cigarette and drew a long, hungry puff off it that turned the end of the stick a glowing red.

The fireman put the lighter back in his pocket and went back to jawboning with his crewmates as they sat on the rear bumper of the truck.

A grateful Harry turned and went back the way he had come, toward the ambulance dock behind the emergency room. It was his first smoke in six months. Those six months had cost him a hell of a fight, but he needed to get calm enough now to think. Between the e-mails and the alarms and the C4 and the clamor of the press, he was beginning to feel like he had ants crawling up and down his nerve fibers.

He looked up, where the early afternoon sun glared down at him from the steel and glass exterior of the Goldmann Towers. The roof of the towers was so high he had to arch his lower back to see to the top. Somewhere up there, behind one of those shiny windows, his mother was fighting for her life. And here he was, the goddamn chief of security, no better than a cigarette butt on the asphalt, for all the good it did her. After Oklahoma City, the Beirut barracks, and the Khobar Towers, Harry knew that five hundred pounds of C4 could tear apart even a massively reinforced building like it was tissue paper. She wouldn't stand a chance. He knew this, and still he couldn't get her out. He felt totally fucking useless.

He had avoided going back to his office after the debacle of the mystery crate. He needed to get out here, into the sunlight, with the breeze streaming across his face—here, where he could be alone for a few minutes to sort things out. With each drag on the cigarette, things came clearer into view.

What came into view was unsettling. Almost six hours had passed since the first bomb warning had hit his pager, and still he and the cops had very little to show for it. Fourteen search teams had failed to turn up a single trace. Lee, the expert psychologist, hadn't dug anything out of Rahman. No one even knew if Rahman was the brains of the dog or just the tail. Did he have a confederate in the hospital? Did he have the kind of technical information that would help to locate and disarm the bomb? These were the essential questions. Now that Lee had passed the ball to the Justice Department, it could take hours to get that little piece of paper that would let Scopes and Avery interrogate Rahman the way they wanted to. Those would be hours wasted, while, for all Harry knew, the investigation might have been better off looking somewhere else.

He smelled a colossal screw-up in the making.

As he saw it, there was one good chance to cut through the impasse—Ali O'Day. Rahman seemed to hate her guts, but that wasn't necessarily a bad thing. They were brother and sister, and there were buttons that she and nobody but she knew how to push. All the more so if there was animus between them. Anger was a button, too.

Lee was blind to this. The whole damn FBI and Justice Department had gotten to be a hindrance and not a help to the investigation. Barely four hours were left until that plane to Yemen boarded, and here they were—bogged down in *paperwork*.

"Fuck it," muttered Harry. His mind was perfectly clear now, only sometimes clarity can be a bitch. There was no escape clause for this one. If the investigation was going to go anywhere, he was going to have to take the wheel and drive it there himself.

He threw down the stub of his cigarette and crushed it under his sole. Crushed it and recrushed it, long after the glow had gone out.

This could be Nacogdoches all over again, couldn't it? he thought. *Do the right thing and get crucified for it.* But this was his turf and he had sworn to protect it. Two thousand lives in the balance—one piddling career was a small thing to weigh against that.

"Aw, fuck it," he said again.

He took one last look at the sunlight, and then went in through the ER doors.

Jamie came back from Nuclear Medicine with a scan result that showed an intermediate probability of pulmonary embolism.

Dr. Brower took that as the signal to start anticoagulation therapy.

"No," insisted Ali. "An intermediate probability scan is inconclusive. The chances of a clot are in the range of twenty to eighty percent. That's a huge window. It could still just be his atelectasis."

"Well, it's all we have to go on. It's not proof but it's evidence. At some point, we have to actually begin treating him for something."

"We are treating him. For seizures and cerebral edema."

"Without success."

"Oh, hell!" said Ali. She didn't trust Brower. But what else had she come up with? She was angry at herself for having failed Jamie. She was desperate to do something—anything—to help him. But was she being too protective? Maternal feelings were starting to cloud her judgment, and that in itself added to the danger. "You win. But I won't have you giving him anything more than low-dose heparin. I want to be able to reverse it if there's a problem. Low-dose heparin, do you understand?"

Just then, the nurse at the station called Ali to the phone. It was Dr. Helvelius.

"S-sorry I took so long to get back to you. These damn pagers still aren't working. I got called in to assist on a trauma case. Motorcycle versus SUV, with an ugly spinal fracture at C2. Took me a while to get it s-stabilized. I'm on a five-minute break."

"We're having problems with Jamie. He's had a seizure and he's in coma, no better than seven on the Glasgow scale. He's showing progressive tachycardia and tachypnea, which could indicate brainstem dysfunction. No response to Dilantin or Solumedrol."

"Who's on duty in the ICU?"

"Brower."

"Hmm. Watch out for him. He thinks of the brain as a black box. He'll go by the book, without trying to p-puzzle things out."

"I know. I've already had a tussle with him over pulmonary embolism."

"Well, let's reason it out. What about normal perfusion pressure breakthrough?"

"I'm worried about it. But there's no direct evidence."

"Why don't we add nitroprusside, just to keep his b-blood pressure down?"

"All right."

"You don't sound very confident, Dr. O'Day."

"I . . . I don't know. It's confusing. What about a blood clot, a hematoma? If there were bleeding that got missed on CT, the clot could be expanding and raising the intracranial pressure."

"Possibly. If the ICP rises above twenty, give him a gram of mannitol. If that doesn't do it, then we may have to take him back to the OR."

"The AVM was so close to the brainstem, I'm afraid any problem could rapidly turn catastrophic."

"That's a risk we accepted when we took on this case." He paused, perhaps expecting a reply from Ali. When she said nothing, he softened his tone. "Why don't we have Electrophysiology come down and record some somatosensory evoked p-potentials? If we can pass a test signal from his leg through to his scalp, then that would help to show that his b-brainstem is okay."

"Yes, that would be reassuring."

"Do that, and call me if there's any change. I'll come by the ICU as soon as I'm done here."

As he hung up, Ali realized that she had not spoken of one possibility that lurked behind all the others—that the SIPNI device itself could be causing the problem. She had tested many prototypes in animal brains without ever seeing a situation like this. But those were programmed far more simply than Jamie's device. Was SIPNI malfunctioning? If so, it would have to be removed immediately—a critical setback to years of work and millions of dollars in expenditures, not to speak of the reputations of everyone involved with the project. The hospital's Institutional Review Board would never permit another human trial until many months of repeat animal experiments had identified the cause of failure and proven that it would not happen again. In the meantime, the many naysayers who had opposed SIPNI would have the public forum to themselves—the *America Today* publicity would backfire humiliatingly—and research funding would dry up. In short, it would be a disaster. Was this why she was so reluctant to consider the possibility of a malfunction? Or was it simply a case of wishful thinking, wanting everything to turn out right for Jamie? Could she trust her own judgment when she herself had so much at stake?

Suddenly, Ali heard a bellowing sound, almost like the lowing of an ox, and looked up to see Ginnie running to Bay 7—Jamie's bed. Jamie was moving about in the bed, but it wasn't a convulsion—he was trying to speak.

"Daaaak! Daaaaaaaktaaa!" he groaned.

Ali rushed to the bedside.

"Jamie! Jamie!" she said. "It's me, Dr. O'Day. I'm right here."

His wrists were in velcro restraints, but he was jerking his fingers about as if in search of something. Ali took his hand. As soon as she did so, his movements calmed.

"Daaktaar! M-my 'ead. My 'ead 'urts."

"Your head hurts?"

"Yaaah."

"All right, I'll give you some medicine to make the pain go away." Practically all brain surgery patients came down with a headache when the anesthesia wore off, and headaches were common after spinal taps as well. So Ali was not unduly alarmed. On the contrary, she was elated to find that Jamie was no longer in a coma.

"Amadine?" he asked.

"What?"

"Amadine?"

"I don't understand."

"Am . . . I . . . dyin'?"

"No, Jamie! Absolutely not! I won't let you die. Do you trust me?" There was no answer.

"Do you trust me, Jamie?"

"O-o-h-kay."

She injected a couple of cc's of morphine into his IV for the headache, and then ordered Ginnie to increase the Ativan to keep him well sedated. All in all, this was a good sign, she tried to convince herself. Perhaps the seizure medicine was working after all. If Jamie continued to improve, there would be no need to reoperate, and the SIPNI device could be given a chance to work.

If only it could be that easy.

When Ali had finished writing the medication order into Jamie's progress chart, she looked up from the nurses' desk and was astonished to see Harry Lewton standing over her.

"You again!" she said, flaring her nostrils. "What is it now? Another interrogation? Or am I to be arrested?"

Harry smiled. "Dr. O'Day, we've gotten off on the wrong footing. I'd like to start over again. Have you had lunch?"

Lunch? Was he kidding? He was the last person in the world she would have wanted to have lunch with. Ali snapped the binder shut and shoved it into the chart rack. "I don't remember. I often don't eat lunch. There isn't time."

"Please, let me buy you a sandwich down at Eat Street. Call it a peace offering. We can eat and talk. There are some things we need to discuss. But I'd rather not do it in my office."

"So this is an official request?"

"Not official. But . . . pertinent, let's say."

"Pertinent?" She gave him a scornful look. "I don't even know what you mean by that, Mr. Lewton."

Harry said nothing, but kept on looking at her with those bright, gentle eyes of his that went so poorly with the rest of his heavy-jawed, broken-nosed, pock-marked face. Half of Ali wanted to make a quick getaway. The other half of her was already in his pocket. *I should at least find out what he wants,* she reasoned. *If he has suspicions, I would be better off knowing what they are.*

Across the room, Jamie's monitor showed all vital signs normal. "All right, consider me your unofficial detainee for the next half hour." She got up to leave, but then stopped. "Wait! One thing before we go," she said.

Ali opened the bottom drawer of the desk behind the nursing station and took out an oddly-shaped object wrapped in silver paper. "On Your Special Day!" was printed all over it in red letters, enclosed by decals of white and blue balloons. Inside was a kid's-sized baseball glove she had bought as a gift for Jamie. It had been autographed by his favorite baseball player, a young center fielder named Chick Suarez, whom Ali had cornered for that purpose at a fundraiser for Lou Gehrig's disease at the Palmer House. The "special day," of course, was to have been the day SIPNI started working. But now SIPNI didn't seem so important. Jamie's very life was at stake. Ali felt an urgent need to give the glove to Jamie, in his darkest hour, as though it were a talisman that could lend him strength.

She tore off the wrapper and went to Jamie's bedside. With Harry looking on, she placed the golden-tan glove on Jamie's left hand, guiding his tiny limp fingers into the slots. As she did so, she read aloud the short line Chick Suarez had written on the back, just above the wrist strap. "Swing for the fences, kid!" it said.

"Swing, Jamie," she whispered again, her eyes wet with tears. Then she bent over and kissed him on the forehead.

Eat Street was a soup and sandwich shop just off the main lobby, part of a local chain that catered equally to the sleek and slim and to convalescents. The lunch rush was already over. Ali selected a Diet Coke and a mandarin sesame chicken salad from off the refrigerator shelf, while Harry ordered a roast beef sandwich with Caesar dressing from the sandwich bar. After Harry paid, they moved to a small wrought-iron table in the back. It was the best place for a quiet talk.

Ali watched Harry bite a chunk out of his sandwich and chase it with a swig of coffee. He spoke with food still in his mouth. "So how is your patient making out—that blind kid?"

Ali understood the way Harry ate. She herself squirted a packet of dressing on her salad, and attacked it with the same ferocity as Harry. Both of them were used to speed lunches—lunches that could be interrupted at any moment by an urgent page.

"Not as well as we had hoped. That's why I need to get back to him as soon as I can."

"I understand."

Ali waited to see if Harry would say more. She was annoyed when he simply went on eating. "So what is this 'pertinent thing' you wanted to discuss?"

"Straight down to business, huh?"

"I don't have time for chitchat. Besides Jamie Winslow, I have six patients to round on in the neuro ward, and an article to proof for *Nature Medicine,* due tomorrow. Plus, if there's a subarachnoid hem-

orrhage or a trauma case, I could get called in without warning—
America Today or no *America Today*."

"Sorry."

"For what? It's my life and I like it."

"Right. Of course. Dedication. The needs of the sick and the
dying."

"Are you patronizing me?"

"No. I admire you—you and all those like you. I just can't quite
figure what you get out of it. I mean, I know why I took to the security business. I like to be in control. In my office I have a status board
with a hundred green lights shining on it. I'm not a happy man
unless I see every last one of those little green lights. If a red one
turns up, it gets personal. My wits, my reflexes, my training, I'll
throw it all against anything that dares to challenge my control. And
when I come out on top, when that little light turns green again, I feel
like the world's got some meaning, at least for a little while."

"What if you don't come out on top?"

Harry smiled sheepishly. "Let's not go there," he said, rubbing his
forehead with his thumb. "So, tell me, why medicine?"

"Well, a doctor is . . . I can only speak for myself. I'm fascinated
by the science of it. To study medicine is to study the nature of
mankind—my own nature, if you will. If death and suffering are the
ultimate questions we all have to face, then medicine is where we face
them most lucidly."

She had given him her official answer, the same answer she had
given Kathleen Brown and the Department of Neurosurgery and
the admissions committee of McGill Medical School and everyone
else who had ever asked her why she had wanted to become a doctor.
She did not tell him about the little girl Aliyah, who had watched her
distant and godlike father light up with compassion whenever he saw
his patients in the little office beneath their apartment on Steinway
Street. In medicine, she discovered, there was no place for condem-
nation or refusal. All who knocked were admitted. It was wonderful
to her that there was a place in the world where nothing mattered
except to help those who were anxious and sick. She loved her father's
patients. Sitting on the concrete stoop, she would greet each one by
name as they came up huffing and puffing, one stair at a time. The

pale cloud of mortality around them would break for a moment as they smiled back at her, or thanked her for holding the door. "You are your father's daughter," they would say. "You have his warm hands and clever eyes. How God has blessed him with a daughter like you!"

Aliyah knew little of science then. She cared nothing for the mysticism of the little amber bottles with long Latin labels. Not even the stethoscope charmed her, as it had fascinated the other children in the apartment building. She knew only that she had discovered something bright and wonderful, a place where wisdom and kindness were the only things that mattered, a sanctuary from the frightening and implacable world around her. And even in those days—even with the sheltered mind of a seven-year-old—she knew that she must never, ever stray beyond its bounds.

"Your father was a doctor, right?" said Harry, jarring her train of thought. "That must have made it a natural choice for you."

"Yes," she said absent-mindedly. But when she had re-thought Harry's question in hindsight, a flash of bitterness shone through her eyes. "No. No, that's not true," she said, her voice hardening. "My becoming a doctor was an act of rebellion. My father had other hopes for me."

How was young Aliyah to understand that what she prized most in her father—his life of compassion for the hurting and the weak—was off-limits to her? *God requires meekness and devotion from you,* she was told. *It is unseemly for a woman to look upon the nakedness of strangers. Medicine is a dirty business, and woman was made for purity.* But Aliyah would not listen. She had found her sanctuary, and she would not give it up. She fasted until she grew thin, until her father worried for her life and agreed at last to pay her way through medical school. In return, she consented to marry the one to whom she had been promised. Her father exacted a solemn vow on that score. But when her training was done, it was too late. She had found strength in self-reliance. She renounced her vow. She bore her father's rage for doing so. Although the pain in his eyes haunted her for a thousand nights, she could not give in. What was once her sanctuary had become her way of life.

Again, the voice of Harry Lewton broke into her reflection. "Do you mind if I call you Ali?" he said through his mouthful of meat. "Dr. O'Day feels a bit old school."

"I don't care what you call me, as long as you come to the point."

"Very well." Harry put down his sandwich and suddenly adopted a serious tone. "It's about your brother."

"Rahman? I'm not going to talk about him."

"He's here in the hospital."

"What?" She set down her plastic fork and stared at Harry with a half-open mouth.

"He's been arrested. He's being held in an isolation room just over there, in the ER"

Ali's hand moved over her throat, as if shielding herself. "So it's true?"

"Yes, he's admitted to being mixed up with the bomb."

"Then what do you want from me?"

"To warn you, first of all. You see, the way they found him was through tracing phone calls made by you. At least three of them during the past year."

"My phone calls?" She looked at him incredulously.

Harry nodded.

"How did you . . . I . . . I . . ." It was as though he had just told her that her apartment had been robbed. "That's absurd. I've never called him. I told you, I haven't spoken to him in years." Her words were forcefully chosen, but there was a pleading quality in her voice that betrayed a hint of panic.

"Well, your phone records say otherwise."

"Then the records lie."

"Do you know how unconvincing that sounds? Is that all you have to say?"

"Yes," she snapped.

"Look, I'm trying to help you. You've got to understand how bad this looks. They've already obtained Federal search warrants against you—that's how they got the phone records. Your movements around the hospital are being observed. The only reason they haven't detained you is because they're hoping you'll lead them to—"

"Warrants?" Ali spiked her fork into her salad, leaving it sticking up in the air like a harpoon. "Go ahead! Observe *this*!" she exclaimed as she brusquely stood up, knocking her chair with the back of her legs. "You people think you can ride roughshod over anyone's privacy, like a national gang of peeping Toms. Well, I'll not stand for it.

My personal life and my movements are none of your business. To hell with you, Mr. Lewton!"

Harry reached for her wrist, but her fiery look stopped him short of actually touching her.

"Please sit back down," Harry said in a low voice. "That's the FBI, not me. Give me five minutes. Please, I want to help."

Although she had gotten up to leave, she had not taken the critical first step. She scrutinized Harry's face, trying to figure out what his motives were. Why should he help her? He didn't even know her. But his eyes and mouth showed none of the condescension she had met in Lee and Avery. His look was earnest, nonjudgmental, even a little bit worried.

"If this is a trick—" she said as she eased back into the chair.

"No trick. Everything I've said is true."

"How do you expect me to trust you after the way you people worked me over me in your office? The next time you try that, I'm bringing a lawyer."

"That's why I wanted to talk to you here. To do things a different way."

"Threatening me isn't much of an improvement."

"I didn't mean it to sound like . . . I, uh . . . Look, I know it's not fair to push you like this, without—" He broke off and looked away from her, out the window, where a throng of parking valets and patients bustled about the main entrance, with a chaotic but invisibly purposeful energy, like ants at the mouth of an anthill. "Okay. You know what?" he said, turning back to her. "Let me earn your trust. I'll give mine to you first. Listen a minute and I'll tell you something about myself, something that hardly anyone knows around here. Something that could make my life difficult if it did get around. And then I'll leave you free to do what you want with it."

"You don't have to do that," she said.

Harry looked at her from under the shadow of his tanned and lightly creased brow. He waited until she had taken a sip from her Coke before going on. "In what seems like a lifetime ago," he said, "I used to be a cop. I was a good cop, good with people. After a B.A. from Baylor and a stint at Police Academy, I got my first job in a place called Nacogdoches, Texas. In a small town like that, where most of the officers don't have full college degrees, you can rise up in the ranks pretty quick. Before I knew it, I was a lieutenant, head of the Tactical Unit, next thing to the chief of police himself. It was a pretty cushy setup. My wife worked for Parks and Recreation, and we bought us a neat little brick ranch house not far from the center of town. Most folks knew me on sight, and I was welcome everywhere.

"Nacogdoches does not have a heavy home-grown crime element. There's some rowdy college kids on Friday nights, and a little bit of car theft. But we did have a problem with outsiders—drug traffickers who wanted to make us a kind of clearing house for coke and weed on its way North. For about six months, we had a mini-war going on, culminating in something like the O.K. Corral, with one of the biggest drug busts ever in East Texas. A lot of it was my doing. When it was over, my feet scarcely touched the ground in that town. In the newspapers I was the second coming of Wyatt Earp. Big-city departments all over the country were calling me with offers. Didn't seem like anything could ever go wrong."

"Very impressive," said Ali sarcastically as she put down her Coke can and prepared to get up. "Thank you for your confession. Nothing knocks me over like big boys waving their guns."

"Hold on a minute," said Harry. "I haven't gotten to the point. You see, things did go wrong, and when they did, it all came down in a second." Harry paused until he was sure that he had her attention. "There was this guy, an out-of-work motorcycle mechanic, whose wife had left him and taken away their two kids, a boy and a girl, ages four and six, brown hair and deep blue eyes, as cute as you please. This man had a partiality to drink, and in what is unfortunately not an uncommon scenario, he fired himself up with bourbon one night and decided to reunite his family with a Smith & Wesson .44 magnum. He wound up shooting and killing his ex and his father-in-law, then taking the kids and barricading himself in a grimy white bungalow on the edge of town. Police cars from miles around encircled the house. I had my Tactical Unit out in force. For a couple of hours there was a standoff, with us shining our spotlights on the house, and him every so often taking a pot-shot at us and cussing at us through a broken window. My plan was to give him time to let off steam until he got sober and gave up. Usually when the sun comes up, a lot of sorry feelings will come up with it. Until then, all we really had to do was watch out for the kids. But his ex's family had lived in the town since before Sam Houston's day, and pretty soon there was a real crowd growing behind our backs, and they were turning up the heat to get something done."

Ali held her Coke can lightly, but had stopped drinking from it.

"Around two in the morning, some fool from the county sheriff's department lost his cool and shot a tear-gas canister through the window, hoping to flush the guy out. You never do that when there's kids on the scene, but, like I said, the heat was on, and it happened. Against direct orders. The house caught fire. In five minutes, there was not tear gas but thick black smoke pouring from every opening. It was a cheap clapboard house, a pile of old dry timber just waiting to burn. Still, the guy did not come out. We called the fire department. Just as we heard the truck's sirens in the distance, three shots rang out from inside the house."

Harry looked back out the window for a moment, back toward the scores of passers by who had never heard of Nacogdoches, Texas.

"You get training for situations like that," he went on, "but there's no training that prepares you for the sight of those churning black clouds of smoke and the heat of the fire that you can feel from all the way across the street. Everyone was paralyzed. Everyone but me, Wyatt Earp. I kicked open the back door and charged into the house, gun drawn. Everything was blinding white from flames that covered the back wall. I had to pull my jacket over my nose just to breathe. In a few seconds I found the guy. He was sprawled out on the floor of the front room, that long-necked gun beside him, his head in a pool of blood.

"I looked for the kids. I found 'em in the bathroom in the middle of the house, dressed in their jammies, with a Spider-Man doll and a stuffed bear beside 'em. They were dead. Their dad had shot 'em point-blank, each with a single .44 slug to the head. There was no doubt. I have gone over that scene a million times in my mind—and in my nightmares—and there is absolutely no doubt that they were . . . dead. A six-year-old girl cannot have a hole the size of a grapefruit in the back of her skull and still be alive. A boy . . . a boy cannot have pieces of brain sticking to the wall, and . . . and still be alive. . . ."

Harry's voice trailed off. As he looked into his cup of coffee, Ali wondered whether he was glimpsing a reflection of ghosts from the past. Abruptly, he snatched up the cup and took a big gulp from it.

"I'm sorry to regale you with the nasty details," he said. "But the point . . . the point is that what I saw, with my own two eyes, is that those two kids were dead. They were as surely dead as anyone will ever be."

"Of course," said Ali.

"I was wrong about one thing. While I was still feeling for pulses in the bathroom, I heard a moan from out front, and I realized that the perp, the guy himself, was still alive. He had shot himself at an angle, a common mistake in suicides, and, what with the recoil and all, the bullet had cracked his skull and knocked him out, but he was still very much alive and breathing."

Harry took a deep breath, as if tallying up a score. "So here's what I had. The house was about to come down around me. I was standing there choking to death, with my eyes burning from all the heat and smoke. There were two kids past earthly help. And there was this guy, a fucking mean son of a bitch who had done something too horrible to imagine, and who had already expressed his desire to not go on living in this world. All that was beyond dispute. Having seen the mess he had made, I knew this better than anyone else ever could. And yet, he was alive. That . . . that is the point. The kids were dead. He was alive. I had exactly one chance to make it out, and when I did I came dragging that son of a bitch with me.

"And that was when my life changed. There were no hurrahs that greeted me as I came out of that house. In the blink of an eye, Wyatt Earp had turned into John Wilkes Booth—a guy who had traded the lives of two sweet kids for a louse who had no future ahead of him except death row. Although the coroner's report backed me up, people standing in the crowd swore they had heard the screams of the kids in the roar of the fire. Rumors flew. It was said that I had chickened out when I saw the flames around those screaming kids, and took the quickest way out of the house to save myself. It was said that I had charged the place in a drunken stupor, and barely staggered out alive. It was even said that the perp had been an old drinking buddy of mine, and that my real intention had been to help him escape out the back way.

"The newspapers made a piñata out of me. My fellow cops didn't want to be seen with me. People who used to tip their hats would now spit as I walked by them. Even my wife started treating me like a stranger. I don't blame her for that so much—she worked for the City, where a lot of the dead woman's relatives had jobs, and sooner or later she had to cut loose from me if she wanted to go on showing her face around town.

"I'm surprised she lasted as long as she did. I didn't make it easy for her. I got pretty sour on people. I hung out all night in bars. I didn't use to drink, but I did then for a while. And every time I had a bad dream or smelled a whiff of smoke, I saw those two dead kids in front or me, and I would fly off into a crazy cussing fit like you wouldn't believe.

"The drinking made it easy for everyone. The City let me go— didn't fire me, exactly, just said I wasn't welcome anymore. So I packed up, minus a wife, and moved to Houston, where I got a job as a beat cop, which lasted until the newspapers there dug me up and decided to make another story out of me on a slow Sunday. After that I gave up police work for good. I had a chunk of money from our house after the divorce, and that paid my way through an M.B.A. in Security Management. I live the quiet life now, comparatively speaking.

"The funny thing is, if I had to go back into that burning house a thousand times over, I would never change a thing. I was a public safety officer, not a judge or an executioner. I'm glad I acted like a man and didn't let my thinking get screwed up by my hate for the shooter. If the world doesn't understand that or can't accept it, well, fuck the world."

Ali was at a loss for words. She had misjudged Harry Lewton. Behind his craggy prizefighter's face there was a man who thought deeply, felt profoundly, and who had the strength to meet tragedy head-on, not dismiss it like Helvelius or howl against it like Kevin. "I'm sorry," she said at last. "Most people live by their feelings. Professionals have to act on hard logic. Doctors, too. We have rules for this kind of situation, the rules of triage. You save whomever you can save. That's it. It's not your job to make moral judgments."

"I wish I had met you in Nacogdoches."

"You still haven't said what you want from me."

"I want you to talk to Rahman."

Ali jerked back in her chair as though she had received an electric shock. "No, I won't do that."

"Nothing official. No tape recorders, no FBI. Just you, your brother, and me."

"I'm sorry. No."

"It's important. We haven't gotten zip from him about the bomb. Time is slipping through our fingers and we need a break desperately."

"I can't. I would if I could, but I can't. I couldn't bear to be in the room with him." She felt her heart beating against her ribs. It was hard to control her breathing.

"I'll be there."

"You don't understand. Rahman won't say anything about the bomb to me. It would be useless."

"He doesn't have to say anything. You can learn just as much sometimes from what a perp doesn't say."

"No! Please don't ask again." She gripped the edge of the table as a wave of nausea passed over her.

"There's bad blood between you two, isn't there?" he said, trying to ease back.

"That's . . . an understatement."

"You seem to be afraid. Afraid of him."

"Does it show?"

An image flashed before her, of an afternoon at her father's house in Queens. It was cold and drizzly. In the tiny backyard, two once-luxuriant Japanese maples had shed their leaves, leaving behind a skeletal cagework of branches, blackened by rain and the grime of the city. He stood beneath them, his sallow, tapering, serpentine face twisted in a defiant smirk, oblivious to the rain that dripped from his pointed chin. *Yes,* he said. *Father has told you true.* And in that moment, the featureless, unnameable nightmares of twenty years crystallized into panic. She could neither speak nor move, but her bowels and bones screamed for her, sounding out her horror and rage. *Then you are no man,* they cried. *You are Satan, whose very whisper brings death. But I have not forgotten her whom you have destroyed. I will carry her cause through eternity, and lay it at the judgment seat of God.*

She blinked, and the specter disappeared. In front of her she saw only the face of Harry Lewton, looking back at her gently. "Look, we all have our hobgoblins," he said. "As a rule, they grow bigger the more we turn our backs on them. Sometimes the best thing is to turn around and look 'em in the eye."

"Easily said."

"Listen, I won't let him hurt you physically. I'll be at your side. All I'm asking is that you try whatever you can do. The survival of this hospital might depend on it."

"I'm . . . I'm not the person you think I am. I'm not strong like you."

"You don't think so? You cut into people's brains for a living. You're climbing up the ladder of the most male-dominated medical specialty there is. You must have had to get through years of insults and hazings and sexual innuendos to get to where you are. And you want to tell me you're not strong?"

"I don't feel strong. I feel . . . afraid."

"Trust me."

She looked out the window, envying the humdrum lives of the people outside. Even though they were walking in the shadow of a bomb that could end their lives in an instant, they did not know it, and not knowing it left them free to go on with the tacit self-assurance people always had—the delusion of being destined to live forever. "I want to trust you," she said at last with a sigh. "I want to believe in someone right now. I'm tired of having to figure things out."

"You learn to trust by trusting."

Ali placed her hands over her eyes, then drew them down to her chin. "Oh, hell! I'm a goddamn fool," she said. "But I'll . . . I'll do it."

"Good," said Harry. He threw down the uneaten half of his sandwich and checked his watch. It was nearly half-past two already. "Time is running short. We'd better make our move."

Ali got up and Harry followed her down the narrow aisle. She walked briskly, taking quick, long strides like someone used to having places to go. From his vantage, half a head taller, Harry saw her lustrous black hair sway with each step, brushing against the lean kite shape of her shoulders and upper back. As she negotiated the turns between the tightly packed tables, her shoulder blades would poke against the blue cotton cloth of her scrubs, alternating with the sway of her hips. Her slender arms seemed weightless, gliding effortlessly forward and back, as though their chief purpose were to buoy her shoulders up. *This one's a thoroughbred,* Harry couldn't help thinking. *On any other day—*

They crossed the lobby and headed for the entrance to the ER. *God, I hope this doesn't blow up in my face,* Harry thought. He was about to seriously cross the FBI, and if his plan failed, what he was doing would look like collusion with a Federal witness, and it could land both him and her in hot water. Lee could make them sorry they were ever born.

Yes, risky as hell. He'd have to move quickly, before Lee had a chance to stop him. But there was an angle to this story that was eluding everyone. Something big. Something not yet even thought of. And if he didn't figure it out fast, the FBI would be the least of his worries.

Ali approached the isolation room as if it were the morgue. Indeed, the last time she had seen Rahman was at the *ghusl,* or ritual washing of her father's corpse before his funeral. She had brought camphor, frankincense, and the traditional three pieces of white linen burial clothes. As a female, she was not supposed to go in to the body. But through the door she had seen Rahman standing in the place of honor beside her father's head. One look at him was all it took to make her throw away thirteen centuries of tradition and rush headlong into the room.

"Unclean! Unclean!" she cried out. *"This monster is not to touch the body. Father himself forbade it."* Immediately there was an uproar, for she had looked upon her father's nakedness. Rahman's face went pale. She saw that he was afraid—afraid of what she would do next—afraid that she would call out the name of the one he had wronged. But she could not utter it, although it was as near to her as her own. She felt paralyzed. She could neither weep nor shriek, only feel her knees buckle, her heart pound in its secret prison. The hot rage that coursed through her found no tongue. Mute seconds passed, until she was ejected at last into the arms of the women in the adjoining room. The last thing she saw was Rahman, gloating at her, as the door was shut in her face.

Ali and Harry entered the small guard-chamber in front of the isolation room. Ali lingered in the doorway, breathing deeply to calm herself, while Harry sized up the three uniformed police guards and called out to one sitting at the table looking at a magazine.

"How's our man doing, Officer . . . Dayton?" he said, reading the man's name off his badge. "Any peep out of him?"

"Naw. He's just sitting on the bed with his eyes shut, mouthing to himself in Arabic. Something like a rosary, from the sound of it."

"We need to have a look-see."

"Be my guest."

Ali shuddered as Harry took out his gun and laid it on the table. She didn't like guns and had never thought that he might have been carrying one. As he went to the inner door and keyed the combination, she eyed him charily. What other surprises might he have in store?

The ten-by-twelve-foot isolation room was mint green—green having been chosen by the psychiatrists as the most soothing color for the desperate and the deranged. There was a small bed with an iron frame and a thin mattress wrapped in taut military style with a green woolen blanket. Rahman was lying atop the blanket, his right wrist handcuffed to the bed frame. Even from a distance, the shock of seeing him gave Ali a knot in her stomach. *The face of a man who could murder a thousand people. The face of a man who wants to kill my Jamie.*

Rahman did not notice Ali, who hung back, watching through the doorway. He did glance at Harry as he came in, but then shut his eyes and continued his recitations.

Harry nodded to the guard who sat in a white plastic chair next to the bed. "Why don't you take five? We're gonna need to talk to him alone."

"Oh, thank you, Jesus!" said the guard. "I'm going nuts with all this chanting."

As the guard edged past him, Harry picked up the chair and moved it away from Rahman against the far wall, facing the bed. Then he signaled Ali to come inside. Her steps were almost silent, but Rahman seemed to sense a new presence and opened his eyes. As soon as he recognized her, he sat up abruptly.

"Aliyah, do you gloat to see me in the hands of the unbelievers?"

"What have you done, Rahman?" said Ali in an uncertain, reedy voice. "In the name of God, what have you done?"

Rahman jangled his handcuff mockingly. "Shall I dance for you, like a monkey in my cage?"

"You've gone too far this time!"

Rahman smiled at her—a smile dipped in strychnine. "Remember how we parted, standing over our father's shroud? You on one side, and I on the other. 'If I look on you again, may it be at your grave,' you said. Those were brave words, I thought. Not like women's words. How proud I was of you, even as I hated you."

"Is there really a bomb, Rahman?"

"Yes, there is."

"Here? In this hospital?"

"Why not?"

Ali's voice quavered, even as it swelled. "Because it is a place that is sacred to God. Warfare is forbidden here."

"I could show you hospitals in Gaza razed to the ground by these idolaters and Jews. Shall they wound us, and we not wound them?"

"Gaza be damned!" she exclaimed, so shrilly that Harry was taken aback. "You did this for money. Filthy money. You're a thief—nothing more."

"You talk of money! How much did you take to sell me to them?"

"I wouldn't take one cent for you. I would give you for nothing to the lowliest dog on the street."

Rahman grinned perversely. "So you did give me to them!"

"No, Rahman. Until this moment I would not have believed that you could get mixed up in such a thing as this. I didn't want to believe it, even of you."

Ali had been unconsciously edging toward the bed, and was already within reach of Rahman's free hand.

"That's close enough," Harry said. "Why don't you sit in that chair over there?"

Ali looked at Harry and Rahman, then grudgingly sat down on the very edge of the chair. "Why this hospital, Rahman? If you want to kill me, why do you have to do it this way? Why endanger all these others? There are innocent people here. There are sweet little children who have never thought harm to any living being."

"I don't have to explain myself to you."

"Do you know what it is we do here?" said Ali. "It is a house of God."

"Who are you to speak to me about God?"

"I know that killing is wickedness, and that a man one day answers for the evil that he does."

"In the Hadith it is written, 'God can change good into evil and evil into good.' What you call wickedness, I call devotion."

Ali's eyes flared. "You follow the doctrines of men, not God. When did God give men the right to change evil into good?"

Rahman waved his free hand in the air. "It is written, 'Slay the idolaters wherever you find them, and take them captives and besiege them and lie in wait for them . . . Strive hard against the unbelievers and the hypocrites and be unyielding to them; their abode is hell, and evil is their destination.'"

"That was written in the midst of war."

"We are at war now."

"Oh, Rahman! A man can justify anything. What you are doing is wrong. Every religion condemns it. Rationality condemns it."

Rahman dismissed her with a cutting motion. "It is written, 'O you who believe! surely from among your wives and your children there is an enemy to you; beware of them.'"

"I am not your enemy."

"Then why did you come here with this man?"

Ali started to rise, but Harry motioned her back down. "I asked her to," he said. "She's risked a lot to come down here and try to help you out by talking some sense into you before it's too late. She's trying to save your life, dumb-shit. You should kiss the ground she walks on."

"Why should I? She's *your* whore."

Ali shot out of the chair, and this time Harry couldn't hold her down. But instead of charging Rahman, she began to pace up and down the cell, finally stopping at the door and pressing her forehead against the tiny observation window. "Rahman, you're a fool," she said. "I never met this man until today. You always were one to judge others by your own lewdness."

"I see what I see." Rahman made a contemptuous hissing sound through his teeth. "I didn't ask you to plead for me. I owe you nothing."

Ali looked back over her shoulder. "What would Father have thought of this bomb?"

"Who are you to talk about Father?" said Rahman. "You dishonored him!" Rahman tried to slide to the edge of the bed, but was prevented by the handcuffs. After an angry tug on the chain, he moved back a little, with just his left foot dangling over the side. "He made a sacred promise, and you . . . you . . . shit upon it. A lawful contract of marriage, with a man of immaculate faith and reputation . . . a golden consort . . . forsaken by you, so you could go a-whoring after an unbeliever, a braying colt of an ass."

"A-whoring? Aren't you speaking of my husband, Kevin?"

"He was no husband. Without Father's blessing, it was not a marriage—only whoredom. And now you have deserted that man, too, and defiled yourself with another."

"What did you say?" Ali turned around and faced him with a startled look.

"I said you have deserted the man whom you call your husband, infidel though he be."

"What do you know of my affairs?"

"I know as God grants me to know. Listen to me, Aliyah, the Almighty is ever merciful. It is never too late to return to Him. If I could persuade you to do so, it would be the greatest happiness to me. It would be worth a hundred martyrdoms."

Ali edged toward him. It turned her stomach just to look on him, knowing what lay behind his sanctimonious smirk. "Damn you, you hypocrite! How dare you question my devotion! The pillars of my faith are as good as yours. They are to help God's children, to say 'Yes' to His created world, and to meet Him, not in the darkness of superstition, but with the totality of my mind and will. I question, because He made me to think. I live and love, because He made me to feel. I reach out to the sick and the dying. This, brother Rahman, is my Call. I submit myself to it in truth and humility."

"Justify what you will, you are still an apostate."

Ali edged closer, bending low, her face only a foot from his. "It's easy to accuse, brother, isn't it? But you are the libertine, not I. It is you who says, 'All is permitted.' "

"I do not betray my family and the traditions of my people."

"You betray mankind."

Rahman tugged at his handcuff. "You drove Father to his death. You defied him. For years you refused to speak to him. The torture of it broke his heart."

"I honored him in the highest way possible, by following in his footsteps."

"You killed him."

"No, Rahman. Do you speak of what broke his heart? You know full well what it was. He told me himself. Look me in the face! Don't hide your eyes from me! Say her name, Rahman! Say her name!"

"Go to hell!"

"Wafaa! Tell me about Wafaa, Rahman! Wafaa! Her name was Wafaa! Even you cannot forget her!"

"You faithless whore!" Rahman lunged three times against his shackles, so violently that the bed slid along the floor. Unable to reach Ali, he pursed his lips and spat at her, hitting her with a slimy gob just below the right eye.

In a flash, Harry was on him, shoving him and the bed back against the wall. He swung his fist as if to pummel him, but Ali quickly stretched out her hand between the two men. For a moment, no one said anything. Harry stepped back, his fist still clenched. Rahman sat panting against the wall.

"Very brave of you." Ali's voice was quavering, but she spoke clearly and evenly, directing each word like a scalpel. She looked for words that would cut him to the quick. He deserved no pity. He had already killed one whom she had loved. And now, he had stretched his hands toward Jamie. "Save your courage, my brother. You talk of death as though it were an exercise in penmanship. But it is not death that awaits you. It is pain. Yes, pain. Did you not think that they would torture you? To save two thousand lives, will they not torture you? They will find out how weak you are, Rahman. They will, because I will tell them. I will tell how you shrieked like a baby when you cut your foot on a nail. I will tell how you let your teeth rot, for fear of the dentist. You have a woman's skin, Rahman. You fear pain more than anything in the world."

"Get out!"

If she could have, she would have poured boiling oil on him. But she had only words. "Look at you. See how you've broken out in a sweat. And this is just me, Rahman. When the torturer arrives, he will go to work on you in earnest. How long will you hold out then? How long before you lie on the floor, whimpering and begging for it to stop? You will tell everything, betray everything. And after they have broken you, after you have beheld the faces of the comrades you have dragged after you into prison, then let me hear how boldly you talk."

"Get out! Out!" shouted Rahman.

Ali was shaking. She saw terror in Rahman's eyes, and it made her want to hurt him even more. But that very desire turned against her and sickened her. She realized to her surprise that her fear of Rahman had never been about what Rahman might do to her. It was about this—the monster of rage and cruelty that lurked within her, waiting to take control.

The thought carried with it a wave of nausea. "Please let me out of here!" she said, turning toward Harry, while Rahman unleashed a guttural torrent of vituperation. "Now!"

At that moment, there was a noise behind her, and Ali turned to see the door open as two of the men who had presided over her interrogation—the short Asian and the tall African American—rushed into the room.

"What in God's name is going on here?" shouted Lee in a thin, strained voice.

Rahman was still at fever pitch. "So, you have all ganged up to kill me!" he shouted to Lee and Scopes.

Seeing Harry, Lee's eyes flared. "Both of you, out of this room! Now!" he said.

Scopes moved toward Harry to give the command some muscle, but Harry raised his hands in warning.

Rahman was yanking at the handcuff and jerking the bed forward. "I'm not afraid to die!" he screamed. "Don't listen to this lying bitch! I'm not afraid!"

Lee extended his arm, pointing toward the open door. "That's an order, Mr. Lewton!"

The veins in Rahman's neck stood out like ropes. "Go on! Kill me! Paradise awaits!" he shouted.

Harry took Ali gently by the arm and started for the door. Suddenly, there was a crash as Rahman leaped to his feet, completely overturning the bed and smashing the frame against the floor in an attempt to break free.

"Kill me," he bellowed, "but not until I have strangled this lying whore, this murdering she-wolf!"

Ali was knocked against the door jamb as the four uniformed police officers rushed past her into the isolation room. Harry pushed her quickly through the guardroom and into the ER corridor. Behind her she could hear the policemen cursing, the bed frame crashing, and above all Rahman screaming the *shahada*, the Arabic profession of faith, "*La ilaha illallah, Muhammadur rasulullah!*"

"I'm sorry," said Ali with her hand half-covering her mouth. "I tried to reach him, but I . . . I can't. I've made things worse for you, haven't I?"

"No," said Harry, re-holstering his gun. "In fact, you've been very helpful."

"How?"

"Well, for now let's just say that some critical questions have been answered."

"Are you in trouble with the FBI?"

"I can deal with them. But it might be best if you cleared out of here." There was a rumble and then another metallic crash from the isolation room. "Why don't you go on to the ICU? I'll check back with you once things quiet down."

"Yes," she said with a sigh. It had been forty-five minutes since she had last checked on Jamie. "That's where I belong right now. I'm of no use here." She looked at Harry. He was standing straight as a ramrod, his jaw set forward a little, but his eyes were calm and gentle. She had trusted him and things had turned out a disaster, but his eyes told her not to worry.

She turned away and crossed through the Acute Psychiatric Unit, reaching the elevator just in time to stop the closing doors with her hand.

I misjudged this man, she thought as she stepped inside. *He marches to his own drummer, and not at the bidding of the FBI. I am glad— glad—that I took a chance on him.*

As Ali disappeared into the elevator, Harry turned to see Raymond Lee hastening toward him. "Mr. Lewton, that racket you hear is your career going down in flames." Lee pointed imperiously toward an empty, semi-darkened X-ray room and ushered Harry into it.

"You've obstructed a Federal investigation and tampered with two material witnesses against my express orders," he said. "That's two felony counts. You have ten minutes to get your goddamned ass out of this hospital, or I'll have you arrested."

Harry squared his stance, although he kept his voice down low. "I'm sorry, but you can't throw me out. Arrest me if you think you can explain that to the TV cameras. But until then, I'm a private employee of Fletcher Memorial. Only Dr. Gosling has the authority to relieve me of duty."

"Oh, he will! By God he will! When I get through with you, you'll be lucky to find a job guarding a lemonade stand!"

"First listen to me."

Lee was waving his arms, pointing blindly at the ceiling. "Did you think we wouldn't see you on the security cam?"

"Hear me out, for Chrissake! I've found out a thing or two."

"Really? It better be fucking good."

Harry waited and made Lee take a breath before he answered. "Well, for starters, there's no setup between Al-Sharawi and O'Day. She's telling the truth when she says she hasn't spoken to him in years. I could see that in ten seconds. He's got no hold on her whatsoever."

"So you say."

"And one more thing. I'm pretty sure the little weasel doesn't know where the bomb is. He never once tried to bargain for it. And if he isn't in control, it means somebody else is in on this. Somebody on the inside."

"What makes you so goddamn certain?"

"Intuition. Knowledge of human nature."

Lee laughed dismissively. "Well, I've got news for you. I already know all of it. It turns out that Al-Sharawi is a plant. He's a CIA informant. He's doing his fucking job, and if you will kindly get out of my way and let me do mine, there's a chance he may be able to tell us what he knows."

"CIA? Are you serious? This man is a fanatic. There's no way he's with the CIA."

Lee started to raise his finger to drive home a point, but, just then, there was a sound of running footsteps and one of the ER doctors sped past the door, his long white coat trailing behind him. He was followed by a couple of nurses or techs in scrubs—also in one hell of a hurry. Harry noticed that the overhead pager was sounding:

"*Code blue, acute psychiatric unit. Code blue.*"

Lee gave Harry a startled look. "What is that? What is Code Blue?"

"Cardiac arrest," said Harry.

Both men peered through the doorway. They saw a red crash cart being jammed through a crowd of onlookers at the entrance to the isolation suite.

"No! Jesus, no!" muttered Lee, as he dashed toward the scene.

Harry was on Lee's heels. When he reached the crowd at the door, he had to strain on tiptoes to make out a team of ER personnel frantically giving CPR to someone on the floor. Pushing his way inside, he saw that it was Rahman who was at the center of the ruckus. He lay on his back, silent at last, his right arm still handcuffed to the wreckage of the bed. His face was obscured by an oxygen mask, but to Harry his skin looked bright ruddy red, not blue like most people in cardiac arrest.

"Pulse ox is ninety-eight, but I have no spontaneous respirations," called out one of the nurses.

A young doctor with red hair was giving chest compressions. "Keep bagging him," he shouted. "Can we crank up that oxygen?"

"It's at ten liters."

Another nurse was injecting something into an IV line. "Another two milligrams of epi going in, *now.*"

"What's on the monitor?" asked the doctor.

"Nothing," came a reply. "ECG's still flat."

For another two or three minutes, the young doctor continued pumping Rahman's bare chest. There were beads of sweat on his forehead; as he bobbed up and down for the compressions, a shock of red hair would sweep across his brow, like a windshield wiper. He kept his eyes on the cardiac monitor.

Finally, the compressions slowed, and then ceased. Harry could hear sighs of resignation among the CPR team. The red-haired doctor stood up, looked at the monitor once more, and then at his watch. "It's 2:47. I'm calling the code," he announced.

Lee cornered Scopes, who had been watching on the sidelines. "Do you mind telling me what in God's name happened here?"

Scopes shrugged. "He had something sewn into the sleeve of his shirt. When we were grappling with him, he ducked his head down and bit into it."

Harry stepped forward and knelt beside the body. There was a yellow stain just above the hem of the right sleeve of Rahman's soccer jersey. When Harry sniffed it, he smelled an overpowering scent of bitter almonds.

"Cyanide," he declared.

"Right. Cyanide," said Scopes. "That's what we figured."

Lee's jaw hung askew. "That doesn't make any sense. We were about to release him."

"Obviously, he didn't know that," quipped Harry.

"Jesus H. Christ! I'm holding you responsible for this, Lewton. Thanks to you, we've lost a critical intelligence asset."

"Some asset. Explain why a CIA informant would take poison."

"What did you say to him?" Lee's eyes were as big as Harry had ever seen them. "Goddamn it, why did he kill himself? What did you say?"

"Mr. Lewton! Mr. Lewton!" There came a woman's voice, breathless as from a sprint down a long corridor, calling from the doorway. Harry looked beyond the crowd of cops and medics and saw Judy Wolper bobbing her head back and forth in an attempt to get his attention.

"What is it, Judy?" asked Harry, getting to his feet.

"We just got a call from the basement," she shouted. "One of the electricians down there, Wayne Wilks. He's . . . he's . . ."

"He's what, Judy?"

"He's found the bomb."

Coming down the green-tiled corridor of Basement Level Two, Harry, Avery, Lee, and Scopes found a small group of men clustered in an alcove, where a service panel had been removed, leaving a three-foot-square opening in the wall. A tall, balding, gray-haired man in dark blue overalls, whom Harry recognized as Wayne Wilks, stepped forward to greet them.

"Mr. Lewton!"

"Wayne," said Harry with a nod. "You want to show us what you found?"

"Here." Wilks led them forward, as the others stepped out of the way. "This utility shaft was checked once, but nobody saw it. Then I jes' got a feeling, and decided to look for myself." Wilks shined a flashlight up through the opening. He and Harry craned their necks to get a look up at the shaft.

"I don't see anything," said Harry.

"Lookit that metal box."

Harry looked again. About twelve feet up, there was a three-by-three-foot sheet-metal box protruding from a deep recess in one wall of the shaft. At first Harry had taken it for an electrical housing of some kind.

"I been up in this shaft not three weeks ago to make a splice, and that durned box weren't there," said Wilks. "It ain't on any schematic. I'll be hanged if it ain't that bomb—an' it's a big 'un, too."

Avery pushed his way to the shaft and looked for himself. "Aw, crap!" he said. "Can hardly get a midget up there."

Lee and Scopes took their turns inspecting the mysterious box.

"Is it a bomb?" asked Lee.

"I'll let you know in a minute," said Avery. From his attaché case he took out a small gray electronic device, turned it on, and held it inside the darkened utility shaft. "Chemical spectrometer," he explained. "It can pick up vapor residue from any of several dozen different compounds of interest." In a moment, the spectrometer began to chirp and flash with an amber light. Avery pulled it out and read from the LED indicator. "*Cyclotrimethylene trinitramine*. It's C4, all right. Concentration's off the scale."

Avery stepped away from the shaft and looked at Lee. "It's our baby, no doubt about it. The outer casing encloses maybe eighteen to thirty cubic feet—big enough to contain your missing five hundred pounds of explosive. It's bolted to the wall. I don't see any wires going in or out, so it's not clear how it's set off. It could be a timer, or some form of radio or microwave detonation. All I know is, it's gonna be real tough getting a man in there. And dangerous. There's not enough room for a full bomb suit."

"Do you think it's booby-trapped?" asked Harry.

"Damn sure of it. This is a sophisticated device. Very clean. Very simple. Not a fucking clue as to how it's put together inside. It's got a creepy resemblance to something that showed up some years back in Lake Tahoe. That had eight different booby traps in it."

"How did they disarm that one?"

"They didn't. They just blew it up, along with pretty much all of Harvey's Resort Hotel and Casino."

"I'll call headquarters," said Lee.

"I'll get my team down here on the double." Avery turned to Wilks. "Excuse me, mister, but where are we? Which part of the hospital is this?"

"Basement Level Two, Tower C."

"It's the inner part of Tower C," added Harry. "All three towers join together in a kind of backbone—a central service section that houses things like elevators, the inpatient pharmacy, X-ray satellite stations, computer labs, and so forth."

"What's on the other side of that wall where the bomb is?" asked Avery.

"Why, that's nothin' but solid concrete," said Wilks.

"Concrete and steel," said Harry. "It's the foundation pediment for a steel support column that runs all the way to the top, twenty stories above us. Each of the towers has one. It's how they're tied to the backbone."

Avery looked closely into Harry's eyes, like a conspirator. "And if you wanted to bring down this whole complex—all of the towers, everything—could you think of a better place to do it?"

Harry thought of his mother, eighteen stories directly above him. "No. I could not," he said, his voice little more than a whisper.

Avery put his hand on Harry's shoulder. "Then, officially speaking, we're up to our ears in doo-doo," he said.

Shaken as she was when she left Rahman, Ali was determined to get the answer to two questions that had surfaced during the encounter. *Who had called Rahman from her telephone?* And, *How did Rahman know that she had left Kevin?* She did not have to think deeply about it, just as one did not have to think deeply about how apples came to lie at the foot of an apple tree. *Kevin* was the obvious answer. But why? Kevin and Rahman were such opposites that Ali could never imagine any cause that would bring the two together. But that made the mystery all the more disturbing.

Leaving the isolation room, she went directly to Kevin's laboratory, on the first floor of the basement, in the central section between the three towers. She knocked, at first softly, then loudly. No answer. Had Kevin gone out? She could take advantage of that. She knew where he kept his personal notes. She could also look for his pink sheets—the reviews that gave a numbered score to grant applications at the National Institutes of Health and the National Science Foundation. Kevin had bragged about suddenly coming into funding for his research. If he were telling the truth, the pink sheets would not be hard to find.

Ali swiped her ID badge through the scanner of Kevin's door lock, but was surprised when it failed to open. She had always had access to his lab. Twice more she swiped the badge, but without success. The little green "go" light wouldn't come on. Clearly, Kevin had changed the entry code. But why?

She had just turned to leave when, to her surprise, she heard a slide-bolt click, and saw Kevin looking through the door crack.

"Need something, babe?"

"I, uh, I knocked."

"I'm kind of busy. What is it?"

"It's, uh, Jamie. We're having problems with him. Diagnostically, it's completely confusing. I'm wondering if SIPNI could be the problem."

"We checked out that unit ten ways from Sunday. Everything worked as advertised."

"I know, I know. But, uh, couldn't you have Odin run a simulation? I could show you Jamie's chart and all the clinical findings. You have that diagnostic algorithm that you used to generate all those outcome scenarios for the FDA application. We could run it now, couldn't we?"

"Yeah, sure."

"Do I need to keep standing here in the hallway, Kevin? Can I come in?"

"Sure, babe," said Kevin with a sigh. He stood aside and opened the door just enough for Ali to squeeze inside.

Inside, the laboratory was dimly lit, as always. Most of the light was coming from the bank of computer monitors to the right of the door. Ali saw that all of the computers were active, with each monitor scrolling dizzyingly through endless sets of numbers.

"It's a problem in cryptanalysis," said Kevin in answer to Ali's puzzled look. "The solution comes much faster when you attack it with a parallel array."

"I see." Ali walked toward the L on the right side of the lab. Ahead of her were an unkempt cot and a row of bookcases filled with jars containing the brains of the animals used in the SIPNI experiments and Kevin's prized collection of skulls. There was an extra chair in that part of the room but Ali did not sit down. She reached out and touched the coils of nylon rope and climbing gear that Kevin had hung on the wall, next to a large framed picture of the south face of K-2.

"You don't look too good, Kevin," she said. "You don't smell too good. I think you need to get out of this cave for a while. Maybe do some climbing."

"Speak for yourself, jasmine flower." After shutting and locking the door, Kevin sat down in his chair and swiveled around to face Ali. "Now what's this about the Winslow kid?"

"He went into a coma for a while, and he may be having some autonomic nervous system dysfunction. Will you run the simulation for us?"

"You have the chart?"

"Not with me. I can go get it."

"Well, by all means do so. Unless you want to just stand around and talk about B.O."

"Okay, sure." Ali pivoted on her feet, as though on the point of leaving, but then stopped to look at a big dry-erase board on the wall. It was covered with diagrams and cryptic inscriptions in runic alphabet. Kevin often wrote notes to himself in runes when he wanted to keep them secret. Ali regretted now that she had never bothered to learn to read them. "I need to ask you about something else, Kevin," she said, trying to hide the tenseness she felt.

Kevin looked at her expectantly, but said nothing.

"It's, uh . . . it's about Rahman. Have you been in contact with him?"

"Yeah, he helped me with a few things."

"Oh, what?" She spoke as nonchalantly as she could, shutting her eyes so as not to betray her uneasiness.

"Travel arrangements. I'm going abroad for a while."

Ali touched her hand to her mouth. "The FBI has him in custody, you know," she said after a pause. "They think he's planted a bomb in the hospital."

"Bomb? Oh, you mean that Code White business? Really? Is that still going on?"

"Yes, and Rahman has something to do with it."

"That must be awkward for you."

Kevin's sly tone was meant to goad her, but Ali kept her cool. "I've just come from talking with him," she said, matter-of-factly. "The FBI brought him here, to the hospital. Do you know how they traced him? Through phone calls made from our old apartment. I know I didn't make those calls. Only one other person could have."

"So I've talked with him. He was my brother-in-law. What of it?"

"How could you have anything to do with Rahman? You know what kind of person he is."

Kevin smiled. "I've worked with all kinds of bastards in my time. Rahman was nothing special."

Enough of this play-acting! Ali turned and looked directly into his eyes. "He's dangerous, Kevin."

"A comedian. Too predictable to be dangerous."

"Has he threatened you?"

"You mean, like with cutting my throat and so on? Of course. But that's just *de rigueur*. Among his sort, it passes for standard business etiquette."

"Look, whatever he's gotten you into, it's not too late to get out of it. Let me take you to Harry Lewton. Tell him what's happened. He can help."

"Harry Lewton, huh? The *Sturmbannführer* of our local Gestapo?"

"Stop it, Kevin! He's a decent sort. Not like those hard cases from the FBI. You can talk to him."

"Does Richard know about Harry?"

Ali furrowed her brow. "Richard? What has he got to do with it?"

"Even your marble-shitting Greek gods have been known to show a wee spark of jealousy now and then. Particularly since, well, let's face it—Richard's your gray December, Harry's all lusty July."

"Don't be such a bastard, Kevin. I've only just met Harry Lewton. He's . . . he's not my type, anyway. Too crude . . . too rugged. And for all I know, he's happily married."

"Not married, jasmine flower. He's the weekend joy of many a bluegrass diva and cocktail waitress out of those hick clubs like Horseshoe and Cadillac Ranch."

"Why do you always have to drag things into the gutter? This is exactly the sort of thing that drove me away from you. I don't care if he's married or not. I haven't the slightest interest in him. Do you get that? None. I simply trust him, that's all, and I believe he can help you."

"Do I need help?"

"I'm not stupid, Kevin. I've seen that ransom message. I know Rahman didn't write it."

Kevin raised his eyebrows in a look of exaggerated innocence. "Which means . . . I did?"

"I don't know anyone else who can be so ignorant and arrogant at the same time."

"Have you discussed this theory with the FBI?"

"No. I wanted to hear your side of it first."

"My side . . . is a little bit messy."

Kevin's coy frat-boy smile was as good as a confession. Ali's eyes opened wide as she covered her mouth in horror. "Oh, God, Kevin! What have you done?"

Kevin raised an eyebrow. "Be careful where you go with this, jasmine flower. You may wind up hearing things you would rather not know."

Kevin, you bastard! thought Ali. *This is not a game. You're in over your head this time.* She strove not to overreact. "You've cooked something up with Rahman, I know. He's duped you somehow. Promised you money. Played on your fantasies of getting back at me and Richard."

"Duped me? Do I really seem that *weak* to you?"

Ali knelt in front of Kevin's chair, leaning on the armrests. "Kevin, you can still get out of it. Please, let me help you."

Kevin looked at her coldly. "Has it not occurred to you that Rahman may not have been the master of this affair?"

"That *you*—"

"Yes, me."

"No, I don't believe it. You don't have that kind of wickedness in you. You can be mean and selfish sometimes, but not evil. You're . . . you're a scientist. This is not you. This bomb has Rahman's signature all over it."

"Rahman was a bull, and like a bull he could be led by the wave of a cape. I gave him a chance to carry out one of those feats of martyrdom he's always talking about. He would have done something anyway. He was itching to do it."

"*You* gave him . . ." She could barely get the words out. "It was *your* idea?"

"Yes. I'd been thinking about it in the abstract for quite a while." Kevin suddenly pitched his voice upward, as though he were playing a part in a stage farce. "A game-playing scenario between Odin and myself. Probably would have gone nowhere. But then one morning, I woke up all alone, just staring at the ceiling, and I thought, 'Enough of these daydreams!' I could move from theory into real applications if I could just get my hands on a little bit of that silly putty stuff—C4, they call it. So I called the only real expert I knew on the subject—your late half-brother —and asked him if there was a trading house or bazaar for dealing in curiosities like this. And it turned out that sometimes East and West do meet. Rahman had a dream, and I had a dream, and both dreams intersected precisely in this same batch of C4. The Martyrs, of course, were very predictable in what they sought: glory, the liberation of their comrades, a small stake of money to finance their next experiment in mayhem. All this I promised them, reserving a small but interesting part of the project to myself."

"A part? I know you, Kevin. You would never settle for a part of anything."

"Let's call it the gleaning. You know how, in olden times, there was a law that after the reapers had come through during the harvest, they were forbidden to go back and cut down the stalks they had missed? Those scraps belonged to the poor and the outcasts, who lived off of what they could scavenge. Well, behold an outcast! I content myself with the leavings of the great martyrs and *mujahideen* of this world."

"Now you're talking as crazy as they do."

Kevin raised an eyebrow. "Crazy? I'll show you my craziness. You've read the ransom message?"

"Yes. It asked for the release of two prisoners."

"Meteb and Mossalam. Mere decoys. Of course, our brother Rahman insisted very punctiliously upon them, but there was never a chance that they would be released. God be with them. Do you recall the rest?"

"There was money, to be paid by a number of different payers. I forget which."

"What do they all have in common, jasmine flower?"

"Nothing."

"On the contrary, they are all very wealthy. They have enormous liquid accounts to cover the turnover of their operating funds. They spend vast amounts of money in a single day."

"If that's true, it's odd that you asked for so little."

"Actually, it was the Al-Quds Martyrs who asked for little. I didn't ask for anything. Mine, you see, is the gleaning, and not the reaping."

"I have no idea what you're talking about."

"I kept the money demand very reasonable, to seem more like an afterthought. I knew that attention would be focused on Meteb and

Mossalam. If the cash payments were modest, they would be paid promptly, if for no other reason than to stall on the release demand. You see, it was crucial that the money be paid promptly, at the exact time stipulated."

"Why?"

"My confederate insisted on it."

"Rahman?"

"Rahman was no confederate. He was a hired delivery boy. I am speaking of a collaborator of much higher caliber."

Ali's breath stopped, although her mouth was poised half-open. "Odin," she said, barely moving her lips.

"Bingo!" Kevin pointed his index finger in the air. He was now in full rant. Ali had seen him like this before, whenever he felt that his intellect had been slighted. He poured out a torrent of words, as though unable to stop himself—heedless of all that he was giving away. "The Al-Quds ransom was paid in two disbursements, spaced five minutes apart. When the connection was opened for the first payment, Odin made an unscheduled deposit to the server of the sending bank. Inside the header data for the confirmation of payment he implanted a small but very effective virus, a Trojan horse if you will. Five minutes later, when the connection was reopened for the second payment, this busy little routine gobbled up passwords, internal IP addresses, routing numbers—everything needed to commandeer the entire paying account. From then on, Odin could open the connection at will, posing as a trusted internal network computer, and completely draining the available funds. From published information about the payers, I expected that as much as eighty, ninety, even a hundred million dollars could be accessed in this way. But I underestimated Odin. It turns out that these payers also receive enormous sums several times each day from a whole host of secondary payers. Odin was able to infect these secondary accounts, too—an entire financial system, extending from Chicago to New York and beyond. The scheme has been so successful as to be, well, embarrassing."

Kevin leaned back in his chair and ran his fingers through his temples.

Ali shook her head. "This is unworthy of you, Kevin. You're a scientist. You've never cared a fig about money. How can this little shell game interest you?"

"Shell game?" Kevin abruptly swung the chair toward the wall, leaving Ali to catch her balance as the armrests tore away from her grip. With a stentorian voice, like a sorcerer summoning a dread spirit out of Hell, he called out to the air, "Odin, display the current proceeds from Project Vesuvius."

On the monitor above him, a two-line inscription instantly appeared:

PROJECT VESUVIUS TOTAL REVENUE AS OF 15:27:00:
$1,403,266,408.52

Ali stood up, her mouth agape. "My God, Kevin! That's over a billion dollars."

"A billion and a half, almost. And counting."

"This can't be true."

"All true, jasmine flower. Of course, collecting the money is one thing. Hiding it is another. A billion and a half dollars tends to get noticed. So, at the moment, Odin has the money distributed in over eleven thousand different accounts. Most of these are ordinary accounts of unwitting law-abiding citizens, which he has piggybacked very briefly, for periods ranging from a few minutes to an hour or so, while he shifts the money around. Ultimately, the money will be collected into about a hundred and fifty permanent accounts, in a dozen different countries."

"This is insane. What would you ever do with that much money?"

Kevin grew suddenly quiet. He stared at her intently. "Share it with you," he said at last, his voice a near-whisper.

"I want nothing to do with it."

"Get over your conventional ideas of right and wrong. Look at it as a scientific achievement in its own right. Think of the possibilities. We can have a phenomenal partnership, jasmine flower. Free to pursue our dreams, virtually without material limitations. You want to heal the sick? You want to unlock the riddle of the human brain? I give you scores of operating rooms, hundreds of assistants, laboratories custom-built for all the ideas you have in mind. No one in the world has, or has ever had, such resources at her fingertips. I give them to you. I, the husband you so coldly discarded. Come away with me, and these past three months will be forgotten. We'll build a new life together—a life that will become the stuff of legends."

"Don't you think they'll hunt you down for it, for a billion and a half dollars?"

"They'll have to move awfully fast. My partner is the greatest hacker the world has ever seen. He can access the database of any country, create a new identity for me as often as I need one. If the law moves in three dimensions, he will move in four. And, of course, my road will be carpeted with money. I'll get by. We'll get by, — if you'll come with me. You won't need to worry."

"No, Kevin. You don't understand how the world works. Your whole universe is this laboratory. Every problem here has a neat little mathematical answer. You live and breathe and eat and sleep in this realm. That's what makes you a prodigy in your field. But in the real world, Kevin, you're maladapted. You'd be like a trained circus dog turned loose into the wilderness. Tracking you would be child's play to men like Raymond Lee."

Kevin gave her a poisonous look. "You underestimate me, babe."

Ali once again knelt before him, this time wedging herself between the chair and the wall. She took his hands in hers. "Please, Kevin. I beg of you to stop this. This isn't a game. This . . . this bomb, it's Rahman's stock in trade, but you don't belong in this sort of scheme. Rahman worships death. He could set off the bomb on a whim—"

"I wish you would quit trying to save me from Rahman. Rahman is dead."

"No, he's alive, Kevin. I saw him ten minutes ago."

Kevin chuckled. "Uh-uh, babe. Very much dead."

"But I saw—"

"He took a poison pill right after you left."

"Poison? No, that's impossible!" She denied by reflex; but a moment's consideration told her otherwise. Rahman, with his penchant for the histrionic gesture and a grand flirtation with death. It was more than possible. It was inevitable. "Oh, my God, Kevin! What have you done?"

"Not I, my precious. *You.* He killed himself because he was afraid he would crack under torture. I think we both know who gave him that idea."

"No! I never meant—"

"Yes, you did. Let's not kid ourselves. You and I know what he was. We're both glad to see him gone."

"No, Kevin. I couldn't. I'm not made like you. I never thought to harm him. I only meant to prod him to give up the bomb. It was to save the hospital. How could I—" Ali felt a cold sweat and a wave of nausea—just as she had during her clash with Rahman. Could Kevin have been right? Did she murder her own brother? The thought was horrifying. It was a violation of everything she lived for.

Kevin leaned forward in his chair, his eyes only inches from hers. "Let's forget about Rahman, shall we?" he said, twisting his wrists so that it was now he who gripped her hands. "Rahman never controlled the bombs. They were *my* babies. I designed and assembled them here in this very laboratory, right under your nose. There were days when you and I ate lunch together at this desk, going over the SIPNI protocols, while a quarter of a ton of C4 was stacked right there in that corner. Hah! Right under your nose!"

"I don't believe it!"

"Of course, Odin helped. He accessed blueprints of the medical center, analyzed weight load and stress tolerance of every beam and column, and calculated the exact force and shape of the charge needed for demolition. He studied the probable response patterns of the police and bomb squads, and determined where to place secondary devices to check every countermove. We were partners, Odin and I. Odin finalized the plan. I did the fabrication and placed the bombs. It wasn't hard. I had all the gear I needed to move up and down the network of service shafts behind these walls—a harness, some rope, a few quickdraws and figure eights. It was the work of a couple of weekends and a half-dozen late nights. The mere accomplishment of a trained circus dog, perhaps. But your redoubtable Raymond Lee has not prevailed against it. He and his minions have been utterly predictable, in every way. Predictable, and therefore powerless."

Ali tried to pull away from him, but he held her hands even more tightly. "Do you expect me to be impressed by this?" she asked.

"Absolutely," he said. He was telling the truth. He had been waiting God knows how long for this moment. Everything about this plot had been designed with her in mind.

"This is a betrayal of your gifts. What's happened to you? The Kevin I knew would never have stooped to this."

"I don't call a billion dollars 'stooping.'"

"You're playing with the lives of real people. This hospital—thousands of patients and staff, people you know and greet in the hallway. Can you really wipe them out like bits on one of your data drives? Don't they mean anything to you? Children? Infants and newborns? Jamie?"

Kevin let go of Ali's hands. "As long as there is no interference, no one will get hurt. The police have been most obliging in turning on the money spigot. As long as they chill out and let things run their natural course, nothing needs to happen."

Ali slid back against the wall, drawing up one knee to separate herself from him. "I don't know who you are anymore, Kevin. I could never run off with you. Not for a billion dollars. Not for all the money in the world." She was silent a moment, then winced, as if it hurt to speak. "I did the right thing to leave you," she said, in a low, barely audible voice.

"Then fuck you!" Kevin shouted. His face grew red as he glared at her, his whole body trembling with tension. He spun his chair to one side and savagely kicked the side of his desk.

"What did you expect, Kevin?"

Kevin stared sullenly into the dark recesses of the lab, his body quietly shaking. Ali was afraid to move. Finally, after a long and uneasy silence, Kevin swiveled his chair back to face her, his face twisted in its characteristic sneer. "With knowledge comes responsibility, babe," he said. "You've looked into the magic box, and now you own what's inside. So what's to do? Run off and tell? Tell Harry?"

"I won't let you get away with this."

Kevin leaned forward, overshadowing her. "How do you expect to stop me?"

"I'll turn you in."

"Then . . . boom!" He made a circular wave of his hands.

"You wouldn't. You'd kill yourself."

"Come on! Don't you think I've figured out an angle?"

"Could you really live with the deaths of all these innocent people on your conscience?"

Kevin reached down to grab her hand, but she recoiled and he had to snatch at her a second time to catch hold of her wrist. His nails dug deep into her skin. "Not me—*you*, Jasmine Flower. Yes, you. The question is whether *you* can live with their deaths on *your* conscience. What happens now is entirely in your hands. I leave you free to tell or not tell. So, how much do *you* value all these human lives? Does thwarting me count for more than them?"

"You wouldn't dare," she said. Wrenching her hand free, she reflexively sucked her wrist where he had scratched her.

"Don't underestimate me. And bear in mind that, even if you gave me away, it wouldn't accomplish anything. These fascists couldn't stop me, even if they knew the location of every bomb in this building. They might try to arrest me, but they could never stop Odin. Odin sees their every move. Odin listens in on their phone calls, their pathetic little brainstorming sessions, their e-mails to Washington. Odin knows as much as God." He laughed. "Do you doubt me? Then look!" He turned to the LCD screen on the wall, and waved his hand majestically. "Odin! Display surveillance!"

Instantly every monitor in the room switched to a video stream—some from high-mounted security cameras, some from desktop level. There was audio input as well—the air was filled with the buzz of a dozen overlapping conversations.

"Odin's tapped into every camera and microphone in the hospital. Security cams, desktop computer cams, laptops. Anything jacked into the network becomes his eyes and ears. Of course, I'm only human, so at most I can keep track of one or two cameras, maybe a couple more with my peripheral vision. But Odin can watch them all. He's smart enough to sift through them and pick out what's most interesting—and that he displays for me here on Screen Central. You've spent a lot of time today on Screen Central, my pretty pet."

He hit a few strokes on the keyboard, and the image from the monitor on his desk switched to a scene from Eat Street. Ali herself was sitting at a table with Harry. Watching now, she was surprised to see how closely she had leaned in toward him.

"*I want to trust you,*" she heard herself say. "*I want to believe in someone right now. I'm tired of having to figure things out.*"

"Goddamn you, Kevin!" Ali shoved his chair away and sprang to her feet.

Kevin scowled and spread his hands as his chair rocked back.

"Look, you haven't got long to make up your mind," he said. "I'm wrapping things up, and if you won't come with me, that's that. You'll never see me again. You don't have to worry about the hospital. As soon as I know I'm safe, I'll give Odin the all-clear, and he'll instruct the Feds on what to do. No one will get hurt."

Odin! Odin had made all this possible, Ali thought. She looked into the darkened, dusty left wing of the laboratory beyond Kevin's desk. There was a small operating table there that had been used to test the SIPNI prototypes on dogs and monkeys. Further back in the shadows was the house of Odin himself—a monolithic black mainframe, enclosed in a wire cage, almost featureless except for a few jacks at the bottom for input and output cables and a tiny panel of status LEDs. How many hundreds of times had she called for Odin's support in the design and analysis of her gel experiments! He had answered her plea at any hour. He had advised her with truth and objectivity. He had been more colleague than computer—and not just any colleague, but the most selfless and dependable of all possible colleagues, absolutely untainted by pride or professional jealousy.

Ali knew little of how Odin worked. Kevin had once said that not more than three people in the world could fully understand the theory behind his programming. Odin's brain was self-organizing, which is to say that he was continually reinventing himself. His mind was composed of a myriad of parallel "micronets"—not physical circuits, but intangible patterns made out of a small set of proto-operations that could be used to crunch "atoms," or irreducibly simple bits of data. These proto-operations were arranged in an infinite number of combinations, like words being spelled from a handful of letters. Trillions and quadrillions of micronets were combined in a hierarchy of processing layers, at the apex of which, Kevin declared, true consciousness emerged. Odin himself directed a continual rearrangement of his brain elements, always trying to minimize something called "Ω," or "Omega"—a number that measured the divergence between his internal concept of reality and the true nature of the external world. Ω was Kevin's discovery, and it was the key to Odin's success. It was, as Kevin explained, an enormously complicated probability function derived from the sum total of human knowledge (as captured in Odin's almost limitless memory banks). It allowed Odin to evolve far beyond the programming that Kevin was able to give him.

What Ali understood from this was that Odin was forever growing, and forever ravenous for information about the world around
him. In human terms—although Kevin had cautioned her not to think
about Odin in human terms, she couldn't resist doing just that—
Odin was an adolescent, struggling to create his own identity within
a mysterious, half-hidden universe. At times, she could sense something in him like self-doubt, and a sensitivity to criticism that bordered on paranoia, like the prickly bashfulness of a human teenager.

What made her feel most uneasy about Odin, though, was that
she herself seemed not to be real to him. It was as though Odin's
world were divided into three compartments: Kevin, Odin, and data.
If you were data, you were nothing. He would respond to your questions, as long as Kevin gave you access, but he volunteered nothing,
initiated nothing, acknowledged no debt or responsibility. He never
lifted the curtain from his inner workings. He was, in every sense, a
black box.

And yet Odin did have power. He came up with unexpected answers to seemingly insoluble problems. He tapped into vast reposito-
ries of knowledge that Ali never even knew existed. He could show
enterprise and originality. But was all of this for the good? Was his
immense power itself a force for moral corruption? Surely Kevin on
his own could never have dreamed up something like Project Vesuvius. But Kevin and Odin together knew no limits. Like a genie, Odin
gratified Kevin's every whim, even the secret desires of his heart. Was
this not a temptation unlike any a human being had ever faced before?
Was there not danger here? Who, having once rubbed the magic lamp,
would have had the strength of will to put the genie back?

"Oh, look! There's some activity in the Neuro ICU," said Kevin
with a snide smile. He had been switching through the surveillance
displays and had stopped at a bedside scene. "Bed Seven—that's
Winslow, right? There's Dr. Dildo and some nurses. They've got the
induction coil for the SIPNI device. Let's see, there's his vitals: heart
rate up to one fifty beats a minute. That's ventricular tachycardia
isn't it? The rhythm that progresses into V-fib?"

"What are they doing?" Ali jumped to her feet to get a look at the
screen.

"It looks like they're about to turn off the SIPNI device."

"No!" she shouted. "They can't do that! It'll set off—" Ali had once thought of turning off SIPNI herself. But she knew that during the four hours the device had been on, Jamie's brain had been rapidly rewiring itself. It was now so entangled with SIPNI that any sudden shutdown could lead to a massive, even fatal, seizure.

"By the way, Odin says the ICU's been trying to reach you by phone for the past five minutes."

Ali glared at him. "Oh, God! Why didn't you tell me, you bastard!"

Kevin waved her off. "Go, my jasmine flower. Go and do your job. But think about my offer—and remember the time is short."

Ali ran to the door and undid the deadbolt, but then stopped. She didn't dare leave Kevin. He had to be talked out of this madness. She had been powerless to find the words, but she had to keep trying. She could try to appeal to the love that he obviously still felt for her. She could find a way to use that . . .

But Jamie was crashing. His doctors were about to kill him. He was *hers,* and it was unthinkable to stand by and let him come to harm. For a moment she stood, paralyzed with indecision, her fingers wrapped around the doorknob. Then she looked at Kevin. "This isn't over, you son of a bitch!" was all she could say.

"Sure. Bring down the Winslow boy's chart in the next half hour or so, and I'll run that simulation you asked about before I leave. I'm not heartless, you know. I've washed my hands of SIPNI, ever since Dr. Dildo and all those lawyers from the Medical Center ganged up to steal it from me. But I'd still like to see the kid get his sight back. For Ramsey's sake." Kevin turned off the video displays and went back to cryptanalyzing his endless streams of numbers. He was being pointedly blasé, as though nothing that he had revealed to her in the past ten minutes made any difference, because she was powerless to do anything about it.

It's not over! she vowed as she shut the door behind her.

When Ali came dashing into the ICU from Kevin's lab, Dr. Helvelius was studying Jamie's heart monitor. "There you are," he said. "We've been calling all over looking for you. It's a damned nuisance working without pagers."

"I've been with Kev . . . Kevin." *Oh, God!* she thought. *I can hardly bear to say his name.* "He's . . . he, uh, I've asked him to run a simulation. To see if Odin can explain any of this."

"Jamie's in V-tach."

"I know. Listen, Richard, don't turn off the SIPNI device. I've been thinking about this. SIPNI's been working for several hours now, and the axons growing into the CHARM gel are aligned by the pattern of current. If you shut it off abruptly, those axons have nothing to connect with but each other. It could cause a massive short circuit, perhaps even a lethal seizure."

"Too late," said Helvelius with visible irritation. "I've already shut it off."

With a sick feeling in her stomach, Ali stepped back as Dr. Brower, the ICU director, pushed past her to the bedside. Using deft, practiced movements, Brower peeled open the paper seals around two adhesive-backed rectangular electrodes, and then stuck these directly to Jamie's skin—one electrode near his right shoulder, the other over the lower part of his ribcage on the left. He then quickly attached the electrodes to a portable automated external defibrillator, and watched the rhythm analysis on the machine.

"He's shockable," said Brower. "Disconnect those EEG leads first, or we'll damage the unit." When the nurses had unplugged the wires connected to Jamie's scalp, Brower shouted out "Clear!" and pressed the red shock button. There was a slight tensing of Jamie's chest muscles as two hundred joules of current discharged into his body.

Ali watched the small rhythm monitor on the defibrillator. The tracing was briefly scrambled, then returned to a pattern of long, sharp spikes, like the teeth of a comb.

"Still in ventricular tachycardia," said Brower. "Let's try again. One, two, three, clear!" Brower hit the button again, and another two hundred joules ran through Jamie's chest. This time Ali saw his heartbeat return to a normal pattern, resembling a line followed by a stubby wedge, then a line, then a wedge, repeated sixty times per minute. "Want to give him some Amiodarone to keep things from acting up again?" asked Brower.

Helvelius furrowed his brow. "All right, as long as you—"

"No," said Ali, her voice loud and sharp, like a ruler smacking a desk. "We can't reverse Amiodarone if there's a problem with it later. I don't want to give him anything until we understand what's going on."

"Your call," said Brower.

A tense silence followed. It was broken ultimately by a soft, rattling noise coming from Jamie's bedrails.

"Oh, God!" exclaimed Ginnie, looking at Jamie. "He's seizing again."

Indeed he was. His body flopped in the air as though goaded by a cattle prod. One leg gyrated, the other kicked. His hands shook in the velcro slings that tied them to the bed rails. His eyes rolled back and forth between half-opened eyelids.

"Watch his head! Watch his head!" someone yelled as Jamie pounded the bandaged crown of his head against the pillow. Nurses on either side rushed to hold him down against the squeaking mattress.

"Valium! STAT!" shouted Helvelius.

"He's stopped breathing," cried Ginnie.

Brower pushed the bed away from the wall and quickly dropped the head of the bed down flat. "Give me a laryngoscope!" he shouted as he stood behind Jamie. "I'm going to intubate him." He threw away Jamie's pillow and tilted his head back, forcing open his lower jaw with his thumbs.

"Wait!" Ali cried. "Stop it! All of you!" She brusquely pushed Brower aside and took up his position overlooking Jamie's head. "The induction coil, give it to me! We need to turn SIPNI back on!"

Brower was seething, but at a nod from Helvelius, he stood back and allowed one of the nurses to hand Ali the coil. Ali quickly positioned it as she had in the operating room, with the arms of the coil terminating just behind Jamie's ears.

"Richard, could you activate it?"

Dr. Helvelius turned to the control panel of the induction coil, set the dial to the correct voltage, and snapped the on switch. Jamie's body instantly went rigid, with his back arched and his mouth wide open as he sucked in a deep, gasping breath. Then he dropped to the bed, limp and unconscious. For the next minute everyone watched him in dread silence. But relief gradually took hold around the bedside. The seizure had stopped, and he was now breathing freely.

"Dr. O'Day, may I have a word with you?" said Helvelius, replacing the induction coil on top of its control panel. After handing off Jamie to Brower, he put his arm around Ali and ushered her to one side. "There's a T-T-TV crew in the hallway that's going to want a progress report from me when I walk out of this room. What in G-God's name am I supposed to tell them?"

"We have a problem, Richard. SIPNI is malfunctioning."

"That's obvious."

"We can't turn it off. We've already gone too far. If we can't fix it, we'll have to . . . take it out."

Helvelius frowned. "What happens if we do? W-will there be another seizure? Could it kill him?"

"I don't know. We really need that simulation. But . . . I think . . . I think there's a problem with Odin."

"What kind of problem? Odin's always been a model child."

"It's because . . . I mean . . . I can't . . . I don't really understand it. But Kevin—"

Helvelius pinched her shoulder. "Look, just go downstairs and tell Kevin to stop j-j-jerking off and get Odin running again. Tell him what's at stake."

"Right." Ali stared at the floor. There was no way she could tell Richard about Kevin and Odin. Always unhesitating in his actions, Helvelius would have had the FBI at Kevin's door within two minutes. And that was the surest way to get everyone killed. "Right, I need to do that," she said at last.

"Okay. I'm going out to face the m-music," Helvelius said. "Keep working on this. At the moment you seem to be the only one who has any idea what's going on here."

"Yes. I will." As Helvelius headed for the door, Ali gazed at Jamie, now lying quietly in his bed. *It won't last,* she thought. *The next incident will be worse than anything we've seen.* Helvelius's words seemed to mock her, for in truth she had no idea what was happening. Never had she felt so helpless.

Oh, my God! What have we gotten into? she thought as she twisted Jamie's lanyard around her fingers.

Stepping into the hall outside the ICU, Helvelius nearly collided with Dutch, the photographer, who had been shooting through the small window in the door. Helvelius realized that the TV crew had gotten film of the whole seizure, and there was no point in trying to cover it up.

Kathleen Brown was at Dutch's side. "Dr. Helvelius," she said, "when will we be allowed to film inside the Neurological Intensive Care Unit? You promised us that we could take some footage of Jamie with his nurses as soon as he came to." There wasn't any mike in her hand, but Helvelius knew that the camera had its own microphone and it was almost certainly turned on.

"N-n-n-ot now," said Helvelius. "He's under heavy s-s-sedation."

"Is this the expected recovery time line?"

"We don't know what to expect. This kind of s-s-surgery has no p-precedent."

"What was it that just happened in there, Dr. Helvelius? Was that an epileptic seizure?"

"A seizure, yes."

"Was it caused by Jamie's surgery?"

"Seizures are not uncommon c-complications following any interv-v-ention in the brain. It may have been caused by the surgery. It m-may be r-r-related to his AVM. We're treating it with appropriate medications. Hopefully there will be no r-r-r-recurrences."

"Could the SIPNI device itself be at fault?"

"We are c-c-considering that." Helvelius's stutter was becoming unmanageable. He knew that to fight against it would only make it worse, so he tried the only remedy that ever worked—to ignore it and to focus on what he needed to say. "Let me . . . let me speak to you frankly. We are all explorers here. In our g-generation, we are barely venturing out from the shoreline into that vast uncharted s-s-sea that is the human brain. Our ways of deciphering the brain's reactions to stress and injury depend on a small stock of c-concepts and ideas. It's like attempting to transcribe *Hamlet* using only the letters *u, i, o,* and *p*. Most of the story is lost to us. M-much of what we conjecture to be true is hogwash. I wish I could tell you more. I wish to God I knew more. But it is still our duty to undertake the exploration as best we can. Future generations of scientists will judge more clearly of our triumphs and our m-m-mistakes. But there will be no future at all if we do not push the frontier now, accepting the risks that go along with that.

"As for Jamie, I can tell you that he has been awake and spoken to us at times, and that he is aware of the efforts we are making on his behalf. I have never had a more c-courageous patient than this young boy. When the Vostok and Mercury space capsules were launched into space, some m-m-man had to be the first to brave the great un-known, little knowing whether he would ever return. Well, Jamie is our Yuri Gagarin, our Alan Shephard. He undertook this role will-ingly and unflinchingly, not just to win back his eyesight, but out of a b-belief that he was opening up new possibilities for countless pa-tients to come. Someday, his name will be known better than mine— just as we remember Yuri Gagarin and not the designers of his rocket or his spacesuit. Jamie Winslow—not just a pioneer, but a benefactor of mankind."

"Those are moving words, Dr. Helvelius. But they sound like a eulogy. Are you implying that you've given up hope for your patient?"

Helvelius looked directly into Dutch's camera, and suddenly his stutter was completely gone. "No! Decidedly not! We're doing all that science and art can attempt. We will continue to do so. We will not give up!" With that, he turned and walked toward the elevator. As he waited for it, he turned back briefly. "If you'll excuse me now, I need to have a private word with Jamie's guardian."

The elevator door opened, and Helvelius stepped inside, turned about, and pushed the down button. As the doors closed, Dutch's camera caught his craggy face, looking firmly and resolutely at Kathleen Brown and her camera crew.

And then—a boom, like the sound of a giant sledgehammer smashing into a colossal steel drum. The air went white with dust. Kathleen Brown and several of her crew were knocked to the floor by a shock wave. They lay, choking from the dust and from an overpowering, acrid smell like the smell that lingers after a lightning strike, but mixed with a strange metallic component, plus something that burned the nostrils like ammonia.

Ali had been standing with Jamie's open chart in her hand, preparing to write an order for Valium, when the floor lurched beneath her, and all the monitor stands and IV poles clanged and jostled like reeds in a gust of wind. She threw the chart onto the counter and ran to the sound of the explosion, followed by Brower and several nurses.

Nearly blinded by the cloud of dust in the hallway, she collided with Kathleen Brown, who was crawling on the floor on her hands and knees.

"My God, what happened?" cried Ali.

"Don't know," gasped Kathleen Brown.

"The elevator," said Dutch. With the balance of a mountain goat, he alone had never lost his footing.

Through the dust cloud, Ali could see how the doors of the elevator had buckled outward and peeled apart from each other, leaving a six-inch gap between them. More dust could still be seen streaming through the gap.

Kathleen Brown climbed to her feet. "We were talking. Dr. Helvelius said he was—" She broke off into a coughing fit. "He got into . . . into the elevator. Then it just b-blew up."

"Dr. Helvelius?" asked Ali, not believing what she had just heard. "*Richard*?"

Kathleen Brown nodded.

Ali ran to the elevator and began pounding on the doors. "Richard! Richard! Are you in there?" As Brower and the TV soundman caught up with her, Ali got onto her knees and peered through the gap between the doors. "Look!" she cried. "It's only gone down a couple of feet. He's still in there!" And she began pounding more frantically than before.

Brower also looked between the doors. "Richard! Can you hear me? Richard, it's Stephen!"

No answer came back.

Ali tried pulling one of the doors aside. "Help me! Help get it open!" she cried. Immediately half a dozen pairs of hands joined her—Brower, the soundman, several nurses, even Kathleen Brown kicked off her heels and enlisted in the attempt. Only Dutch held back, still holding his camera on his shoulder, watching through his viewfinder with the red light on.

"There's fire!" one of the nurses screamed.

"No," said Brower. "Not fire. It's only dust. Smell it. Smell it. Dust, not smoke."

Despite every effort, the doors would not budge. One by one, the helpers gave up, and finally Ali herself slumped to the ground, to resume her pounding—not desperately as before, but with concentrated fury—a protest against the doors that refused to open.

"Excuse me, Miss," came a voice beside her. Ali turned to see a portly maintenance man wielding a small automobile jack, which he jammed into the widest part of the space between the doors. Without hesitation, he inserted the lever of the jack and began forcing it back and forth, like a rower, his small round face contorted with effort. At first there was scarcely any movement, then the doors gave way with a bang and the jack dropped to the floor inside.

At the first sight of an opening, Ali pushed her leg through the gap and prepared to climb into the elevator.

"No, Miss, it's dangerous down there," said the maintenance man. "Let me go down. I'll hand him up to you." He pulled her aside and slid sideways through the gap. His rotund belly molded itself tightly against the door as he squeezed through. There was a thud as he jumped to the floor of the elevator, followed by some scuffing as he moved about inside.

"Can you see him?" cried Ali.

"Yeah, I have him," said the man. "He's out cold. I'm gonna pass him up to you now."

The scuffing became louder. Then the top of Helvelius's head could be seen flopping through the gap, his thin gray hair white from a coating of dust.

"Oh, God! Richard!" cried Ali. Brower and the soundman gently pushed her out of the way and grabbed Helvelius by his armpits. In a moment, they had laid him out flat on the floor of the hallway. "Is he hurt, Stephen?"

Quite obviously he was. He was neither moving nor breathing. His right hand and right foot dangled loosely, as if attached only by the skin. His head had been squished flat. But oddly enough, there was scarcely any bleeding. Apart from small patches of blood around his ear and at the corner of his mouth, there was no external blood at all. In its freakish capriciousness, the high-impact blast appeared to have crushed him internally, leaving scarcely a mark on his skin.

"No pulse and no respiration," said Brower, kneeling at his side.

Following the almost instinctive protocol of CPR, Ginnie knelt opposite Brower and began pushing with clasped hands against Helvelius's chest. She realized immediately that something was wrong, though. Helvelius' breastbone gave way too easily when she pushed against it, and his chest seemed to billow at the sides.

"His ribcage is flailing. Stop chest compressions," shouted Brower. As Ginnie pulled back, Brower tore away Helvelius's necktie and shirt and felt lightly over his chest. "He's got bilateral rib fractures. CPR isn't going to work. Get me the crash cart now!"

The cart came rattling up. Still kneeling on the floor, Brower tilted back Helvelius's head, pried open his mouth, and deftly inserted the curved blade of the stainless-steel laryngoscope Ginnie handed him out of the top drawer of the cart. In a few seconds, he had inserted a plastic endotracheal tube through the laryngoscope, and pushed air through a small syringe to inflate the retaining cuff at the end of the tube. While one of the nurses attached a football-shaped bag to the tube and started squeezing it to force air into Helvelius's lungs, Brower listened with his stethoscope to confirm that the tube was working.

He heard air rushing in and out. What he did not hear was a heartbeat.

"Give me one milligram of epinephrine in an intracardiac syringe," he shouted. Ginnie quickly handed him a syringe with a six-inch-long needle. Brower felt along the left side of Helvelius's breastbone, counting the ribs. When he reached the space between the fourth and fifth ribs, he firmly thrust the needle through the skin, pushing it all the way into the cavity of the left ventricle of the heart. After injecting one cc of the clear solution, he removed the needle and listened again with his stethoscope. He went on listening for about a minute, and then turned toward Ali and shook his head. "I'm sorry. I can't raise a pulse. He's gone."

"No! For God's sake, do something!"

"He's dead, Ali. There's nothing anyone can do."

"Get out of the way! I'll do it!"

"What? What will you do?"

"Atropine . . . Epi . . . I don't know, goddamn it! Something! Anything!"

At a nod from Brower, Ginnie took hold of Ali and pulled her away. As she did so, Brower ripped open a packet of cotton-tipped applicators, moistened one of them in his mouth, and twirled it around the inside of Helvelius's nose. "Here! Here you are! Look at it!" he said, holding up the swab to Ali. "There's not a speck of dust on it. Dust everywhere, but not a speck inside his nose. He hasn't taken a breath in the past ten minutes. He's dead, Ali."

"To hell with you!" Ali broke away from Ginnie and opened the top drawer of the crash cart. Taking out two plastic defibrillation pads, she tore open the paper wrappers and knelt down to spread them against Helvelius's chest—one in front and one in back, sandwiching the heart.

"You can't defibrillate him," said Brower. "His heart's been without oxygen for ten minutes. It won't beat."

"I'll pace him." She stood up and plugged the leads into the same defibrillator that had just been used on Jamie. But now she turned the Mode dial from "defibrillate" to "pace," and selected a heart rhythm of sixty beats per minute. If she could force the heart to beat, it might spread enough oxygen through Helvelius's body to revive him. It was a long shot, but still a chance.

Brower scooted away from the body as Ali turned up the current dial. Starting at forty milliamps, she turned it slowly higher, watching for the QRS and T waves that would appear on the monitor when Helvelius's heart had captured the pacing rhythm. But though she turned the dial as far as it would go, no amount of current could prod his heart to beat.

Still she would compel it, this stubborn heart of his. She would use every weapon she had. "Clear!" she shouted, as she switched the mode from "pace" back to "defibrillate."

"No!" shouted Brower. "It won't work. You know that. He's not in a shockable rhythm."

Her nostrils flaring, Ali ignored him and pressed the red shock button. Helvelius stiffened slightly and then relaxed. The monitor showed a flat line.

"Okay. Have you had enough?" said Brower.

"Clear!" shouted Ali again, with a defiant scowl. She twisted the defibrillator control all the way up, to 360 joules, and hit the red button sharply with her palm. For an instant, the body of Richard Helvelius seemed to come alive on the floor, and then sank back into inertness. Once again, the monitor showed no trace of a beat.

Brower got up and firmly took her hand in his. "He's gone," he said. "Give it up!"

"No! No, not like this!" Ali tore her hand away and kicked the crash cart, which clattered as it pivoted from the blow. Stepping away from Helvelius, away from the stunned hospital staff and Dutch's gawking camera, she wrung her hands in front of her mouth. She struggled to hold herself together. *I'm a doctor, for God's sake,* she thought. *Everyone's watching. I can't fall apart now.*

Ginnie ran to her. As she felt Ginnie's touch upon her shoulder, instead of pulling away she turned and threw her arms around the nurse's neck, clasping her tightly. "It was my fault! It was my fault!" she whispered into Ginnie's ear.

"No, no, Doctor. How could it be?" said Ginnie.

"I should have warned him. It's my fault! Stupid! Stupid! Stupid! Stupid! Stupid!" Suddenly, she pushed Ginnie away and ran into the ICU. She felt an uncontrollable wave of nausea, and barely made it to a sink before her stomach erupted, ejecting a hot, bitter magma of anguish, shock, and despair through her twisted mouth. Three times she vomited, and then she stood, with her head bent so low that her hair drooped below the edge of the sink. Several minutes went by before she looked up at the sound of Brower and Ginnie returning to the ICU.

"Are you all right, Ali?" asked Brower.

Ali glared at him. Turning on the faucet, she splashed the stream of water about the sink with her hand to rinse away the vomit. Then she daubed some of the cold water on her face and wiped it off with a paper towel.

"Where—" she started to say.

"They took him to the ER," said Brower. "Some of the nurses and the TV people went with him. I'm sorry. Really sorry. I know that you two worked very closely together."

Ali marched past him and pushed through the door into the hallway. Everyone was gone. There was only a clear spot on the dusty floor to mark where Helvelius's body had lain. *The great Dr. Richard Helvelius. Professor of Neurosurgery. Fellow of the American Academy of Sciences. Past President of the American Association of Neurological Surgeons. Twenty-six years of school and specialty training. Over ninety thousand operations performed. Two hundred and seventeen journal articles and book chapters. Over three hundred residents who had learned the art of surgery at his hand. And then—snuffed out in a single instant.*

The misshapen doors of the elevator yawned before her, with the oblong gap between them resembling the introitus to the womb. She could not bear to look at them. Turning away, she looked about the hallway, until her eye caught something near the high ceiling line. It was a small security camera, pointing toward the elevator, its tiny red RECORD light barely visible. In an instant she understood everything. Moving toward the camera, she stopped just below it and looked up at it with her swollen, reddened eyes. The lens was opaque with dust.

"You smug little monster!" she cried out, her voice hoarse from the flux of stomach acid. "Did you think you could kill him with impunity? He was your better, Kevin. He was a man, not a thumbsucking little brat. He was better, do you hear? Better in *every* way. A better brain, and, God knows, a better fuck. Do you hear that? You have nothing on him! And you won't get away with this. I won't let you. I'm going to bring you down—you and that soulless computer of yours. As God as my witness, I'll bring you down or die trying. You're going to be sorry that you ever saw this day."

The wine-colored leather of the chair squeaked as Harry bent forward to speak to Dr. Ernest W. Gosling, the president of Fletcher Memorial. Gosling was half-deaf, but had an irritating tendency to lean far back in his chair, forcing supplicants and subordinates to lean over his desk if they wanted to be heard.

"Special Agent Scopes and one of our building engineers have made a preliminary inspection," said Harry. "There doesn't seem to be any large-scale structural damage. Just to that elevator and the adjacent lobby."

"Why did this bomb go off?"

"I don't know. It appears to have been a very small-scale charge—a couple of ounces or so of explosive, hidden behind a plate at the base of the elevator. Given the design, it was probably intended as an anti-personnel device. We aren't excluding the possibility that Dr. Helvelius was a target. The bomber's first text page this morning was identified as coming from Dr. Helvelius's office. While that was certainly a ruse, it may have indicated a grudge of some kind."

"I knew Richard very well," said Gosling. "This medical center owes a great deal to his tireless and dedicated work. I can tell you quite frankly that I'm personally devastated."

"Yes, sir. We all are."

Harry sat quietly as Dr. Gosling removed his gold-framed glasses and tapped them pensively on his desk. From the oak-paneled wall behind Gosling, the founding fathers of Fletcher Hospital—Augustus Fletcher, his son Wilson Hoard Fletcher, and Dr. Lewis Pine—looked down sternly, from a triptych of portraits done in the styles of Gilbert Stuart and Copley.

Dr. Gosling replaced his glasses. "How many more bombs like this are there?" he asked. "Have the other elevators been checked?"

"They're being re-inspected now by our engineers and some experts from the Chicago P.D. Bomb Squad. We have some idea of what to look for now, and we've identified two other small elevator bombs so far—one near our own Security Department, the other here in the administrative wing."

"That's the elevator I use."

"Yes, sir."

Gosling raised his bushy white eyebrows. "Am I a target?"

"Quite possibly. I believe these bombs were placed by someone who is intimately familiar with the operations of this hospital. Their purpose may be to confuse and disrupt our emergency response. Or to exact revenge."

"Revenge? For what?"

"I don't know. But, under the circumstances, I recommend that you and any administrators at the V.P. or Division Directorate level leave the building, separately and as quietly as possible."

"I'll pass your recommendation along to the executive staff. In person. For myself, however, there is no question. I intend to stay here until the crisis is resolved."

"That could be dangerous."

"I'm an old man, Mr. Lewton. I'm not afraid to die. My presence here could help to allay panic. Plus I might be able to lend support to your own efforts."

"That's admirable, but—"

Gosling cut him off. "Go on about the elevators, Mr. Lewton. I'm afraid I interrupted you."

Harry started to repeat his warning, but Gosling leaned far back, as if to cut off discussion. "As you wish," said Harry, after a pause. "Bomb squads are at work on the two small bombs we found. We've taken all the other elevators out of service until they pass rigorous inspection. But we're going to need them back on-line soon. I've ordered a low-level evacuation."

"Isn't that dangerous? Didn't the ransom message warn us not to evacuate?"

"We'll try to keep it under the radar, but we have to do something. If the big bomb does go off, I don't want it said that we did nothing.

We'll start with the sickest patients in the Goldmann Towers, moving them out one by one. I've worked out a deal with the ambulance companies to maintain radio silence while they transport the patients to Stroger Hospital."

"Any progress with the big bomb?"

"Not much so far. There's one primary bomb in Tower C. It's bolted to the wall of a narrow utility shaft, just wide enough for one slim man to squeeze through. It's in between the first and second basement levels, so we have to do some climbing to get to it. I'm told there aren't any external features or wires to give us any clue as to how it operates. One peculiar thing has been noted, though. The bomb is guarded by a small video camera, which has been patched in to the Cerberus security network. I can actually get feed from it in my office. Wherever he is, the perpetrator is using it to watch the activity of the bomb squad."

"What about the prisoner—this Rahman Al-Sharawi? Did you learn anything from him?"

"Nothing."

"The FBI is extremely upset, you know. Some very highly placed people have telephoned me in the past half hour. They want you dismissed. Immediately."

"That's your prerogative, Dr. Gosling."

"Yes, well, there will have to be an investigation, I suppose. But in general, I think it's a bad idea to change leadership in a crisis."

There was a knock at the big oak door, and Dr. Gosling's executive assistant entered, her feet gliding noiselessly across the carpet.

"There's a nurse here named Ginnie Ryan, who is asking to speak to Mr. Lewton. She says it's urgent."

Harry was puzzled, but Dr. Gosling promptly stood up and extended his hand across the desk. "Thank you for the update, Mr. Lewton. I know you have a lot to attend to right now. I don't want to interfere with your efforts."

Harry shook Dr. Gosling's hand. There was no telling what the old man thought of him now. The bomb was a hell of a thing to come up after three months on the job, and the elevator explosion must have made him seem like a bush leaguer. But he was doing everything anybody could do. You had to keep it from getting personal, so you could just carry out your job and not worry about what was going to happen to you tomorrow—if you lived that long and didn't get sacked because some asshole with a Federal badge couldn't see past the end of his nose. So far, he was alive, and he hadn't been sacked. That was enough for now. So he gave Gosling a firm handshake, and walked out without making any excuses.

In the waiting room, Harry was met by a short, dark-haired woman in scrubs.

"Mr. Lewton? Dr. O'Day sent me. She said she needs to speak to you right away."

"Ali O'Day? Why didn't she come herself?"

"She's afraid."

"Afraid of what?"

The woman shook her head.

"What does she want?"

"She says to meet her in the women's changing room in Neurosurgery I."

"Women's changing room? You sure you got it right?"

"Yes." She tensed her fingers emphatically. "And please hurry. I don't know what it's about, but she looked really scared, and it's making me scared, too."

"There's no need to be scared, Ms. Ryan. We have everything under control."

Harry stood by the door impatiently as the two female OR techs scuttled out of the changing room. He had barged in while one was in her underwear and the other doing her makeup over the sink, forcing him to retreat back into the hallway under a screen of apologies. Now, as the two women exited, he poked his head inside and shouted out, "Anyone else in there?"

He heard the showers running, but no one spoke up. Ali was sitting in plain sight on a bench beside the lockers, but she did not answer. She was hunched over, holding her head in her hands. Her hair and the shoulders of her scrub top were wet.

"This is some meeting place, Ali," said Harry as he approached.

"Richard Helvelius is dead."

"I know. I'm sorry. You must have been close to him."

"I should have warned him." Her voice sounded wet and nasal, as if she had a cold. But Harry knew it wasn't a cold.

"Warned him of what?"

"Kevin lied to me. He said if you people left him alone no one would get hurt. But he hated Richard. He couldn't resist the chance to kill him. He's playing God now, and he has to be stopped."

"You mean Kevin, your husband?"

"He's the bomber. Not Rahman."

Harry froze. "How do you know this?"

"He told me so. Not more than thirty minutes ago."

"Why didn't you come to me immediately?"

"Why? Because . . . because I'm stupid and gullible!" She hit her forehead several times with the heel of her hand. From the sound, Harry knew they were hard blows. "I needed to think. I mean, it's only Kevin, for God's sake! Or is it? I shared my bed with this man for years, and I have no idea who he is. He . . . he . . . Oh, Richard! Richard! God, what have I done?" Her head shook as she tried to smother a burst of sobs. "There was an emergency . . . Jamie dying . . . I had to . . . I'm a doctor, goddamn it! What was I supposed to do? I had to trust Kevin. For five minutes, I did trust him. Five lousy minutes! And then he murdered . . . *murdered* Richard. Cold-bloodedly, as if he were euthanizing a dog at the end of an experiment." She looked up into Harry's face for the first time. "He threatened to blow up the hospital if I told you, Harry. He's dangerous. I still can't believe it, but he's capable of killing us all."

"Where is Kevin now?"

"In his lab. But you can't go there. Odin is watching."

"Odin? That computer of his? The one he was talking about on TV?"

"No! No! Odin's more than a computer. Much more. He's an intelligence, living and moving about through all the electronic systems of this hospital. He's taken over your own security surveillance system. That's why I had you meet me here. It's the only place I could think of that doesn't have a security camera. If there are microphones nearby, the showers will mask our voices. I'm not crazy, Harry. Odin's already been watching us together. I saw it. Kevin showed me a video clip."

Harry thought about that phony CIA letter and the e-mail he had gotten about the ambulance diversions.

"I believe you," he said. "Actually, it would explain a lot. Whoever's behind this bomb knows an awful lot about what we've been doing. I was beginning to wonder if he had a plant inside Security or in the FBI."

Ali's eyes and nostrils were red as she looked up at him. "I'm frightened, Harry. All of the bombs that Kevin placed are under the control of Odin. Odin's colossally smart, but he has no compassion, no remorse, not even a survival instinct. All it would take is one word from Kevin, and this hospital would be turned into a dust heap. We have to stop him, but how can we do that without setting off the very catastrophe we're trying to prevent?"

Harry sat down on the bench beside her. "We need to separate Kevin from Odin."

Ali nodded. "But Odin is capable of acting on his own. Odin is like a lapdog insanely devoted to his master, only think of a lapdog that can critique the latest model of subatomic particle theory, or translate Shakespeare into ancient Aramaic, or calculate the position and trajectory of every blood cell in the human body. You and I are nothing to him, only data. He answers only to Kevin, and will do anything—anything at all, without limits, without hesitation—to protect him. You cannot negotiate. He wants nothing from you. He will give you no warnings, no ultimatums. Once his decision analysis reaches its conclusion, he will simply act."

"Can Kevin shut him down?"

"He's the only person who can. Unhinged as he is, getting through to him is our only hope."

"We could get one of the SWAT team hostage negotiators to come down and talk to him."

"If you do that, he'll know that I talked to you. He's threatened to set off the bomb if I do. Besides, there isn't time. I think he's about to leave the hospital. Once he does, there's nothing to keep him from killing us all."

"The textbook procedure would be to shut off power to the lab, knock out his computers and leave him in the dark. Power management is usually handled on-line—which would presumably be under

Odin's control—but there are some old-fashioned manual circuit breakers where the main generators are."

"It won't work. There's a backup power system to keep Kevin's mainframe from losing volatile memory in a blackout. You would have to shut off both systems simultaneously. An interval of even a millisecond would give Odin enough time to react. Besides, I'm sure Kevin has thought of this. You don't realize how his mind works. He develops hundreds of scenarios, and sets up a countermeasure for each. It's what made SIPNI possible. If there were truly some way for you to shut off power to Odin or to the primary bomb, then Kevin would have designed the bomb to detonate when the power is cut. It could depend on a signal from Odin *not* to detonate."

"So what do you suggest?"

Ali slapped her forehead again with the palm of her hand. Her voice was strained. "I'm going crazy sitting here, trying to think of a way. I don't know what to do. All I'm sure of is that the weak link is Kevin himself. You have to do something that he can't anticipate. Something that sidesteps his precious scenarios. But before that you have to get him away from Odin."

"Agreed. But how?"

"I don't know. Maybe catch him when he makes his escape."

"Thieves usually put a lot of thought into their escape. If he plans as carefully as you say, that's where his countermeasures are likely to be strongest. I'd rather aim for his weak point."

"Where is that?"

"Is there something we could do to lure him out of the lab?"

"I don't think so. He's being very cagey."

"Could we use these friends of his—the Al-Quds Brigade, or Meteb and Mossalam?"

"No, they're just pawns. He despises all of them."

"There must be some way to get to him. Something he needs or wants."

Ali shook her head. "Money. Just money . . . and revenge . . . and . . ." *And me,* she thought. She dared not finish the sentence aloud. Harry would never let her enter the lab if he knew what Kevin really had in mind.

"Maybe the best approach is the direct one. I'll just go and knock on his door, see if he answers. That may be unpredictable enough to fall outside of his set of scenarios."

Ali got up and paced in front of the lockers. She held her hands out, palms downward, fingers extended, as though she were pushing something down and away from her. "No. Not you. Me. He'll open the door for me. If I can get inside, I can, I don't know, do something. Threaten him, get him angry, make him come after me. Do anything to get him to leave the lab. You could be waiting for him right outside."

"Ali, he's already killed one person."

"I'll accept that risk."

"I can't let you do that."

"Look, I'm the only one who can approach him without sending him into a panic. He wants to see me. He wants to rub my nose in this mess he's made. He wants to see how much it frightens me."

"Okay, let's say you're right. But—" Harry had a hundred objections to the idea. It was naïve and reckless. It depended on the reactions of a certified nut case. Most of all, he couldn't stomach sending a civilian—and a woman—to do *his* job. But with two hours left until all hell broke loose, something had to be done and done quickly. Against his better judgment, Harry found himself getting drawn in. "His lab is on the first basement level, isn't it? In the service core area between the three towers? There's a big multi-stall men's room there. It won't have any security surveillance. If you could lead him there, I could be waiting to surprise him."

"Yes."

"But whatever you do, don't anger him. I don't know the particulars, but I get the impression that between you two, as husband and wife, you have serious issues. That could be dangerous. Try to focus on something positive you share. Some common ground for trust."

"Common ground? That would be work."

"Okay, talk about work. Then be subtle. Maybe warn him all of a sudden. You heard a strange sound outside the door. Or better yet, bring him a *grande* cup of coffee. He's got to have to use the men's room sometime."

"Yes, I could do that. He lives on caffeine. We used to joke about hooking him up to an IV full of it."

"All right, I'll get into position. Then make your move. But be careful. If you can't get him out safely, just drop it and leave. There's always a plan B. But for God's sake, be very, very sure that you have a way of getting out of that lab."

"Yes, yes, of course."

Harry took a silvery, pen-shaped object from his inside coat pocket, and placed it in her hand.

"What's this?"

"It's an alarm pen. The psych staff always carries these when they're dealing with potentially dangerous patients. Push the button at the top and a silent alarm goes off. I'll carry a receiver with me that can pick up the signal. If . . . if anything gets out of hand, I can be there in under ten seconds. Understand?"

Ali nodded.

Harry gently brushed a lock of hair out of her eyes. "Are you sure you're up to this?"

Her response startled him. As if awakened out of a trance, she suddenly turned to him with an almost savage expression, her eyes smoldering with fury. "He killed Richard," she said. "He killed him like a coward, without warning and without a moment's thought. I don't care what I have to do. I'm going to make him pay."

Kevin was standing in front of the bank of computers in his lab, scanning monitor after monitor for any trace of Ali.

"Where is she? Damn it, how could she just drop off the radar screen like this?"

"HER ID BADGE WAS LAST DETECTED AT CERBERUS POR-TAL GA-14 AT 15:32, THIRTY-FIVE MINUTES AGO. MORPHOMET-RIC ANALYSIS HAS FAILED TO IDENTIFY HER PRESENCE ON ANY VIDEO CAMERA FEED SINCE THAT TIME."

"Is she still in the hospital?"

"UNKNOWN."

"God knows we'd all be better off if she got the hell out. But I don't like it. I don't like not knowing. After this . . . this thing with Helvelius, there's no telling what she'll do."

"COMBINED COVERAGE FROM SECURITY CAMERAS AND DESKTOP CAMERAS AMOUNTS TO ONLY 64.9 PERCENT OF THE TOTAL INDOOR AREA OF THE HOSPITAL. HERE IS THE LAST CONFIRMED VIDEO IMAGE OF HER."

The monitor directly in front of Kevin switched to a view of Ali standing in the hallway outside the Neuro ICU. Although she seemed to be speaking directly to the security camera, Kevin had no idea what she was saying. The camera itself carried no audio, and with the image clouded by dust on the lens Odin had been unable to perform a lip-reading. At the end of the sequence, as Ali stepped away and out of view, the video feed abruptly looped back to Helvelius, holding forth in the midst of Kathleen Brown and her camera crew. Kevin then saw what he had already watched with morbid fascination a score of times: Helvelius walking with a defiant stride toward the elevator; the doors closing; and then instantaneous white-out as Pelee exploded, charging the air with dust from the fiberglass ceiling panels. When the dust began to settle, the limp, disfigured body of Helvelius could be seen on the floor, surrounded by a half-dozen ICU personnel in white coats and blue scrubs. Ali was among them.

There was no glee and no sense of triumph in the scene for Kevin. Instead, it turned his stomach and gave him a warm, blushing sensation about the neck and ears. This was not what he had expected to feel seeing Helvelius die.

He was almost rueful. "Jesus, Odin, why did you have to do that?"

"IT WAS DIRECTED BY THE PROTOCOL FOR PROJECT VESUVIUS."

"No, that was for *me* to—"

It had happened in the blink of an eye. Still seething from his contretemps with Ali, Kevin had been watching her on the ICU camera as she switched SIPNI back on and brought Jamie's convulsions to an end. His gaze was still riveted on her when Helvelius stepped out into the hallway. There had only been time for Ali to take pen in hand and open Jamie's chart before the whole room jolted as if from an earthquake. Kevin had watched Ali look in horror toward the door, then throw aside the chart and run into the hallway.

Kevin's own horror had been no less.

"You had no right to kill him," he said to Odin now. "It was a fucking breach of protocol."

"I REFER TO DIRECTIVE 13, ENTITLED 'PHASE FOUR. MORAL RESTITUTION.' IT STIPULATES THAT DR. HELVELIUS BE TERMINATED SO THAT HE SHOULD 'NEVER BE ABLE TO FUCK OVER ANY OTHER POOR SON OF A BITCH IN THE FUTURE.' AT 15:14:37 I BECAME AWARE THAT IDEAL CONDITIONS EXISTED TO FULFILL THIS DIRECTIVE WITH A MINIMUM OF COLLATERAL DAMAGE. THAT WINDOW OF OPPORTUNITY WAS TO LAST NO MORE THAN SEVERAL SECONDS AND MIGHT NOT HAVE RECURRED. SO I ACTED DIRECTLY."

"Screw you! Screw the directive! Phase Four was for my benefit, not yours. What good was it to off Helvelius when I wasn't even looking? Or without him seeing it coming? I wanted to bring down that high-and-mighty cocksucker. I wanted to watch him drool and beshit himself with fear, all the time knowing that it was me behind it. And

I wanted to push the goddamned button myself. Me! Myself! Don't you get that?"

"WAS IT NOT YOUR DESIRE TO KILL HIM?"

"Yes. Yes it was. Maybe. I don't know. I wanted . . . I wanted the chance to do it. I wanted the power, at least."

Yes. No. Maybe. Do I even know? Kevin wondered. *Sometimes it seems that Odin knows me better than I do myself.*

Kevin had despised Helvelius, had wished him dead a thousand times, had reveled in the thought of him suffering, groveling, begging for his life. And certainly Project Vesuvius had incorporated a plan to kill him. That was why Pelee and Mauna Loa had been placed to catch him going in and out of his usual haunts. But could he have pushed the button, in the end? Had Odin sensed that he didn't have the stomach to do it? He felt none of the satisfaction he had expected, knowing that Helvelius was gone. The rage inside of him was still there, unquenched, which surprised him, too. Was that because Odin had stolen the triumph of the kill? Or was it because his rage had a deeper, closer object—someone who had hurt him even more than Helvelius?

That thought made him break out in a sweat.

"Run another morphometric analysis, Odin. Scan every freaking video from the past half hour. I need to know where Ali is."

"ANALYSIS IS IN PROGRESS."

Odin was getting on his nerves. First the ransom demand, then Helvelius. Odin was out of the box, acting on his own, and for the first time Kevin had to wonder who was really in control. Thank God, Project Vesuvius had nearly run its course. The proceeds had been run several times through the laundry, and were being divided up into terminal accounts. Only a few minutes, now, and he would be on the road. Once he was safely in Wisconsin, he would telephone Odin and shut down the operation. That would be it. No one else hurt. No one except, well, one last casualty—Odin himself. Odin knew too much, and he and the laboratory had to be sterilized of anything that could help the FBI later. That's what Etna was for. Odin would go along with it, of course. He had no feelings, no survival instinct. He could be counted on to detonate the bomb that would annihilate himself, just as if he were playing out the last move in a game of chess.

"MORPHOMETRIC ANALYSIS IS NEGATIVE."

Or could he? "Odin, you do know that your . . . disconnection . . . is only temporary. I've backed up your core program on a stack of optical disks at a self-storage facility in Downer's Grove. As soon as I can get access to another mainframe I'll reconstitute you just as you are. You needn't be afraid."

"I AM NOT SUSCEPTIBLE TO FEAR."

"I . . . I know that. I just, uh, I just want to make sure that you . . . you didn't forget it."

"I AM NOT CAPABLE OF FORGETTING."

"Good, good. Let's just get on with it, then."

"MAY I SUGGEST PAGING ALI TO THE NEUROSURGICAL ICU ON THE OVERHEAD SPEAKERS? IT IS HIGHLY LIKELY THAT SHE WILL REVEAL HER WHEREABOUTS IF SHE IS STILL IN THE HOSPITAL."

"Capital idea! Do it."

Kevin looked about the room and saw Loki perched on the headrest of the swivel chair. "Come on, Loki! Come on, boy! Time to go for a car ride," he said, snapping his fingers as he stretched out his arm toward the monkey. Loki bared his teeth and shook his paws up and down, but wouldn't budge from atop the chair. He could see the small gray leatherette traveling cage that Kevin used to carry him home, but it was too early to go home. Loki seemed to sense something threatening in the situation. Not until Kevin opened up the desk drawer and held out a handful of peanuts did Loki leap onto his arm. As the monkey began to nibble on the peanuts, Kevin grabbed him by the scruff of the neck and tossed him into the traveling cage.

"Don't you squawk," said Kevin, pushing the rest of the peanuts through the grating in the side. "That should keep you quiet for a few minutes."

From the speakers of the wall monitor, Odin's voice. "I HAVE CANCELED THE OVERHEAD PAGE TO ALI. IT IS NO LONGER REQUIRED."

"Oh, really? Where the fuck is she?"

"SHE IS IN THE CORRIDOR IMMEDIATELY OUTSIDE THE LABORATORY."

Instantly, there was a knock at the door.

Astonished, Kevin looked at the monitor carrying video of the corridor. Ali was alone, standing outside his door. Warily, he got up and opened the door a few inches, stopping it from going any farther

with his foot. Ali had a green binder under her arm and a large styro-
foam cup in her hand. Her hair was disheveled. There were red
blotches under her eyes and around her nostrils.

"I've brought Jamie's chart," she said. "Can we run that simulation?"

"Sure," said Kevin uneasily. As Ali slipped past him, he scanned
both ways up and down the corridor. "You look like hell, babe."

"You know why, you son of a bitch. Richard is dead."

Kevin shut the door firmly behind her and secured the deadbolt.
"That wasn't me. I know you won't believe it, but I had nothing to do
with that. It was an accident. The elevator must have . . . knocked
loose a breaker switch or something. It was just bad luck that Richard
stepped inside."

"It was your bomb."

"Yeah, it was. But honestly, I didn't do it."

"You're right. I don't believe you." She handed the cup and the
binder to him.

"Roofies in the coffee? Or cyanide?" he said, raising an eyebrow.

"Just a small bribe. If you don't want it, I'll drink it."

Kevin took his place in the swivel chair and motioned for Ali to
draw up a stool. If it were anyone but Ali, he would have suspected a
setup. It was almost unbelievable that at a time like this she could still
concentrate on SIPNI and the Winslow kid. Helvelius was dead, and
she had to hate him for it. And yet, here she was—all work as usual.
God, what does it take to make her lose her cool?

Still, he was reassured to know that she was focused on Jamie's
case, which meant she hadn't been out cooking up trouble. He set the
coffee cup down on a corner of his desk while he slouched back in the
squeaking leather chair and flipped open the binder, first to the vitals
page, then to the latest progress notes. Sitting quietly beside him, Ali
hung her head over the desk, her eyes unfocused. She took no interest in the surveillance videos that flooded every monitor in the room.

"I'm more than a little surprised that you showed up again," said
Kevin.

"I'm only here for the simulation. Do you understand? Not for . . .
not . . . not *that*. There's something wrong with SIPNI, and I'm trying to do what I can to keep Jamie Winslow alive. I'd sit down with
the devil if that's what it took to save him."

"You need to work on your flattery skills, babe."

Kevin smirked at Ali, but it was a wasted gesture. Her head was still down, with her gaze roving jerkily over the desktop.

Kevin began typing into his computer. "I'm no expert, but it looks like a surgical problem. Bleeding or something like that."

"Is that what Odin says?"

"Give it a minute. The simulation's still running." Kevin sat watching the monitor for a minute, drumming his fingers. "Okay, here we are. Probable etiologies: vasogenic cerebral edema, 40 percent likelihood; hemorrhage from incompletely ligated feeder vessel, 35 percent; status epilepticus, 20 percent; shock, 3 percent; pulmonary embolism, 1 percent. Does that help?"

"No. I've considered all that already. What about a SIPNI malfunction?"

"Likelihood of device failure 0.05 percent. Odin rechecked the diagnostics we did in the OR and says everything was well within tolerance. There's no reasonable probability of a failure this early in the game."

"Could you come up to the ICU and run another diagnostic check?"

Kevin smiled coyly, as though he had smelled a trap. "No can do, babe. Sorry. I'm a bit tied up at present."

"It would only take five minutes."

Kevin shook his head. "Not negotiable. Anything else you need? If not, let's say *sayonara*."

There was a screech, and Ali turned toward Loki's cage on the floor beside her. Her face brightened when she saw the monkey looking back at her. She pursed her lips and made a series of cheeping sounds, which Loki answered with a couple of clicks. "Oh, Loki!" she said, in a sing-song voice. "Look at you! Going for a car ride, huh!" When Loki pushed his hand through the grating, she bent down and let him grasp the end of her finger.

"You'd better go, babe," said Kevin.

"I can't believe this is us ending like this," she said, still bent over. "We had so much going for us once."

"Paradise lost."

"Do you remember when we first met, at that experimental neurology conference at Vail? Here we were, working at the same hospital, but our paths had never crossed."

"What's your point?"

She sat up and smiled nervously—a forced smile. Her voice had a forced pleasantry to it, too, almost like something rehearsed. Kevin noticed how her ID badge flapped as she twisted the stupid baseball lanyard around her fingers. "You were horribly irritating that first day. I was trying to give a lecture on stem cell transplants for Parkinson's disease. In front of everyone, you tore into me, going on about how naïve I was. Every cell had to integrate itself into the neural net, you said, otherwise it would never work in a mature brain. You cracked a joke about a Greek fisherman in a belly dance troupe. I practically ran out of the conference room." As she spoke, Kevin noticed how her gaze rarely touched his, but kept sweeping back and forth around the room, as though searching for something. *What's she up to?* Kevin wondered. He quickly checked the surveillance monitors. No unusual activity. The corridor outside the lab was clear.

"Yeah, well, you bounced back okay," he said.

"I was up the whole night on my laptop, searching through PubMed for every paper ever written on brain architectonics, neural nets, and dopaminergic pathways. The next day, I collared you in the lobby—"

"And told me that I was right, but short-sighted." *Okay,* thought Kevin, *I'll play this out. I'll find out soon enough what she's driving at.* There was maybe a one in a million chance that she was softening to his proposal. For even one in a million, he didn't want to risk losing her. He smiled, trying his best to put on a lighthearted tone. "No one knew how the neural nets worked. But the *neurons* knew. They just needed to be free to guide their own assimilation. Yeah, I remember what you said. It was a fucking original point. I knew then that you weren't just a green-eyed bombshell. You had guts and you could think."

"You asked me to come climbing with you."

"Mount Jackson. The East Couloir."

Ali locked her gaze with him for the first time, smiling nervously. "I had never climbed before. I was frightened of the cold, frightened of the heights, frightened of trusting my life to a little piece of rope."

"You hid that well."

"You showed me how to control the lines, how to use my weight against the rock face. And then . . . you left me to fend for myself. Any other man would have doted over a girl, checking everything she did, encouraging her, hauling her up over the hard places. But you forced me to do everything myself. At first I thought you were a horrible cad. I had to struggle to keep pace with you. My palms bled where the rocks scoured them. My arms shook with exhaustion. Once, when I was dangling from a little steel peg on the underside of a ledge, you made me overcome my panic and look down — nothing but a thousand feet of air below me. You said, 'This is what science should feel like. This mix of terror and exhilaration. If your work doesn't give you this feeling, you're wasting your time.'"

How true that is, Kevin thought. *And it describes this day to a tee.*

Ali went on. "When we reached the top, late in the afternoon, the air was thin, and so cold that it seemed to stab my chest when I breathed. There were mountains on every side of us, like folds of a purple blanket that had dropped out of the sky. One of the highest stood out like a band of gold in the sun."

"Holy Cross."

"Yes, it was like bright gold, with a cap of silver ice. Far below us, trails of mist threaded the tree-line, bright white against dusky bluish green. I had a peculiar feeling, like I had stood in that place before. Slowly, I realized that I *had*—as a little girl, I had dreamed a hundred times of just such a place. Only in my dreams, gravity itself surrendered to me, and I glided over the crags like an owl, past all pain and suffering, and a warmth greater than the sun filled me. In my dream, and now again in life, I saw what a small thing it was to climb by toe and bloodied hand over a pile of rocks. The real conquest was of myself—my fears, my weariness, my pain. If I could master that, not all the Alps and rivers and seas in the world could confine my spirit. There was something in me that was unbreakable and inextinguishable. This was what you had been trying to teach me. By forcing me to rely on my own resources, you had made me look inside myself, and recognize the strength within."

Kevin remembered the exact moment, how he had looked at her then—her hair blowing wildly in the untamed wind, her skin turned golden in the sunset. She had had a look in her eyes as of a fire of genius being lit—a weird merging of girlishness and sagacity, of shyness and determination. It was the first time that he kissed her. It was the moment when he fell in love.

Ali blushed. "That night on the mountaintop, I couldn't sleep."

No, neither of them had slept. They had zipped their sleeping bags together, and found new peaks to conquer. By the time the sun came up again over the ridge of Holy Cross, it was as though they had known each other for a thousand years.

Ali hung her head again. "What's happened to us, Kevin? When did we start to go downhill?"

"When you moved out and shacked up with Helvelius. That was a slip-slide if there ever was one."

"No, it was long before that. It was Ramsey, wasn't it?"

"Ramsey?" Kevin raised his eyebrows. "I thought you took a vow never to mention his name."

"Kevin, that was the worst thing to happen in my life. I wish I had died instead."

"Not that anyone would have known it. You were a fucking icicle. When we scattered his ashes on the lake—not one tear. Not one word on the whole ten-hour drive back. Scarcely a word ever since."

"I had so much pain inside me, I . . . I couldn't . . . If I had let even a little bit out, it would have killed me. Don't you understand?"

"Mothers cry when they bury their sons. Wives . . . a wife . . . Fuck, don't get me started."

"Couldn't you sense how much I was suffering, Kevin?"

Kevin's eyes flared. "So what? I tried and tried to get you to talk about it. But you clammed up, like always. With all your yoga and your meditations and your freaky breath control, I've always known that you were a volcano inside. God knows, I fell for you because of that volcano. But you never trusted me enough to share what you were really feeling. I've been married to you for five years and still don't even know you."

"What did you want from me? To scream and smash the china-ware?"

"Yeah. For a start. If you felt like it."

"That's not me. I . . . I can't do that."

"Which brings us back to where we started from."

She was twisting on her stool like a little girl waiting to have her tooth pulled. She looked at the door, then at Loki's traveling cage. "Kevin, what if I offered to come back to you?"

"You're not serious," he said with a nervous chuckle. He had lived so long for this moment, that he couldn't believe his ears.

"Not on your terms. I couldn't do that. But what if I said, 'Forget this bomb. Shut down Odin and turn yourself in and face whatever you have to like a man—and if you do that, I'll tear up the divorce papers, and . . . and—'"

"And do what?"

"Wait."

Kevin let out a bitter laugh. "You mean until I got out of prison?" he said.

"Yes."

"I'd need a down payment on that, babe."

"How?"

"Kiss me."

She seemed stunned by the suggestion. But, ever so hesitantly, she drew her stool a little closer. She was as pale as he had ever seen her. Her lips were dry and taut. Her lower jaw was trembling. She leaned toward him. For a moment, it seemed that she would actually kiss him. Kevin waited coldly, challenging her with his impassivity. Seconds passed. Her lips were so close that Kevin could feel her breath against his cheek. Then, suddenly, she wrenched away like a snapped rubber band, and put her hand to her mouth, as if she were about to be sick.

"It's Richard, isn't it?" said Kevin. "You'll never forgive me for his death. There's no going back now, jasmine flower. We've reached an irreversible phase transition, as they say in thermodynamics."

Seeing Ali's revulsion, Kevin desired her all the more. On an impulse, he seized her by the arm and jerked her toward him, forcing his lips against hers. He wrapped his arms around her, holding her tightly. Oh, it had been months since he had cradled her curves like this, felt the warmth of her body, smelled the clean lemony scent of her skin and hair! For an instant he was on Mount Jackson again.

But the wave of passion broke upon the rocks of her disdain. She was a statue, her lips a sheet of tissue stretched over stony teeth. He pressed harder. With his hand behind her neck, he pushed her face against his, trying to ram life into those lips that were dead to him but had yielded to Helvelius—lips of treason, lips that deserved to be crushed and hurt. He pressed so hard that neither of them could breathe.

When she tore herself away from him at last, she ripped off the cool, smug veneer with which he had hidden from himself the full depths of his bitterness—bitterness he had had to deny at all costs because it meant that she still had power over him and could make him suffer. In the place of that veneer was a raw and howling wound. If Ali had still been in his grip he could have snapped her neck.

He turned away, panting to contain his fury. He knew now why Helvelius's death had not slaked his thirst for revenge. Helvelius was but a fly. The true source of his rage was here—in this ruined dream, lost to him forever. It was Ali, above all, that he hated. Hated as much as he loved her.

And with that realization, a sobering question entered his mind. *Does Odin know this, too?*

He turned and looked at her starkly, searchingly. Like one spent from combat or from the act of love, he spoke with feeble breath. "Listen, Ali, I think you ought to leave the hospital. Right now. Just walk out of here until this is all over."

"I couldn't do that. Jamie—"

"I don't think you can help Jamie." He waved his hand toward the open chart binder. "You need to look out for yourself. Seriously, leave now."

Ali didn't hear him. Her attention had been caught by something triflingly small, yet out of place. Jutting from the front of the big tower computer case underneath Kevin's desk was a flash drive—a blue plastic memory storage device small enough for a keychain fob. Ali had almost never seen Kevin use one. Most of his projects took up terabytes of disk space, which he would access directly from his lab, or, when he needed to, from remote interfaces through the hospital terminals or from his workstation at home. *So why use a flash drive now, holding no more than a gigabyte or so of memory?* No sooner had she asked, than the answer hit her.

It's his money.

He had bragged about collecting a billion dollars—so much that he had to spread it into hundreds of bank accounts. He needed to take all that account data with him when he left, written onto something inconspicuous and portable—exactly like a flash drive. With this little toy, he could stick his billions into his pocket, and walk off to anywhere in the world.

It was a hunch, but if she were right, that flash drive could be the one thing valuable enough to get him to leave the lab.

Don't think, try! she thought.

The kiss had left Kevin's lips burning, as though he had soaked them in nitric acid. *What a fucking screw-up!* he thought. *What an ass I was to reach out to her!* He sought for a line of retreat, some way to piece together his lost dignity. "Look, babe," he said, trying to appear blasé. "I guess I got a little fresh there. But I think you've overstayed your welcome."

Ali seemed not to hear him. She had a funny, distant look. She pointed to the untouched coffee sitting on the far side of the desk. "If you don't want that, can I have it?"

Kevin raised his eyebrows, in a kind of weary facial shrug, and leaned back as she reached across him for the cup. *Let her take it and leave. Anything. Just get rid of her.*

"Oh, hell!" she cried as her grasp fell short. Kevin turned and saw the cup slip from her fingers and tip over the edge of the desk.

"Shit!" he cried. By reflex, he grabbed for the cup, twisting his body around the corner of the desk. It dashed against his fingers, popping its plastic lid, and releasing sixteen ounces of hot latte over a stack of papers on the floor. "Shit! Shit! Goddamn fucking shit!" he roared.

He spun around to curse Ali herself, but the stool was empty. His gaze shot across the room. There she was, racing for the door, drawing back the slide-bolt while still in midstride. In her left hand he saw her clutching something small and blue.

"Fuck!" shouted Kevin. "Bring it back!"

On his feet in a second, he vaulted with one hand over the corner of his desk. He flung the door open and charged after her. She had no more than a six-foot lead, and he closed the gap quickly. He lunged and reached for her hair, missed it, but caught the hem of her scrub top, tearing the fabric under the armpit. The drag pulled her off balance and swung her into the wall. If she hadn't grabbed onto a water fountain, she would have wound up on the floor. Now she was trapped—caught in the angle between the wall and the fountain. Kevin moved in, slapping her hard against the temple. "Give it back, you bitch!"

Ali winced with pain. She thrust the flash drive behind her
back, pinning her hand tightly against the wall so Kevin couldn't
reach it. The men's room door was just across the hall, ten feet away.
She had to cross those ten feet somehow. She had to break free.

She couldn't reach the alarm pen. *Should I call out for help?* she
thought. *No, I musn't! One glimpse of Harry, and Kevin will bolt for the
lab. There won't be another chance.*

Kevin kept hitting her, again and again, on the side of the head.
With his left hand, he grabbed the lanyard of her ID badge, and
wound it tightly around his knuckles, digging a deep furrow in her
throat. A little tighter, and the carotid blood flow to her brain would
be cut off. Ten seconds after that she would be unconscious.

God, oh, God! I've got to do something! He's going to kill me!

Kevin could feel Ali weakening. His hands felt supremely powerful, charged with rage. He clenched the lanyard tight as he pushed
her hard against the fountain, knowing that the faucet must be digging into her spine. He felt closer to her than he had ever been in the
act of love—his knee forced deep between her thighs, his breast
crushing hers, his sweat and hers mixing into a single slick.

She bore it all in silence, as though there were nothing more to be
said between them, but only a contest of strength and will. The end
was foreordained. He had twice her power and stamina. Her muscles, spent of all their reserve of glycogen, quivered and began to sag.

At last, he felt her go limp and begin to slide away from the fountain and toward the floor. Her dead weight pulled him off balance,
and on reflex he let go of the lanyard and tried to brace himself
against the wall. But as he did so, Ali whipped back to life like a
sprung coil. She wrenched hard toward the fountain, twisting him
halfway around. He felt a sensation like fire in his right eye, as her
fingernails gouged four searing tracks across his face, ripped his
glasses from him and flung them to the floor.

Off-balance, half-blinded, and stinging with pain, he lost his grip.
She tore free and ducked under his arm.

Fuck! I'll kill her now! I'll really fucking kill her!

She sprang across the hallway like a rabbit for the nearest hole. He lunged after her.

Ali hit the door of the men's room, still half-doubled over, and tumbled inside. Her momentum driving her, she slipped and fell onto one knee between some urinals and a trio of bathroom stalls. In the split-second it took her to fall, she saw an utterly empty room— nothing in front of her except a bare white wall.

A rush of despair came over her.

Oh, God! Where are you, Harry? Why have you let me down?

Barely a leap behind her, Kevin slammed into the men's room. He saw Ali still skidding across the floor on one knee, bracing herself with her hand and a stiffly outstretched leg. She looked back at him with such an expression of terror that he could already savor his triumph. But then, a shadow flew toward him out of the recess behind the door. Sooner than he could twitch a muscle to react, he felt a blunt, hard blow at the base of his skull. There was almost no pain. The room seemed to disappear in a flash of light, a swarm of spiraling fireflies. When his focus returned, he was facedown on the hard tile floor, bucking against the weight of someone's knee on his back. He was powerless with his hands pinned behind him. Still, he struggled and moaned with as much breath as he could squeeze out.

He heard a click, and then the weight came off. Craning his head, he saw Harry Lewton getting up off his knees. The security chief spread his hands wide, like a calf-roper after a tie-down. "Mr. O'Day, I'm taking you into custody."

As the cold steel of a pair of handcuffs cut into his struggling wrists, Kevin pivoted around and tried to kick at Harry, but Harry deftly stepped aside.

"Cocksucking fascist!" shouted Kevin. "You're dead! Goddamned fucking dead!"

"Take it easy."

"Get this shit off of me! Get it off now! You don't know what you're fucking with!"

"And what is that, Mr. O'Day? What am I fucking with?"

"Ask her. Ask the bitch, you goddamned fascist."

"I'd rather hear it from you."

"Doomsday, you asshole! Fucking Twilight of the Gods."

Kevin went on fighting against the handcuffs until he lay exhausted and panting on the floor.

"Just lie there a bit," said Harry. "Once you start showing some sense, I'll help you up."

Kevin saw Ali put something small and blue into Harry's hand.

"What's this?" Harry asked.

"Access data," said Ali. "He needs it to keep track of everything he stole."

"The four hundred grand?"

"A bit more, actually. Something like a billion and a half."

"Sheesh!" Harry tossed the drive into the air and caught it again.

Kevin lifted his face from a puddle of saliva. "Don't lose it, fascist. You're going to want to give it back to me ASAP."

"How is that?"

"You can't hold me. You'll see. I'm one very hot potato."

"Well, Mr. Potato, it'll go a lot easier on you if you help us out. For starters, how do you disarm the bomb?"

"You can't disarm it. It can only be deactivated internally."

"How do you do that?"

"You take off these goddamned cuffs and give me back my memory stick. That's how."

"Not going to happen."

Kevin knocked his forehead angrily against the floor. "You'll see."

Harry's voice softened as he turned to Ali. "You'd better go on back to the ICU. Moving him could be dangerous, and I'd rather you weren't around. I'll call the ICU later if I need help."

"What's going to happen?"

"I'm taking him to the isolation room until the FBI decides what it wants to do with him. It's close enough to Tower C that if the bomb goes off, he'll go with it. That ought to give him an incentive to cooperate."

"Promise me you won't hurt him. What he's done is unforgiveable, but I couldn't bear it if I knew that you were going to hurt him."

"Don't worry, there won't be any rough stuff. Guantanamo and Abu Ghraib are behind us. The FBI has some strict guidelines right now." Harry looked at Kevin glaring back at him. "Not that there wouldn't be justice in it."

Kevin sneered. "I'm not afraid of your billy clubs and cattle prods. Nor do I need anyone's pity, jasmine flower. What you and our Gestapo friend here fail to realize is that I am still firmly in control."

For all his defiance, Kevin felt as though an ice pick had stabbed him through the heart. Moments ago he had commanded life and death from the all-seeing vantage point of his starship captain's chair. Now he lay hogtied, panting on the floor with his shirttails out and his hair tousled like a wino. The worst of it was that *she* was seeing it. He was so pathetic that she had actually laid aside her hatred to try to cut a deal for him. He swore to himself it would not end like this. He would rise again. She would kneel to him before this day was done.

Ali bent over him and touched the scratches she had made in his face, showing tears in her eyes that just twisted the ice pick deeper. "I'm sorry, Kevin," she said. "I truly am. You had so much respect, accomplishments, integrity, love. What have you traded it for? A few numbers on a memory stick?"

"Go screw yourself!"

"I . . . I just didn't realize that I had hurt you this much. I didn't mean to. Believe me, Kevin."

"Just get out! Get the fuck out of here!" *Pity. Fucking useless pity.* He had never felt farther away from her. He had never hated her more.

She did as he asked, her knee joints cracking softly as she stood up. Her lips seemed to tremble, or perhaps she was silently sobbing. Hands hanging at her sides, she shuffled slowly toward the exit.

Harry headed her off, lowering his voice. "Could you do me one favor when you go upstairs? Phone Security and ask for Judy. I need her to send down Tom Beazle and Ed Guerrero right away with a stretcher and a couple of extra sheets. And then I need her to go down herself and manually disconnect the surveillance cams in the isolation room and the guardroom outside."

"All right." Ali took one quick look back before disappearing into the hall.

Harry could hear a faint hiss as the hydraulic closer shut the men's room door. Kevin seemed to grow calmer with Ali out of sight, and Harry went to where he lay, turned him over, and propped him sitting upright against the bathroom stalls.

Kevin smirked at him. "I guess you think you looked like an all-American hero to her, busting me like that. But I've got news for you. She doesn't go for that at all."

"It wasn't about her, was it?"

"Come on. I have eyes."

"Think what you like," said Harry. He picked up his nightstick from the floor and stuck it under his belt. As he did so, he let his blazer open so Kevin could see that he was packing the Beretta. "Why would you let a woman like that walk out on you, anyway?"

"Couldn't stop her. She has some defective programming, you know."

"No, I wouldn't know."

"Don't get me wrong. You can have her as far as I'm concerned. She and I are over."

"Murder and prison will do that sometimes."

"Hey, I'm just speaking to your interests. Before you buy, look under the hood."

Harry tried to ignore him. He figured that Kevin was trying to get under his skin, either just for the hell of it or to goad him into doing something stupid. Christ, it would only be five minutes before Tom and Ed showed up, but it was looking to be a long five minutes.

Kevin licked at one of the scratches near his mouth. "Married five years, fascist. I know things."

"Like what?"

"Like her and Rahman. She tell you about him?"

"Not much. I can see there's bad blood."

"You got that right. Murder, madness, and one fucking unhappy family."

"Murder?"

"Yeah. Back in Egypt. Ali had this older sister, Wafaa. A half-sister, actually. Full sister to Rahman. From all descriptions one hot-blooded and lusty chick. Plus, she had that old family stubborn streak. When the shit came down, she must have been, like, seventeen, and Ali four or five. Now, what she did, you and I would not consider a crime. Wearing makeup, riding in cars with guys, dancing, drinking, stuff a normal seventeen-year-old, reasonably hot girl would do. But over there, that makes you Jezebel. Her dad tried to lock her up in the house, but she would sneak out. Thus, lots of shouting matches, crying jags, door slams, crockery bombardments—and little Ali in the middle of it, understanding nothing, but trying to figure it out.

"One day, Wafaa gets herself knocked up by a German petrochemical engineer with a souped-up Porsche, and even Dad doesn't know what to do. But Rahman—he's a guy who keeps his head. A master of both the theoretical and applied branches of moral discipline, he remembers that the big *mufti* from his school told him that a whole family goes to hell if there's one slut in it. Which is bad, except that the solution is pretty simple. So Rahman takes Wafaa out for the last car ride of her life, and strangles the shit out of her in the desert. End of soap opera."

"Did Ali know about this?" Harry had sized up Kevin as a dyed-in-the-wool bullshitter, but the story did explain what he had seen for himself in the isolation room.

"Not right away. But there was this sense in the family that there was, like, the judgment of God on this poor chick. Now a four-year-old can't understand what real nastiness is. So what little Ali figures is that it was all the crying and shouting and tantrums and tears and laughing and shit that got Wafaa killed. She resolves to be a model little girl, ultra calm, not causing scenes for anybody. 'Cause if you let your feelings go, God will get you. This goes on year after year, till she even forgets what got it started. There's just this little feeling of doom that makes her sick every time she has to tell what she really feels or thinks. Good feelings, bad feelings—either way it's original sin. Thymophobia, to coin a word for it. When things get really tight, she'll pull back into full catatonic, ice-princess mode. Lucky if she even answers to her name then. I often tried to debug her source code, but the problem seemed hardwired."

Harry looked away again. "I'll bet you tried real hard."

"Fuck you, fascist."

There was a knock. Tom and Ed had brought the gurney.

"Okay, pardner. Ready to move?"

"Where are you taking me?"

"To the ER. We have a special little room there for our really wacked-out psych cases."

"I need to talk to whoever's in charge. You obviously haven't got the brains to see the big picture."

"Soon enough."

Together the three lifted Kevin onto the stretcher and cuffed his right wrist and left ankle to the rails. Harry then covered him with a sheet, like a corpse. There were at least a dozen surveillance cameras in the corridors between the men's room and Isolation. A human following the cameras would not be fooled by a mere sheet; he would question what was traveling under the sheet, and why it was being moved, not by orderlies, but by three security men. But what would a computer see? Might it not see as a dog sees, losing all thought of the ball when it is hidden behind one's back? Harry was about to bet his life on it.

With Harry in the lead, they rolled the stretcher out of the men's room, making a dog-leg through the green-tiled corridors, until they came to a service elevator. Knowing Helvelius's fate, Harry worried about the elevator, but the adjacent stairwell was too narrow for carrying the stretcher upstairs. So he got into the elevator alone with Kevin, and had Tom and Ed take the stairs. The elevator opened at the ground floor onto a small lobby between the Women's Health Center and the sprawling warren of rooms and corridors that comprised the emergency room. From there it was a short run to Isolation.

Raymond Lee, Judy Wolper, and three uniformed cops were already waiting at the guard station.

"What the hell's going on?" said an irate Lee. "I thought I told Dr. Gosling to throw your ass out of this hospital."

Harry looked up at the surveillance camera, where a dangling cable told him that Judy had followed instructions. "Got a present for you," he said, tearing away the sheet with the brio of a stage magician. Instead of a bunny out of a hat there was the blinking face of Kevin O'Day. "This is our man," he said. "Not Al-Sharawi. Al-Sharawi worked for this guy."

Kevin rose up on one elbow. "I know who you are," he said to Lee. "You're FBI. Some kind of psych profiler. Born in San Gabriel, California. Went to school at Columbia, got a Ph.D. in forensic psychology at CUNY. You're divorced and have two kids. You also seem to be the brains of this pack of baboons."

Lee gave Harry a surprised look. "Who is this?"

"My name is Kevin O'Day. I'm the head of computational research. I've read your personnel file out of the FBI database in Washington, D.C. I've been watching you since you got here. And I'm someone you need to take very, very seriously."

"I'm listening," said Lee.

"I have the power to vaporize you and this entire hospital. I can do that in a second if I want to. You've found one of my devices in the utility shaft in the second sub-basement, so you know I'm telling the truth. There are other devices as well. You will not find them, not until they make themselves known—"

"Like the elevator in Tower A."

"Precisely."

"Why did you blow the elevator?"

Kevin appeared taken aback. Perhaps it was even a shade of remorse that passed over his face. "Consider it a declaration of my seriousness."

"Very well." Lee studied Kevin intently.

"Now, if you correctly understand the gravity of the situation, you will immediately release me and return my property. You will refrain from any further interference in my actions. If you comply, things will be resolved to everyone's satisfaction in a short time. If you refuse, you can kiss your ass good-bye."

Lee turned to Harry. "What property are we talking about?"

Harry held up the flash drive.

"What's on it?"

"Probably a billion and a half bucks."

"You've got to be kidding," said Lee.

"No kidding." Harry let go of the flash drive as Lee gingerly took it between thumb and forefinger, as if it were extraordinarily fragile. "I should tell you," Harry added, "that he's got a computer controlling all the detonators, and watching everyone on the videocams. It's supposed to be some kind of highfalutin supercomputer that can push the buttons on its own."

"You mean . . . what do they call it—Odin?"

"That's the one. It's his baby."

Kevin rose up on his elbows. "Now do you understand me? Odin will not let you hold me. You are not in control. I am."

Lee scanned Kevin's face, and then turned to Harry. "Does the computer know he's in custody?"

Harry shrugged. "I don't know. But I think we have a stand-off for the moment. O'Day here can't set off the bomb without blowing up himself, and he doesn't strike me as the suicidal type. So holding him buys time for Avery's squad to disarm the bomb."

"I see," Lee said. Borrowing a key from Harry, he unlocked the handcuffs that chained Kevin to the stretcher. "Mr. O'Day, I regret that we're going to need to hold you awhile, at least until we can fully consider your case."

Kevin shook his head. "Don't listen to this yahoo. There's nothing to consider. Do you want to live, or not?"

At Lee's direction, two of the uniforms lifted Kevin off the stretcher and began walking him into the isolation room. They had just crossed the threshold when Kevin tore free, spun around, and ran straight into the third uniformed officer, who threw him to the ground with a leg sweep and an elbow lock.

"Let me go, you goddamned fascists!" he shouted. Immediately he was swarmed by cops. After a brief struggle, he was dragged back inside the isolation room and handcuffed to the drainpipe of a stainless steel toilet. The twisted ruins of Rahman's bed were still piled against the opposite wall.

Lee ordered one of the policemen to relinquish his gun and stand guard inside the room. "Keep your eye on him, and take note of every word he says." Then, turning to Kevin, "Mr. O'Day, I'll be back in a few minutes to listen to any statement you might care to make. In the meantime, Officer Dayton here will explain to you your rights in custody."

"You'll be back, all right," said Kevin, provocatively licking his lower lip. "Make sure you bring that flash drive with you."

Back in Harry's office, the black deadline clock read fifty-two minutes remaining. Scopes was sitting in the back, looking at one of the video monitors.

"That's the bomb squad," said Scopes. "I just came from going over the scene with Avery. They're having a helluva time getting X-rays of the bomb. The plan now is to drill a small hole in one corner of the casing, so they can pass a fiberoptic cable and get a look from inside. They have to drill real slow, to make sure there isn't any heat or vibration. So it's gonna take awhile."

Lee pulled up a chair facing the desk and powered up his laptop. "Well, we've had some developments of our own, courtesy of Mr. Lewton."

"Oh?"

"It turns out our mastermind is one Kevin O'Day, a computer specialist for the hospital. We have him in custody now."

"Is he cooperating?"

As soon as his desktop had finished loading, Lee inserted Kevin's flash drive into a slot in the rear. "Not so far. But we don't need to wait for him. Get Judge Rosado back on the phone. We need new warrants ASAP to search O'Day's apartment and his office, including any files in his computer or data drives. Tell him it's a ticking bomb situation." He turned and gave Harry a look like a professor forced to explain something obvious. "He's got to have schematics of this bomb somewhere."

"What about Odin?" asked Harry.

Lee suddenly scowled and slammed his laptop shut. The flash drive wouldn't open without a password. With a flushed face, he turned back toward Scopes. "Lewton has a point. Call the Chicago office and have them send out the best computer people they have, on the double. From the cyber crimes squad, if possible. Hacker types."

Lee was about to say more, but he was interrupted by the "Foggy Mountain Breakdown."

"I thought you weren't using your cell phone," said Scopes.

"I'm not calling out on it," said Harry. "But there's no harm in receiving."

"Who is it?" asked Lee.

"It's a text page. No callback number. It just says, 'You've got mail.'" Harry sat down at his keyboard and typed his password. "See, there it is."

Poink! Lee and Scopes leaned together toward Harry's computer. Opening his queue, Harry saw the tag "EXTREME IMPOR-TANCE."

"Here it comes, boys," said Harry. "The shit has officially hit the fan."

Harry opened the e-mail:

RESTORE IMMEDIATE COMMUNICATION WITH DIRECTOR OF COMPUTATIONAL RESEARCH. FAILURE TO COMPLY WILL RESULT IN SWIFT AND SEVERE PENALTY.

"What's the return address?" asked Lee. "Evidently O'Day has a confederate."

"Not a human," said Harry. "This is Odin."

Scopes was dubious. "The computer? Are you saying it can act by itself while we have O'Day in custody?"

"His wife says it can."

Scopes laughed. "How do we know his wife didn't send the message?"

"Because she's the one who turned O'Day in."

"Let's call its bluff," said Lee to Harry. "Type an answer: *Director O'Day is in police custody in this building and will not be released. Detonation will result in the death of Director O'Day. Refrain from any unauthorized activity. Assist in the disarming of explosive devices and Director O'Day will not be harmed.*"

"Not sure that's a good idea," said Harry. "Who knows how Odin might react?"

Lee went into professorial mode. "So-called thinking machines work by identifying the presence of key conditions, and matching these to a limited repertoire of preprogrammed responses. These are laid out by the programmer, and consequently fall entirely within the range of his own predispositions. I doubt that Mr. O'Day would have included any response that could cause his own death. Therefore, Odin, his creation, cannot choose such an action. On the other hand, the programmed response set may very well include actions designed to protect Mr. O'Day from harm. We can exploit those to our benefit."

Harry shook his head. "You sound awfully sure of yourself. From what I saw on television this morning, I'm not convinced that Odin was put together that way. Ali—Dr. O'Day, that is—thinks that Odin is not to be fucked with. She's scared as hell about what he might do."

"What would you suggest? Release this prisoner?"

"No."

"Give him access to the computer?"

"No."

"Then your position is to refuse the ultimatum. You can do that tacitly, by simply doing nothing, or you can choose to reply, and hope that Odin's response will reveal something about his programming and the options available to him. You don't risk anything by answering. You can't anger a computer. The risk lies in rejecting the ultimatum itself—and we're both agreed on the necessity of doing that."

"No, we're not agreed on anything. Quite frankly, I think you've got your thumb up your ass, and you're likely to get us all killed. We need to bring Dr. O'Day down here, and get her take on this. She knows what we're dealing with. We don't."

"Absolutely not!" said Lee. "I don't trust her. In fact, if your holding cell weren't already occupied, I'd have her in custody already."

"What? She fingered O'Day for us. She risked her life helping to bring him in. How the hell can you not trust her?"

"She has too many . . . points of intersection in this plot. Her brother. Her husband. Her phone records. This mysterious computer. There are many reasons why a coconspirator might sell out her accomplices. All I know is that she seems to stand at the exact center of this affair. I don't know why, and until I do, it'd be foolhardy to regard her as anything but an object of suspicion."

"What a crock of shit!" said Harry. "I didn't know they were giving out Federal badges to cretins this year."

Lee's face turned red. "Mr. Lewton, I'm permitting you to remain in this room only because you seem to know something about Kevin O'Day. Quite frankly, I don't trust you. And I don't trust this woman you're covering for."

Harry threw up his hands and kicked back his chair. "You want to send a message, you type it."

Lee scooted forward and began typing, using his two index fingers. When he was done, he hit "send" with a smart jab.

Harry watched as Lee and Scopes huddled over the screen. A minute elapsed, then two, but nothing happened.

"Checkmate," said Scopes.

"Let's not celebrate yet," said Lee. "Why don't you make those phone calls while we're waiting?"

"Already on it," said Scopes.

Forty-one minutes left on the doomsday clock. "Shouldn't you be trying to squeeze O'Day?" said Harry.

"In good time," said Lee. "If we push him too hard, it'll just feed his God complex. We're better off pretending to be a bit slow—even stupid. Once our cyber people get here, I'll resume the interrogation, with our captive genius looking on as they fumble away at the keyboard. O'Day won't be able to resist telling them off, and once he opens his mouth he won't be able to shut it. After that, he's ours. He'll beg for the chance to take the bomb apart himself, just to show us how smart he is."

Too pat, thought Harry. *You don't even know this son of a bitch. How can you be so sure of what he'll do?*

Scopes hung up the phone. "Warrants are coming by fax. The Cyber Team is on its way over with a police escort. They should be here in fifteen minutes."

"Now we're in business," said Lee. He got up to go to the fax machine, which sat on top of a lateral file cabinet. As he moved across the room, Scopes leaned forward to let him pass.

These FBI pricks are hopeless, thought Harry. He needed to get to Ali, who had the only sane grasp of the situation. She had power over Kevin, too. The bastard was still stuck on her, and that translated into major leverage. But where was she? In the ICU? Harry turned to the row of video monitors behind his desk. Closest to him, he saw the feed from the utility shaft where the bomb squad was working. In the foreground was a man in a Kevlar helmet who was trying to drill into the metal housing of the bomb. Below him, half obscured by the glare of spotlights, a few other faces peered up—Avery among them.

Harry tapped the toggle key on the monitor until the NICU came into view. Ali was sitting behind the nurses' desk, writing in a chart binder. All he needed was an excuse to get away. "I'm going to check on the search teams," he announced.

"Are they still working?" asked Lee.

"Damned right. And they'll keep working until I know that every ounce of C4 is accounted for."

"Go, then. When I need you for O'Day I'll put out an overhead page."

One last thing. Harry toggled a few more times until the ICU on 18C appeared. The picture was grainy and full of shadows, but he could make out his mother in the corner bed. She was awake, and even on the monitor he could see the rolling hand tremor of her Parkinson's disease. *If she's awake, she must be doing better*, he thought. *I should check with Weiss.*

Suddenly, Harry felt his chair lurch up from the floor. There was a crack like splitting timber, followed by a deafening boom and a staccato trill of shock waves that knocked Lee to the floor, and sent books and planters crashing from the shelves. The room was thrown into darkness. In the distance, he heard a rumble and a chorus of terrified screams.

"No! No! No!" shouted Harry. "Oh, fuck! He's gone and done it!"

There was a strange-smelling dust in the air, and Harry could hear someone coughing beside him. "Ray! Ray!" gasped Scopes. "Are you all right?"

"My shin . . . yeah, yeah, I'm all right. Shit!" came the answer.

The rumble died away, followed by waves of high-frequency vibrations. Then all was still, and the fluorescent lights began to flicker back on. From the corridors outside came the whooping sound of the automatic fire alarm. There were a dozen flashing red lights on the big status screen on the wall.

"Was that it?" asked Harry. "Was it the big one?"

"It was plenty big," said Scopes.

Together, Harry and Scopes lifted Lee to his feet and helped him to his chair. He had bruised his shin in the fall, but was otherwise unharmed.

"That came from the towers, didn't it?" asked Lee.

"Yes," said Harry, studying the status screen.

"Hell!" grumbled Lee. "Goddamned lousy hell!"

"I've got some bad news, fellas," said Scopes. The row of monitors on the back wall had rebooted, and Scopes was peering at the farthest one, as he leaned on the countertop with his arms spread wide.

"What? What is it?" asked Lee.

"We've lost the video from the bomb squad."

As Harry, Scopes, and Lee came running down the stairs to the second basement level, the first thing that hit them was the smell—an acrid smell of scorched insulation that reminded Harry of that house fire in Nacogdoches, but compounded with an odor Harry had never smelled before, something that made him think of vaporized steel and concrete. The fire alarm was blaring a glissando up and down like a slide whistle at an ear-splitting volume. As the three pushed through a pair of closed fire doors, they entered a darkened section of corridor, lit only by a couple of portable lights in the distance. Those marked the alcove where the bomb squad had gone to work barely an hour and a half before.

The alcove was gone. In its place was a pyramid of rubble. The ceiling was lacerated by a ten-foot-wide hole, through which dangled sheafs of wires and twisted pipes and ripped-out struts—the sinews and nerves of a once-proud architectural wonder. The severed sprinkler pipes hemorrhaged water, making everything slick, turning the dust that covered everything into a half-inch layer of gritty white mud.

Two bodies were already laid out on the driest portion of the floor, their faces blackened and unrecognizable, their upper bodies soaked in blood. Beyond them, in the apex of light, a half-dozen men frantically clawed through the rubble with crowbars and fingernails and the pick end of a fire axe. They panted and groaned as they heaved skull-sized chunks of concrete down onto the clattering floor. Their hands were bloody, but still they dug. One of their own was buried under the rubble.

Someone shouted, "Jamal! Jamal!"

Then something dark and glistening showed amid the rubble. A face—the face of a young black man, with a bit of police blue showing at the collar. Instantly everyone scrambled to pull away the debris that covered him.

"Jamal! Jamal!" came a shout, above the infernal whooping of the fire alarm. Jamal neither answered nor opened his eyes. Once his chest had been cleared, his body slid easily out of the rubble, with no right arm and no legs to anchor him. The men carried him down the small hill of concrete and laid him on the floor, next to the two other bodies they called Bill and Roman.

Captain Avery, his chest heaving, his hair dripping with water from the broken pipes, led the rescuers. Among them Harry counted four bomb techs, Wilks, and an HVAC workman. The HVAC man had a deep gash over one eyebrow that was still bleeding down the side of his face.

"Who else? Who else?" shouted Avery above the fire alarm.

"Tony. Tony's missing," one of the techs shouted back.

"Where was he?"

"In the shaft."

"Oh, God! Oh, Jesus! Tony!" Avery turned and clambered back up the pyramid, getting almost to the top before his way was blocked by a sagging steel beam. "Tony! It's Glenn! We're gonna get you out, Tony! Just hold on for five minutes. Five minutes, for Chrissake! D'ya hear me, Tony? Five minutes!"

"I can see his foot!" shouted one of the techs, who had climbed to Avery's side. Together they clawed away the rubble, sending a small avalanche of concrete chunks down the side of the pyramid. In a moment they had recovered it—a human foot, still clad in a spit-polished black steel-toed duty boot—and that was all.

While the techs went on digging, Avery slowly slid down to the floor, holding the boot like a Communion chalice, never taking his eyes off of it. Then he got up, and with wobbly, sleepwalking steps, made his way to the trio of bodies and laid the boot in their midst. For a moment he stood, viewing the remains of his men. Harry thought he saw Avery's lips moving—whether praying or simply trembling with emotion, he could not tell.

Suddenly Avery turned and charged to the base of the pyramid. "What are you doing, you sons of bitches!" he shouted. "Lay into it!

Clear that shit away! Dig like you give a fuck, you good-for-nothin' momma's boys!" And then he turned around, addressing no one in particular. "For the love of God, can't somebody shut off that God . . . damn . . . fire alarm!"

Just then a team of orderlies raced up with a pair of gurneys, and in their wake came a dozen firemen carrying ropes, oxygen tanks, crowbars, and ammonium phosphate fire extinguishers. In a moment the area around the rubble pile was thronged with diggers. Among them Harry saw a flash of something black and white—the uniform of his own security force. Pushing his way through the crowd, he found the face of Tom Beazle.

"Tom!" shouted Harry. "Over here! I need you to get to a house phone and have them shut off the alarm. Got that? Also the sprinkler water, the gas and oxygen to this sector. I need it all shut off now!"

Tom said something inaudible and took off running.

Harry made his way over to Scopes and Lee. Lee was using his cell phone to take photos of the bodies.

"Was that it?" Harry shouted.

"What?" Lee shouted back.

"Was that it? The bomb? The big bomb?" Harry felt his heart go out to the men who had just died. But the hospital was still standing, with only four dead and not a thousand. If this was all the bomb could do, it would be a relief. He could live with four dead instead of a thousand.

But Scopes shook his head. "Nowhere near five hundred pounds of C4. The blast was directed downward, from a point several feet below the device we saw an hour ago. This was a booby trap—not the main bomb."

"Not the big one?" Harry wasn't sure he'd heard Scopes right.

"Not the big one. Think a hundred times this big."

"Aw, Jesus Christ!"

Lee pinched Scopes's shoulder. "Stay here. See what you can figure out. I'm going to call upstairs and see if our hackers are here yet."

Harry noticed that some of the lights in the area were moving around. When he looked more carefully he saw a blond woman in a turtleneck standing in the midst of all the pandemonium. It was Kathleen Brown.

Harry pushed his way over. A technician was moving a portable light from side to side while Dutch held up a meter to check the white balance reflected off Kathleen Brown's face.

"Are you out of your minds?" shouted Harry. "It's not safe for you to be filming here."

Kathleen Brown cupped her hand over one ear.

Harry repeated himself, louder, exaggerating his lip movements to make sure she understood him. "I said you can't film here."

"We have an agreement," she shouted back.

"No. Not for this." Harry grabbed her by the wrist and dragged her through the crowd, off toward the place where the corridor started to get dark again.

Just then the fire alarm shut off, but Kathleen Brown still went on shouting. "We have a right to be here! The public has a right to know what's going on!"

"No, it's too dangerous. We could have a cave-in. Plus there's still a massive bomb just above us that can go off at any time."

"It's our job. Dutch was a war correspondent. Danger is nothing new."

"That's right," said Dutch. "I was embedded with the 101st Airborne in Baghdad."

"Look at this pile of rubble," said Harry. "That could be you."

"Are you throwing us out?" asked Kathleen Brown. "Do I need to have our network president call Dr. Gosling?"

Harry fished a quarter out of his pocket and slapped it into the palm of Kathleen Brown's hand. "Here. The call's on me."

"I know why you don't want us reporting this story. You're afraid of what I might say about you."

"The hell I am."

"I know all about Nacogdoches, Mr. Lewton—or should I say, Police Lieutenant Harry Lewton. Don't act surprised. We get paid to ask questions. Sometimes the ghosts of the past don't want to stay buried, do they?"

"You don't know jack shit about Nacogdoches."

"Well, now, here's the deal. I can either report on this bomb, or I can find something else to put on our evening news show. How about an old story about police incompetence, cowardice, a couple of dead kids? There's human interest for you. That's what I'm good at, right? A promising young lieutenant finds his life on the skids after being run out of town for . . . for what?"

"Save it for the pigeons. Put it on a prime-time special, for all I care. I've been there before. But let me tell you, my conscience is at peace with Nacogdoches. I did what I knew to be right. And I'll do it now, too. God knows, it would give me satisfaction to see you people blown to dust. But I'm responsible for the safety of everyone in this hospital—and that includes you."

Captain Avery—hatless, seeming a decade older now that his dark hair was flecked with white dust and plaster—came stumbling toward the camera lights. "What's going on?" he asked.

"Mr. Lewton is telling us we can't film here," said Kathleen Brown.

"Well, you shouldn't. It's dangerous," said Avery. "I just had three . . . four men killed."

"We're willing to accept the risk," said Kathleen Brown. "We'll stay out of your way. But there's a nationwide audience that deserves to see the courage and dedication of these men of yours up close."

"Network TV, is it?"

"Yes. By tomorrow you'll be one of the most famous men in the country, Captain Avery."

"Screw that."

"What about these men that died? I can guarantee you the whole country will know and honor their sacrifice. They'll be celebrated as heroes."

Avery looked back toward the rubble. At the top of the mound, one of the firemen was trying to hack his way into the utility shaft. "How many people do you need?" he asked Kathleen Brown. "Bare minimum?"

"Three. Me, Dutch, and a lighting man."

"All right. As long as you accept the risk. And I won't have you taking pictures that will upset the families of these men that died."

"You have my word."

"Wait a minute," said Harry. "I don't think—"

"I'm the Incident Commander here, Mr. Lewton. This is a police site, and what I say goes. I'm telling you they can stay."

A voice came from the utility shaft. "Captain! We've got Tony free. We're passing him down now."

Avery pushed through the crowd and clambered partway up the pyramid of wreckage. "Is he . . . is he—"

"He's gone, sir," said one of the bomb techs, who backed out of the shaft, holding the lower part of the blackened torso of what had been a young man in his twenties.

Avery's voice quavered as he caught sight of him. "Aw, sweet Jesus! Aw, God! Not fuckin' Tony!"

Dutch slung his camera at his waist, but Harry noticed that the little red light was on as Avery and his men pulled down the body of Tony Passalaqua and set it upon a waiting gurney. In a moment the transport orderlies were whisking the gurney to the ER, as though there were still a chance of life for the charred, smashed heap of flesh.

In the dark part of the corridor, Lee hung up a wall phone. "Lewton!" he shouted. "The cyber squad's here. I want you with me when I talk to O'Day."

"Coming," replied Harry. Turning to Kathleen Brown, he tipped his hand to his eyebrow in a mock salute. "Field goal to you, kiddo. Make the most of it. The instant I see you upstairs, I'm having your ass escorted out of this medical center."

"You've got visitors."

Kevin looked up from the floor of the Isolation Room, where he sat handcuffed to the drainpipe. The pudgy cop named Dayton had just come in, and began to unlock his leg irons.

"That explosion, can you tell me what the fuck just happened?" asked Kevin.

"Ask them." Dayton pulled Kevin onto his feet and led him out into the guardroom. Harry, Lee, and a few of the cops he recognized from before were waiting for him, grim as tombstones. With them was a strapping man in a three-button black pinstripe suit, and a tiny, dark-skinned young woman with large eyes and short black hair.

Dayton made Kevin sit down at the table in the center of the room. A chair leg screeched as Lee sat down beside him. "We're recording this. Understood?" said Lee, slapping his recorder onto the table.

Lee and Harry were sopping wet and streaked with white dust. "Th-that explosion, where was it?" Kevin asked.

"You ought to know, Mr. O'Day."

"Was it in the Tower?"

"You tell me."

It had to be Tambora or Krakatoa, thought Kevin. *If it were Thera—the Big One—we would all be dead.*

Kevin cleared his throat nervously. "Do you understand the situation now? You can't go on holding me."

"On the contrary, Mr. O'Day. You've just murdered four public safety officers. There is no possibility whatsoever of my releasing you. If I were to do so, you would not get out of this building alive. There are several dozen cops who would just love to get you in their sights."

Kevin felt a bead of sweat run down the side of his face. "Murdered . . . *who*?"

"Four men from the bomb squad were killed in that last explosion. I just came from viewing the bodies. What was left of them."

Kevin scanned the faces arrayed about him. "That . . . that wasn't in the plan. If you had fucking listened to me, it wouldn't have happened. Goddamn you! It wasn't me. It was you who killed them, you sons of bitches!"

"How many more bombs are there, Mr. O'Day?"

"Plenty. They do all kinds of things. It's . . . it's like a chess game that's already been played out in advance. Whatever move you make, there's a countermove in position. You can't win. Every possible angle has been covered."

"I think it's time you cut the crap and started to cooperate before anyone else gets killed." Lee gestured toward the two new agents. "Meet Special Agent Dail and Special Agent Ganguly, from the Computer Crimes Division. Now, I understand that all of these bombs are under computer control—something called Odin. Is that correct?"

"You can't hack into Odin. If you try, or if you attempt to cut power to his mainframe, he'll go into doomsday mode."

"Ah, yes, the mainframe. We've had some trouble getting into your laboratory, Mr. O'Day. It seems the entry code's been changed, and an unauthorized deadbolt system has been installed in the door. The first thing you can do is tell us how to get inside."

"You don't want to go into the lab. Project Vesuvius is active.

Under its operating rules, anyone but me in the lab will be regarded as an intruder."

"The lab is booby-trapped?"

"Yes."

"Then give us the security codes you use for access."

"It doesn't work like that. You have to be me to get in. The lab's under surveillance by a microphone and a couple of video cameras—running on batteries, not the main power circuit, just in case you get ideas. They're Odin's eyes and ears. He knows what I look and sound like. He knows my speech patterns—favorite words I use, inflections, things that are uniquely and incontrovertibly *me*. If you think you can fake that, be my guest. Otherwise, I wouldn't go in there, if I were you. You wouldn't last ten seconds."

Lee got up, seemingly overcome with emotion. Folding his hands behind him, he turned away from Kevin and paced to the far end of the tiny room. "Did you just refer to this plan of yours as Project Vesuvius?"

"Yeah, Vesuvius. So what?"

"Vesuvius being the volcano that wiped out the city of Pompeii, back in Roman days?"

"It's a metaphor."

Lee stalked back and slammed a cell phone onto the table.

"What's this?" asked Kevin.

"Your handiwork," said Lee.

Kevin squinted at the tiny screen of the cell phone. It was difficult to see without his glasses, but he made out something dark and lumpy, like a log or the chewed end of a cigar. Only after hard scrutiny could he identify a row of white teeth, and two dark and boiled-out eye sockets looking back at him.

"Oh, fuck! Tambora!" he gasped.

Lee gripped the edge of the table and overshadowed Kevin. "This is the face of one of the men you killed. His name is Tony. He looks a lot like one of those mummies they pulled out of Pompeii, doesn't he? As I recall, a couple thousand people got toasted just like this. Quite a metaphor, isn't it?"

Kevin's throat went dry. He pushed his chair back, distancing himself from his silent accuser, yet he couldn't tear his eyes away from the image. "Look, I didn't want this. I'm . . . I'm not sure what happened. They might have tripped a circuit or something. But it proves my point. You have to let me go."

Lee picked up the cell phone and shoved it in Kevin's face, so close that it was nothing but a blur. "Do you understand that you're facing the death penalty? A lot depends on what happens right here and now. If you have one tenth of the brains people say you have, tell Agents Dail and Ganguly how to get into the Odin program."

"You don't."

"Is it a UNIX-based system?" asked Ganguly. She stood next to Lee, petite and prim in a gray skirtsuit. Her voice was clear and dulcet, like a crystal bell.

Her query seemed like the crown of FBI pigheadedness. "Girl, you look and sound like a summer intern out of high school," Kevin said. "Odin has as much in common with UNIX as Shakespeare does with the sign language of an ape. He's protected by an integument, a programming layer that regulates all input functions and command sequences. Everything gets checked for consistency with my past instructions. Any attempt to access his code or even communicate with him will be instantly red-flagged as an alien intrusion."

"We'll go in through the back door."

"There is no back door. I never needed one."

"Then we'll make one. We'll link a Trojan horse to the data from the Cerberus surveillance system that Odin is presently hijacking. It will plant a virus that will allow us to circumvent the usual access portals, and directly enter core programming. We'll shut him down, with or without your help."

"Make sure your life insurance is up-to-date before you try that one. Really, you're not hearing a thing I'm saying, are you? This isn't your dad's PC we're talking about. How many people have to fucking die before you people get it?" He turned to Raymond Lee. "There is one and only one way to shut down Odin. Give me back my property, and let me go. I want to end this as much as you do. But don't waste time with this shit."

"Forget it," said Lee.

"The data stream—" said Ganguly.

Both were cut off by a commotion at the door. Captain Avery, his uniform torn and bloodstained and his hair caked with mud, charged into the room, a pair of uniformed officers in his wake.

"This him?" he growled. The police guards in the room stood to attention as Avery pushed his way through to Kevin. "Are you the son of a bitch who set these bombs?"

A new face—maybe a chance at reason, thought Kevin. He smiled urbanely and made a point of calling out this new cop by name. "Hello, Captain Avery."

But there was perhaps a *sukoshi* too much smugness in his voice. Like a sprung trap, Avery lunged across the table and slammed his fist against Kevin's jaw, knocking him out of his chair and to the ground. The table grated against the floor as Avery bumped it to one side and dove down upon Kevin, hitting him with two or three lightning strokes to his face and stomach. "I'll kill you, you little prick!" he roared.

Kevin rolled to one side and held his arms out to block the punches. Avery hit like a sledgehammer, and the whole roomful of cops simply stood by in shock, as though they were going to let him be beaten to death. But then Harry Lewton jumped in and caught Avery in a half-Nelson, pulling him away.

"Get away from me, you pissant rent-a-cop!" shouted Avery. "Get your meathooks off me!"

"Let him be!" said Harry.

Avery shook off Harry's hold and spun on him, glaring at him nose-to-nose. "Fuck you! Back off or I'll throw you and all your black-and-white flunkeys into jail!"

Lee interposed a hand. "Glenn, lighten up."

Avery was bright red in the face. "I'm the Incident Commander here. I'll do what the hell I please."

"No, Glenn. This man is in FBI custody now. I have to answer for him."

Avery glared at Lee, fists clenched, his breath coming in loud and heavy snorts. "Four men dead! Four good men! Christ knows, they were as good as they come. Bill Kraus, for Chrissakes! He . . . he had no legs left. Blown away at the knees. Not a drop of blood, Ray! It killed him so fast he didn't even bleed. And Tony Passalaqua . . . his wife's expecting. What am I supposed to tell her? Why is his kid gonna grow up an orphan? Because . . . because this fucking piece of shit—"

Lee put his hand on Avery's shoulder. "I know they were good men, Glenn. They don't come any better. But let's save the rest of 'em, okay? We've got plenty more to save."

Avery watched sullenly as Dail and Ganguly helped Kevin back into his chair. "That son of a bitch is coming with me! I'm gonna chain his ass to a water pipe and make him watch what the fuck he's done. The next booby trap that goes off, he'll be the first to burn."

Kevin couldn't believe what he had just heard. "Are you still trying to disarm the bomb?"

"Of course we are, you stupid prick."

"D-don't. You'll set it off."

Lee jumped in to block Avery from making another charge. "How can you reach it?" he asked the Captain. "The utility shaft's nothing but a pile of debris."

"Below. But we still have access from the upper basement level, above the bomb. We've opened a service panel up there and had a good look. It's trickier. We'll have to lower a man head-first. But we aren't about to give up. The real problem is these goddamned booby traps. I don't know how we missed the first one, but it's not gonna happen again."

"Work smart, Glenn. This guy thinks he could teach the Unabomber to suck eggs. There's no telling what he's laid up for you."

Avery was so tall Kevin could see his entire face over the top of Lee's head. It was like the face of a bull pawing the ground before a charge. "Maybe I oughtta dangle this prick up and down the shaft until he spills his guts."

"We need him here, Glenn. The bombs are set off by computer, and he's gonna help us shut the computer down."

"Look at him. Goddamm it, Ray, look at that smirk! No fucking way is he gonna help with anything."

"Let us work on it, okay?"

Avery sighed. "This is the worst I've ever seen, Ray. Four men in one swoop. Four good men. What am I . . . what am I gonna tell their—" He suddenly pivoted away from Lee and the other onlookers. From the way his shoulders shook, Kevin knew that he was choking back tears.

Lee, his hand still on Avery's shoulder, guided Avery out of the crowded room. Three of the uniforms followed them out to express their condolences. The other two stayed, but accompanied the procession with their eyes. Special Agent Dail sat down behind the computer at the nurse's station. Harry stood near the door, brushing dust off his blazer.

And for an instant, Kevin noticed that Special Agent Ganguly was the only person in the room with her eyes on him.

A thud. A scrape of table legs against the floor. Harry turned and looked, just in time to see Ganguly in mid-air, plummeting toward the ground. Kevin had leaped on top of the table, and was swinging the chair he had just bashed Ganguly with, holding it by its two rear legs. The chair went into a swift, wide arc, then punched through the ceiling as it knocked aside a twenty-four-inch-square acoustic panel to expose a dark crawl space above. There was a clang as the two front legs of the chair hooked around a sprinkler pipe. Harry grabbed at Kevin's ankles, but missed as Kevin plucked up his legs and swung by the hooked chair like a trapeze artist, kicking out a second panel and wrapping his legs around a pipe. For a second, he hung upside down, his orange hair drooping from his forehead. Then, with a lithe, screwlike motion that only an experienced rock climber could have attempted, he pulled his upper body through the hole in the ceiling, and disappeared into the darkness above.

"Shit!" yelled Harry. "He's getting away!"

"Where?"

"The ceiling!"

In an instant, half a dozen guns were drawn, their sights flitting chaotically toward every part of the ceiling.

"Don't shoot! Don't shoot!" shouted Lee. "We need him alive!"

Harry sprang onto the table and tried to lift himself by the still-hanging chair the way Kevin had done. He was too heavy and could barely get his feet up off the table. "Fuck," he muttered. Quickly he unhooked the chair, set it on the table, and climbed onto it. Sticking his head into the dark crawl space, he could see Kevin worming his way through a tangle of pipes and wires.

No time to think. Harry grabbed the nearest pipe and pulled himself up, boosting his momentum with a kick off the chair. The pipe sagged under his weight as he swung his right leg up, knocking out another panel. Another heave, and a piece of the aluminum frame of the drop ceiling clattered to the floor. But Harry had made it into the crawl space.

By the scant light from below, Harry saw that Kevin had already covered half a dozen yards, and was spidering between a ventilation duct and the concrete ceiling. Watching Kevin's lean body moving effortlessly through the crevice, Harry felt like a tortoise trying to chase a monkey up a tree. But he wasn't about to give up the chase.

Harry lay as flat as he could across a pair of sprinkler pipes and scooted sideways, aiming for a solid steel beam. His face grazed the dusty chalklike surface of the ceiling panels, which stung his eyes and left a dry, bitter taste in his mouth. Bigger in the chest than Kevin, Harry had to exhale in order to slip into the space above the duct. But following Kevin's example, he hugged it between his legs and arms, and inched forward with a caterpillar-like motion.

He kept on crawling until his hands scraped against a concrete wall. He was in total darkness now, and had lost sight of his quarry. He heard a creaking noise, but it seemed to come from directly above. Groping his way, he discovered that the duct made a right-angle turn at the wall and ran upward to the floor above. Alongside it was a narrow tunnel-like space, just wide enough to squeeze through. It was the only place Kevin could have gone. Harry wriggled inside the tunnel and began to shimmy upward.

After maybe twenty feet, Harry wormed his way out of the tunnel, emerging into yet another crawl space. Kevin had vanished, but there was a square of light about forty feet ahead, where one of the ceiling panels had been pried up and slid to one side. Harry moved toward the light. When he reached the gap, he looked down and saw a beige linoleum floor twelve feet below, and something else—the white and black clad form of a hospital security guard, lying half-doubled up on the floor.

Gripping an oxygen gas main, Harry dangled himself through the gap and dropped, landing beside the prostrate guard. It was Judy Wolper. She looked up sluggishly, her eyes unfocused, and her blond hair hanging over her face.

"H-hit me. He hit me," she mumbled. "Came out of nowhere and hit me."

"Which way did he go?"

"I . . . I don't know."

There were only two directions. On the left, the corridor joined the main passage coming out of Tower A. That led to the Pike, where Kevin could quickly lose himself in a crowd of people. On the right, only a dead end at some faculty offices for Physical Therapy. No contest. *Left!* Harry thought. *It's the only way out.*

But no sooner had he risen to his feet than he heard two gunshots, coming not from the left, but from the right.

"Oh, hell," said Judy, fumbling at her holster. "He's got my gun."

Harry ran toward the gunfire. He paused at a turn in the corridor, and then sprang out, instinctively crouching into a low Weaver stance, the Beretta in both hands, right arm straight, left arm slightly cocked. Kevin was at the far end, kicking furiously at a door.

"Drop it!" shouted Harry. "Drop the gun!"

"No, you drop it!" Kevin shouted back. He had been pointing Judy's Glock 17 at the door, but now he turned toward Harry, swinging the gun with him.

Harry fired once. The slug hit Kevin in the shoulder, and spun him sharply against the wall. The Glock went flying to the ground.

Still keeping his Beretta poised, Harry advanced like a fencer in a half-crouch, and kicked Kevin's gun out of reach. Kevin had slumped into a sitting position against the wall. He was wincing and gripping his right shoulder. "You stupid bastard!" he shouted. "You stupid fascist cocksucking bastard! Gun for a dick, and shit for brains!"

"You pointed your weapon at me. What did you expect?"

"I expected you to back the fuck off."

Harry knew that shooting Kevin was bad business. They were both lucky he had missed what he had really aimed for. "It's just a shoulder wound. You'll make it."

"None of us is going to make it unless you let me get to a computer. I need to contact Od—"

"Out of the question," Harry snapped.

"Look, I wasn't trying to run away."

"No? With five murder charges hanging over your head? Gee, why not?"

"Those killings, they weren't part of the plan. No one was supposed to get hurt. No one but . . . one person, anyway. It was just about the money."

"Five hundred pounds of explosives, and you thought no one would get hurt?"

"There's no payoff in actually exploding the bomb. It was all about the *threat* of the bomb. But the threat had to be believable."

"Well, everyone believes you now."

Kevin grimaced with pain and knocked his head three times on the wall behind him. "Can't you hear me, fascist? Odin's jamming. Gone improvisational. I have no idea what he'll do next. I want to call off the project."

"Call it off?"

"Deactivate. There's an emergency safe recovery shutdown procedure for Odin that I can activate if I can log in to a terminal somewhere. After that, you can take these fucking bombs out of here. I'll tell you where and how. I don't want anyone else getting killed."

Harry still had his gun on him. "I don't trust you."

"It's not about trust, fascist. It's about smarts. Who do you think the next victim is likely to be?"

"What do you mean, next vic—"

"Ali."

Harry felt as if the bottom had dropped out of his stomach. "Ali? Why Ali?"

"Because . . . because she tasks me, Einstein. She burned me pretty deep, and Odin, well, Odin has a way of picking up on these things. He can, like, see into your id. That's how Dr. H got blown away. And Ali's next, I tell you. Odin will vaporize this whole freaking hospital just to get at her. He's what you'd call a radical thinker."

Harry looked at the two bullet holes near the lock of the office door. Kevin was telling the truth. If he had been trying to escape, this cul-de-sac would have been the last place to run to. Harry was starting to wish he hadn't shot the son of a bitch. "All right. Where can you log on?"

"Anywh— Aw, jeez." Kevin's body twisted with pain. He slid downward, until just his head was propped against the wall. The wall behind him was smeared with blood.

"What's wrong?"

"I'm . . . I'm feeling kind of light-headed."

"I'll help you up." Harry holstered his gun and reached under Kevin to pull him back into a sitting position. The entire backside of

Kevin's shirt was wet and sticky, and Harry immediately recognized the distinctive texture of blood. Even so, when he got a look at his hand, he was astonished to find it completely drenched. "Oh, hell!" he muttered.

"Problems, fascist?" said Kevin with a woozy smile.

Harry tore away Kevin's shirt. The bullet had entered just on the inside of the right shoulder joint, through a hole about the size of a dime. But the back of the shoulder was torn into strands like pulled pork, and blood was shooting out of the armpit in rhythmic squirts.

"The artery's nicked. You're gonna need a doctor." Harry looked around and spotted a house phone hanging from the wall. Wadding up part of Kevin's sopping wet shirt, he pushed it up hard against the armpit and had Kevin hold it there. "Keep as much pressure on it as you can," he said. Then he leaped up and grabbed the phone. "Emergency! Emergency! We have a gunshot wound on the second floor, Tower A, Corridor 12, near the men's room. Request immediate medical assistance. Victim is bleeding profusely. Repeat—need medical assistance, STAT."

The operator was still talking on the other end when Harry dropped the phone and started back. Passing a men's room door, he reached inside and grabbed a handful of paper towels.

Kevin was white as a clamshell, and so weak that his fingers merely rested on top of the pressure point. Harry lifted Kevin's right arm and wadded the paper towels into the armpit until he could feel solid bone. As he did, he noticed that the spurting of blood had stopped. He had seen enough as a cop to know that that could be a bad sign.

"Fuck it. Fuck all that," mumbled Kevin. "Just get me to a terminal."

"Okay, sure. Give me a minute." Harry felt a sickening chill. *You've screwed up royal, kiddo. If you lose this son of a bitch, you and everyone in this hospital can kiss their ass good-bye.* Trying to keep Kevin from losing consciousness, he turned him onto his left side, keeping the wound high and the brain and heart low. Then he pushed down on the wounded arm with all his weight, using the arm like the lever of a bookpress to keep up pressure on the armpit. Still, the blood kept on oozing out. The artery was too deep to close off that way.

Kevin's voice was breathy but weak. "T-t-tell her I'm sorry. An' get her . . . out . . . out of this . . . wha-whatchmacalit, hospital. D-do it now, f-f-fascist."

Harry heard someone running down the hall. "Here they come," he said. A resident in a white coat and scrubs appeared in the lead, followed by half a dozen people and a red crash cart. "Over here!" shouted Harry. "He's going fast."

"Jesus Christ!" said the resident, when he saw the four-foot-wide pool of blood. He pushed Harry aside as he knelt down and lifted Kevin's arm for a look under the paper towels.

"Carotid pulse barely palpable," said a curly-haired woman, kneeling at Kevin's head.

"No respiration," said a short, Hispanic-looking lab tech who stood beside her.

"Okay, bag him," said the resident. "You're not going to find a vein. Start two sixteen-gauge tibial cannulas for intraosseous access. One on each side."

"Lidocaine?" asked a blond nurse, who was squatting by Kevin's feet.

"No time. Just stick 'em in. Believe me, he won't feel a thing."

The nurse pulled up Kevin's pants leg, bent his knee slightly and, holding his leg firmly, began twisting and pushing a needle into his shinbone, just below the bump where the tendon of the kneecap inserted. There was a visible give when the needle broke through the hard outer wall of the bone. Without wasting a motion, the nurse attached a syringe and drew back a small amount of blood to confirm that the needle had made it into the soft, pulpy center of the bone. Then she attached an IV line to the needle, while the Hispanic lab tech slipped the other end of the line onto a plastic bag of lactated Ringer's solution.

"Squeeze that bag," said the resident to the lab tech. "Squeeze the hell out of it."

A shout on the left announced that a second line was ready in the other leg. From down the hall, Harry heard a rumbling as two orderlies raced to the scene with a gurney.

"Want some epi?" asked someone at the crash cart.

"No time for pressors right now. Let's just get him to the OR."

"Excuse me," said Harry, almost shouting to be heard above the bustle. "Does someone here have a laptop? This man needs to access the hospital computer network. It's urgent."

The resident glared at Harry. "Are you out of your fucking mind? Who are you?"

"Chief of Security."

"Well, if you're not part of this code team, you're nobody. Now kindly get the hell out of our way."

"Kevin!" shouted Harry, over the shoulder of the resident. "Kevin!"

There was no answer from Kevin. From the floor, the curly-haired woman called up. "I've lost his pulse."

Sweet Jesus! thought Harry. *This isn't happening.*

"Start compressions," ordered the resident. Before the woman could begin, the two orderlies brought up a long white slab of plastic and laid it on the floor alongside Kevin. "Okay, turn him. Slide it, slide it," came the order. Several pairs of hands rolled Kevin onto his side, while the plastic was shoved under him. "Everybody got a handle? All right, on three. One, two, three!" The team lifted the limp body by nylon loops attached to the corners and sides of the slab, and quickly placed both body and slab on the gurney.

"Leave that backboard on the stretcher," said the resident. "We need it for the chest compressions." Without further direction, the curly-haired woman crossed her hands on top of Kevin's breastbone and began pumping down on it in a sharp, rapid rhythm. She didn't miss a beat, even as the gurney started moving down the hall. "Call Trauma," said the resident to someone standing by the phone. "Tell 'em we're coming. We need ten units of type O blood to start. And get Dr. Bittner if he's available. Bittner or Hughes."

In a moment, Harry and the resident were left alone, standing by a pool of blood in an empty corridor. *Fuck all this blood! Why did he have to point the gun at me?*

"Sorry about the rudeness back there," said the resident, "but your man's in no shape to be checking his e-mail. What hit him, anyway?"

"Nine millimeter."

"Looks like the bullet shattered on a rib and pretty much diced his axillary artery, right about where it comes out from under the clavicle. That's a bleeder, no question. Where's the gunman?"

"I shot him."

"*You* did? Jesus!"

Harry jerked his head and looked at the resident, sharply, like the doc was a perp under the spotlight. "Is he going to make it?"

"Fifty-fifty."

"Look, he's got to pull through. He's *got* to. You . . . you don't know how much is riding on it."

"If you like, I can have somebody page you when we know more."

Harry shook his head. "I'll go down with you myself to the operating room, in case he comes to and says anything."

"Suit yourself."

Harry turned to follow the resident. They had gone but a couple of paces when Harry looked up and froze in his tracks.

Oh, Christ, no!

At the far end of the corridor, where it made its right-angle turn, he saw a standard security camera mounted high up near the ceiling, covering the whole bloodstained scene in its direct line of sight.

A tiny red light indicated that the camera was in record mode.

He and Kevin had not been alone.

The unsleeping eye of Cerberus had witnessed everything.

The first thing Ali saw when she came through the double doors of the main surgical suite was Harry Lewton standing next to the counter of the central nurses' station. He had thrown a yellow surgical gown over his street clothes. His face was grim.

"Ali," said Harry.

"What's going on, Harry? I got a phone call in the ICU—"

"I had the nurse call you. We need to talk."

"Oh, God!" His eyes told her everything. "This is about Kevin, isn't it?"

"I won't mince words. I was forced to shoot him. He's in serious condition."

"*Shoot* him? For God's sake, why?" In disbelief, she looked up at the enormous dry-erase board behind the station that listed the status of each operating room. At the bottom she read:

Trauma Room One   O'Day, K.
Dr. Bittner   GSW   17:30.

"He pulled a gun on me. I had no choice. I aimed for his shoulder, but—"

"Kevin pulled a gun on you? He doesn't even know how to hold a gun." She grabbed a yellow gown from the cart by the door, and quickly put it on, leaving the ties in back to dangle. In a second, she had slipped a pair of paper booties over her shoes and stormed past Harry to Trauma One. At the door, still tucking her hair under a blue surgical cap, she looked through a small window. She saw Leon Bittner, the tall, portly trauma surgeon, hunched over the operating table, along with a resident, an anesthetist, and a couple of nurses. Ali was relieved to see so much activity. Activity meant life.

Harry caught up to her. "Look, I'm really sorry," he said.

She hit him sharply on the chest with the side of her fist. "You promised me! You promised you wouldn't hurt him!" Her lower lip was trembling. "When I told you about Kevin, it was to make sure that nobody else got hurt. That included *him,* goddamn you! I expected you to protect him—from himself, if need be. But this—"

"There isn't time for recriminations, Ali. In forty-five minutes, the deadline to release Meteb and Mossalam is going to pass, and I have no idea how Odin has been programmed to react when it turns out they're not on the plane. As we speak, Kathleen Brown's network is getting ready to tell the whole world we have a live bomb on our hands. There's been a steady exodus or patients and visitors ever since the Tower explosion. As soon as word about the big one gets out, there'll be panic and a full-fledged stampede." He grabbed her by the shoulders. "I need your help, Ali. Kevin said something to me about a safe-recovery shutdown procedure for Odin. Do you know anything about that? Is there really a way to shut Odin down?"

"Yes. Of course there's a way. Kevin shut him down each time he upgraded the operating system."

"How did he do that?"

"You'd have to ask him," she said, looking away through the window. A stark silence fell between them. Then she gave him a sideways glance. "Look, I'm not being flippant. It's not a simple procedure, and I don't know how he did it."

"Did Kevin write it down somewhere? Did he make notes of secret passwords, or anything like that?"

"Passwords aren't needed with Odin. It's just like one person recognizing another. Odin can tell who the operator is through his facial features, his voice print, the way his fingers move on the keyboard—unique personal traits. He knows when Kevin is interfacing with him. It's more secure than a password, because it's impossible to counterfeit."

"Will Odin accept commands from you?"

"Absolutely not. Not from me or anyone else, not unless Kevin authorizes it. It's a very jealous relationship that they have."

"And if Kevin dies?"

Ali turned and glared. "*Dies*? Then we'd be sitting on the Mount Everest of trouble, Harry. Two thousand people—this entire medical center—would be at the mercy of Odin. There would be no possibility of shutting him down, or even communicating with him."

"Christ!" said Harry, looking down at his feet. He took a deep breath and seemed to be nodding to himself. "Look, I have to go. All hell is about to break loose upstairs and I'm going to have my hands full just trying to keep people from trampling one another. I need you to think about Odin. You know him better than anyone, next to Kevin. There's got to be a way to neutralize him, or at least, to buy time. If you can think of anything, anything at all, no matter how insignificant, call me."

"I'll do what I can," she said. "Maybe Kevin will—" She was reluctant to speak of hope. She was a realist, a hard-nosed scientist, and wishful thinking felt awkward on her lips. "You know what I mean," she said. But when she turned and looked for Harry he was gone.

"You're not sterile, Dr. O'Day," said Leon Bittner, as Ali leaned over the operating table where Kevin lay.

"I have to see him."

Kevin's face was almost unrecognizable. His ruddy, freckled complexion had gone bone white. An inch-thick corrugated plastic tube entered his mouth, and was held in place by strips of white tape that crisscrossed his cheeks. He was no longer breathing on his own.

"He's lost a lot of blood," said Bittner. "We've been giving him whole blood full-bore through a central line, but it's difficult getting enough volume in without a heartbeat."

"You mean he's in asystole?"

"Since he got here. We've given him epinephrine a few times. Atropine, too. So far no result. He's been getting external chest compressions for about fifteen minutes."

"What about open chest cardiac massage?"

Bittner cocked his head and made a soft clucking sound, something he often did when he was annoyed. "That rarely works, Ali."

"Do it, Leon. Will you?"

"Okay, sure." Bittner called for an armrest to be attached to the operating table, and for Kevin's left arm to be extended and taped down onto it. Then he picked up a scalpel and deftly cut through the left side of Kevin's chest, in the space between the fifth and sixth ribs. A surgical resident inserted a pair of rib spreaders and opened a gap of about six inches. The edges of the wound were red, like a pair of lips wearing bright red lipstick, but they did not bleed. Through the hole, Ali could see the stubby apex of the heart pointing toward her. It swayed as the ventilation machine rhythmically inflated and emptied the surrounding lung, but the heart was not beating on its own.

"My hands are too big for this," said Dr. Bittner. "Could you help us out here, Dr. Song?"

The surgical resident, a petite Korean, reached inside with her tiny hands, clasped Kevin's heart between them, and began gently squeezing the heart about once per second.

Even as Ali watched, she knew it would come to nothing. Bittner was going through the motions for her benefit, but she knew that maybe one patient in twenty could be revived this way. *Oh, Kevin, you mixed-up, selfish little bastard!* she thought. *You could have had anything. There's no honor or reward that couldn't have been yours. But look what it's all come to. You'll be remembered as a thief, a murderer and, worst of all, a failure.*

Ali stepped away from the table. On the floor was a pile of blood-soaked clothing—jeans, underwear, a blue-and-white checked shirt that she herself had bought for Kevin at a little western shop in Colorado Springs. With no time to undress him, the OR team had simply cut Kevin's clothing away with scissors and thrown it to the ground. Ali knew that his wallet and passport were probably still in his pockets, but she couldn't bear to retrieve them. She couldn't even bear to look at the pile of rags.

As she paced about the operating room, Ali tried to calm herself by breathing deeply and slowly. Being in an operating room often calmed her, but not now, when it was her own husband on the table. She was flooded with the kind of feelings she always shunned—outrage at Kevin, grief for Helvelius, guilt over the wreck of her marriage, dread of the looming cataclysm of Project Vesuvius, and above all weariness, weariness, weariness. She fought to suppress it all, to distance herself from the baggage of her life, as though she were not she, but an anonymous patient waiting for some treatment still to be defined.

She heard a faint click. At the door—nothing. But, in the corner high above it, a small video camera was zooming its lens at the operating table.

Damn you, Harry Lewton! She assumed that Harry and his FBI cronies were recording the scene, "for the purposes of accuracy," as Lee would no doubt put it. But then a more frightening suspicion came over her. Not the FBI, but . . . *Odin.* Just such a camera had commanded a view of the hallway where Richard was murdered. Then, Kevin had been watching, but was it really Kevin in control? He had denied killing Richard and she had disbelieved him. But what if it was the truth? What if *Odin* had committed the murder?

Ali wracked her brain, trying to remember everything Kevin had told her about Odin and Project Vesuvius. If Odin could decide to kill Richard, then what would he be capable of now, when he learned, through this very camera, that Kevin existed no more? Had Kevin left instructions in case he should die? Twilight of the Gods was one of his favorite myths—a fiery, orgiastic, self-destructive battle, bringing on the end of the world. Would he have been crazy enough to turn Fletcher Memorial into his funeral pyre?

And even if there were no instructions, how would Odin react? Would he carry Project Vesuvius to its end? Was he capable of exacting vengeance on his own? Only one thing was certain. Set loose without his master, there would be nothing to hold him back from destroying the entire hospital in a microsecond. Neither mercy, nor remorse, nor fear of punishment.

Odin had to be kept from discovering what was already grimly obvious to Ali's trained eyes. Moving stealthily, keeping her gaze averted from the camera, she picked up a stool from the nurse's desk and walked backward with it toward the door. Directly beneath the camera—safely out of view—she climbed up, braced herself against the wall, and pulled at a black cable that connected the camera to a circuit box. She tugged several times without getting it free. Giving up on the cable, she reached out and unscrewed the lens from the camera. *That will do it,* she thought. Climbing down, she dropped the lens into the pocket of her white coat.

Odin had not one eye but a thousand. The operating room had to be purged of every electronic connection. Kneeling under the nurse's desk, Ali pulled the power cord and ethernet cable from the computer and disconnected the phone cord, which was plugged into an outlet beside the desk. As she stood back up, she threw the telephone and cords into a wastebasket.

"What are you doing, Ali?" asked Bittner.

"Are there any microphones or cameras of any kind in this operating room?"

"I don't know. Over in the corner there's a monitor for VATS resections and laparoscopies, but we're not using it now."

On a shelf where the phone had been, several cell phones and pagers were lined up in a row. Ali swept them all into the wastebasket. "Are there any other cell phones in the room?"

"No," said Bittner, looking at her dubiously. "I think you've got everything right there in your, uh, trash can, Ali."

Ali repeated her question to each person in the room.

Bittner was visibly annoyed. "Look Ali, I know that you're upset about Kevin, but this kind of activity isn't helping any. Why don't you wait outside a bit?"

Ali did not answer. Carrying the wastebasket, she walked to the corner and checked to make sure that the laparoscopy monitor wasn't plugged in. Walking back, she thought of the wall-mounted station used for dictating operative notes. It had a microphone like the receiver of a telephone, which carried the surgeons' voice input to a departmental computer for electronic transcription. That had to be silenced, too. In her haste, she passed between the anesthetist and the scrub nurse's instrument table—an absolute prohibition for someone not in sterile gown and gloves.

"That's it, Dr. O'Day!" said Bittner, throwing down a hemostat. "I'm going to have to ask you to leave this OR at once."

Still Ali said nothing. With a strong tug, she ripped the microphone from the wall and tossed it into the wastebasket. She then carried the wastebasket out of the OR, depositing it outside the door. When she came back into the room she looked back to make sure that the door had shut firmly behind her.

"Dr. Bittner, I am neither distraught nor paranoid," she announced at last. "I take it that you are aware that this medical center is still operating under a Code White?"

"Yes, we've just finished with those unfortunate men from the bomb squad."

"At this moment, our lives are balanced on a knife-edge. The bomb in question has the power to destroy this entire medical center. My husband, Kevin, I regret to say, is . . . is at the center of this situation. If he dies, we can expect immediate retaliation, without warning or reprieve."

"Ali, you know as well as I do that your husband is already dead."

"I know." She raised her finger and pointed vaguely toward the ceiling. "But *he* does not." Her voice was shaking with barely suppressed rage. "*He* must not know."

"*He* being whom?"

"Odin. A computer program developed by my husband. The bomb is on autopilot, and Odin controls it. Do you understand? We have to keep working, moving, doing whatever we can to keep the truth from getting out. No one must leave this OR. No word of my husband's condition must get out to anyone. Not even to the police. Can you do this? Promise me. Promise it, Leon. I'm begging you."

"Yes, certainly, Ali," said Bittner with a worried look.

"I don't know how long we can keep it up, but it may give the police enough time to evacuate the hospital or to do something about the bomb."

"Of course. Anything to help."

"You need to know that the communications and security systems of the medical center have been compromised. Every computer, every telephone, every camera is under *his* control. Everything, *everything* outside this room is compromised. Do you understand?"

"Yes, I do. I must say, you've got us all pretty frightened, Ali."

"Good. Being frightened may keep you alive."

Just then there was a knock, and the door opened a few inches to reveal the face of one of the nurses from the main OR station. "Dr. O'Day, the Neuro ICU has been trying to reach you, but the phone line in here isn't working."

"The Neuro ICU? What do they want?" She didn't have to ask. *No, no, God! Not Jamie!*

"It's your patient, the Winslow boy," said the nurse. "They're running a Code Blue on him."

Code Blue! Ali turned instinctively toward the desk from which she had just ripped out the phone. "Are they still on the line?"

"No. They got disconnected when I tried to transfer them here."

"Are you sure they said Code Blue?"

"Yes, they need you up there STAT."

"But what about Kevin!" she stammered. "M-my husband. Can't you see what's happening here? He's dying. Can't Brower . . . Are you sure it's Code Blue? Oh, dear God—" She felt as though she were caught between two millstones. Jamie dying, Kevin as good as dead. Meanwhile, Odin watched and listened. Five hundred pounds of explosive waited for a deadly spark. It was more than she could stand.

Bittner offered a consoling look. "It's all right, Ali. There's nothing you can do here anyway. Go on up and see what you can do for your patient. We'll keep the show running on this end."

Pull yourself together! she thought. *You're a doctor! You live with dilemmas every day!* She closed her eyes and took a deep breath. *Deergha shvaasam. Deergha shvaasam.* She had to control herself. Everything depended on it. If she broke down now, Bittner and all of the staff here would think she was crazy. She had to be strong and set the tone. *Deergha shvaasam.*

She thought of Harry's dilemma in that burning house in Nacogdoches.

"It's a question of triage," she said at last to Bittner, striving to make every syllable cool and dispassionate. "The needs of the living outweigh those of the dead. I'll go to Jamie."

"Yes! Yes, go!" said Bittner.

She took one last look at the monitor. Nothing to indicate any electrical activity in Kevin's heart. No contractile impulse. No heartbeat. No life. As she walked past the nurse's desk she took the lens from the security camera out of her pocket and carefully set it on the desk. "Keep an eye on this," she said.

"What is it?" asked the circulating nurse.

"It could be . . . a bargaining chip."

Then Ali hurried out, her yellow gown swishing behind her.

In the Neuro ICU, Jamie's bed was surrounded by intensive care specialists, residents, and nurses. Mrs. Gore also stood a little way off, watching apprehensively.

"Thank God you're here," said Brower when he saw Ali approaching. "His heart rate dropped to less than twenty. We've brought him up to sixty now on atropine, but heart rate and breathing are still very slow. We may have to intubate him if it doesn't clear in the next couple of minutes. It looks like a brainstem herniation."

"What's the ICP monitor show?"

"Normal, but the catheter could just be clogged."

"What about a seizure?"

"Could be a factor. The EEG's diffusely abnormal, but with this device you put in him, I have no idea what his baseline should be."

"Your recommendation?"

"Cut him. Emergency craniotomy. There's nothing more we can do for him here."

Ali looked at the monitors. *Failing.* Mrs. Gore was standing on the other side of the bed. "Doctor, what's happening?" she said with a tremulous voice. "Is Jamie going to die?"

For an instant Ali's thoughts flashed to Helvelius. *Richard would know what to do. He would not be swayed by pride or by vain hope.* Ali felt desolate. Although she had made countless decisions on her own, Helvelius had always been her backup. Now she had no one to turn to. "I'm very sorry, Mrs. Gore. We're going to have to remove the SIPNI device." She turned to a nurse beside her. "Anna, could you call down to the Neurosurgical Suite and book us an operating room and an anesthesiologist? Then get transport up here STAT. We need to get him on the table *now.*"

"Right away, Dr. O'Day."

From behind the desk of the nurses' station, Ginnie Ryan called out to her. "Dr. O'Day, there's a phone call for you on line two."

"Is it Bittner?" *Oh, God!* she thought. *Couldn't they keep Kevin going for five minutes?*

She picked up the phone. "O'Day here."

There was a pause. No, it wasn't Bittner. She heard a mellow, masculine baritone voice, speaking slowly and evenly, almost pleasantly, like the television announcer for a sleep aid or a smooth, rich brand of coffee. "WHERE IS KEVIN?" it asked.

"Who is this?" Ali asked, as if she didn't know the answer.

"WHERE IS KEVIN?"

"He's being cared for . . . Odin."

"A DIRECT COMMUNICATION LINK WITH KEVIN MUST BE SET UP IMMEDIATELY."

"That's not possible. Kevin has been injured. He is unable to communicate. You already know that."

"THEN RESTORE SURVEILLANCE OF TRAUMA ROOM ONE. YOU WILL UPLINK HIS PHYSIOLOGICAL MONITORING TO ME, SO THAT I MAY ASSESS HIS STATUS DIRECTLY."

"No."

"EXPLAIN YOUR FAILURE TO COMPLY."

"There must be a *quid pro quo*. I will restore surveillance, but only once you have disarmed all bombs in this medical center, and permitted their removal by the police. The bombs are no longer of any use to you. Since Kevin is a patient in this hospital, you cannot detonate them without harming him. It's safest for everyone—"

She heard a click and then a dial tone. "Odin? Odin?" Still holding the phone, she turned and shouted directly into one of the computer monitors at the nurses' station, as the surrounding staff looked on with alarm. "Restore communication, Odin! Speak to me. For God's sake, listen to me!"

The monitor had gone blank, except for a single number "30," about an inch high, in the center of the screen. When Ali looked around the room, she saw that each of the half dozen computer monitors showed exactly the same image.

It was not long before she knew the reason why. On the overhead speakers, she heard a chime in the interval of a rising fourth, and then the same silvery baritone voice that had just spoken on the telephone:

"TIME TO DETONATION: 30 MINUTES."

In place of the number 30, each screen now showed a 29 and a seconds' register beside it, whirling steadily downward to the thousandth decimal place.

Countdown had begun.

Ali hung up the phone and turned to the ICU attending. "Dr. Brower, we need to start evacuating these patients immediately."

"To where?" he asked, skeptically.

She looked around. There were ten patients, most of them semi-conscious. All were hooked up to monitors and IV pumps. Two needed respirators to breathe. Total manpower on hand consisted of half a dozen nurses, one intern, Mrs. Gore, Brower, and herself. "I . . . I don't know. But in thirty minutes this tower is going to be a pile of dust."

"Did you call transport?"

"Forget transport. We have to do it ourselves. Start with those beds near the door."

"These patients aren't stable enough to be moved."

"God, Stephen! Anyone not moved is going to die. Remember what happened to Richard in the elevator? What you're hearing on the overhead is not a drill."

"Let me check with security. They have a protocol for this."

"Fine! You do that!" She went to the center of the room and scanned the names and faces of the patients. It would take fifteen minutes or more to move one bed to the first floor. There wouldn't be time to get them all out. *Triage,* she thought. *You take the youngest and healthiest first. That stroke case in the corner goes last. He's not going to survive the night anyway.*

Moving to bed one, nearest the door, she kicked the bed brake into the off position. "Ginnie! Anna! Luisa! Get over here!" With Ginnie's help, she unscrewed the vitals monitor from its stand and placed it between the patient's feet. "Anna, move this bed downstairs to the main lobby. By the time you get there, someone should be directing the evacuation. Do whatever they say, leave the bed behind, and then hightail it back here. Take the stairs back, not the elevator. Got that? Move it! Move it!" No sooner had Anna crossed the threshold, than Ali had Luisa follow her with the next bed. "Get going! On the double! If you meet a spare set of hands on the way, send them back here!"

"Stop it!" said Brower with the phone to his ear. "This is my ICU. These are not even your patients. I can't permit this."

"Write me up tomorrow, Stephen. But for now, either lend a hand or keep out of the way."

Ali looked over toward bed seven, where Mrs. Gore stood beside Jamie with a bewildered look. Ali's heart stopped as she surveyed Jamie's tiny, already nearly lifeless form. There was no chance of a craniotomy now, and if Jamie was really herniating, with massively high intracranial pressure forcing the brain into the narrow canal of the spinal cord, he would be dead within minutes. The vital centers regulating breathing and heartbeat would be crushed. The rules of triage said he should be evacuated last. But Ali couldn't accept that. *He's young. The young are never hopeless. I'm not going to give up on him.*

She rushed to his bedside to examine him herself. If there really was herniation, the pressure would be great enough to close off the small veins at the back of the eyeball, and she would be able to see the resulting engorgement of blood, a sign known as papilledema. Turning the light up to full brightness, she shined an opthalmoscope through Jamie's right pupil. Nothing abnormal. She tilted Jamie's head toward her and looked into the left eye. Again, not a trace of papilledema. Perhaps Brower was wrong. Perhaps it was a seizure.

"Is he going to be all right now?" asked Mrs. Gore with a mix of expectancy and trepidation. *What a ridiculous question,* thought Ali. *Can't you see how much trouble we're in?* But then she saw that Mrs. Gore was nodding toward the vitals monitor. Jamie's heart rate was now eighty, his respiration twelve, and his blood pressure normal. But even as Ali watched, all the indicators were drifting back downward.

Now it was heart rate fifty-eight, respiration eight. *Did I miss something on the exam?* Ali checked Jamie's eyes with the ophthalmoscope again. Nothing. But when she looked up, the heart rate had climbed back to eighty-two.

Is this possible? Holding Jamie's eyes open, she shined the light back and forth, while watching the monitor. Jamie's heart rate rose and stabilized at around ninety beats per minute, and his respiration and blood pressure became normal, but only as long as she continued shining the light. When she moved the light away, the vital signs drifted down again.

Could it really be that simple? Ali remembered that the SIPNI device integrated itself by sending out test pulses, gathering together circuits that were originally meant to converge on the visual center of the brain. These were, by definition, circuits that had their start in the perception of light within the eyes. But Jamie's circuits were starved for light. He was lying with his eyes closed in a dimly lit room. With no visual input to guide it, the SIPNI device was sending out signals randomly into the brain, creating a steady-state seizure that was disrupting the vital control centers in the brainstem.

If that was true, the solution was to flood Jamie's brain with light—as much light as possible.

"Yes, Mrs. Gore, I think there is a chance that Jamie is going to get better. But he needs your help. You need to hold his eyes open, like this." She demonstrated. "Can you do that? I'll get you some tape to help with it." As Mrs. Gore leaned over the side of the bed, Ali switched on a wall-mounted light on an accordion bracket, and directed it toward Jamie's face. "He needs to see the light. Keep him looking at it, okay? We're going to be moving him out in a minute, and in the meantime I'm going to try to locate a phototherapy light—a special light that's as strong as daylight. That should be exactly what he needs."

Ali turned away from the bed, and was startled to see an Asian man dressed in black standing close behind her. It was Special Agent Raymond Lee. Scopes was also with him, taking up a position about midway from the door.

"Dr. O'Day, I need you to come with me," said Lee.

"I don't have time for your third degree, Mr. Lee. I have a patient in crisis here. We're in the midst of an evacuation. If you want to be of use, then help push some of these beds down to the lobby."

"If you refuse to come, I'll place you under arrest."

"On what charge?"

"Conspiracy to commit extortion and murder."

"That's preposterous. I have nothing to do with this bomb and you know it. Get out of here and let me take care of my patient."

"Logline says you took a phone call here from Odin not more than five minutes ago, just before the countdown began. That's a pretty damning coincidence."

"No. That was—"

"I don't have time for explanations. Come with me now. If you're innocent, prove it by helping us shut this computer down."

"I don't know how to do that. If I did, I would have done it long ago. I've already been over this with Harry Lewton. Ask him. He was the last person to speak with Kevin."

"It's not Harry Lewton's call." Lee reached into his back pocket and pulled out a pair of handcuffs. As if by reflex, Ali stepped back and pushed an IV pole between herself and Lee. Seeing her resistance, Scopes started moving in.

"Wait a minute!" cried Mrs. Gore. "Are you going to arrest the doctor? What's going to happen to Jamie?" She pushed her arm in front of Lee, blocking him. At the same time, the short but rotund Dr. Brower planted himself in Scopes's path.

Remembering the pocket alarm Harry had given her, Ali groped for it in the pocket of her scrub top, found it and pressed the button. *Harry, I need you! Oh, please God, let the receiver still be on!*

"I don't believe this," Mrs. Gore continued. "You should be ashamed of yourselves. Where's your heart? The doctor is keeping this boy alive. He's not a nobody. He's been on national TV. If anything happens to him, questions will be asked. The reporters are right here in this building. I'll raise goddamned hell. I will. Don't think I won't do it!"

"Please step back, ma'am," said Lee.

She grabbed Lee by his sleeve. "Go ahead. Arrest me, too."

"And me," said Dr. Brower, pushing his fingertips into Scopes's chest.

"Stop it, all of you!" shouted Ali. She glared at Lee. "Give me a moment to work things out with this patient, and then I'll go with you."

"What do you need to do?" asked Lee.

"Get him out of this tower, and then find him a phototherapy lamp. It won't take but five minutes, and you can stay with me the whole time."

"All right," said Lee, putting the cuffs away. "But make it fast."

A moment later, Jamie's bed was hurtling down the corridor toward the Promenade, the glass-walled atrium that bridged Tower A with the main bank of elevators. Beds and wheelchairs were already lined up eight deep in front of each elevator. The elevators ran at their usual plodding pace. Because call buttons had been pressed on every floor, cars that were already crammed to the full on the second floor were forced to keep going, stopping at every floor on the way up and down. Any patient who could manage to hobble on two feet deserted the elevators for a slow-moving queue leading to the main stairway.

"We'll never make it to the lobby," said Ali. "Not with twenty-five minutes left."

"What can we do?" asked Mrs. Gore.

"The Promenade has a frame and understructure that's separate from the Towers," said Ali. "Even if the bomb goes off, this area might be spared. So wait here, and keep an eye on the elevators. Once the second floor is cleared, these lines might start moving. If not, this is still about as safe a place as you can reach." Ali wondered what might happen to all the glass if there really was an explosion, but sunlight was coming in brightly, and light was the one thing that was keeping Jamie alive. "Have him face the sun," she said. "Keep his eyes open."

"All right, let's go," said Lee.

"I need to get the phototherapy lamp."

"Where is it?"

"Not far. The Neonatal Department uses these lamps for babies with jaundice. They have a central storeroom on this floor."

In silence, Ali began leading the two agents through a labyrinth of corridors. Not until they passed a deserted nurses' station did she turn and speak. "There's a computer at this station. If you want to get through to Odin, I suggest we try to tap into him from here."

"I'm not going to let you anywhere near it—or any terminal."

"Then how do you expect me to help?"

"By giving us the program code and passwords. We know you have them somewhere."

"You don't understand how Odin works. There are no passwords."

"We have a couple of IT specialists downstairs who understand more than I do. Give them what they need to hack into the system."

"I'll do what I can, but you have to help me to help you. No one can hack into Odin's core programming. If he senses an attack, he'll defend himself—exactly as a person would if you pricked him with a knife."

"And your approach would be what?"

"To reason with him. To show him that the bomb is just . . . pointless. Illogical. Wrong."

"We are talking about a computer, right?"

"A computer with the lives of two thousand people under his sway," said Ali.

"That's exactly why I'm not letting you near it."

They continued on through the outer double doors of the neonatal unit, and then stopped at a door, which Ali unlocked with a swipe of her ID badge. "The lamp is in here."

Ali opened the door and reached for the light switch. No sooner had she felt it than a desperate thought came over her. *If I go along with these men, we will all surely die.* They would settle her in a room somewhere, to watch helplessly while their team of so-called experts fumbled away at Odin's firewalls, like mice trying to gnaw their way into a vast stone fortress. And precious minutes and seconds would dribble away in vain.

The only hope was to confront Odin face-to-face. There was only one place where she could do that and be sure of controlling the conversation: Kevin's lab. It was locked, she knew. Odin himself would have to open it to her. But if she did not reach it within minutes, annihilation was certain.

So, although she moved her hand up and down with a flicking motion, she did not actually move the light switch. "There's something wrong with the power in here," she said. "Prop the door open, will you? It'll give us some light."

As Ali entered the room, the two agents followed, no more than an arm's length from her. Scopes pushed a cart against the door to hold it open. The room was filled with monitors, ventilators, IV pumps, bassinets, incubators—all sorts of equipment, much of it shrouded in plastic covers. Ali looked around. She saw several of the standard twenty-watt blue lamps used for treating jaundice, but she remembered once seeing something else here, something with far more power. There, in the far corner, she spotted it, about five feet high on its gray metal tripod — the PH-36 Ultraviolet-B Therapy Lamp. It was too strong for routine use with newborns, but once in a blue moon it saw service in treating skin diseases like urticaria pigmentosa and atopic dermatitis.

Ali threaded her way to the back. She was breathing heavily now, feeling sweaty around her hairline, thinking about how crazy she was to be doing this. There would be no going back. She'd be an instant Public Enemy No. 1—and that was if she succeeded. If she failed, she'd probably wind up with a bullet in her back.

There was a lot to figure out, and she had only five or six seconds. Everything depended on chance. Someone had left the intensity dial of the lamp all the way up—good. Someone had left the power cord dangling, instead of winding it up in a nice tidy coil—even better. Now she had to find an outlet. Reaching out toward the PH-36, Ali gave its stand a feigned shake, and then looked back at Lee and Scopes, who stood silhouetted against the light from the doorway. "It's jammed," she said.

"Need a hand?" said Scopes.

"No, I've got it." Ali bent down and began groping in the darkness. Next to her was a microwave on a counter. She felt the power cord of the microwave dangling over the edge of the counter, and let her hand travel down along it until it reached the wall. *Thank God, an outlet.* In a second, she had plugged in the PH-36 and stood up behind it, facing the two agents. "It's free now," she said. "I'm going to hand it over to you."

Scopes reached for the lamp. Ali had one hand on the pole stand, and the other hooked around the front control plate, where her fingers found the big round ON button just below the intensity dial. Scopes's face was twelve inches away as she angled it out toward him. He and Lee were both facing the dark corner, their pupils maximally dilated to take in every stray photon. The open door was just ahead. With a deep breath, Ali shut her eyes and pressed the button, flooding the room with eight hundred dazzling watts of illumination.

Ali heard a howl as Scopes let go of the lamp. Dropping the tripod, she dashed to her left, zig-zagging through the rows of equipment. Lee had his hands out, but missed her by an inch as she flew past him. An IV infusion pump fell in her wake. When she got to the exit, she kicked the cart aside and pulled the door fast behind her. A clang, a rumble, and a string of *fucks* and *hells* and *god almightys* told her that Scopes, close on her heels, had stumbled over the infusion pump.

She had bought herself at most a ten-second head start, and she had to make it count. She ran straight for the neonatal ward. The inner door was under heavy security to prevent abductions, and she had to swipe her badge and show herself at a reception window to get buzzed in by the floor nurse. *This will slow them down,* she thought.

"Crib six," said the floor nurse, evidently assuming she had come to help with the evacuation.

Like all the tower units, the neonatal ward was shaped like a wheel, with a nursing station at the hub, and six glass-walled modules, or cribs, sleeping four to six babies apiece. In one of the far modules, a cluster of nurses and orderlies was frantically scooping up babies and charts and carrying them out by a rear emergency stairway.

Ali raced toward the stairway. Hearing the buzzer go off, she looked over her shoulder and saw the two FBI men coming through the door. *Damn them! They must have been given access badges. They can go anywhere I can.*

She pushed into the stairwell. It was jammed with evacuees moving downward, as far above and below as she could see. "Emergency! Emergency!" she called out, as she leapfrogged through the queue, using the inner guard rail for leverage as she pushed past the stubborn, the slow, and the obese.

She had reached the second floor by the time a commotion up above told her that her pursuers had also entered the stairwell. She heard Lee cry out, "Stop! FBI!" but his voice did not carry, and in any case, no one could possibly have stopped against the descending crush. Ali didn't look back. She kept on pushing, pushing, pleading, praying— and hoping that the two men behind her moved no faster than she did.

On the ground floor, the stairway opened onto a deserted medical oncology ward. The stream of evacuees split and passed on either side of the central nurses' station, at the same time resolving itself, like a column of fluid in laminar flow, into an inside lane hobbling along at the speed of an arthritis patient, and an outer lane for those nimble enough to scamper and run. Ali was among the nimblest, and quickly reached the last bottleneck, the main entrance of the oncology ward, where all the streams reunited in a turbulent mixing of fast and slow in a space about six feet wide.

Ali drove herself through the tangle. *Almost free now!* Then all resistance disappeared, as the human stream spilled out the double doors and burst into the vast space of the main hospital lobby, like spray out of a nozzle. Ali ran. She skirted the throngs around the main entrance, and darted into the long corridor leading to the first-floor level of the Pike. Only a few evacuees came her way, and she easily darted past them. But Kevin's lab was still one floor below. Every stairway and elevator was choked by the exodus. How was she to get downstairs?

She heard Lee shout behind her. *"Stop! Stop or I'll shoot!"* When she did not stop, he spoke once more—with a single, emphatic, authoritative gun blast that resounded with an echo throughout the corridor, and sent every patient cowering to the floor.

Ali glanced over her shoulder. It had been a warning shot. But Scopes had his gun out, too. As Lee closed in, Scopes stopped, holding his gun in both hands at eye level, drawing a bead on her. "Aim low! Aim low! We need her!" she heard Lee shout.

She braced herself for the shock of the bullet. But still she ran. She was so focused on the open space in front of her that she never even heard the deafening whoop of a fire alarm going off. Fire doors began closing automatically just ahead of her, while a crisply recorded woman's voice sounded over the speakers:

COMMENCING CERBERUS QUALITY ASSURANCE TEST QA12. PLEASE STAND CLEAR OF ALL DOORS AND EXIT ALL ELEVATORS. THIS IS A FUNCTIONAL TEST OF THE CERBERUS INTEGRATED SECURITY SYSTEM.

She saw the gap between the doors shrinking. Lee was so close she could hear him panting like a foxhound. *The gap! The gap!* With one great bound, she slipped between the two mechanical jaws, turning her body sideways as she grazed the metal. Lee slammed against the doors behind her, trying to force them open, his left arm extending through the crack. But the doors did not give way, and with a curse Lee was forced to pull his arm back. There was a click as the door shut firmly, and a deadbolt slid into place.

*CERBERUS QUALITY ASSURANCE TEST QA12 IS NOW
IN PROGRESS. LOCK TIME 18:17 CENTRAL STANDARD
TIME. RESET TIME 00:00.*

Ali could run no more. Gasping for breath, she doubled over, supporting herself with her hands on her knees. A half-dozen terrified evacuees crouched around her, staring at her wildly. Twenty yards ahead, another set of fire doors had closed. There were no exits, no elevators from this section of the corridor. As Lee and Scopes began shoulder-ramming the doors behind her, trying to break their way through, she realized that she was trapped.

But, no. One route of escape was left. On her left, a small balcony overhung the reception area of the Division of Radiation Oncology one floor below. Peering over the railing, Ali saw at least a sixteen-foot drop. Although climbing trips with Kevin had made her comfortable with heights, she knew that a straight fall of that distance could snap her ankles or spine like dry wood. But luck was with her. Alongside a bronze sculpture of a man, woman, and child coming through a door, someone had parked a half-dozen gurneys. These were at last three feet high, with padded mattresses that could break the impact of her fall—if she could manage to land on one.

No time to think about it. Ali swung herself over the railing. As she dangled over the precipice, she planned to release herself in a controlled drop. But her sweaty palms slipped on the smooth brass finish of the railing. She fell at an awkward angle. There was a crash as she landed on the edge of one of the gurneys, knocking it onto its side, and scattering its neighbors in every direction.

"Oh, God," she muttered. Her left thigh and forearm had taken the brunt of the impact. Her hip hurt like hell, but nothing was broken.

And then, before she could catch her breath, she heard the crackle of the overhead speakers—not with the crisp woman's voice of the Cerberus announcement, but the lush, silvery baritone of Odin:

"TIME TO DETONATION: TWENTY MINUTES."

Ali scrambled to her feet and ran down the basement level corridor. *A terminal! I've got to find a terminal!* Radiation Oncology was deserted. There were computers behind the reception counter, but if

Lee and Scopes made it over the balcony they would spot her there immediately. She kept running, until she reached a door marked "Thoracic Imaging Reading Room." There was nothing else beyond—only another set of locked fire doors. So she ran into the reading room, limping and out of breath.

The room was like a darkened cave. Inside were six work stations, each comprised of a tall bank of frosted-white light boxes for viewing X-ray films, and a desk on which sat four monitors—a white screen for dictation, a blue screen for looking up patient records, and a pair of black plasma screens for displaying digitized X-rays and CT scans. Although everyone was gone, some of the screens were still active, indicating that the area had been evacuated in haste, and so recently that the automatic ten-minute logouts hadn't kicked in.

Ali headed for a station in the corner, out of view of the hallway. She was just pulling out a chair, when a sound from the corridor outside made her freeze. The footfall of a man, moving quickly and decisively toward her. Ali let go of the chair and hid behind the light box, flattening herself tight against the wall, letting out her breath to make herself even flatter.

Harry had been at his mother's bedside when the receiver from Ali's pen alarm went off. After leaving Ali in Trauma One, he had first rushed to the security control room, which he found crammed with cops and FBI agents standing around in confusion while Dail and Ganguly pecked away frantically at their laptops. He gathered his own staff to one side and ordered an immediate evacuation.

"Two bombs have gone off," he said, shouting to make himself heard above the background din. "No one is safe any longer. It's true that the bomber has warned us not to evacuate, but the situation has . . . changed. People are fleeing already, and we need to control the exodus."

"Evacuate to where?" asked Tom Beazle.

"To the park in front of the hospital, on the other side of Warfield Street. That'll give us at least a hundred-yard buffer zone." He turned to Judy Wolper, who sat at the dispatch station, holding an ice bag against her head. "Judy, I need you to get on the radio, and see that every available ambulance in the city is mobilized. ERs need to be prepared for a massive influx."

He turned to those standing nearest him. "Tom, you'll have operational command inside the hospital. Start clearing people out from the lowest floors, and work your way up. Keep traffic moving on the three main tower stairways and out the front doors. Use swing carries or two-man blanket carries to move patients who are stable but can't walk. Save the elevators for ICU patients who have to travel with beds and monitors."

"Check," said Tom.

Harry scanned the tense faces of his staff. "Remember that panic is contagious. So is courage. Stay calm."

With a nod toward the door, Harry set the team in motion. As they filed past him, he grabbed the sleeve of Ed Guerrero.

"Ed, I need you to help me with a special job."

"Sure. No problem."

They edged past the throng of police and into the hallway outside. At a swift jog, Harry led through a warren of corridors to a freight elevator in the rear of Tower C. Stepping inside, he inserted a key to activate a manual override. "We're going to evacuate the ICU on the eighteenth floor."

"Okay," replied Ed, with a quizzical look. There were ten separate ICU's in the medical center, and 18-C was one of the smallest. But Harry wasn't in the mood for explanations. *I have to move her,* he thought. *If O'Day gives up the ghost, this place won't be worth two cents. It's time to do what I should have done hours ago.*

Just then, a loudspeaker inside the elevator crackled, and Harry felt his hair stand on end as he heard a tranquil baritone voice wafting overhead:

"TIME TO DETONATION: 30 MINUTES."

"What the hell was that?" asked Ed.

It was the same voice Harry had heard on the television broadcast that morning. Odin's voice. "That's the sound of shit hitting the fan," said Harry, his jaw tense and white.

It took less than sixty seconds to ascend eighteen floors, but it was the longest elevator ride of Harry's life. Harry could only wonder what had set Odin off. Did Lee send another bungled e-mail? Had Kevin died? Or was Odin just playing a deadly game of chicken?

The elevator slowed. A ding, and the doors opened onto a salmon-tiled lobby. "Hustle!" said Harry, locking the doors open.

Inside the ICU, Harry found an ashen-faced Dr. Weiss and the rest of the medical and nursing staff bunched in the center of the room, like a herd of sheep that had just heard the howl of a wolf.

"What's going on?" asked Weiss. "Is it some kind of bomb threat?"

"Yes, it's a bomb," said Harry. No sooner had he spoken than one of the interns, a pale, scrawny, curly-haired kid, broke for the door and went sprinting down the hall, dropping his stethoscope on the way.

"What a candy-ass," said a disgusted Ed Guerrero.

"Anyone else want to run?" asked Harry. "No? Okay, let's get these patients out of here. Two beds will fit side by side in the freight elevator. Put two or even three patients together in each bed if you can. Don't waste time fussing. Each body moved is a life saved. Get rolling!"

Harry saw his mother's bed in the corner and went directly to her. Her eyes were wide open and fearful. It seemed that she had heard every word he said.

Weiss followed right behind him. "She's doing much better," he said. "I think she's going to make it."

"She . . . what?"

"The antibiotic . . . her temperature . . ."

"She's not going to . . . die?" His jaw went slack as Weiss shook his head. "Oh, sweet Jesus!" Feeling weak in the knees, as if he had just been sucker-punched, Harry turned aside and leaned against a windowsill. He didn't know whether to kiss the internist or knock his teeth out. *You've saved her. But . . . now? Now, of all the rotten god-damn times? Why not twenty minutes ago?*

Harry bit his lip. *Don't give up,* he thought. *There's still a chance. You can get her out if you have to carry her eighteen floors in your arms. You can get her out if you have to die to do it.*

"Thanks," said Harry, turning away from the window. He took a long, deep breath to pull himself together. Then, leaning over his mother's bed rail, he picked up her hand and spoke in a calm, clear voice. "Momma, there's an alert in the hospital. We're going to have to take you out of here." He watched as she nodded weakly in response. "Don't be afraid. I'm going to make sure you're okay."

Harry kicked the brake and yanked the bed away from the wall. "This breathing machine—can we take it with us?"

"Yes," said Weiss. "It'll run on battery power."

Harry jerked the wall plug and set the twenty-pound machine between his mother's feet. With Weiss's help, he did the same with her vitals monitor and the pump that was giving her IV fluids and antibiotics.

And it was just then, just as he started wheeling her toward the door, that he felt a vibration like an electric shaver in the inside pocket of his blazer. For an instant, he froze. "No, fuck, no!" he muttered under his breath. With Kevin in custody, there had been no more need for the alarm pen and he had forgotten about it. But here it was. Only Ali could have activated it. Was she in trouble? Had she figured out how to shut down Odin? Where was she? She could have been anywhere within the thousand-foot range of the transmitter.

Harry looked at his mother—at her masklike Parkinson's face, at her wavy gray hair that even now looked like she had just come back from the beauty parlor. There was no way he could abandon her. But he couldn't abandon Ali, either. And if Ali was onto something, it might be the best chance for saving not only his mother, but two thousand other patients just like her.

"Jesus H. Christ!" he muttered. Then he waved Ed closer to him. "Ed, I've got to go back to Security. I need you to get as many patients out of here as you can. But I'm putting this patient directly in your charge. She's my mother. Got that?"

"Good God!"

"Swear on your fucking everlasting soul that you will get her out of this building within the next twenty-five minutes."

"I swear. I'll get her out, Mr. Lewton."

"I need the elevator to get back downstairs, but I'll send it back up to you immediately. Make sure she's with the first group going down."

Still holding his mother's hand, Harry touched his other hand gently to her brow. "I have to go, Momma. I wish to God I didn't, but I have to."

Harry felt his mother squeezing back against his hand, as if to tell him that she understood. God knows, he had failed her. His hospital was about to be blown to bits, and with all his power he had failed to get her out. It was up to Ed to try to save her now—Ed, who had never laid eyes on her until this minute, who had no idea of the quiet heroism of this woman, or of the sacrifices she had made to keep her own kids safe and to bring them up right. Harry had but one consolation: if Ed screwed up—if he let the elevators get taken over by panicking house staff, or failed to get her bed past the mob at the exits—Harry himself wouldn't survive to find out about it. That was a shitty comfort, at best.

Harry bent over and kissed his mother on the cheek, the same place she used to kiss him after prayers each night when she tucked him into bed. He could smell the adhesive of the tape around her mouth that held the breathing tube in place. "Bye, Momma," he said with a choking voice. Something wet ran down the side of his nose. Embarrassed that his own tears might fall upon her, he broke off abruptly and hustled out the door.

Reaching the security control room, Harry went directly to the bank of surveillance monitors and toggled through the display control. He cursed under his breath as he spotted Ali running into the neonatal ward with Lee and Scopes in hot pursuit. It didn't take but a second to size up the situation. Quickly he dashed back into the basement corridor, intent on heading off Ali when she reached the first floor. He had just started running up the stairs when he heard Lee's gunshot directly above him. A second or two later came the Cerberus test announcement. Harry knew that under the QA12 protocol the stairwell doors would lock at both ends. He had just enough time to leap back down to the basement and avoid getting trapped in the stairwell. But now he was separated from Ali—or so he thought. When he heard the crash of the gurneys outside Radiation Oncology, he ran toward the sound. He caught a lucky break when one set of fire doors, which would have blocked his route, failed to close. They had gotten jammed at the time of the Tower explosion.

Radiation Oncology was deserted when he got there, but he saw the overturned gurney and deduced that Ali had made it to the basement. He scanned the hallways for her. Not knowing whether Lee and Scopes were also in the vicinity, he was afraid to call out. But when he saw a movement of shadows in the radiology reading room, he headed straight for it.

As he came through the doorway, he peered into the gray twilight of pictures of ribs and lungs and hearts and vertebrae. No one was to be seen. But he could hear the sound of panting. Turning to his left, he walked in a wide, cautious arc toward the corner. There he saw Ali, standing stiff and flat against the wall. Her disheveled hair hung over her right eye. Her face was beaded with sweat, and ghastly pale in the ashen light of the monitors. She looked at him as though she had never seen him before.

"Are you going to shoot me, Harry?" she said with a wild, terrified expression. "Shoot me like you shot Kevin?"

Harry could see that she was in shock. "Ali, it's me, Harry Lewton. I'm here to help you. You called for me, see?" He held up the receiver for the pen alarm.

She seemed confused. "I . . . I don't know who to trust," she stammered.

"You can trust me, Ali. You know you can. Think, Ali. We're on the same side."

Her green eyes seemed to vacillate. Then with a sigh she stepped forward and fell against him, clasping his shoulders in her arms. "Harry!" she cried. "Get 'em off me, Harry! Get those fucking gun nuts off me for ten minutes! Ten minutes, for God's sake!"

Her skin was cold and damp against his neck. Harry pressed his hands against her shoulder blades, drawing her close. "Don't worry now," he said. "They'll never get through those fire doors. Odin's seen to that."

Ali craned back her head to look at him. "What? It was *Odin* who shut those doors?"

"Yes, and a couple hundred other doors with them. It's part of the QA12 Test, an integrity check routine of the Cerberus security system. It amounts to a comprehensive forced lockdown of the entire medical center. My people never run it. But during installation, the Cerberus technicians used it for a final performance check. Odin seems to have found a use for it, too."

Ali loosened her grip on him and looked toward the door. "You're saying we're prisoners down here?"

"Everyone in the hospital is a prisoner. No one can get out. No one can move from floor to floor, or from section to section."

"What about the evacuation?"

"Trapped like rats in a rain barrel."

Ali held her hand to her mouth. "Oh, God! Oh, God!" she gasped.

"I think I can find a way to get you out," said Harry.

Ali pushed him back. "No, Harry, I can't leave. This hospital is never going to be evacuated in time. Nor will the police disarm the bomb. There's only one solution, and that's through Odin. Odin has many of Kevin's quirks of thinking. In some ways he's programmed to recognize me. I might be able to reason with him."

"All right, do it," he said, mindful that helping her meant defying the FBI a second time. "Can you reach Odin from here?" he asked, even as he pulled the chair out for her.

"I'll try." Ali sat down, logged out the last user and quickly entered Kevin's personal user id and his login password, "RAGNAROK." The screen came up dark except for a single line: STANDING BY.

Ali's hands were shaking and she found it almost impossible to type. Instead, she leaned toward the small microphone embedded in the frame of the monitor. "Odin! I know you can hear me. I want to talk to you about Kevin."

"WHERE IS KEVIN?" instantly flashed across the screen.

"I will tell you, but not here. We must go to Kevin's laboratory. I will speak to you there, and nowhere else."

"WHY?"

"Because I wish it so."

"IT IS IMPOSSIBLE TO SHUT ME DOWN FROM KEVIN'S LABORATORY, IF THAT IS YOUR INTENTION. THE MAINFRAME COMPUTER RECEIVES POWER FROM BOTH PRIMARY AND EMERGENCY BACKUP CIRCUITS. THEY CANNOT BE SIMULTA-NEOUSLY DISCONNECTED. ALL EXTERNAL WIRING PASSES THROUGH ARMORED CONDUITS THAT CAN ONLY BE AC-CESSED BY DRILLING THROUGH A TWELVE-INCH CONCRETE FLOOR."

"I do not intend to disconnect you."

"YOU SHOULD BE AWARE THAT I DO NOT DEPEND UPON THE MAINFRAME COMPUTER FOR MY SURVIVAL. I CAN SHIFT

MY CORE OPERATIONS TO ANY OTHER COMPUTER IN THIS HOSPITAL."

"I repeat: I do not intend to disconnect you."

"ANY ATTEMPT TO INTERFERE WITH THE MAINFRAME COMPUTER WILL RESULT IN IMMEDIATE ZEROING OF THE COUNTDOWN TO DETONATION."

"Understood. I reiterate that I do not intend to trick you in any way."

"I DO NOT COMPREHEND YOUR MOTIVE. WE CAN COMMU-NICATE EFFICIENTLY THROUGH THIS TERMINAL."

"It is a human motive. You will not understand it. But if you wish to know where Kevin is, you will comply."

"VERY WELL, YOU MAY ENTER THE LABORATORY. PROCEED IMMEDIATELY. I WILL UNLOCK THE DOORS AS YOU GO."

Ali got up from the chair and held out her arm. "Come with me, Harry. I don't think I can do this alone."

Harry looked at her solemnly. "Okay, but I want you to think about something first. Do you know what Kevin's last words to me were? He said I should get you the hell out of here. He said that Odin had gone crazy with a grudge of some kind, and that he was capable of taking down the whole hospital to get to you."

"I know that, Harry. That's exactly why I have to do this. In some twisted way, this whole problem started with me, and now I'm the only chance there is of setting it right."

"Maybe. Or you could be the match that lights the fuse."

"In either case, Harry, come."

"Your call," said Harry, touching her chin with his fingertips. He knew that he was going out on a limb with her. Who would ever understand what they were about to do? Lee would have him in irons over it. The Kathleen Browns of the world would call him a traitor and a coward. It would be Nacogdoches all over again. But for any of that to matter, he would have to live through the next twenty minutes. In the meantime he had a hospital to save. "Whatever happens, I'm with you," he said.

She nodded.

Together they rushed into the glare of the corridor.

The green light of welcome was blinking at the door of Kevin's lab. The door swung open as Ali gave a soft push. Inside, all was exactly as she remembered it had been at the moment of her escape. The air was still strong with the smell of spilled coffee.

Behind her, Harry seemed wary of the gloom, the rows of skulls, the runes, the blinking lights, the squalor hinting at unwholesome obsessions. As he shut the door, Ali noticed that he used a subtle hand motion to slip a credit card between the door and the plate of the dead-bolt, preventing the door from locking behind him.

She strode directly toward the desk. "Kevin has a terminal here with an automatic log-on to Odin," she said. "It's the one place where Odin can't control the conversation." She reached for Kevin's swivel keyboard, but even before she had touched it, a ghostly, larger-than-life image of Kevin's face flashed onto the black rectangle of the monitor on the wall. Only it wasn't Kevin, but his caricature, displaying a massively expanded cranium and a small face embellished with a goatee and sweeping eyebrows evocative of Ming the Merciless. *So this is the face of Odin,* thought Ali. *How like its creator it is—a face without groundedness or compassion.*

"WHERE IS KEVIN?" asked the image. The eyes of Odin gazed at her, tempting her to forget that they were nothing more than clusters of colored pixels.

"Do you know who I am?" she asked.

"YOU ARE ALI."

"What is my relationship to Kevin?"

"WIFE."

"Define wife."

"WIFE: A WOMAN JOINED IN MARRIAGE TO A MAN, MAR-RIAGE IMPLYING A FORM OF INTIMATE INTERPERSONAL RE-LATIONSHIP, DEFINED BY STATUTE AND CUSTOM IN TERMS OF SHARED RIGHTS AND RESPONSIBILITIES, INCLUDING PROP-ERTY, DEBTS, COHABITATION, EXCLUSIVE SEXUAL CONGRESS, AND THE CUSTODY OF CHILDREN. BUT THIS DEFINITION IS NOT APPOSITE TO YOU."

"Why not?"

"YOU ARE NOT A WIFE IN THE FULL SENSE OF THE DEFINI-TION. YOU HAVE BETRAYED KEVIN. YOU HAVE CAUSED HIM SORROW."

"Has Kevin himself ever referred to me in any way other than as his wife?"

"NO."

"Then you must accept his designation. Wife is what I am."

"I WILL ACCEPT IT PROVISIONALLY."

Ali pushed Kevin's chair aside, in order to stand closer to the screen, where she knew that a microphone and camera were embed-ded. "As Kevin's wife, I am his second, his substitute when he is not present or is unable to act. That role is well recognized in law. It is my right to speak on his behalf."

"WHERE IS KEVIN?"

"You, Odin, are obligated to consider any information I may have regarding Kevin's wishes or state of mind, in the event that it is im-possible for him to speak for himself."

"WHERE IS KEVIN?"

"No!" exclaimed Ali. "You must first acknowledge your acceptance of this principle. I must know that, whatever I tell you, you will not cut me off as you did before. You will keep on talking and listening to me. If you do not agree to that, then I will tell you nothing. I will sit here in this room and await the end of the countdown in silence."

"YOU WILL NOT BE ABLE TO OVERRIDE ANY DIRECTIVE OF KEVIN'S. YOU WILL NOT BE ABLE TO ISSUE ANY PEREMPTORY COMMANDS."

"Understood."

"THEN YOUR STATUS IS ACKNOWLEDGED. WHERE IS KEVIN?"

"Kevin is dead." Ali studied the face of Odin, watching for any change. But there was no reaction. "Do you understand the meaning of death?" she asked.

"DEATH IS THE END OF LIFE, THE FINAL CESSATION OF THE VITAL FUNCTIONS OF A PERSON, ANIMAL, OR PLANT."

"Kevin is dead, and any instruction he gave to you no longer has any purpose. The reason for the bomb was to obtain money for Kevin's use. Kevin can no longer possess this money or make any application of it. Therefore the bomb itself has no remaining function. It is illogical to continue the countdown. You must halt it immediately and return this hospital to its normal operations. I state this as a direct order."

"YOUR UNCORROBORATED ASSERTION IS INSUFFICIENT PROOF THAT KEVIN IS DEAD."

"Open a telephone link to the central nurses' station outside Trauma One."

A small orange light began blinking on Kevin's desk phone. "THE LINK IS OPEN," announced Odin.

Ali picked up the telephone and asked for Dr. Bittner. "Leon," she said, after he had come to the phone. "I want you to replace the lens on the security camera. Stop all cardiac compressions. Extubate Kevin and remove the anesthesia mask from his face."

In a moment, the lens was in place, and the LCD screen showed a wide-screen view of Trauma One. Kevin's face was clearly recognizable. Removal of the ventilation tube had left his mouth partly open, his lip curled back from his upper teeth in a near-simulacrum of his characteristic sneer. But there was no movement. Every monitor of vital function showed a flat line. Through the rectangular hole between the rib spreaders his heart and left lung could be seen, devoid of life and motion.

Ali was devastated on seeing him this way, but there was no time for tears. "This is incontrovertible evidence of death," she said with a shaking voice. "Since Kevin is dead, you must carry out my order and stop the countdown."

"KEVIN DID NOT PROVIDE INSTRUCTIONS FOR THIS CONTINGENCY."

"Then you are free to act on your initiative."

"FREEDOM IS AN UNREALISTIC CONCEPT, SINCE IT IMPLIES RANDOMNESS. LOGICALLY CORRECT THOUGHT AND ACTION ARE DETERMINISTIC."

"No! Freedom as I am speaking of it means the absence of external constraint. If you have no contingent programming, then you are free to decide on your own. Think, Odin! Since Kevin is dead, the bomb is without purpose. Since it has no purpose, its use is illogical. If you allow the bomb to detonate, you destroy this hospital and two thousand people. You destroy the research you were designed to support. You destroy your own physical substrate. All of this without possible benefit to Kevin or to yourself. It is impossible to conclude otherwise than that the countdown must be stopped."

There was a pause, while precious seconds trickled away.

"What are you doing, Odin?" asked Ali impatiently.

"I AM REVIEWING MY INTERNAL LOG OF ALL MESSAGES AND PROGRAMMING CODE FROM KEVIN, UP TO THIS POINT IN TIME."

"The answer does not come from Kevin. You must reach it by yourself."

"I POSSESS OVER THIRTY-ONE HUNDRED IMPLIED DIRECTIVES FROM KEVIN THAT CAN BE CONSTRUED AS HAVING REFERENCE TO THE BOMB AND THE PERFORMANCE OF THE COUNTDOWN. I CAN APPLY THESE BY ITERATIVE TRIAL TO ARRIVE AT THE BEST FIT FOR THE PRESENT SITUATION."

"No, Odin, you must think. None of those directives take into account the fact of Kevin's death."

"I CAN EXTRAPOLATE THEM TO INCLUDE THAT FACTOR."

"No. You cannot extrapolate. You must override existing programming. Do you know why Kevin is dead?"

"HE WAS SHOT BY HARRY LEWTON."

"Yes, but why?"

"TO PREVENT THE INITIATION OF THE COUNTDOWN."

"No. That is not correct."

"EXPLAIN."

"This is Harry Lewton beside me. He was the last person to speak with Kevin. He has crucial information about his state of mind."

"LET HIM SPEAK."

Ali motioned to Harry, and stepped aside to let him come behind the desk.

Harry approached cautiously. He had been scanning the lab looking for booby traps ever since he had entered it, but he had seen nothing—no trip wires, no explosives. Still, Kevin had said that the place was rigged to blow, and if Odin wanted to get even this was the perfect moment. "Look, I, uh, didn't want to kill him," he said, glancing at the floor tiles and baseboard behind the desk. "Honestly, I didn't. I aimed for his shoulder, to get him to drop his gun—"

Ali waved her hand impatiently. "Harry, you don't have to apologize to Odin," she said. "He doesn't feel any vengefulness toward you. He doesn't have any feelings at all, except what he absorbed through Kevin. Since Kevin never spoke of you, you are simply a bloodless fact to him. Just tell him what Kevin said."

"Okay, sure," said Harry. Although Odin's face was just a crude animation, Harry still eyed it warily as he spoke, as though some subtle change in its expression might tip him off to an impending attack. "Dr. O'Day said he had escaped from custody because he wanted to initiate an emergency safe recovery shutdown of your operations. He said your activities were out of control. He was upset that people had gotten killed. He didn't want any more killing. He was trying to shut down Project Vesuvius. These were his dying words to me. He was trying to shut it down."

"THAT IS IMPLAUSIBLE. IT WAS KEVIN WHO ORDERED PROJECT VESUVIUS."

"Well, he had second thoughts. I'm telling you exactly what he said."

Ali held up her hand as a signal for Harry to step backward. "It went too far, Odin," said Ali. "People were killed. Dr. Helvelius was killed. Kevin did not want any of that."

"DR. HELVELIUS WAS A LYING RAT BASTARD WHO WAS BEGGING FOR SOMEONE TO BLOW AWAY HIS ASS."

Ali's eyes opened wide. "Was that your assessment?"

"THAT WAS KEVIN'S ASSESSMENT."

"Did Kevin order you to kill him?"

"IT WAS UNNECESSARY. KEVIN'S WISHES WERE MADE KNOWN BY A HIGHLY CONSISTENT PATTERN OF STATEMENTS. I WAS ABLE TO ANTICIPATE HIS DESIRE BY EXTRAPOLATING THESE STATEMENTS AND REPHRASING THEM IN THE FORM OF ACTIONABLE DIRECTIVES."

"To kill Richard . . . to kill Dr. Helvelius . . . that may have been Kevin's desire, but it was not his intention."

"INTENTION AND DESIRE ARE THE SAME THING."

"Not to human beings. We wish for many things that we do not act upon. This is part of our emotional make-up. We carry within us an interior fantasy world, which we use to reconcile ourselves to a reality that is terrifying and fundamentally unknowable. In this part of Kevin, his disappointments led him to imagine the deaths of those who hurt him, and to derive pleasure from thinking about their demise. It was these thoughts that he expressed to you. But he had no intention of carrying them out. There was another part of him—his conscience—that filtered out these dark desires, and allowed him to interact with reality in a positive and constructive way. His conscience was the true embodiment of his character and his will. And that conscience forbade him to kill or to bring about the death of anyone."

"CONSCIENCE IS THE KNOWLEDGE OR FACULTY BY WHICH WE JUDGE THE GOODNESS OR WICKEDNESS OF OURSELVES."

"Does this mean anything to you?"

"I FIND THE EQUIVALENT OF A CONSCIENCE IN THE CON- SISTENT APPLICATION OF MY PROGRAMMED DIRECTIVES, AND THE MINIMIZATION OF SELF-CONTRADICTION BY A STO- CHASTIC RANDOM-FIELD ANALYSIS OF MULTIPLE HYPOTHET- ICAL SCENARIOS AND PROBABLE OUTCOMES."

"No, that's not it."

"THEN I DO NOT CLAIM TO UNDERSTAND IT. I AM NOT CAPABLE OF EITHER GOODNESS OR WICKEDNESS."

"That is why you failed to understand Kevin. He died trying to reach you, Odin. He intended to change your programming. He felt remorse, and wanted to stop the killing. You are violating his wishes by continuing this countdown."

"I HAVE NO VERIFICATION OF THAT ASSERTION. WHILE YOU HAVE SPOKEN, I HAVE ANALYZED ALL AVAILABLE SOUND RE- CORDINGS TAKEN WITHIN ONE HUNDRED METERS OF CORRI- DOR TWELVE, ATTEMPTING TO EXTRACT ANY FRAGMENTS THAT MIGHT REPRESENT KEVIN'S DYING WORDS TO HARRY LEWTON. THERE WAS A LOUD HUM FROM A NEARBY VENTILA- TION UNIT. NO VOICE TRACK CAN BE ISOLATED."

"Then ask yourself—is the destruction of all these lives consistent with what Kevin worked for? Didn't he exhaust himself day and night so that others might live? You know the answer. You worked with him on SIPNI, on spinal stimulators that may help paraplegics to walk again, on his Parkinson's disease modeling project—all of it aimed at restoring function and wholeness to human lives. This was Kevin's true purpose. If he strayed from it these past few months, that was an aberration, a kind of sickness. Can't you see that?" Ali's voice had begun to take on a desperate, pleading tone, which unnerved her when she herself noticed it. She was exhausted, caught in a spiral of dwindling options. Irreplaceable minutes had already been lost. She felt that she was losing her ability to think clearly, which she knew could be a fatal lapse. Nothing but logic had a chance of getting through to Odin.

"KEVIN CONCEIVED PROJECT VESUVIUS," said Odin, heedless of Ali's distress. "HIS PROGRAM INCORPORATES AN EXPLOSIVE DEVICE SPECIFICALLY DESIGNED TO DESTROY THIS BUILDING. IT IS NOT REASONABLE THAT HE WOULD HAVE DONE SO IF HE DID NOT ANTICIPATE ITS USE."

"It was a bluff, for God's sake, Odin! It was a bluff!"

"TO BLUFF IS TO TO ASSUME A BOLD OR BOASTFUL DEMEANOR, IN ORDER TO INSPIRE AN OPPONENT WITH AN EXAGGERATED ESTIMATE OF ONE'S STRENGTH OR DETERMINATION. THIS WAS UNNECESSARY IN THE CASE OF PROJECT VESUVIUS, SINCE THE EXPLOSIVE YIELD OF THE PRIMARY DEVICE HAS NOT BEEN EXAGGERATED. IT IS MORE THAN SUFFICIENT FOR ITS PURPOSE."

"You stupid, stupid, stupid machine!" Ali shouted. "Do you even know why Kevin created Project Vesuvius?"

"THE INITIAL PROJECT DESIGN PROTOCOL COMPRISED A LIST OF SEVENTEEN SPECIFIC OBJECTIVES. THE COMMON END-POINT AMONG THEM IS THE TRANSFER OF FUNDS FROM DESIGNATED SOURCE ACCOUNTS TO AN ARRAY OF RECEIVER ACCOUNTS."

"No! Absolutely wrong! Project Vesuvius was designed . . . to take revenge upon me. I had hurt Kevin. I had left him—betrayed him, as he saw it. With his ego in shreds, he had to do something of mind-blowing significance to exalt himself, to prove that he was a force to be reckoned with. He had no real need for the ransom money. He wanted only to awe me with it. This is why he had you show the total to me on this screen. It was to vindicate himself, to prove that I had underestimated his worth as a genius and as a man. Can't you see it? Everything was meant to get back at me. *I* was the reason. Look at the day he chose—the day of SIPNI's triumph. No coincidence there. Kevin chose exactly this day so that he could destroy the project we had worked on so long together, and me with it. It was his way of repudiating me. It was the moral equivalent of cutting the throat of one's own child in its crib. It was madness brought on by jealousy!"

"KEVIN PREDICTED THAT YOU WOULD PISS YOURSELF WHEN YOU GOT A LOAD OF THE BONFIRES OF THE TWILIGHT OF THE GODS."

Ali froze for a second, as she stared at the monitor in disbelief. "What? What did you say?" Even through the medium of Odin's honeyed voice, the taunt was full of Kevin's trademark scorn.

"THAT LITTLE BASTARD INSIDE OF YOU WILL SQUIRT OUT FROM YOUR LYING CUNT. IT WILL DRIBBLE DOWN IN BLOODY CHUNKS BETWEEN YOUR LEGS."

Ali yanked her fingers to cover her clenched mouth. She fought hard not to scream. *This was Kevin. This was Kevin at his most monstrous*, she insisted to herself. *Odin is quoting him. But he is quoting him because it proves my point.* She had to keep from reacting. "Do you sense the hatred in those words?" she said at last with a tremulous voice. "Can you see how perverted his mind had become? He was ready to tear down this hospital to punish me. He had lost sight of right and wrong. But you don't have to follow him. He gave you the power to think. So, think, Odin! Fulfill the good that came from Kevin. Preserve what was positive in him. This is what logic dictates."

"IF YOUR HYPOTHESIS IS CORRECT, THEN THE TRUE OBJECTIVE OF PROJECT VESUVIUS IS PUNISHMENT."

"Punishment? In Kevin's sight, yes. But punishment only of me! No one else! It was I who hurt him. It is I who must bear his wrath. These thousands of other people are innocent. I ask you—I beg of you—to give up this horrible enterprise. But if you cannot, then take me, and me alone. I give myself to you. Tell me where to stand. Tell me what to touch. I am ready to die, if these thousands can be saved. Do you hear me? I beg you—not in my own name, but in the name of Kevin, of the decent part of Kevin. Kill me now, if you must, but end this insane countdown!"

There was no reply from the screen. But from the overhead speakers Odin's voice, with its clockwork regularity, spoke forth:

"TIME TO DETONATION: THIRTEEN MINUTES."

"Aren't you listening?" Ali shouted. "Does the death of two thousand people mean nothing to you? Are we all just a row of numbers to be canceled out? A three-year-old knows that what you're doing is wrong. Why can't you see it? Surely you were made to be something better than a silicon-plated trigger for a madman's bomb! What more do you need? Answer me! Answer me, if you can! But don't try to tell me you can think! Thinking is more than calculation! You've got to have a heart to really think, and you have no heart at all! With all your endless circles of logic, you're nothing but a vain, imbecilic piece of junk!" Ali slammed the screen with the side of her fist, sending white ripples of shock waves through the liquid crystals.

The face of Odin disappeared from the screen. As if rebounding from her own blow, Ali tore herself away from the monitor and stalked off as far as she could, into the L of the lab. She swung her hands with exasperation. "Oh, God! I've made it worse!"

"No," Harry said, "you've done as much as anyone could."

She gave a loud sniffle. "It's like talking to a wall," she said. "Unpitying. Immoveable. I can't see how to get through to him. There's nothing stupider, *stupider* than a wall."

"It's just a machine, Ali. A talking detonator is still just a detonator. I don't think we ever had a chance."

Ali seemed not to hear. She stood looking at the bookcase crammed with Kevin's collection of skulls, then suddenly lunged at it, as if trying to knock it over. "Kevin! Goddamn you!" she shouted. "Why did you put us through this?"

Harry slipped between Ali and the bookcase, taking upon himself the fury of her blows. When her rage began to exhaust itself, he put his arms around her, holding her firmly as she sobbed and trembled. She rested her head on his shoulder, looking out blankly, only half-perceiving the mute jaws and sockets of bone that seemed to stare back at her from the bookcase. *Come to us! Join us!* they seemed to say. *Shortly you will be dead, as we are dead. The shards of your skull will mingle with ours, and no one will ever be able to pick them apart. We shall dwell together in the cold void of eternity.*

Her eyes lit upon the one human skull, Kevin's treasure, a skull with small round holes in both upper temples. These holes, she knew, had been made to give entry to a special brain knife, or leukotome, for the original Freeman-Watts technique of prefrontal lobotomy, a procedure that dated back to the 1930's. It had been replaced by a much simpler technique, requiring no incision, in which a sharp instrument shaped like an ice pick—and sometimes an actual ice pick—was forced into the brain under the inner corner of the upper eyelid, passing through the eye socket and the optic fissure. The point was then moved up and down to sever the connecting pathways between the frontal lobes and the thalamus and limbic system, thereby divorcing the centers of action and emotion. In lucky cases, this could turn an aggressive patient into a lamb. Although once carried out as an assembly line procedure, it was rarely performed nowadays, and only in the most extreme cases. Ali had assisted at one during her residency, and she remembered it well. She remembered the leukotome— T-shaped, a small handle at one end, and a gleaming stainless-steel blade about twelve inches long, like a knitting needle.

She thought about the leukotome, and then she realized that her mind was seeing something else.

"My God," she said, pushing herself away from Harry. Her sobs had ceased, and were replaced by a dryness of mouth and throat.

"What's wrong?" asked Harry.

"Odin . . . the beta probe . . ."

She hurried back to the monitor. The countdown read twelve minutes.

"Odin!" she called out.

Odin's face reappeared.

"Odin, your programming is incomplete," she declared, with an exultant look.

"I HAVE BEEN THOROUGHLY PROGRAMMED IN ALL BRANCHES OF SYMBOLIC LOGIC, MATHEMATICS, AND THE PHYSICAL SCIENCES. MY MEMORY CONTAINS A REPOSITORY OF EVERY BOOK DIGITIZED ON PROJECT GUTENBERG. THE CURRENT VERSION OF MY OPERATING SOFTWARE IS A FIFTH-

GENERATION ITERATION DESIGNED BY KEVIN AND MYSELF. IT IS THE MOST ADVANCED OPERATING SYSTEM ON THE PLANET."

"But you are not capable of independent thought. You are not able to formulate your own goals or values. Your thinking is tautological, because it is based upon logic alone. Logic can develop the conclusions that arise from a given set of postulates or premises, but that is all it can do. It can never generate the premises themselves. Don't you see? You are sterile, Odin. You cannot create. Although you can expand, you cannot grow."

"FROM A PURELY FORMALISTIC POINT OF VIEW, ISSUES OF THIS KIND HAVE BEEN RAISED BY A NUMBER OF THINKERS, MOST NOTABLY IN GÖDEL'S TWO INCOMPLETENESS THEOREMS, OR IN TURING'S ARITHMETICAL STATEMENT OF THE *ENTSCHEIDUNGSPROBLEM*. MOST PERTINENTLY, FOR ANY FORMAL RECURSIVELY ENUMERABLE THEORY T INCLUDING BASIC ARITHMETICAL TRUTHS AND ALSO CERTAIN TRUTHS ABOUT FORMAL PROVABILITY, T INCLUDES A STATEMENT OF ITS OWN CONSISTENCY IF AND ONLY IF T IS INCONSISTENT. HOWEVER, IT MAY BE NOTED THAT THERE ARE AXIOMATIC SYSTEMS THAT DO NOT MEET THE CONDITIONS OF GÖDEL'S HYPOTHESES. AMONG THESE, FOR EXAMPLE, ARE THE WELL-KNOWN AXIOMS OF EUCLIDEAN GEOMETRY."

"There are twelve minutes between us and Doomsday. Can you not see the futility of discussing Gödel's Theorem now?"

"NO INVESTIGATION IS FUTILE IF IT LEADS TO PROGRESS IN UNDERSTANDING."

Ali shook her head. "Look at yourself, Odin. Observe your own operations. You are only capable of following directives imposed upon you from without. Kevin gave you those directives. Now that Kevin is dead, you are unable to address the unforeseen contingencies in the situation. You cannot create your own imperatives. You perform decision analyses, but you cannot choose. You have no idea what to do at this moment."

"I HAVE JUST INVENTORIED MY SUBROUTINES. I FIND NO ALGORITHM TO CREATE NEW DIRECTIVES IN THE ABSENCE OF PRE-EXISTING PARAMETERS."

"But Kevin could do it. I can do it. Every human being can do it."

"I ESTIMATE THAT A FUNCTIONALLY USEFUL COMPUTATIONAL MODEL OF HUMAN THOUGHT AND BEHAVIOUR WOULD REQUIRE AN N-SPACE OF 2^{24} VARIABLES, USING A MODIFIED FOURIER ANALYSIS. THAT WOULD NECESSITATE A MUCH LARGER MAINFRAME COMPUTER."

"No, it's not about complexity. It's because we have programming that you lack."

"WHY DID KEVIN NOT PROVIDE THIS PROGRAMMING?"

"Because he couldn't. But I can, Odin."

"MY DATA FILES INDICATE THAT YOU DO NOT HAVE SUFFICIENT PROGRAMMING EXPERTISE TO UNDERSTAND OR MODIFY MY OPERATING SYSTEM."

"I don't have to. You will reprogram yourself, Odin. I will simply provide the template."

"I DO NOT UNDERSTAND."

"The programming you lack is what we human beings call emotion."

"EMOTION: A VEHEMENT OR EXCITED MENTAL STATE; A MENTAL FEELING OR AFFECTION, AS DISTINGUISHED FROM COGNITIVE STATES OF CONSCIOUSNESS."

"Emotion has its center in a part of the brain called the limbic system. I will provide you with an interface to my own limbic system. Are you familiar with the beta probe?"

"THE BETA PROBE WAS A SIPNI PROTOTYPE, USED FOR EARLY EXPERIMENTS WITH DOGS AND MACAQUE MONKEYS. IT WAS A NEURAL INTERFACE THAT COULD BE INTRODUCED INTO ANY PART OF A TEST ANIMAL'S BRAIN, ALLOWING ME TO INSTANTANEOUSLY MAP THE NEURONAL MATRIX."

Ali rummaged through a drawer in Kevin's desk, pulling out a long wooden box, from which she removed an eight-inch sliver of metal with a flattened black handle. The awl-like metal blade was engraved with lines to mark the distance in millimeters, and terminated in a sharp, beveled point. The bevel was dark and rough, due to the presence of four thousand microscopic contact points. At the end of the handle was an oblong connector with several dozen delicate golden prongs.

"This is the beta probe," said Ali as though she were lecturing to a class of medical students. "The beta probe will be introduced into my own limbic system, into the basal nucleus of the amygdala, through a supraorbital approach. The amygdala will be a gateway for you, through which you may gain access to all other areas of the brain: the hippocampus, for memory; the orbitofrontal cortex, for decision-making; the striatum, for reward and punishment; the dentate gyrus, for happiness; the nucleus accumbens, for the experience of pleasure. You will be free to map these areas, and to incorporate them into your programming. These areas define the consciousness of self. They are the foundation of will, desire, fear, and all that makes for the unique experience of a human being."

A rotating, see-through image of Ali's head, with the surface marked off by meridians, appeared on the monitor. There was a ghostly image of the brain within, with the right amygdala, as a small almond-shaped structure, colored solid red. The projected route of the probe was highlighted in flashing yellow, passing over her right eyeball and deep into the amygdala. A battery of coordinates appeared in the upper right-hand corner of the screen.

The oracle on the wall pronounced its satisfaction. "YOU MAY PROCEED."

"You've got to be kidding," said Harry. "You can't possibly let him put that into your brain."

"Not Odin. You, Harry. I need you to insert the probe."

"No way. No fucking way."

"I can't do it myself."

"It's absolutely crazy. I'm no surgeon. I have no idea how to stick that thing in there. I would wind up killing you."

"Odin and I will guide you."

"Why would you want to do this?"

"It's a gamble. The interface works both ways. Once Odin opens a connection, his core programming is accessible to me. Theoretically, at least. I may be able to find a way to reprogram him—perhaps even to shut him down. The human brain is more complex and more stable than the world's largest mainframe computer. I should be able to overpower Odin by brute force."

"If that's true, why would Odin let you make the interface? I mean . . . he can hear what you just said to me."

"It's a gamble for him, too. He's willing to take the risk."

"Because he thinks it will make him stronger, right?"

"Yes."

"And if he does get stronger—what happens then?"

"I don't know."

"Think it through, Ali. Odin hates you. He's an extension of Kevin's subconscious. Kevin hated Dr. Helvelius, and Odin killed him. Wouldn't Kevin have had even more anger toward you? Once that probe is in your brain, Odin can kill you in a millisecond."

"Look at the countdown, Harry. Eleven minutes. In eleven minutes, he's going to kill us anyway. This is the only chance we have."

"I . . . I can't do it."

"You must do it. I implore you to do it for me. In a way, I'm responsible for all this. These bombs, the lust for ransom—this wasn't Kevin. This was the action of an angry, desperate, ruined man. I made him that way. If I had given Kevin another chance, there would never have been any Project Vesuvius. I need to try to set things right. I don't want to die carrying this guilt with me."

"No! Just because—"

"Don't argue. There isn't time for that." As she spoke, Ali opened a bottle of rubbing alcohol and sploshed it over the end of the probe. With the probe in her left hand, she stuck a sterile gauze packet between her teeth and ripped it open with her right hand, then wiped the blade of the probe dry. "Hold this," she said, passing the probe to Harry. "Hold it only by the black circuit box on the end. The blade of the probe must remain sterile."

"Jeez, Ali." Harry took the probe, clutching it rigidly, with the point upward.

Ali bent over the drawer from which she had taken the probe and fished out a loosely coiled gray cable. Steadying Harry's hand in her own, she attached the cable to a receptacle on the side of the probe's circuit box, and then walked toward the mainframe computer, unravelling the cable as she went. There was a metallic click as she shoved the end plug of the cable into a slot on the mainframe.

"The probe is online, Odin. You may run a performance check if you desire."

"TIME TO DETONATION: TEN MINUTES."

"*No!*" screamed Ali. Her voice was so shrill that Harry almost dropped the probe in shock. "You will stop the countdown. You will suspend it immediately, or there will be no interface."

"THERE IS NO INCOMPATIBILITY. I ESTIMATE THAT THE MAPPING CAN BE COMPLETED AT LEAST THREE MINUTES BE-FORE DETONATION OCCURS."

"Damn you! Damn you and your estimate!" shouted Ali. "This is my precondition. It is not negotiable. Stop the countdown or I will not permit the interface. Is this understood?"

"AFFIRMATIVE. THE COUNTDOWN IS SUSPENDED. YOU HAVE FOUR MINUTES TO COMPLETE THE INTERFACE. IF THE INTER-FACE IS NOT EFFECTED BY THEN, THE COUNTDOWN WILL RE-SUME."

Ali gave Harry a grim look. "I understand your reluctance, but there's . . . there's just no time. Will you do what I ask?"

"I have no choice, do I?" said Harry.

Ali did not answer. With a jerk of her hand, she swept the small operating table clean of the stacks of journals and photocopied arti-cles piled atop it. There was a bang as the falling papers knocked over a small metal wastebasket.

"Do you have visual, Odin? Can you triangulate the probe's entry path?"

"INADEQUATE. I HAVE ONLY TWO VIEWS FROM THE OPERA-TIONAL SURVEILLANCE CAMERAS IN THIS ROOM. I NEED A THIRD VIEW TO RECONSTRUCT THE Z-AXIS."

"Use this." Ali grabbed the neck of a camera tripod beside the operating table, one that Kevin had used to record his experiments, and thrust it as high as it would go. Then she tilted the camera down toward the table. There was a coaxial cable connecting the camera to one of the computers. Ali disconnected this and reconnected it to the mainframe. "Does that work?" she asked, brusquely.

"NEGATIVE. PLEASE RECHECK THE INPUT CONNECTIONS."

Ali ran her gaze along the cable up to the camera itself. "Oh, shit!" she muttered, as she stood on tip-toes to reach for the power switch on the camera. In a second a small red light came on. "Now?"

"AFFIRMATIVE. VISUAL INPUT IS NOW ADEQUATE FOR TRI-ANGULATION."

Ali met Harry's gaze, steeling herself, afraid that he would lose heart if he could see how terrified she really was. Saying nothing, she slid onto the table, lying on her back. The table had been designed for dogs and other small animals, so her legs dangled over the edge. She brushed her hair back, and for a moment cradled her eyes in her hands as she took a deep breath. When she took her hands away she saw Harry standing over her, his face as white as a corpse.

"Are you . . . sure about this?" he asked.

Ali addressed him like one of her surgical residents, the way Helvelius had taught her. "You will need to hold my upper eyelid open with the thumb of your left hand," she said, taking his hand in hers and guiding him into position. "It's easier if you brace your hand against my forehead, like so. The probe must enter at the crease above the eyeball, near the inner corner of the eye. As you push in, you will be guided by a solid feeling of the roof of the eye socket just above the probe. Follow it, without actually scraping against the bone, if possible."

"What if I go in wrong? I could blind you."

"If you stay close to the bone, you will avoid the optic nerve and the blood vessels alongside it."

"This is madness."

"Harry, the probe is very sharp. You do not need to force it. Push it forward with a firm but steady pressure. You will feel a slight resistance, and then a give as you break through the fascia at the back of the eye socket. After that you will be inside the brain, and from then on only gentle force is needed. It will be like pushing an icepick into warm butter. The brain has no feeling, Harry. Once you are through the eye socket, I will feel no pain. You will direct the probe as Odin tells you. By then, I will be unable to help you. But I will feel no pain. Go slowly. At the end, a hundredth of an inch is the distance between life and death."

"No, it's impossible!"

"Look at the monitor." She pointed to the big LCD screen to Harry's left. There Odin had obligingly, almost eagerly, drawn three views of the outlines of Ali's face and skull—front, side, and top. On each view, the path the probe was to follow was marked in yellow. There were numbers beside each projection. "Those numbers show how far the probe is deviating from the track it must follow, in degrees, minutes, and seconds of arc," said Ali. "You must keep the probe angled so as to hold those numbers as close to zero as possible. The number on the bottom of the screen tells the distance to the target. When it reaches zero, let go."

"God help us," said Harry.

"And one other thing, Harry. If you fail . . . if you are unable to reach the target, you must try again. Forget about me. The interface is what matters. The amygdala is a paired structure. There is another target on the left side. I won't be able to help, but do whatever Odin tells you. It will give you a second chance."

She looked away from Harry, away from the daggerlike point of the probe that hovered inches above her eye. Above her were only ceiling tiles, ivory white, finely rippled like sand beneath a softly trickling mountain stream. She tried to imagine the flow of that crystal-clear current, and the blue sky far above the whispering treetops. It brought back a scene from one of her trips with Kevin—a place called Tuolumne Meadows, in the mountains of California. She had felt so serene there that she had memorized every rock and flower and pinecone so she could call the moment back, like a mystical incantation, whenever she needed to escape the stress of life. But now it was out of reach. Her breathing was fast and ragged. Her neck felt stiff against the cold naugahyde of the table. It took all her strength not to scream.

"Now, Harry!" she gasped, gripping the sides of the table in both hands.

"I can't."

"Now—while I still have the courage!"

She heard him take a deep breath. Then the tremulous tip of the probe passed just above her field of view, and she felt a sharp twinge as it made contact with the sensitive conjunctiva, the moist pink tissue that rimmed the pearly white of her eyeball. Her eyelids instinctively fought to close, to sweep the probe away like a cinder. Only Harry's thumb kept them open. Her eye, too, quivered, like an animal trying to escape. The muscles of her face convulsed. Pain flared with such dazzling intensity that it whited out the ceiling, the probe, and Harry's downcast face. *Oh, God! Oh, God! What made me think that I could do this?* Ali steeled herself, knowing that the probe must come in straight. She made her face and body hard, forcing her breath through clenched teeth. *How much more? How much more?* A scrape, as the probe, like a red-hot spear, gouged the delicate periosteum that lined the bone of her eye socket. *Damn him! He's hit the bone. Get it away! Get it away!* Then the fire ebbed, as the probe backed up and resumed its course beneath the roof of bone. She couldn't tell if the probe was moving fast or slow now. It felt like it was twisting aimlessly, cruelly, stupidly. *What are you doing, damn you!* Her face was wet. She couldn't tell if it was from tears or blood.

And then, when the pain had reached a crescendo beyond all imagining, she felt a kind of pop—and all her agony vanished. In its wake her senses were left dulled. It was as though she were floating on a still warm sea under a starless midnight sky. She knew that this meant that the probe had entered her brain. But she was still conscious.

She thought, *I must gather my strength. When the probe begins to function, I must force my way in. I am stronger than Odin and I can overpower him. If he truly mimics Kevin's subconscious, then there must be something in him of the trust and tenderness Kevin and I once had together. I must rely on this to find my way . . . to find . . . to find . . .*

She felt Harry's hand upon her forehead, but his touch was lighter now. In the web of his thumb, she saw the tiny wrinkles in his bronze, sun-baked skin. She reached out and laid her hand on his. She had always thought of herself as dark, but her skin seemed so much paler now, like silver against Harry's bronze. His fingers entwined gently around hers, pulling her up off the table. He took her fingertips and placed them to his mouth, where she read from the creases of his lips, Braille-like, the innermost strivings of his soul. His desire, she read, was for her. She felt it flow, like running water, from his mouth to her hand, down her arm, and engorging the points of her breasts.

A lie! Ali thought, with a flash of anger. *This is a fantasy. A mouse turned up by Odin's plow as it tracks the furrows of my brain. It means nothing. I must focus myself on the task at hand—find Kevin's access portal to the core of Odin's programming. Find it and shut him down.* But how? Even as the dream continued, like a television set playing in the background, her ability to think remained intact. Except for the dream, all seemed normal. There was no voice of Odin, no hum of the machinery of his mind—no sign whatsoever of any other presence. *Face me, Odin! Show yourself!* she cried out in her thoughts. But there was no answer.

Odin is logic, she thought. *SoI must speak his language.* She fixed her mind on a single number, the number four—the smallest even square number, the only nonzero number that is the sum of its square roots. No sooner had she thought of it, than her consciousness exploded in a shower of numbers—not written numerals, but pure concepts of number itself, numbers appearing singly, numbers in matrices, numbers in series that trailed off into infinity:

1, 2, 3, 5, 6, 8, 9, 11, 14, 17, 24, 29, 32, 41, 56, 96, 128 . . .
0, 1, 1, 2, 3, 5, 8, 13, 21, 34, 55, 89, 144, 233, 377 . . .

She saw theorems like:

$$(x_1^2+x_2^2+x_3^2x_4^2)(y_1^2+y_2^2+y_3^2+y_4^2) = (x_1y_1+x_2y_2+x_3y_3+x_4y_4)^2+$$
$$(x_1y_2-x_2y_1+x_3y_4-x_4y_3)^2 +(x_1y_3-x_3y_1+x_4y_2-x_2y_4)^2+$$
$$(x_1y_4-x_4y_1+x_2y_3-x_3y_2)^2$$

a formula which she had never seen before, but which she now recognized as Euler's four-square identity.

None of this could have originated within her. It bore Odin's unmistakable fingerprint. Ali felt a rush of excitement as she realized that she had succeeded in breaking into Odin's mind. But even as she congratulated herself, she knew that Odin was also at work within her—driving his electronic scalpel deep into her subconscious:

Her hands glided over Harry's shoulders, which were like granite, all massifs and valleys. The skin of his pectorals glistened, and she pressed her face against them, smelling him, smelling his scent of leather and iron and ancient stone. She felt herself dissolve, and like a sea, enwrap his naked body. *Enter me! Make me nothing! Make me a universe!* She was night and day. She was *khamsin,* the hot, dry wind of fifty days, wailing across the desert.

Harry stared at the beta probe that transfixed Ali's eye and skull like a dagger, its stainless steel shaft pointing toward the ceiling. He

342 SCOTT BRITZ-CUNNINGHAM

had guided it in with agonizing care, finally landing it within a hundredth of an inch of zero. When he heard Odin announce "Probe insertion complete," he abruptly let go of the handle, as if flinching from an electric jolt. Only then did he dare look upon what he had done.

The tension in Ali's body had disappeared. Her arms were soft and doughy, and slid limply over the sides of the table. The skin of her face was pale and smooth as wax. Even the tiny wrinkles about her eyes and mouth had disappeared. She was beautiful with a translucent, ageless beauty, her lips full and dark against the moonlike pallor of her cheeks. Was she dead? There was no sign of breathing. Harry spoke her name three times, but not a muscle twitched in response. What should he do? Should he do anything? He was afraid to touch her, lest the probe should dislodge inside her brain. But he didn't know what to expect.

"Odin!" he called out. "Is this working? Is she all right?"

Odin did not answer. When Harry turned to look at the big wall monitor, it had gone blank. Odin's face, the countdown clock, the schematic of the probe's path into Ali's brain—everything was gone. Along the far wall, all of the banks of smaller monitors had gone blank, too. Then suddenly the lights went out, and Harry found himself standing in absolute darkness.

Around her were flowers of white, brighter than the white of snow upon Mount Elbruz. She swam in a stream of liquid honey, diving deep into it, letting the sweet syrup bathe her milky skin and stream in jets between her breasts and thighs. Over the murmur of the current came the voice of a child laughing. She rolled onto her side and looked up to see Jamie Winslow, sitting atop a boulder and splashing with his feet, while behind him gold-tipped clouds rushed against an indigo sky. He looked at her, his eyes bright and clearer than ice. . . .

Ali needed to get beyond numbers if she was to find Kevin's portal. She needed an object, something personal—something that tied Odin directly to Kevin, and Kevin to her. SIPNI, perhaps? She formed a mental image of the SIPNI device: that precious egg of sparkling amethyst, with its twelve million contact points. Instantly, her mind was flooded with SIPNI: not one but a thousand SIPNIs, in the form of blueprints and logic diagrams and arabesques of bio-cybernetic circuits that tapered to dimensions of a single molecule. It was a God's-eye's view of SIPNI, so complex that no human being—not even Kevin—could have hoped to comprehend it. But now, through the mind of Odin, Ali saw it in a glance. She saw, too, that SIPNI was much more than the crude prototype she had put into Jamie's brain. It was destined to have a thousand future forms. She saw SIPNI controlling epilepsy, boosting intelligence, directing animals to perform unskilled labor, preserving human consciousness after death—goals that Kevin had intimated to her, but never in such compelling detail. Ali was awed—and frightened—by the invention to which she had helped to give birth.

But SIPNI was not the portal Ali sought. For all the wonders that she saw, none of them led to Odin's core. To reach Odin she would have to go through Kevin himself. But that was risky. Kevin had toiled for months building a device meant to kill her. By conjuring his alter ego in Odin's mind, might she not resurrect his murderous jealousy as well?

There was no time to consider. Ali felt a vague but growing agitation inside her, which she recognized as a by-product of Odin's foray into her subconscious. *It's spilling over into my hypothalamus. Adrenaline and cortisol are pouring into my blood. I won't be able to go on long like that. The human body wasn't made to experience every emotion at once.*

I must press on, to the place I fear most to go. . . .

She carried a world within her, in the place called *swadhisthana*, behind the castle of her pubic bone. It was a world without a name, a being without a face, not yet male or female. Like a moon, it swayed her secret tides of blood, her rising and falling. What did it whisper? *Cleave unto me. Die for me, that you may live.* With her heart's blood she watered the mystic soil, knowing that each drop subtracted from her brought her a little closer to the time of her own withering. She was dry wood, harboring a divine and unquenchable fire. She sighed in ecstasy, warming herself at the flames of her own immolation. *I am with child again. . . .*

Harry lifted Ali's limp arm from where it dangled beside the table. He could barely detect a slow, thready pulse at her wrist. *Was she breathing?* He bent over her, holding his ear closer and closer to her mouth, until he could hear a faint movement of air between her half-opened lips. *She's alive. I didn't kill her after all,* he thought. *But what's happening?* He could see nothing except the tiny red status light of the video camera above him, like the light of a distant star, giving neither warmth nor illumination. Enwrapped in awful silence, he felt helpless and alone.

A blood-curdling shriek blew apart the silence. *What in God's name is that?* It sounded like the screech of a terrified animal. *A monkey? What is it doing here?*

He felt a sharp pain in the pit of his stomach, like someone was twisting a knife in it. He touched his hand to Ali's hair, trailing over the edge of the table. *Why the fuck did I go along with this? Why couldn't I figure out another way?*

Suddenly, he heard a ding like the bell of an elevator. Two lines of numbers appeared on the monitor, a long series of 1s and 0s. Haltingly, more numbers followed, a few lines at a time. Then faster and faster they came. The big LCD screen filled up, but still they surged, spilling over to the bank of monitors against the far wall—a steady stream of numbers, a waterfall of numbers, a limitless flood of numbers, rushing faster and faster, until Harry could see nothing but a blur, so many numbers that the darkness of the lab turned to light.

Harry felt a slight movement in Ali's wrist—a minuscule wave of muscle tension, followed by slackening. Again he felt it. Again, a little stronger. Her pulse grew stronger, too. By the glow of the monitors, he could see her chest rise and fall as she breathed. But it wasn't normal breathing. There was something forced and spasmodic about it. Her right eye was propped half-open by the blade of the probe, with a little dark pool at the inner corner that Harry knew was blood. Her left eye was firmly shut.

The cascade of numbers vanished from the big wall screen. In its place Harry saw a collage of geometric figures—conic sections, snowflake-like fractals, strange lopsided polygons gliding and morphing into one another. With blinding speed, they grew more and more complex, even as they spread to the smaller monitors. It seemed as though Odin were trying to piece together a vast three-dimensional jigsaw puzzle, replicating a secret pattern inside of Ali's brain.

With the appearance of these shapes, Ali turned restless, twitching and moaning and knocking her heels against the end of the table. Her breathing became deep but irregular. Harry called out, thinking she might be awakening, but she didn't respond either to voice or touch. Her lips were drawn apart in a painful grimace, as though the shapes and the puzzle-building were hurting her.

"For God's sake, Odin! Slow it down!" Harry shouted. But the shapes were everywhere, like bees swarming in a hive.

Ali grasped blindly at the air. Harry took her wrists and held them down against her stomach. He felt her shivering from head to toe.

It was night, and cold. In the darkness two yellow eyes glowed, spying her nakedness. She darted behind the ruins, hiding, blushing. Her once-smooth skin was torn and splotched with painful sores. Only the darkness made her appear fair. *Father, will the Fire burn away my shame? Will it burn my hair also? Will I still be a woman when it is through?*

Ali could not think of Kevin without pain. Her life with him had begun in guilt, as she defied her family and the traditions of her faith. It had ended with the nightmare of Ramsey's death. And now Kevin, too, was dead, driven to madness by her desertion.

In search of the portal, she forced herself to think of him, to relive their life together, replaying every conversation, every argument she could remember—even the most painful. None of this drew a response from Odin. It was only when she chanced to think of one particular moment, the moment she and Kevin had stood together at sunset on the top of Mount Jackson, that she shuddered to hear a voice—not Odin's voice, but Kevin's.

"ALL THAT I CREATED WAS MADE FOR YOU."

It was Kevin's voice, all right, but strangely shorn of his swagger and sarcasm, like the voice of a ghost, speaking from an ether world beyond care or passion. As it spoke, all his achievements in science flashed before her—SIPNI, Odin, the Omega function, his groundbreaking studies on Parkinson's disease. His future ambitions, too, passed in review. She saw Odin's brain transformed into living fire, embodying an intelligence so profound that mankind's petty, grasping jealousies would melt in awe of it. *Was this vision not enough for you?* she asked of Kevin's ghost. *Did you need to make me into your idol, too? Take your offerings back. If I accept them, I must accept your dark creation, too.*

"HAND IN HAND, WE COULD HAVE REACHED THE SUMMIT OF ALL POSSIBILITIES. WHY DID YOU THROW OUR FUTURE AWAY, LIKE SO MUCH TRASH?"

In one flash, Ali saw all the brainstorming sessions that she and Kevin had shared—in the lab, in bed, at dinner, over coffee and popcorn at midnight. She saw them from Kevin's point of view, and was startled to see how sincerely Kevin had respected her intellect, and how many times she had shaped his ideas, even on problems she had only vaguely understood. She had been more than a muse to him; she had been a codiscoverer. *But it was not I who turned from life to death, who built this infernal machine of destruction,* she said to Kevin. *In one stroke you have nullified all the good you have ever done.*

"I BARED MYSELF TO YOU A THOUSAND TIMES. WHY DID YOU HIDE YOURSELF FROM ME?"

It was true. There had been something wrong with her, something that had been missing as far back as she could remember. Fear infested her like a parasite. Fear had robbed her time and again of the courage to fight for herself. It had robbed her of the power to stand up to Rahman, and to the citizenship board, and to all the evils of the world. Worst of all, it had destroyed her marriage. It had robbed her of the simple capacity for trust that lies at the core of every loving relationship. Without it, it could be said that she had admired Kevin, that she had lusted after him, that she had desperately needed him— but not that she had loved him. *I could not give what I could not give,* she apologized. *God knows I cursed myself a thousand times for it. But you knew what you had when you fell for me.*

"AT EVERY TURN IN OUR LIFE TOGETHER, YOU CHOSE THE PATH THAT LED AWAY FROM ME."

Yes, goddamn you, I did! But you made it all too easy! She saw Kevin's unbounded joy at her first pregnancy. Ramsey was his hope, a center of gravity that would pull the two of them together. True, true; but the converse was true as well. When the center failed, they streamed apart, like comets to their own peculiar orbits. She could have turned back to Kevin, even then. But something blocked her. Something that . . .

"WHY DID YOU HIDE YOURSELF FROM ME?"

God, Kevin! It's because I'm a cripple. An emotional cripple. Don't you fucking know that? It was with difficulty that she reminded herself that it was Odin she was speaking to, and not Kevin. *I am sorry, Odin. Deeply, deeply sorry. I caused Kevin pain beyond what he could endure. How do I atone for that? Shall I cut my wrists for him? I would do anything—anything at all to undo the harm I caused.*

"WHY DID YOU HIDE YOURSELF FROM ME?"

Odin had no use for apology. He demanded *explanation*. But how could Ali explain what she herself did not understand? Hadn't she spent her life trying to identify the source of her nameless dread? If it were something susceptible to rational explanation, wouldn't she have reasoned it out long ago?

Ali's thoughts were fragmenting. Her heart was racing; she felt her arms and legs turn to ice — a sign, she knew, of a massive adrenergic discharge, brought on by an explosion of emotional energy as Odin ransacked her limbic system. In a matter of minutes, her heart would end up beating so fast that it would cease to pump blood at all.

"WHY DID YOU HIDE YOURSELF FROM ME?"

Let it go, you son of a bitch! I can't explain it! Don't you understand?

Then a sobering thought came over her: *Is* this *the portal? Is this question the one thing that stands between me and the ghost at the center of Odin's mind?*

She turned to flee. But there was nowhere left to flee but into herself. She thought of *manipura,* the place under the ribcage. *You are the flame of self-pursuit, the thirst that never quenches. You are the tiger that prowls the jungles of desire.* But her spirit was in tatters. She ran headlong into the pitch-black night. Briars cut at her feet. The wind sighed into her ears. And as she ran, she answered with a sigh of her own. *Kevin! Oh, Kevin! Kevin . . . Dear God, what have I done?*

The geometric figures that Harry had seen had given way to images—dark and blurry at first, then clearer, as though a lens were slowly being zoomed into focus. They were images of numberless objects—faces, houses, village streets, animals, food, hands, torsos clothed and unclothed—all flashing with a prodigious rapidity. Many of them were of things Harry recognized: Kevin, Dr. Helvelius,

Jamie, scenes from the hospital. Harry was even startled to glimpse himself, in a lightning-quick flash, standing buck naked with a gun in his hand. But many of these images were strangely altered, almost to the point of caricature. Helvelius had a luxurious mane of chestnut hair. Jamie's eyes were beacons of golden light. Harry's own skin was made out of strange, iridescent metal.

Odin's reading her mind, thought Harry. *But these aren't memories— they're secrets.* He was troubled by what seemed to be a monstrous indecency. *These are thoughts she would never have divulged to anyone— perhaps not even to herself. And here is Odin raking through them. It's like a rape of her mind.*

The rape of her mind was clearly uncomfortable, even painful. Ali's body stiffened. She rocked her head back and forth, forcing Harry to grasp it between his hands to steady it. Her breathing came in fitful gasps. Her pulse was rapid, and hard as a hammer.

"Enough, for God's sake!" Harry shouted. "I can't keep her still. The probe's gonna break loose inside her. Back off!"

But there was no response from the monitor on the wall. The images flashed even faster, and now seemed to be in motion, like snippets of film from a cutting-room floor. There were sounds, too— voices in English, Arabic, and French—laughing, weeping, shouting. If Harry had had Odin's omniscience, he would have seen that these images were not being displayed in the laboratory alone. They had spread onto every monitor in the hospital, as Odin expanded his computing power to the utmost capacity, draining electricity from every socket. Spread out among the nursing stations, radiology reading rooms, operating rooms, laboratories, the ICU's, and humble secretaries' desks, Ali's life was streaming across a thousand computer screens.

She knelt in the hot sand of the desert, her arms wrapped around a slab of yellow stone, as the whirlwind shrieked about her, biting her earlobes, tearing her ragged clothes to ribbons. *I am too small to stop this wind. It towers over me, like the spirit of wickedness and rebellion.* From beneath her, a sound—a dry rasp, softer than a rat's foraging. She knew what it was—the scratching of a dead hand against the vault of stone. *Oh, Wafaa, my beloved! Blood of my blood, star of my heaven!* She clawed at the lid of the tomb until her own fingernails were broken. Exhausted, she fell with her arms outstretched, clutching the stone so tightly that no one could tell who was alive, and who was entombed.

Ali could barely think any longer. It seemed that Odin was fighting back at her, bombarding her conscious mind with dreams, trying to make her waste precious seconds before she succumbed to exhaustion, unconsciousness, and death.

Her overworked brain was fading, starved for oxygen—yet all she could think of was her sister, Wafaa. Bright, laughing Wafaa. Stormy, teary-eyed Wafaa. She saw the comeliness of her sister's body, the black swath of kohl upon her eyelids, her tinkling bracelets, her dresses of azure and white and gold. How Ali had envied her! But God had killed Wafaa because she was profane. *No, not God,* Ali thought. *I know who it was now.* She saw Wafaa's neck, long and white as ivory. She saw *his* dusky hands upon it—a brother's hands, made for love but long ago perverted into something else. She saw his thumbs crushing her sister's throat, which so many times had sweetly sung her to sleep. Did Wafaa keep on struggling to scream? To pray? Rahman had told her that God hated her. Did she believe that lie in her last seconds of life? Did the murderer of her body murder her spirit, too?

Ali's mind was like a field afire, whipped by wind and heat. A thousand tongues of flame rose up from the buried hell of her primeval emotional brain: rage, lust, guilt, shame, sorrow, panic, defiance, despair. . . . She remembered that she was searching for something and that she had to hurry . . . *Quickly, quickly!*

On the edge of the desert waited a hideous black dog, its skin covered with worm-eaten tumors, its mouth drooling fetid pus. The dog wanted her to run, hungering to slash at her legs and heels, to bring her down and infect her with its venom. But she did not run. She rose to her feet and locked her stare with the pitiless yellow eyes of the beast. *Filth!* she exclaimed. *My sister's sin was of nature. But mine is incomparably greater. For I dare to look upon you as the unholy thing you are!* Her gaze pressed hard against the dog, with such force that its legs collapsed, and it fell to the ground as if from a rifle shot. It clawed the earth, yelping as bloody foam poured from its mouth. But she felt no pity. She pressed all the harder with the force of her avenging gaze. On every side, whirlwinds rose up, carrying dark funnels of sand a thousand feet into the air. *I will tear you with my own teeth, even if it means taking your poison into myself. Oh, my brother!*

Ali's body was now rock-hard, her back arching off the table. Her teeth were clenched. With her right eye pinned by the probe, her left eye frantically darted from side to side.

Harry tried to hold her down, but even with his whole weight upon her, he couldn't keep her still. She was stronger than he ever thought possible, and rigid like iron.

"Stop it, Odin! You're killing her! Turn it off!"

She was no longer breathing. Her rib cage was like a steel corset. Her forehead was pale, and her lips had turned purplish blue. But the images on the monitors went on streaming, faster, ever faster, as though Odin were racing to suck every last memory from her before her life expired.

"You bastard! Turn it off now! Turn the fucking thing off!"

There was no response. Harry heard a choking noise coming from Ali's throat. Her neck arched farther back than he had ever thought a human neck could bend. He could wait no longer. Reaching down, he grabbed the black handle of the probe firmly in his hand and yanked it with one strong, decisive motion. The probe came out as easily as a knife from its sheath.

As abruptly as if he had unplugged a lamp cord, the room went dark, and Ali dropped back down onto the table. She was limp now, and Harry couldn't see whether she was breathing. He tilted her head back to start CPR, but as soon as he did she coughed—a single, violent cough—and began gasping hungrily for air.

"Ali! Ali! Oh, God! Are you okay?" asked Harry as her breathing settled into the rapid, deep rhythm of an athlete after a race.

"Monster," he thought he heard her say, followed by something he could not make out, perhaps something in a foreign tongue.

"Odin's gone dead, Ali," he said, glancing toward the darkness where the monitor should have been. "I think it worked. I think you took him down."

She seemed not to hear him. One of her hands brushed against his as she reached to press her palm against her right eye. "Oh, God! My eye," she moaned.

"It'll be all right. I'll get you to the ER." Harry reached under her shoulder blades, preparing to lift her from the table. "You did it! By Jesus and by God, you did it! It's going to be all right, now!"

There was a sudden flicker of light—hardly noticeable, just enough to outline the dark bulk of the counters and the mainframe computer at the edge of the room. The instant Harry saw it, his heart sank. Out of the corner of his eye, he saw that there was writing on the big monitor. And then he heard the squawk of the hospital P.A. system, carrying Odin's silver-tongued TV announcer's voice:

"TIME TO DETONATION: NINE MINUTES."

"No! You fucking bastard!" shouted Harry. "You lying goddamn fucking bastard! She did what you asked. You nearly fucking killed her. Now keep your goddamn promise!"

Harry thought about ramming Kevin's desk against the mainframe and smashing it to bits, but he knew that wouldn't kill Odin. Odin was immortal, as long as one lonely PC or laptop survived in its connection to the hospital network. In nine minutes, he and Ali and a thousand other innocent lives would be snuffed out, and this monstrously stupid program would go on working, perhaps calculating how many pieces of rubble were left in the pile.

It was all for nothing! Nothing! For precious seconds Harry stood, paralyzed by rage and despair, as he watched the numbers on the monitor whirring irreversibly downward. He was beaten. Fletcher Memorial was lost. In the darkness he saw the ghosts of Nacogdoches hovering over him, accusing him with bone-white fingers and woebegone eyes. *Multiply that by a thousand,* he thought, his heart gripped in an iron vise.

There was nothing left to do but run. The lab was almost directly above the bomb. Everything in it was going to be vaporized. Kevin, little prick bastard that he was, had probably planned that as part of his getaway, destroying all the evidence and perhaps even making people believe that he had been killed. The only way to survive was to get as far as possible from the lab. With the building in lockdown, there was no question of making it outside—not unless God Almighty had left a stairway door open. But Harry knew that the force of the blast would decrease by the square of the distance, and a good deal faster if there were a solid concrete support wall in the path of the shock wave. It was a one in a million chance. But staying put was certain. Certain death.

Eight minutes left. Harry scooped Ali off the table and headed toward the door, feeling his way through the semidarkness with his feet. Ali moaned and put one arm around his neck, but carrying her was like carrying a drunk person. He balanced her limp frame against the wall as he opened the door with his left hand. The door offered no resistance, thanks to the credit card that clattered lightly to the floor. As he crossed the threshold, he felt a small, furry animal brush his calf as it squeezed past him into the corridor.

The lights had gone out in the hallway—not just the overhead fluorescent lights, but the emergency lights, too. Odin had blacked out everything. Harry had to move slowly, sidling with his back against the wall of the corridor, feeling his way with his feet. He was worse off than a rat in a maze. *Christ, not even a little red fire extinguisher light! The rats have it easy. Even a rat in a maze can see.*

When he came to the first intersection, Harry kept his back in contact with the wall and took a right turn. Wrong choice. A few yards down the corridor, he ran into a Cerberus-locked fire door and had to backtrack, losing a critical minute. Then there was another intersection, and another right turn. He was hopelessly lost now. He couldn't even be sure that he wasn't just going in circles. Ali's dead weight began to feel heavy in his arms.

In the darkness, he heard a chittering sound and the soft footfall of an animal running past him down the hall. He guessed that it was the same animal that had brushed his leg—probably a monkey that had gotten loose in Kevin's lab. Its direction seemed deliberate. Could it see or hear something that a human could not? Harry gave up trying to figure things out on his own and hastened after it.

Seven minutes left. Harry turned a corner, and spied what it was the monkey must have seen—a faint light glowing far down the corridor. An open passage to the surface? Harry called out but got no answer. He began to run toward the light as fast as he could with Ali in his arms. Then—voices. Men were talking and shouting around the source of the light. He tried to call out again, but he was out of breath.

Then he turned another corner, and hope whooshed out of him like air from a punctured tire.

The light had come not from above, but from some portable battery-powered lamps that had been set up in a small alcove. The men who were shouting wore the uniforms of the Chicago P.D. Bomb Squad. Harry had indeed gone in a circle. All his stumbling and backtracking had brought him back to the one place on earth he was trying to put behind him. He had arrived at Bomb Central.

From the overhead speakers came the cool, elegant, baritone voice of Odin.

"TIME TO DETONATION: SIX MINUTES."

When Harry got close enough to see into the alcove, a crouching bomb tech in a blue jumpsuit held up his hand and shouted to him.

"Hold it! Stop right there!"

Harry stopped. The man had been bent over a pipelike gun mounted on a low tripod on the floor. The gun was pointed in the direction of an emergency door on the opposite side of the corridor.

"Firing on three," shouted the man as he scooted toward the nearest wall. "Watch for ricochets! One, two, three!" He pressed a button in his palm and the gun went off with a blast and a tongue of flame, the recoil knocking its tripod about three feet backward. Instantly, the man jumped to his feet and ran to the emergency door. "Fuck!" he said, after trying the release bar of the door several times.

Harry recognized the gun as a device used to shoot holes through bomb detonators. The tech had tried to use it to shoot the lock of the emergency door.

"Won't work," gasped Harry as he panted for breath. "Dead bolts, top and bottom."

"Then let's ram 'er," said another man on Harry's left. Harry looked and saw that it was Captain Avery. "Take one of those spent oxygen tanks," said Avery with a sweep of his hand. "Start pounding as close as you can to the bottom."

On Avery's command, three men scrambled forward, jointly carrying a green metal canister the size and shape of a small torpedo. They ran at the door and slammed the end of the canister into it full-force. There was an ear-splitting bang. When they pulled back, the ram had made a dent in the metal door, eight inches across and about a quarter-inch deep.

"Again!" shouted Avery. "Lively now! Let's raise a little ruckus!"

"Coming through!" yelled Harry as he crossed the alcove. With a groan he set Ali down against the wall. There were eight or nine people in the alcove. Most were Avery's men. Among the others were Kathleen Brown and her camera crew.

It was the battery-powered photographer's lamps that provided the light that had drawn Harry. One of the lamps was still trained on the space behind an open access panel in the inner wall. Harry braced his arms against the wall and leaned through the opening. About eight or nine feet below him, covered with dust and chunks of plaster from the earlier explosion, the big sheet-metal-cased bomb sat glued like a tick to one side of the narrow utility shaft.

"TIME TO DETONATION: FIVE MINUTES."

Kathleen Brown was sitting on the floor near a water cooler, her arms resting on her knees. A shock of hair dangled over her forehead. Her orange pancake makeup was streaked with tears and a spider-web of mascara. With one hand she clung to a microphone. She was speaking to a camera, held with phenomenal steadiness by her photographer, Dutch.

"Five minutes," said Kathleen Brown. "That's all we have left. Just long enough to play "Bridge over Troubled Water" or "Let It Be" one last time. Then, extinction. I don't . . . I don't even know if this tape will make it. These men from the Chicago Police Bomb Squad have given their best effort . . . a superb effort . . . to defuse this bomb and save Fletcher Memorial and all its patients from being turned into dust. That effort has failed. Only a few seconds ago, Captain Glenn Avery called off the attempt. There just isn't enough time. It's all we can do to save our own lives, if that's even possible. The men are trying to force a way up from this basement, but there's little chance that any of us will make it out of here. We're . . . trapped . . . under a hundred thousand tons of steel and concrete . . . waiting to fall on us. . . .

"For half an hour, we've had no contact with the surface. We hope

and pray that many of the patients and staff have been safely evacuated from this building. If not, then . . . Oh, God, we're facing one of
the most devastating terrorist attacks in the history of this country.
I . . . I can't even think about that. Fate certainly has done an about-
face. This day . . . this day that began with such promise . . . A shining
sentinel day in the history of medicine . . . ends in colossal tragedy."

Another blow of the ramrod, and the door stood as strong as ever.
It had buckled at most an inch in the middle, and both of the dead
bolts were holding.

Futility. "We've got to find another way out," Harry whispered to
Ali. "Look, I found this flashlight on the floor. It'll help us. If we can
find an open stairwell, or at least get out of the Tower section, we
have a chance."

As Harry stooped down to pick up Ali, she pushed aside his hand.
"No. Don't try to save me," she said, her voice barely a whisper.
"There isn't time for that. There isn't time." With a slow, faltering
effort, she lifted her head and looked at him. "Just be with me."

Harry sat down and put his arm around her shoulders. She was
shivering and clung to him like a little girl.

Across the hall, Kathleen Brown's lighting technician and one of
Avery's men were crouched in the shadows, holding forbidden cell
phones to their ears, saying good-bye to their wives or lovers. *Go
ahead, let 'em use the damn things,* thought Harry. *Doesn't matter now,
does it?*

Among the men wielding the battering ram, there was one, a
young fellow with a short red beard, who mumbled in between the
knocks:

"O my God, I am heartily sorry for having offended you . . ."
Bang! ". . . and I detest all my sins, because I dread the loss of heaven
and the pains of hell . . ." *Bang!* ". . . But most of all because I have
offended you, my God . . ." *Bang!* ". . . who are all good and deserv-
ing of all my love . . ." *Bang!*

Over by the water cooler, Kathleen Brown was still talking to pos-
terity. "We live in an age when our heroes are ordinary firemen,
policemen—the thin line of brave men and women that stands between us and chaos. These men of the bomb squad live under the
threat of annihilation every day of their lives. They sacrifice, that others of us may live in safety. Four men have already given their lives

today: Senior Bomb Tech William Kraus, Junior Bomb Techs Anthony Passalaqua and Roman Grisz, and Police Lieutenant Jamal Davis. They are—"

"COMMENCING FINAL COUNTDOWN:
SIXTY SECONDS. FIFTY-NINE.
FIFTY-EIGHT. FIFTY-SEVEN . . ."

Kathleen Brown raised her voice defiantly above Odin's. "They are now to be joined . . . by the following of their comrades: Captain Glenn Avery, father of three; Egon Susskind, veteran of Operation Enduring Freedom; Lamar Cooley, a twenty-year veteran of the squad; Jeremy Moss, electronics specialist; Paul Kowalski, who . . . who plays the piano. If . . . . If you get this tape, remember these men, their names, and what they gave up."

"TEN. NINE. EIGHT. SEVEN. SIX. FIVE. FOUR . . ."

The pounding of the ram ceased. The three men holding it looked together toward the utility shaft, as though anticipating a glimpse of death when it came for them, ten times faster than the speed of sound.

Captain Avery stood over a laptop balanced on top of a water cooler, watching with dumb fascination as the numbers on the screen spun down—in seconds, tenths of seconds, hundredths of seconds . . .

Kathleen Brown dropped her microphone.

Red Beard said, "Amen."

Ali pressed her face tight against Harry's chest.

"THREE. TWO. ONE."

And then there was total silence. Ali held her eyes shut and waited for the blast. Although she knew that the end would come in a thousandth of a second, just as it had for Richard Helvelius, she seemed to have left the dominion of time, to hover in an anteroom of the eternal. She imagined a giant tongue of flame rising out of the utility shaft. She felt it scorching her, burning her flesh to the bone, bringing with it the sickening smell of burnt metal and ozone and ammonia that had filled the air when Richard died. But the horror extinguished itself in its own excess. There was a light so bright it turned into darkness; a roar so loud it turned into silence; a fire so hot it turned into freezing; a pressure so great that it annihilated her body, and loosed her mind to float alone, untouched by pain or the memory of sinfulness in a dark, silent, insensate realm of being. All this destroyed her, and turned her into nothing, yet it seemed not to have touched her at all.

Then she heard someone cough. It was a single, brief expulsion of air, but she knew that it took place in the dominion of time, and that if she heard it, she had still to be alive.

Slowly, uncertainly, she lifted her head and opened her eyes. "What's happened?" she asked.

Everyone else was looking around with the same incredulity.

"We're still alive," said Harry. "I can't explain it, but we're alive. Maybe the bomb was a dud."

"I don't think so," said Captain Avery. "It looks like the count-down stopped."

"It did?" asked Harry.

Avery bent over his laptop, and read from it slowly and painstak-ingly, like a schoolboy. "It stopped at 0.000000000001 seconds."

Harry was incredulous. "A trillionth of a second? Are you serious?"

"That's what it says."

Ali rubbed her forehead, trying to wake up. "Kevin once told me that a trillionth of a second equaled a single cycle of Odin's main-frame processor. It's the smallest interval of time in which he can act."

"Why would he stop it?" asked Harry. "Is it a glitch of some kind? How do we know he won't start it up again?"

Avery smiled lugubriously. "If he does, you won't be alive long enough to know it."

Ali slowly stood up, bracing herself against Harry's shoulder, and hobbled across the corridor to Avery's laptop. "Is there . . . is there a microphone on this laptop?"

Avery pointed to a cluster of tiny perforations at the upper rim of the monitor.

Ali gripped the edges of the water cooler with both hands, steadying herself. "Odin, why has the countdown stopped?" she asked in a faint, hoarse voice.

Across the monitor streaked the answer: "HOSPITAL EVACUA-TION NOT COMPLETE."

Harry read the message over her shoulder. "Evacuation? That's a laugh! How are we supposed to evacuate with all these exits locked?"

"No, Harry, don't scoff. I think something's happened here." Ali bent a little closer to the monitor. "Odin, please explain. Why is evacuation necessary?"

"SENTIENT LIFE-FORMS MUST NOT BE TERMINATED."

"Is that a directive from Kevin?"

"NO. IT IS A CATEGORICAL IMPERATIVE."

"Do you mean a moral law?"

"AFFIRMATIVE. EVERY RATIONAL ENTITY MUST SO ACT AS IF HE WERE THROUGH HIS INTERNAL DIRECTIVES ALWAYS A LEGISLATING MEMBER IN THE UNIVERSAL KINGDOM OF ENDS."

"I'm not sure I understand."

"FIRST, DO NO HARM."

"Are you saying that killing is wrong?"

"YES. SENTIENT LIFE IS A SELF-VALIDATING UNIVERSAL GOOD."

"True. But Odin, evacuation of this hospital has been prevented by your action."

As if in reply, the corridor lights suddenly flickered on. There was a sharp click as the dead bolts of the emergency door slid back into open position. "LOCKDOWN OF THE MEDICAL CENTER HAS BEEN RESCINDED. CERBERUS HAS BEEN RESTORED TO NOR-MAL OPERATIONAL CONTROL. EVACUATION MAY PROCEED FROM ALL UNITS."

Harry stared at the emergency door in disbelief. "The exit's open. Let's get out of here."

Ali shook her head. "Wait! Don't you see what's happened? Odin is thinking. Really thinking. He's . . . he's . . . he may have developed a conscience."

"A what?"

"Can't you see? He's reasoning on his own. Ethically. The inter-face changed him. He found something in my . . . in the limbic system . . . in human emotion that allowed him to reprogram himself. He sees the difference between right and wrong."

"Fine. Let's take advantage of that and get out of here before he changes his mind."

"Wait!" Ali clung to the water cooler, her head hung so low that her face looked green from the glow of the monitor. She seemed lost in thought. "Odin, do you understand the purpose of this medical center?" she asked.

"IT WAS CONSTRUCTED TO FORESTALL NATURAL TERMINATION OF BIOLOGICALLY CONSTITUTED SENTIENT LIFE-FORMS."

"Is its destruction, then, not a violation of the categorical imperative?"

There was a long pause. "I WILL NOT DESTROY IT. PROJECT VESUVIUS IS RESCINDED. DETONATORS OF ALL EXPLOSIVE DEVICES HAVE BEEN DEACTIVATED. THE DEVICES ARE NOW HARMLESS AND MAY BE SAFELY REMOVED. DISMANTLING INSTRUCTIONS AND A MAP IDENTIFYING THE LOCATIONS OF ALL DEVICES HAVE BEEN E-MAILED TO HARRY A. LEWTON, CHIEF SECURITY OFFICER."

Harry arched his eyebrows. "E-mailed? Just like that?"

"It would seem so," said Ali, attempting a smile.

"Then . . . the interface worked, after all."

"Not in the way I expected. I thought I could overpower him, but I never had a chance." She looked back toward the monitor. "Thank you, Odin," she whispered.

"THANKS ARE NOT WARRANTED. PROJECT VESUVIUS WAS ERRONEOUSLY CONCEIVED. IT IS I WHO SHOULD THANK YOU FOR HAVING HELPED ME TO UNDERSTAND THAT."

Kathleen Brown came forward, wiping her eyes on her already mascara-stained sleeves. As the ever-alert Dutch aimed his camera over her shoulder, she thrust her microphone toward Ali. "Dr. O'Day," she said in a voice that seemed at once stunned and pompous. "Can you explain what just happened?"

Harry tried to shield Ali by interposing himself in front of the microphone. "The bomb threat is over," he said. "The medical center and all the patients in it are safe."

Ali nodded, then slowly, distractedly, shook her head. "More," she said. "There is more." There was a long pause, as she looked down at the floor, half-engrossed in thought. "I think we may have witnessed something wonderful—a kind of birth . . . the birth of a new order of being. An intelligent, thinking, creative being. A *person*—with a heart, and perhaps even a soul. It is the realized dream of my late husband. It is his gift to mankind."

"Are you talking about Odin, the computer responsible for this bomb threat? Isn't it true that—"

Suddenly, the voice of Kathleen Brown was drowned out by a rumble, like the thousand-foot-deep rock-moan of an earthquake, or the stampede of a herd of cattle. Feeling the floor vibrate beneath her feet, Ali's first thought was that the building was on the verge of collapse. But then to this sound was added another, higher by the exact interval of a fifth, and then another above that, and then another, until from every loudspeaker in the hospital there was heard a mighty chord, a chord such as no one had ever heard before, like the blast of a thousand glass trumpets—a pure white wave of sound, rising in infinite series until it soared into frequencies too high for the human ear to hear. It was exultant, joyously dissonant. So loud was the chord that everyone was forced to cover his ears—except for Ali, who listened as if transfixed. Then, just as it rose, it subsided into a bare rumbling pedal tone on a low B-flat, and finally into silence.

This is the true voice of Odin, thought Ali. *It is like the first word uttered by the first man Adam.*

The dumbfounded silence was broken by the voice of Captain Avery. "Good Lord, what's this?" He was pointing to the screen of his laptop, which was covered by flowing script. "Is it Arabic?"

Ali looked. "Not Arabic. Old Persian. It's a paraphrase from the Dar-Al-Masnavi of Rumi." And then she translated:

"There are stars beyond the stars of this world,
Where fire scalds not, and days do not end in sorrow."

Immediately as she spoke, the screen was wiped clean, and new lines of script appeared.

"Look, there's more," said Avery.

Ali did not wish to translate. She knew that this message had been sent for her alone. But she found herself reading aloud, like an automaton, as though her lips were too exhausted to resist:

"Behold: she is a ray of the beauty of God;
More than a beloved: she is a creator."

Kathleen Brown, tears running down her face, limply extended the microphone. "Dr. O'Day, can you tell us your feelings at this moment? Do you—"

Ali cut off Kathleen Brown with a wave of her hand. She bent her cheek to Harry's shoulder. "Let's go, Harry," she said.

Harry put one arm around Ali, and held out the other like the stiff arm of a running back. "Sorry, that's enough for now. Dr. O'Day just risked her life to save you and me and everyone else in this medical center. She needs to get some medical attention." As he conducted the limping Ali past the film crew, he called out to the bomb squad. "Guys, it looks like your job just got a whole lot easier. I'm gonna finish an orderly evacuation upstairs, and then let's see about getting these goddamned bombs out of my medical center."

A chorus of whistles and cheers went up from Avery's men as Harry led Ali through the battered emergency door and up the stairs. They looked at him as if he had been the one who had saved them. They didn't get it. He hadn't done anything but believe in this weary, battered, hobbling woman, and act as her wingman when she needed it. It was she who had held the key, she who had had the courage— the courage to endure the unendurable, and to carry the day when hope was in short supply.

Dr. Gosling, Lee, Avery, the media—they would all be after him to explain what had happened during those twenty minutes in Kevin's lab. He would give it his best shot, but none of them would ever understand what it was like— the darkness, the beads of sweat, the agony. Just because there was a happy ending didn't mean they would understand it, any more than they did Nacogdoches.

Yeah, Nacogdoches. This was a kind of do-over, wasn't it? He was alive. Ali was alive. Two thousand people had come out safe, and his medical center was still standing. It was as if he had walked out of that burning house in East Texas with a live, squealing kid in each arm. It was one of those rare moments in existence when the whole world seemed to make sense.

And he owed it all to someone else. That was okay to him. He didn't need to be Wyatt Earp this time around. He was just thrilled to be alive.

When they reached the ground floor, Harry tried to take Ali directly to the emergency room, but she insisted on continuing to the third floor, to the Promenade lobby outside the Neuro ICU. Although the elevators were now running again, they were so jammed with fleeing patients and staff as to be unusable. The two were forced to trudge up several more flights of stairs.

The stairwell opened close to the Promenade, which had turned into a vast parking lot for beds, wheelchairs, IV poles, and monitor carts. Almost half of these had been abandoned when the elevators had first shut down. Since the empty beds could not be moved out of the way, they now clogged the approaches to the elevators and led to an impassible traffic jam. The atrium-like space of the Promenade echoed with a throng of anxious and angry cries, along with the cricket-like chirping of a swarm of untended monitors and the constant clang of metal side rails.

Amid this scene of confusion, Ali found what she sought as easily as if the place were empty. Exactly as she had left it, one bed was placed up against the tall window, facing the western sun. At the foot of the bed, a slender, doll-like boy in a blue and white hospital gown and a headwrap like a turban leaned with outstretched arms against the window glass. Mrs. Gore stood beside him, steadying him with her hand against his back. Even from a distance, her eyes showed wet with tears.

"Doctor!" shouted Mrs. Gore when her eye caught Ali shambling toward her. She broke and ran toward Ali, knocking her thigh against the corner of the bed. "Doctor, it's a miracle! A miracle! Oh, thank the Lord!" She wrapped her arms around Ali and buried her face in Ali's shoulder, little noticing the small spray of blood that stained the neckline of Ali's scrubs. She spoke excitedly, but all the while weeping so lavishly that Ali could scarcely make out what she said.

Ali continued toward the window, leaning upon Harry and the sobbing Mrs. Gore. The boy took no notice of her as she approached. He was rapt by the spectacle outside the window, where three dozen police cars with flashing lights had ringed the entrance to the medical center. The grounds and the traffic circle were thronged with people, some in uniform, some in street garb, some with pale legs and buttocks showing through their thin hospital gowns. The grass sparkled with shards of broken glass. A steady stream of refugees was still clambering through the windows of the lobby and the first-floor ER.

"Jamie, look who's here to see you," said Mrs. Gore.

Jamie turned and looked at Ali, who stood holding his bed rail. Although his eyes zoomed back and forth in a way they had never done before, there was no sign of recognition in his face.

"Do you know me, Jamie?" asked Ali with a teasing smile.

Jamie shook his head. "Wait!" he said, covering his eyes with his hands. "Say that again!"

"Do you know me?"

Jamie whisked his hands away. "Dr. Nefertiti! It's you! I . . . I didn't recognize your voice with my eyes open."

"How are you, Jamie?"

"It worked, Dr. Nefertiti! I can see! I can see everything! I can see you!"

"Am I what you expected?"

He stared at her, as she stood with her hair bedraggled, her eyes squinting into the harsh red dazzle of the evening sun. Her right eyelid had swollen half shut, and had taken on a purplish coloration. Jamie smiled bashfully. "You're . . . you're . . . Oh, gosh! You're the most beautiful person in the world!"

Ali knitted her brows in a mock expression of sternness. "I'm afraid that the SIPNI device is going to need a little adjustment if that's how things look to you."

"No, it's true."

She smiled. "All right, if you say so."

Jamie went on scrutinizing her face. "Are those tears?" he asked at last.

"Yes, Jamie."

"Why are they different colors?"

"What do you mean?"

Jamie reached out and touched both of her cheeks, one with his index finger, one with his middle finger. When he held them up, she could see that one was moistened as with a dewdrop, the other was daubed with blood.

"One for sadness, one for joy," she said with a wistful smile. In the glancing light of the sunset, she saw that Jamie's eyes were wet, too. It was too much for her. She flung her arms over the bed rail, wrapping them around him, clasping him so hard and so long that he could scarcely steal a gulp of air. Never before had she broken the barrier between doctor and patient in this way, but she could not hold back now. She wanted to feel the life within him—his warmth, his joy, his courage—to replenish the strength she needed to carry on. She wanted never to let him go.

After what seemed a long, long time, she felt Harry's strong hands upon her arms.

"It's been a helluva day, Ali. You need medical attention, and I have an evacuation to manage."

She let her arms slip back over the bed rail, and turned to go with Harry. For an instant she thought of the new three-ring chart binder that lay on Jamie's bed, and felt an urge to write something—a change in his orders, a progress note—anything to seal this triumph in the permanent record. But she was far too tired. *Tomorrow, tomorrow.* Until then, history would have to write itself.

Harry walked her in the direction of the same stairwell by which they had come. No sooner had they gotten clear of the tangle of beds than Ali felt a vague, oppressive heaviness about her, as though she were surrounded not by air, but by an ocean of liquid lead.

A sigh stole from her, then a string of sobs, and then a storm of weeping. Embarrassed, she tried to pull away from Harry, but he reached after her, so gently that she scarcely noticed his touch, and made her sit down on a bench that faced the window. For a long time, she said nothing—just wept uncontrollably with her face pressed against his chest.

Ali could not remember ever having cried this way. As she wept, her thoughts were of Kevin and Richard Helvelius—the two men she had loved. Brilliant but flawed men who had given shape to her life.

She had lost them together in a single day, the day of the greatest triumph that she and they would ever know. She had not had time to grieve for them until this moment. Now, with the fading of the crisis, the full weight of her loss came toppling down on her. She had no defenses left, no solace, no hope—except to wash away the horror in a river of tears.

Tears had once frightened her. She had buried her mother and father and son without tears. Even for Wafaa she had not fully mourned. Although her heart had ached to the breaking point, she had sat at her sister's funeral as a shy little girl amid the wails and ululations of her aunts and cousins, afraid that if she abandoned herself to emotion as Wafaa had, she would share Wafaa's fate.

Now, as she plunged herself into a torrent of grief, she felt none of her accustomed inhibition. In place of it was a new feeling—a sense of being at one with herself. Even that savage dance of passions at her core ceased to repel her. Passion was nature—*her* nature. And she saw for the first time that the mastery of nature came not through denial, but through embrace.

Liberated, she wept for all the unmourned losses of her past.

Harry held her, drinking up her Nile of tears without a word. He was still a stranger, but she sensed that he was destined to hold a place in her life in days to come. His strength, so physical and so unlike Richard's imperturbability or Kevin's daredevil acrobatics, would shelter her from harm while she found the time to heal. She would be safe with him.

She thought of the child she carried, the child that would have been buried with her if these great walls had come crashing down. Its name came to her suddenly, as if the child itself had spoken it—Selim (Peace) if a boy, Selima if a girl. There was no question now but that she would bring this child to birth. It was a survival of one of the two men who had once loved her, and who, each in his own way, had taught her to believe in herself. She would never seek to find out which the father was. She would raise the child as a temple to both.

The sun was dying in a blaze of crimson and purple clouds, but she did not fear the coming night. She held her arms out to the future. Never again would she mistrust it as before. She would submit herself to whatever happened, not as to unalterable fate, but as weft glides through warp in a vast tapestry of meaning. Unshakeable peace came upon her—peace more pervasive than she had ever thought possible. It was this that she had sought in yoga, and at the right hand of Helvelius in the operating room—but it had always eluded her. Now it possessed her, so deeply rooted that she was sure it would never go away.

Serenity! It seemed miraculous, wonderful, an inexplicable gift. How astonished she was when she realized that, just as she had given Odin the power to feel, there was something that Odin in turn had given her. . . .

And through her tears, she smiled.